HER
WICKED
MARQUESS

HER
WICKED
MARQUESS

USA TODAY BESTSELLING AUTHOR
STACY REID

Entangled Publishing, LLC
10940 S Parker Road
Suite 327
Parker, CO 80134
Visit our website at www.entangledpublishing.com.

Amara is an imprint of Entangled Publishing, LLC.

Edited by Stacy Abrams and Amarilys Acosta
Cover design by Bree Archer
Cover art by
Model Illustrator: Chris Cocozza
Photographer: Malkovstock/Gettyimages
Interior design by Toni Kerr

Print ISBN 978-1-68281-519-9
ebook ISBN 978-1-68281-520-5

Manufactured in the United States of America

First Edition January 2021

AMARA

ALSO BY STACY REID

Du'Sean, always and forever.

CHAPTER ONE

There were degrees of wickedness, and tonight Lady Maryann Eleanor Fitzwilliam was going to be *terribly* wicked.

She was determined to take revenge on Lady Sophie, a beautiful, reigning diamond of the *ton,* who thought it amusing to harass those she deemed inferior to her because of their lack of wealth and connections.

Unfortunately, this meant the wallflowers of the last few seasons, to which Maryann had been relegated, were forced to the sidelines by Lady Sophie and her coterie's idle gossiping. Maryann and her friends had become thoroughly tired of the sobriquet of "wallflower." Four years ago, for a moment in time, she had been well-loved by the fashionable set, until she had found it impossible to be as mean-spirited and vindictive as many of their number. Then they had cut her from their coterie, avidly whispering and laughing about her behind their fans to all who would listen.

And that, unfortunately, was the majority of young society women.

Lady Sophie might be the sister of a most sought-after duke, but she and her beautiful coterie were bully-ruffians, and tonight she would surely discover her cruelty had a price. Maryann would be the instrument of Lady Sophie's lesson. After all, Maryann had recently impressed upon her dearest friends that it was time to be daring and take whatever they needed, for waiting like biddable ladies had garnered them *nothing*—not love, or family, or any measure of independence or happiness.

Maryann glanced surreptitiously about the gardens, tapping her feet impatiently, wondering why her older brother—Crispin—one of her closest confidants, was taking so long. They had agreed to meet at this section of the gardens once the supper waltz ended.

Pushing her spectacles up the bridge of her nose, she worried her bottom lip, hoping that she hadn't sent him to his death when she had urged him to collect a few grass snakes and critters by the pond. The summer night was overly warm, but a few days ago, he had been abed.

It was that very reason the family split their time between their town house in Berkeley Square and Vanguard Hall, their manor on the outskirts of London. Vanguard Hall was close enough to town that many were more than willing to travel to the Countess Musgrove's home for one of her balls or garden parties, and it was far enough away from the pollution of London to help Crispin recover whenever the shortness of breath that sometimes plagued him reared its ugly, frightening head.

A shuffle amongst the potted flowers had her whirling around.

"There you are!" she softly cried, hurrying over to the dark figure stooped in the shadows. "Crispin, thank you! I knew you did not approve of my revenge, but you came through for me. Where is the bucket?"

The figure went remarkably still, and a niggle of an uncomfortable awareness bloomed inside Maryann. She bit back her cry of protest when, with an almost imperceptible motion, the man melted deeper into the darkness and vanished the way he had come.

"Crispin?"

A few moments later, he appeared with the bucket.

"Oh, thank goodness," she said with an approving smile. "I truly could not do this without you."

He nodded once, and she turned around to peer into their parents' massive and overflowing ballroom. Crispin had originally suggested it should be a masked ball; however, that had been considered too scandalous by her mother for the Musgroves to carry out. Still, a few of Crispin's friends had worn masks to enter, but most discarded them when the countess had discouraged such frivolity. But that was enough if anyone should see her and Crispin now. They would report of two people in masks, and the countess would have to recall that it was several guests who had worn those artful coverings.

To Maryann's mind, revenge was an art, which took careful plotting and execution. She had ensured that at Lady Pilkington's ball last week, her brother danced with Lady Sophie and encouraged her to be here tonight. Not that she would have refused an invitation to their mother's sought-after balls, but Maryann had to be incredibly cautious to prevent her plan from falling through.

"I must rely on your strength and good sense for the next part, Crispin. May I trust in your assistance?"

The slightest of hesitation, then he nodded.

Relief burst inside her chest. "I am not contrary, but you are awfully accommodating tonight. Have you given up on quoting Marcus Aurelius?"

She felt his silent stare in the dark—deep, penetrating, and questioning, and it caused a rush of discomfort to curl through her. "You know, the one about the best revenge is to be unlike the person who performed the injury? But I assure you, nothing I can do will make me endure that odious Sophie for another day!" Maryann gasped. "And speak of the devil's wife, here she comes."

Her brother shifted closer as they peered through the windows into the ballroom, where the radiant blond head of the voluptuously curved darling of the season stepped into view. Her silver-threaded pristine white gown floated around her like gossamer. She held court with her coterie (the members of the mean ladies' club) like a queen, and not the termagant who had been insolently tyrannizing other debutantes of the season.

With her actions, so many young ladies had fled balls in tears with a cloud of shame and scandal hovering over their heads, which Lady Sophie maliciously kept alive. Of course, no one saw the depth of cruelty beneath the pleasant veneer of good-natured countenance she presented.

Only her victims were fully aware…

"Look how sweet and innocent she appears," Maryann whispered, nudging Crispin in his side. "Did you know she was the instigator of the scandal which prompted Hyacinth's mother to rush her off to Cornwall? How ghastly can it be to spend the season, or the rest of her life, buried there because of an overindulged wretch?"

A rough choking sound came from her brother, which he quickly stifled.

Maryann lowered her voice conspiratorially. "Lady Sophie had been piqued that Mr. Humboldt *dared* to turn his attention from her to Hyacinth, so Sophie arranged for her to be locked in the conservatory with a footman!"

An elusive sensation whispered through her, and Maryann frowned.

"No one believed Hyacinth's protests that she had been innocently led astray by a note. But I analyzed the note she got, and it matched perfectly with Lady Sophie's handwriting. And I should know what that looks like, since I found the pretty poems she wrote to you! And what is most terrible about it is that Sophie has no interest in the man. She is the daughter of a duke with a dowry of fifty thousand pounds and an estate in Wiltshire. Poor Mr. Humboldt stood no chance with her, and he rightly fell in love with Hyacinth, who is so good-natured."

A lump formed in Maryann's throat as she watched Miss Louisa Nelson, a young lady the same women frequently whispered about and called the "dowdy wallflower," enter the ballroom. She wore a slightly fussy rose-colored evening gown, which unfortunately did not really flatter her florid complexion and short stature. Her sweet, rounded face appeared excited as she scanned the room. Louisa then made her way over to the refreshment table.

Dread crawled through Maryann at the vicious spite that settled on Lady Sophie's face. She waited until Louisa was close enough, then Sophie stuck out her delicate foot and tripped her.

"Oh no!" Maryann pressed a hand to her mouth when Louisa crashed to the floor in a very indecorous sprawl. Her pink dress was rumpled and one of the flounces was torn at the hem.

The orchestra's violins faltered, the dancers performing the minuet stopped, and the silence in the ballroom was awful and resounding. No one hurried to help the young lady who might be hurt, and to

Maryann's disgust, Sophie and her cronies merely tittered.

That seemed to encourage those eager for her admiration and approval to lift their fans to their mouths and cast poor Miss Louisa disparaging glances. She tried to stand, but in her mortified haste somehow slipped once more. Thankfully, a young man whom Maryann did not recognize hurried to help her up. Louisa covered her face and rushed from the ballroom.

Maryann's temper sparked. "Do you now understand why I must act in the manner I am about to? Lady Sophie is full of spite!"

Maryann was acquainted with the underbelly of cruelty that existed in the glittering world of the *ton*. How easily with words and deeds they could ruin someone's reputation or remind society of a scandal that had long been buried. Maryann had watched Sophie turn her spite on many—even herself for the last two seasons—and had done nothing. *No more*, she thought darkly.

"We must be patient," she whispered, grabbing his arm and tugging him farther into the shadows. "Lady Sophie will make her way to this window, and then we must act."

They waited in silence, and she cast him a few worried glances. "You are uncommonly quiet tonight; is your throat still bothering you?" she fretted, tucking away a note in her mind to summon Dr. Gervase in the morning.

The manner in which he turned his head to stare at her felt unfamiliar and oddly intimidating. Perhaps it was a trick of the light, but she found herself shuffling back, noting how Crispin had perfectly cloaked himself in the shadows so that she was barely able to discern his features.

Still, the golden mask he had donned for this clandestine meeting was familiar. They had agreed that even if they were skulking around in their own home, it was best to do so with a measure of protection. "Do you prefer not to talk?" she asked.

He nodded.

"Are you still feeling under the weather?"

Another nod.

Worry curled through Maryann. But before she could probe further, Lady Sophie said, her voice carrying clearly, "Did you see how perfectly humiliated that sweet Miss Louisa was?"

Maryann shuffled closer, her heart jolting. "Bring the bucket, Crispin," she whispered.

The bucket was pushed to her, and she peered at it, aghast. "*I* cannot do it. I am afraid of snakes."

His lips curved slightly, and the oddest sensation fluttered in her belly. Before she could assess the strangeness of the feeling and *why* it happened, her brother crept forward, and she turned back to the ballroom.

"She is almost here. Pour them out quickly!" *Mama, forgive me for the commotion.*

He complied and poured the bucket full of small snakes and other dreadful crawlies through the window to splat on the parquet floor of the ballroom. Astonishingly, no one noticed. Least of all Sophie, who would soon be upon them. Perhaps the well-placed potted plants hid the invasion. Maryann almost felt sorry for her.

Almost.

"Oh no, I think she is about to make her way over to Phineas Hadley! She won't—"

An ear-splitting scream lifted, and then madness descended. In her haste to get away from the slithering mess she had stepped on, Sophie jumped into the arms of a gentleman, refusing to put her feet on the ground. He wobbled under her unexpected weight. In truth, the flustered gentleman seemed as if he had no notion of what to do with the lady holding on to him and sobbing hysterically. He grabbed her hips—how shockingly improper—and she then turned her wrath on him, slapping his cheek with her folded fan. They both tumbled to the floor…into a few terrified snakes.

Maryann never imagined anyone could scream so loudly. A few of Lady Sophie's clique hurried to help her up, while some had the temerity to laugh. Sophie's glare threatened retribution before her lower lip trembled, and her face crumpled.

Ignoring the confusion erupting inside, Maryann grabbed Crispin's elbow and urged him to run with her from the scene of the crime. She started laughing only a few steps away. They hurried toward the hidden garden alcove they had often played in as children.

The memory of Sophie's horror just now sobered Maryann briefly. But only briefly. Once in the deepest part of the gardens, she wheeled toward her brother. "Justice was served!"

He stepped back, pressing against the shadows of the neatly clipped high-hedged maze. Shrugging the coat from her shoulders, she dropped it to the soft verdant grass and lowered herself to the ground.

Lifting a hand in the air, she began dramatically, "If you prick us, do we not bleed? If you tickle us, do we not laugh? If you poison us, do we not die? And if you wrong us, do we not *revenge*?"

Maryann sighed. "Crispin, I do feel wretched but

also glorious that she has been given a taste of her own bitter medicine. I am certain tonight's incident will be in tomorrow's scandal sheet and on the lips of everyone for weeks. We know how fickle society is about what they consider *news*."

Lifting her face to the cloud-shrouded sky, she asked, "What do you think? Dare I hope that tonight might show Sophie the errors of her ways, or at least let her reflect on the torment she has afflicted on other ladies who have done nothing more than bravely wade out in the *ton* to attempt to secure their bit of happiness? Or do you think I might have to be more extreme with my lesson?"

She hoped she would not have to be more ruthless. For the satisfaction she had felt in seeing Lady Sophie shrieking and then staring at her giggling friends in horror was hollow. It took a lot to compromise her values of kindness and forgiveness, even as she felt satisfied that she had done something.

He slowly lowered himself to sit on the grass, his back pressed against the architectural base of a moss-covered statue showing Venus carrying a vase. Once again, he had picked a spot that perfectly ensconced him in shadows. One long leg was stretched out, while the other was drawn up, his sole flat against the grass. His feet seemed unusually larger.

Maryann frowned. "Perhaps I should have met with her and given her a severe tongue lashing, instead of acting in such a childish manner." She sighed. "Now I've gotten that out of the way, I must contrive of a brilliant plan that will allow me to escape marriage to Lord Stanhope. Mama is being frightfully persistent, Crispin, and I am on the brink of doing something *most* scandalous."

Another long silence. Maryann peered at her brother. She had expected him to splutter his outrage at the mere mention of scandal and their family. And her plan involved convincing him to help her deter their mother from her infuriating machination. Had her brother always been this...still? There was something about him she could not quite put her finger on. "Crispin? What do you think?"

Maryann did not like how timid her question came out.

He took an audible breath. Deep. And released it lazily. "I think you are terribly fascinating," a resonant baritone voice—which was definitely *not* Crispin's—drawled.

Visceral shock tore through Maryann's heart, leaving it to beat weakly. She froze, her fingers curling into thick tufts of grass, as if that were enough to anchor her in the suddenly spinning world. The slow drum of her heart against her chest was painful in its uncertainty. The man before her, perfectly hidden in the private alcove of her parents' gardens, was not her brother.

It was then her senses absorbed everything she had ignored earlier in her eager need to execute her revenge. His height...the breadth of his shoulders, the muscles in his thighs and calves. His scent...dark, subtle, fragrantly spiced musk...a hint of rain. He waited like a predator for her reply, which she could not dredge forth, for she was dispossessed of all rational thoughts.

He is not Crispin. He is not Crispin. He is not my brother. Oh God!

She scrambled to her feet, her haste making her slip a few times. Light-headed and knees shaking, she finally managed to stand. A deep, provoking chuckle vibrated in the air, and Maryann almost collapsed at the sheer menace and mockery in the sound.

This was not her imagination.

A breath-crushing tension wrapped its cruel arms around her. She stared at where he lingered in the shadows for so long, her eyes smarted. The shadows twisted, the feet which had been splayed disappeared, and he slowly uncloaked from the darkness. She took a steady breath, and it was then she observed the lethal stillness to his lean, powerful body, an unfathomable watchfulness in the hooded eyes that caressed over the length of hers.

"Ah...you are going to faint or descend into hysterics. And here I thought you were brave," the voice drawled.

Forgetting her coat, she turned and sprinted away, her heart a pounding drum in her ears.

• • •

Nicolas Charles St. Ives, Marquess of Rothbury, found himself chuckling with genuine amusement for the first time in months, perhaps years. He had never seen a lady move with such speed. But it did the job, taking her away from him as quickly as possible.

Good.

As she rounded the corner, the moonlight revealed something had dropped from her. A letter perhaps. Nicolas walked toward the area the girl had dashed off to, as if something monstrous and unholy lingered in the dark. And perhaps he was a monster, for it had been years since his heart had turned black.

His path for the last few years was revenge driven.

He did not fool himself and pretty his actions by saying he was meting out justice to those who deserved it. He was not the law of the land or the country. What he did was purely to satisfy the hatred in his heart. And tonight, his path had led him here, to this house, and to the surprising encounter with his mysterious and incredibly intriguing lady.

His plan had been to break into the lord of the manor's study, which was on the third floor, and discreetly search the desks, hidden bookshelf, and floor panels, even the safes, for any evidence that might connect the earl's son, Viscount Crispin Fitzwilliam, to the black Dahlia.

A person Nicolas was most interested in finding.

Nicolas had not been invited to the earl and countess's house party, which would have made his task a bit easier. His lips twisted in a rueful grimace. His deliberately constructed reputation of a depraved libertine was simply too clever and believable for the countess to have invited the likes of him to her home. Many matrons who dreamed of landing a wealthy, even if disreputable, marquess for their daughter were happy to open their doors to him.

But the reputedly very proper and exacting countess tended to sniff her nose and lift her chin as high as possible whenever she saw him, showing the lines in her now wrinkly neck and décolletage clearly displayed to all the world. From his foot-taller height, Nicolas still got the sensation she stared down that pointy, oh-so-elegant nose at him.

Pausing, he stooped and collected the paper that had dropped from the lady's pocket. It was carefully folded, like a letter to a secret lover. Interest stirred, for he was a procurer of secrets, believing every information necessary when dealing with powerful families who thought themselves untouchable in the empire.

The gardens were too dark for him to read it now, so he slipped it into his pocket as footsteps crunched over fallen leaves and echoed on the chilly night air. He surged to his feet only to falter as the girl returned, her willowy frame as she strolled toward him graceful and perhaps even a bit dangerous.

Odd that this slip of a girl gave him momentary pause.

Sheathed in a light blue ballgown, she appeared at times ethereal in the shadows. Her figure, though slender, had more than a handful in all the right places. Her hips were lush, and from what he'd seen earlier, her derriere was just as sensually rounded. The pale mounds of her breasts at her lace décolletage invited his eyes to linger, then he lowered his gaze, wondering what was in her hands.

There was a flash of silver, and his heart jolted.

What in God's name?

CHAPTER TWO

Nicolas blinked, but the apparition of his mysterious lady gripping a shovel with its glinting sharpened edge did not disappear. The gardener was overzealous to possess such a damn sharp shovel. And the lady, she was no longer scared but filled with determined anger. It delineated every inch of her body, and that small pointed chin lifted high to give the appearance that she stared him down.

Suddenly he knew this to be the countess's daughter—surely no one else in the country could imitate that arrogant and disdainful mien.

"Intend to bash me over the head for frightening you?" he asked.

The shovel was lifted higher with surprising ease and steady arms. The waif was stronger than he would have imagined.

"I *will* impale you if you do not reveal to me the whereabouts of my brother."

Her brother was clearly the man Nicolas had come upon with the bucket in his hand. "Ah, so it wasn't your sensibilities I offended?"

Her stance shifted, and he expected to hear her feminine cry of *en-garde* any moment. How unusual— she possessed some skill and was not afraid to wield her knowledge.

"You are wearing my brother's mask, so what have you done with him?"

The slight tremble in her voice had an odd sensation twisting through Nicolas's gut. "How brave you are," he murmured, taking a step closer. "You are clearly frightened but ran for the nearest weapon and returned to save him. Brave but foolhardy. What if I am the dastardliest villain?"

The eyes behind the face mask narrowed. She did not back away from him but thrust her weapon forward, holding it steady despite its evident weight. He waved carelessly to encompass the privacy of the gardens. "We are alone, and I can easily disarm you."

Her wide lips curved, and for a precious moment he forgot even his own name.

Nicolas knew then he would never forget that smile, even if he had only been treated to a mere glimpse of its full ravishing potential.

"You can try," she invited darkly. "But I promise you shall lose a limb in the process. Now I demand—"

"Maryann?" a voice creased with astonishment asked.

She whirled around. "Crispin! Upon my word, you are safe!" The shovel was dropped, and she rushed toward the man tumbling from the hedges, rubbing the back of his neck.

The threat of Nicolas's presence had been dismissed with astonishing speed. *How insulting*. Nicolas melted into the darkest pocket of shadow in the garden and waited, all his senses attuned to the night and its possible dangers. Yet a part of him remain fixated on her, and he held himself still at that awareness.

"Who was that gentleman you were talking to?" her brother muttered, glancing behind her. "Where did he go?"

Both turned to stare at the spot he had been, looking around the gardens warily.

"I do not know who that man was, but Crispin, he

was wearing your mask!"

Her brother clasped her shoulder. "Did he hurt you?"

"No."

"Then why did you have that shovel warding him off if he did not act the bounder?"

"It was meant to be a threat for him to reveal what he did with your body," she said with a light huff. "I was certain he had done you in!"

Nicolas found himself smiling at her dire imaginings. He hadn't planned on knocking out anyone; the young man had come upon him by surprise, and Nicolas had reacted swiftly, gently pinching that nerve that would put him to sleep for a few minutes. That Lord Crispin had been wearing a mask was a stroke of luck for Nicolas, and it was a good thing he had donned it himself.

"Of course I was not dead," her brother muttered crossly, and with a heavy dollop of reproach. "You really do need to stop reading those gothic books."

"What happened to you, Crispin?"

He frowned and glanced toward the hedgerows where Nicolas had left his body after gently knocking him out.

"I was coming to meet you with the critters from the pond and I...I believe I startled something that lingered in the dark. I *think*...it was a man and not an apparition."

She lightly punched his shoulder. "Now who is the one reading all those books! Of course it was a man. He clearly did something to you and took your mask. That is rather frightening, for he could have truly done you in!"

She took a deep breath and looked around.

"Crispin, he…he actually acted in your stead. Isn't that simply astonishing? Whyever would he do that?"

Because you caught me by surprise…and I was too captivated to not participate, Nicolas thought, a bit amused with her earnestness.

"Good God, are you smitten?" he asked with a measure of alarm.

No, my good fool, she went back for a weapon. She was a brave spitfire.

Her brother glanced around warily. "Clearly he was up to no good—the bounder knocked me out and stole my mask! Perhaps he is a thief."

"Do not be a buffoon. Why would I become smitten with a stranger?" she said, whirling around. "Let's hurry and rejoin the ballroom. Remember you are to act considerably alarmed and appalled when you hear of what happened to Lady Sophie."

"Never say you went ahead with your mad plan and this man truly helped you."

"I say!"

She bent to retrieve her discarded coat and then headed back to the house. Her brother muttered something under his breath and obediently trailed behind her. Nicolas waited in the shadows for several more moments before he stealthily made his way around the side of the house, away from the ballroom and revelry. Once there, he peered at the trellis covering the side walls and the balconies. He went around to the back, noting the steps along the walls, the ones the sweepers would use to climb to the roof to unclog the chimneys, tend to any slipped slates on the roofs and the downpipes in winter.

Using the steps, vines, and trellis, he silently climbed to the second floor and hauled himself over the nearest balcony. He tested the window, not surprised to find it had not been latched from the inside. Out here on the edges of Town, a family like the Fitzwilliams would never give a second thought to safety or security. Even if they were in the city, where crimes were rampant due to the poverty and the aftereffects of the war, they would still sleep unafraid and undisturbed, protected by their vaunted wealth and privilege.

Slipping through the window, he entered a darkened room. The pale wash of moonlight revealed it to be a small study. He expected their mansion to be furnished with all the latest modern conveniences and ostentatiously displaying their wealth. He was not disappointed in his assumptions. The room he had entered, though shadowy, was lavish in the extreme.

The sound of laughter, the orchestra, and clinking of glasses echoed through the thick walls and opened windows below, and the music reverberated enough to assault his ears. Despite the advantage of the gathering to cover his steps, Nicolas moved with care as he circled the room, feeling as he went along until he located the tapers and lit them.

He removed the mask and lowered it to the large oak desk flushed against the wall. It took him several minutes to search the room. There he only found a few ledgers, unpaid bills from a society milliner and a notable dressmaker in town, and some letters from one of the Musgroves' stewards in Hertfordshire. They only discussed some land drainage that the steward considered necessary. There was no hidden panel in the walls or secret compartment in the desk or bookshelves.

Slipping through the door, he made his way to the library. The door was ajar and low, intimate murmuring wafted out to the hall. He waited for several minutes before moving on, listening as the noises became more frenetic and passionate in nature. Whoever occupied that space had no intention of leaving anytime soon. He knew from careful research that there was a larger study a few doors down, and he entered that room after ascertaining no one lingered inside.

Nicolas ensured he clicked the door handle shut so no one could surprise him. A pile of ledgers rested on the surface of a desk and were strewn upon a sofa by the hearth. Those he ignored. People like the Musgroves did not leave their dirty and ruinous secrets in the open. They buried those festering cankers deep where men with purpose like him had to ruthlessly unearth them.

He searched in the blind, not sure what he looked for, only knowing that should he see it, the instincts he had relied on for the last several years would surge to life and guide him. A thorough search of the room—under the Aubusson carpet, bookshelves, wall panels—yielded nothing suspicious.

An irritated hiss slipped from Nicolas, and he reined in the anger stirring to life within. It had taken him almost a year of investigating the pasts of a few noblemen to lead him here. He'd had his investigators study their past travels, their interests, and their secrets.

Crispin Fitzwilliam fit the description of the man Nicolas searched for, however there was nothing here to indicate Lord Crispin could have been involved in the matter of which Nicolas believed him guilty. The ghost of Arianna whispered to Nicolas then as a line from the letter she had left behind, which was seared onto his memory, rose to the forefront.

The black Dahlia is the cruelest. He offered hope

then silently watched as they shredded my soul.

Nicolas threw himself into the large wing-back chair by the fire, leaned back, and stared at the ceiling. If the information he sought was not here, perhaps he needed to be inside the ballroom, subtly prying information from those close to the young lord. Nicolas wanted to understand who the young viscount was as seen through the lens of others.

A curl of amusement went through him at the thought of crashing the countess's ball. He couldn't show up dressed as he was now in unrelenting black. The *ton* believed him a feckless dandy concerned with wickedness and fashion. He had taken lodgings only a couple miles away, so Nicolas could slip away and be back in as little as an hour. This was a golden opportunity to observe the young lord in his domain.

He shifted, and something crinkled in his pockets. The ashes of his torment wafted away, and dipping his hand inside, he withdrew the paper that had fallen from the girl in the gardens. Nicolas stood, turned up the wick on the lamp, and unfolded the paper.

The first line read,

How wicked does one need to be to achieve the illusion of ruination?

The script was flowing, elegant, and quite feminine. He lowered his gaze to the next line.

Steps on how to lose one's reputation without truly compromising one's virtue, freedom, and independence.

-Persuade Mama to invite London's most debauched lord, Nicholas St. Ives, to one of her balls or entertainments. (I doubt that will be possible. Mama strongly disapproves of him, but I must try.)

-Discover which events the marquess will attend. He is not friends with Crispin, who would not tell me even if

I asked, but if I eavesdrop on some of the faster set, perhaps they will mention where the marquess will be.

-If I can get him alone, even briefly, perhaps that will be enough for a rumor to spread about me leading him on.

-Kiss him or allow him to kiss me, but I must make certain someone will witness it, someone who is known to gossip disgracefully.

-Persuade Nicolas St. Ives to be wicked with me! Even one stolen kiss will mortify my mother. I have no idea how to arrange that? Would he do such a favor if I simply asked?

-Declare myself ruined.

-Prepare for the scandal and the whispers.

-Prepare for an extended stay in the country.

"How silly you are," Nicolas murmured, surprised at the measure of amusement he felt. She wanted him to kiss her. Flicking his eyes over the ridiculous list once more, he amended that: she wanted him to *ruin* her.

Ah yes, he recalled that the next plan she'd been about to discuss with her brother was how to escape a marriage. With a low chuckle, Nicolas replaced the note in his pocket and left the study.

He took his time walking down the hallway, hugging to the shadows so that he remained unidentified to the few guests he passed in the hallway. At the wide-open doors that led to the ballroom, he paused, keeping to the edge and scanning the room. *There.* It did not take long at all for him to find her.

She stood with a group of young ladies on the sidelines, speaking with animation. It was clearly a habit of hers to push her spectacles up the bridge of her nose, but such a charming one. She must have been out in society for some time now, yet he had never seen her before.

If not for her returning to the garden with that shovel, perhaps she would not have attracted his attention beyond their unusual encounter. A nameless face in the crush of a ball, or someone he might walk past in the shopping district. And he wouldn't have taken a second glance.

Now that something about her had captured his regard, Nicolas had an odd sense that he might never *unsee* her, that she would be a prickly thorn in his side he might never be able to dislodge.

She lifted her chin and with uncanny perception stared right back at him. It was impossible for her to see him in the darkness of the doorway, yet she stared as if she could. For a brief moment, he stepped into the light and her eyes widened, her hands fluttering to her throat. A delicate and protective gesture.

Even with the distance, it felt as if something shifted in the air between them.

They stared at each other across the expanse of the ballroom. Her gaze seemed to linger on his mask, and from where he stood, he discerned the curiosity of her mien. She wanted to know his identity. He offered her a short, mocking bow, not understanding what possessed him.

Liar. Nicolas wanted her to know that he knew her identity.

A smile curved her lips, and he spied the unusual beauty of it, and that it held a dare. But a dare to do what?

Then she lifted her chin, hauteur and confidence settling over her like a second skin, and she returned a mocking curtsy. So bold, yet so wonderfully oblivious to the dangers of a man such as himself. Something primal in his gut stirred, a direct response to that unique defiance peeking back at him.

Three of her friends turned around, no doubt wondering to whom she bowed. Before their gazes could narrow in on him, Nicolas was back in the shadows, melting away from the ball and the unusual temptation of a wallflower.

Be careful what you wish for, Lady Maryann, for I am of a mind to be wicked with you, too.

• • •

Maryann couldn't credit that Nicolas St. Ives would be this outrageous! Her mama had not invited him to tonight's ball, yet here he was, descending the wide staircase from the upper bowers, confidently striding, casting sardonic glances at debutantes, and with a sensual smirk about his mouth, declaring him every inch the rake society bemoaned.

He *was* considered improper, disreputable, and was even whispered by some to be cunning. He was also appallingly handsome, and many ladies who should have known better flirted with him shamelessly. He clearly did not give a fig what society thought about him, a thing Maryann had come to believe, since the scandal sheets reported on his exploits weekly.

"Is it really him?" a young debutante asked. "Oh my, he is terribly handsome."

Her friends dissolved into giggles and drew her away, as if they were saving their fair gazelle from the lion drawing closer. The man seemed sublimely unaware of his masculine beauty and the stir he caused whenever he entered a room. His expression was insouciant; she could not conclude what kind of man he was.

A few gentlemen of the *ton* were vain about their appearance to the point of being rather excessive. And it seemed Nicolas St. Ives was one of them, dressed in black trousers and jacket, with a bright golden waistcoat and a matching cravat. A cravat pin studded with a large diamond winked at his throat, and his hair seemed carelessly styled, yet curled at his nape and on his forehead perfectly.

The rakehell! How dare he crash her mother's ball?

The twitter of excitement that went through the throng echoed in Maryann's veins, and she scowled. Mama would curse his name tomorrow, but the scandal sheets would celebrate his wicked daring, the debutantes would excitedly trade stories about how close their gowns had brushed against the lord the scandal sheets referred to as "the daring and the wicked." And perhaps a few married ladies and widows would share among themselves some delightful and naughty things they suggested having done with him.

Maryann silently snorted, thinking it all ridiculous. Yet she couldn't help staring at him, couldn't help the manner in how her heart ached, yet she didn't know what she longed for. Certainly anything in regard to a notorious rake could only lead to inevitable disgrace.

Lady Porter, a young widow with a racy reputation, sashayed over to him, and he did nothing to mask the admiration in his gaze as he perused her. A few ladies gasped, and several fans unfurled. The marquess's smile drew Maryann's eyes to his mouth and made her think of matters a respectable lady should not wonder about, like kisses from his beautiful lips and whether he would use his tongue.

Fanning herself vigorously, she looked away from him and strolled through the opened French doors leading to the gardens to cool her suddenly heated face. Then she made her way to a small private alcove that was empty and dark enough to hide her should anyone follow.

With a gusty sigh, she kicked off her dancing shoes and wriggled her toes in her silken stockings, then lifted her face to the sky. The soft footfalls crunching on leaves alerted her that someone approached, so she stiffened, clutching her fan.

"Nicolas," a soft voice called. "Where are you going?"

Maryann stood, her heart jerking. The marquess had come outside…and someone had followed him? A spurt of intrigued amusement shook her.

"Lady Trentman," his voice said chidingly. "I wasn't aware you followed me."

A sweet, affected giggle lifted in the air. "I am astonished you came to Lady Musgrove's ball. No one expected you."

"That, my sweet, was the idea," he replied teasingly.

"I've heard whispers that you are a man devoted to sensual pleasures. I have been wanting you in my bed for some time now."

Maryann was shocked—and keen to hear his reply.

The marquess made a soft purring noise that set Maryann's heart to racing. It felt like a stroke against her skin. How odd that the sound of St. Ives's voice could produce such feelings.

"And you wish to affirm the rumors for yourself, Lady Trentman?"

Maryann stifled a gasp. The countess was a married lady!

"Perhaps," she murmured in a husky, intimate tone.

"Ah, if you are not sure, then I urge you to return inside."

The lady's laugh sounded breathless. "I *am* certain. I sent you three letters of invitations, which you've ignored. It is my fortune you showed up here tonight."

"Half the pleasure lies in the anticipation," he said charmingly.

"I do not want to wait anymore!"

"As a gentleman, I can only oblige." His voice was warm, heavy with teasing and sensuality.

The scoundrel! Was this all he did?

"It astonishes me that you would dare to compare yourself to a gentleman," the countess said flirtatiously.

"And are those hard because you are cold...or are you aroused?"

Shocked, Maryann glided soundlessly toward their voices, peering around the fountain. The marquess's back was to her, and he still stood some distance away from the woman, but the countess— Good heavens! The front of her dress was lowered, and the pale globes of her breasts were on wanton display, her voluptuous figure arched toward him in scandalous invitation.

"I am not cold," she replied in an intimate murmur.

Clutching her fan, Maryann took a few steps back, blotting out the provocative sight of the countess offering her breasts to the marquess.

"I heard your prowess between the sheets...or in other places is neither gentlemanly nor genteel."

Maryann felt a shameful pulse of primal curiosity. What kind of behavior did the countess imply, exactly?

"Ah, *mon coeur*, you have listened to such gossip and offer yourself up for ravishment?"

The countess giggled, and Maryann rolled her eyes.

"Is it true?" she demanded breathlessly.

"What?"

"Am I really your heart?" Lady Trentham sweetly purred.

His rich chuckle held a careless charm. "So that's what it means," he said a bit drily. "My French is terrible. I had no idea."

Maryann slapped a hand over her mouth to stifle her laugh, but something slipped out, for there was a sharp rustling.

"Oh, Nicolas! Someone is out here," the countess squeaked, sounding genuinely alarmed. "I cannot be found with you."

"But you knew the risk…"

Another rustling sound and them a soft *oomph*!

"I do not think throwing yourself into my arms would help the matter." Now he sounded tolerably amused and very unconcerned by the idea of discovery. "Off you go and return inside."

"But Nicolas, we haven't—"

"Go," he said firmly, all traces of the careless libertine vanishing from his tone.

And the sound of delicate footsteps hurried away. Maryann slowly shrank back on the bench, knowing she was perfectly hidden in the dark. The scent of a cheroot perfumed the air, and his presence grew closer. It was more of an awareness than a sound. It was as if she felt him.

She gripped the edges of the stone bench, her heart quickening.

"Do you not plan to come out?" he drawled with lazy amusement.

Maryann froze, glancing down. The alcove was dark enough that she could not make out her gown.

The marquess could not see her; he was hazarding a deduction. She remained quiet, and the scent of his cheroot drifted closer.

He chuckled, and she stiffened, for it sounded so familiar. Very much like the laugh the man in the gardens had given only a couple hours earlier. Was the marquess and the masked man one and the same?

The idea was outlandish. The masked man had been dangerous. She'd sensed it. Several minutes ago, Crispin admitted he wasn't sure if he had fainted or if someone had acted in a dastardly fashion. Maryann wasn't certain if it was possible to make someone pass out without them sensing it, but either way, the man had taken Crispin's mask and left him unconscious on the ground. Not the act of an honorable gentleman. And despite her mask, he had ascertained her identity. She'd seen him in the shadows of the ballroom doorway, and that mocking bow had made her heart pound with a strange secret thrill *and* alarm.

She only knew St. Ives by reputation, but there was nothing serious or dastardly about the man. Maryann was so very tempted to ask, her mouth parted, but she bit down on her bottom lip.

"I thought a lady of your daring would like a taste of ruin," he murmured provokingly.

Her heart jolted at his words, and Maryann scarcely dared to breathe. Suddenly the very air in the gardens felt perilous. Had he been aware of her when she slipped from the ballroom? *Impossible.* They hadn't met before, and a man like Nicolas St. Ives had no reason to notice Maryann.

And if he knew beyond a doubt she was there, *and* her identity, why did he not reveal his hand? They were playing cat and mouse…no…*he* was playing. Who was the cat? *I am most certainly not the mouse*, she thought and tossed her head.

Somehow his air of expectancy tempted her to be spontaneous, insolent…*scandalous*. Every prudent instinct hungered to be tossed to the winds, but she disciplined her reckless heart. Rakes were still dangerous to ladies like her who were declared wallflowers and soon-to-be spinsters. Even if she had once wished to dance and risk being burned by his fire, that would have been done from a safe distance, not this close—where she could be fully consumed.

A few weeks ago, she had declared to her dearest friend, Kitty Danvers, that Nicolas St. Ives was the wicked path that she, Maryann, needed to encroach on to achieve her measure of happiness. The plan had been to deliberately walk into his path and try to proposition him to a mutual bargain. The idea was outrageous, but she had been desperate to make the attempt. Maryann had spent days wondering what she could offer him to partake in her ruination and had discarded dozens of ideas.

When she'd heard of Lady Peregrine's house party, Maryann had thought to sneak into the marquess's room, just the very edge of it, and allow for the man her parents were forcing her to marry to see or hear she was there. St. Ives would not have been in that chamber, of course; the plan had been to insinuate she was waiting for him in her nightgown at his scandalous invitation. It was the death of the previous marquess and her niggling conscience that had seen Maryann altering her designs on St. Ives.

And that worry had been for naught.

The latest action that had the *ton* in an uproar was that St. Ives did not seem to be mourning the death of his late father, who had been known to be ailing for some time before his demise.

It had only been a little over six weeks since he attained his inheritance and the marquessate, and the man seemed determined to ignore all the proper etiquette and continue with his raking. He certainly was not avoiding the entertainments, as he had been sighted at balls and the theatre, which was considered shocking so soon after his father's interment. Of course, noblemen were allowed to get away with so much more than ladies, especially if the nobleman concerned was as devastatingly attractive as St. Ives.

She silently snorted. Given his scandalous behavior, her using him to start a minor scandal probably would have only amused the marquess. The sound of laughter and revelry filtered on the night air, yet she did not move. Nor did the marquess. They stayed like that in the dark of the gardens, him smoking his cheroot and Maryann reposing on her bench, prepared to wait out the marquess.

"You are a worthy and unflappable opponent," he said.

Perhaps we are both cats, she thought a bit smugly, leaning back against the bench to wait him out.

CHAPTER THREE

"A most delightful tidbit has flown its way to Town. I have it on good authority that the recently minted Marquess of Rothbury has been seen climbing from the bedchamber of a lady at a certain house party. N. St. Ives is notorious for his wicked, salacious pursuits, and has never been known to act in a circumspect manner before. This very odd and suspicious behavior has led this author and her coterie to believe that the lady whose chamber he climbed from is believed to be an 'innocent'! Is London's most notorious and sought-after marquess up to his usual naughty debauchery with a lady of quality? I promise, dear readers, to conduct a thorough investigation to who could have captured St. Ives's wicked attentions." -Lady Gamble

Maryann read the scandal sheet a third time, her mind churning, skipping ahead, opening possibilities and assessing their plausibility. *This* was it; she was certain. The way forward, the path toward freedom. A most timely providence.

"Oh, Maryann, what are you really thinking?" she muttered, pacing by the windows of the small sitting room she had commanded for her personal use in her family's town house in Berkeley Square.

With a sigh, Maryann lowered the paper. She had not been brave enough to see through her previous plans, and now she might have lost the opportunity to use St. Ives. Maryann winced at the notion of using anyone but consoled herself that she was only borrowing the reputation of someone truly disreputable and who would probably not mind in the least. "Oh, Kitty, I wish you were here!"

A few weeks ago, Kitty had bravely acted in a far wickeder manner than Maryann by pretending to be the fiancée of a reclusive duke and had ended up finding something wonderful. Even Kitty's sister, Miss Annabell, was engaged to Baron Lynton, and their union was being celebrated as a love match. Maryann and their other friends who belonged to their intrepid Sinful Wallflowers club felt greatly inspired by Kitty's success, for it proved enjoying life on their terms could lead to a most desirable happiness.

The door to the drawing room was shoved open, and her brother sauntered inside. His rich auburn hair, very much like her own, was tousled by the wind, and when he smiled wide, his green eyes twinkled. He had clearly been riding earlier and made no effort to tidy his appearance after a vigorous trot around Hyde or Green Park.

Her heart lightened as it always did whenever she saw Crispin. He was one of the only people who understood her, and they'd had the best relationship for as long as she could remember.

"Mother tells me you need an escort to tonight's ball. She has a headache and will not be able to make it," he said by way of greeting.

With a scowl, Maryann flung herself into the single sofa by the hearth. "Why does Mama bother to worry about a chaperone for me? No one ever asks me to dance or take a turn in the gardens."

No bouquets of roses and lilies filled the hallways

and parlors for her the morning after a ball. Yet she stubbornly attended those she was invited to because she enjoyed the music and the gaiety. While she hardly danced, Maryann had great fun at balls catching up with her friends, the other merry members of their club.

Ha! *Sinful*. Pitiful lot they were, promising to be wicked and grab life by the horns, but here she was, unable to think of a way out of the life her parents had planned for her.

"As I understand it, your soon-to-be betrothed will be in attendance."

"I will not marry that man!"

Her brother frowned. "Maryann, will—"

"I will not!"

Crispin sighed and made his way over to her, then stooped. "What is your aversion to the match?"

It felt baffling to explain how scary it was to commit her life and happiness to a man with whom she had no connection. Her throat ached with the need to yell as frustration bubbled inside her. "It is awful to not be able to make a choice for myself, Crispin! And what is the rush in me marrying?"

"You are already three and twenty," he said gently. Her brother hesitated slightly. "Could a part of your objection be because of Stamford's age?"

Maryann scoffed. "Can a lady not have a dream to be a happily independent spinster?"

Her brother appeared contemplative. "Even as a woman of some means and independence, you will be under the scrutiny of society."

"Perhaps I shall live away from the eyes of the *ton*, or perhaps by then I won't give a fig what they think."

Crispin sighed. "Stamford is a good friend of Father's. Do not let the age gap be a deterrent to you making such a good match. Papa is still very handsome and is in the prime of his life; perhaps Stamford will be just as charming to you."

She waved her hands in a dismissive gesture. "We met once, Crispin, and I felt no warmth or connection between us. How do we move from that indifference to a marriage and intimacy? The earl does not invite me to ride with him in Hyde Park or even to stroll through Mayfair. We do not converse or dance at balls. This man does not care to know me, and I daresay this supposed courtship is an indication of how cold and loveless any potential union might be, and I am angry that my opinion was not considered. It is I who will be marrying the man, for heaven's sake!"

At Crispin's silence, she asked, "Do you approve of Lord Stamford as a match for me?"

"I do not disapprove. The earl seems to be a good sort. I only want your happiness, and poppet, I have suffered so many tea parties with you over the years and indulged in talks of the large family you were going to have someday. I *know* your dreams, and as you have said, no one has looked your way in the four years you've been out in society. I have heard the whispers calling you a wallflower. I am aware you have only danced with me this season."

Her throat burned with the need to cry. "I see."

He took her hands between his and gently squeezed. "I overheard Papa and Mama just now in the smaller drawing room."

She met his eyes, alerted to the discomfort in his tone. "Tell me," she demanded hoarsely.

"It seems there are plans to announce to the newspapers that a match has been made."

Maryann jerked. "When?"

"In a few days. The marriage negotiations are almost finalized."

She pulled her hands from Crispin and surged to her feet, walking over to the wide sash windows. The press against her heart grew even heavier. "How can they ignore my wishes in such a manner?"

"Perhaps they are thinking of your happiness. You are three and twenty," he reminded her again.

"Yes, I am such a *hag*," she said with biting sarcasm. "You are seven and twenty, and I am not seeing you being pressured into a match that will only make you miserable."

Her brother stood beside her and placed his arm around her shoulder. "Give him a chance, Maryann. Tonight, take the opportunity to speak with him. Mama said she has it on the highest authority he will ask you to partake in at least two dances, signaling his intention to the polite world. So you must attend, I am afraid; our mother will not accept any excuses that will muddle her plans."

"I suppose I must go."

"You must," he said gently. "But when you converse with him, be very mindful of your tongue."

"Crispin!"

"Come now, poppet, in the early days of your come out you were too free and decided with your opinions, and what did that lead to? A rumor that you will not be a biddable sort of wife but one who believes herself equal to her lord. A lady who is too uncompromising with her tongue is considered a shrew."

He rubbed the back of his neck with his free hand and had the grace to flush. "I do not believe it to be so, you know that. I simply urge you to be mindful with Stamford."

Maryann folded her arms below her bosom, unable to sort out the emotions tumbling through her. At her come out she had been so thrilled and eager to meet the young lords who had also seemed eager for her attention. After all, she was the daughter of an earl and possessed a handsome dowry.

The first time she had given her opinion on the misery of orphaned children and widows of war, ladies had tittered, and men had acted as if she committed a *faux pas*. The gentlemen had been discussing it freely, but she had learned that was not an invitation for the ladies to join their conversation.

She'd come to realize her disconcertingly direct manner of speaking was an affront to the gentlemen's arrogance and conceit at their supposed innate superiority. This knowledge had really been driven home when at a picnic at Kensington Gardens, she'd given an opinion of a farming technique she had read about in an Agricultural report on her father's desk some months prior. It hadn't been an expert opinion, but it had not been valued.

With distress, Maryann had realized the indulgent ear her father granted her whenever she spoke on diverse subjects was because he loved her. He valued her. He had cherished the time they spent walking in the gardens in Hampshire chatting and laughing, or when they rowed on the lake and she read to him. And in that moment, when other debutantes had tittered, the gentlemen had looked suitably irritated.

That very night, the honourable Nigel Huntington, who had been paying her attention for the season, informed her that a lady did not own the intellectual capacity to understand politics and matters men discussed. Maryann still recalled the shock and discomfort she had felt upon overhearing a gentleman she found amiable and charming referring to her as "too plain to inspire any true attachment, too mouthy to be marriageable, but her dowry *was* tempting."

She had only been eighteen at the time, but Maryann had known she could not marry a gentleman of wealth and connections if he, too, did not treasure her. For what would such a marriage be like? One without genuine affections and a willingness to laugh and speak on any matter that came to the heart?

She closed her eyes against the memories, and the reasons society had contrived to stack against her in order to render her unfit to marry in the opinion of their best and brightest.

But Lord Stamford is interested.

Her heart ached, and she leaned forward to press her forehead to the window. The coolness of the glass centered her. "There was a time I dreamed of marrying a handsome gentleman, being courted with poetry, long walks, and perhaps stolen kisses," she whispered.

"And do you not have those dreams anymore, poppet?"

"I see something hovering beyond those earlier hopes. I close my eyes to sleep and I feel it…a presence at the edges of the shadows…waiting for me….to maybe leap."

"That's it, I am taking those bloody books away," Crispin muttered.

Maryann laughed lightly, masking the tumultuous feelings rioting inside. "I will dance with Stamford tonight."

At that moment, the man lingering in the shadows of her dreams rose in her thoughts, and she inhaled sharply.

Nicolas St. Ives, the Marquess of Rothbury. Her heart fluttered like wild birds were in her stomach as some undefinable sensation hooked inside her chest. The marquess had only to be in the same room with Maryann, or she only had to think of the wretched man, and the response came unbidden.

I must not think of him, she reminded herself fiercely. The marquess had no notion of her existence, and he was nothing but a speck that crossed her path occasionally, even if he had always done so with such enigmatic allure. She would not recall the night in the gardens, either, for after finishing his cheroot, he had merely returned to the ballroom.

A heavy sigh of relief left her brother, and she knew then that their mother had asked him to convince Maryann of the suitability of the match. Swallowing down the discomfort rising inside, she rested her head on Crispin's shoulder, hoping she had made the right decision.

• • •

Several hours later, Maryann stood on the sidelines of the Countess of Metcalf's impressive ballroom, tapping her feet to the lively music leaping from the orchestra's bows. Stamford had appeared a few minutes previously and made the rounds with a few of his cronies. He stood by one of the impressive Corinthian columns which was swathed in swirls of golden silk, then the man had engaged in deep conversation with the Prime Minister, Lord Liverpool. Stamford did not stay long with their prime minister and soon moved on to speak with Lord Metcalf. Maryann discreetly assessed him, reluctantly admitting that the earl was very handsome for a man over fifty. Nor did he carry obvious excess weight that so many an older man was prone to gather.

On the opposite side of the ballroom stood the popular set of the last few seasons, led by the incomparable Lady Sophie. Since the screaming incident in the ballroom a couple weeks prior, she had been licking her wounds in private. They existed in a society where a favored belle of the season could become a pariah with nothing more than a whisper in the right ear, and it was normally Lady Sophie's devilled tongue doing the whispering. But it would take more than one embarrassing incident to teach her a lesson and see her toppled from the lofty pedestal on which she'd placed herself.

Her coterie had been silent and not up to their usual mean-spiritedness since their unelected leader had withdrawn from several events. And that was enough for Maryann to celebrate as a victory. Those they normally tormented would get a reprieve from their cutting snide remarks and cruel pranks and might even be allowed to shine a little.

Lady Sophie's bully-ruffian set consisted of James Foundry—a young lord who had been declared the most eligible viscount in all of England, Sir Thomas Belfry—an impoverished young man only made popular because he was reputed to be the *cicisbeo* of the Marchioness of Deerwood. There was also the ravishing Lady Minerva and Lady Justine, both daughters of distinguished earls and celebrated beauties, and Lady Henriette, daughter of the Marquess of Gilmanton. The six reigning young lords and ladies were inseparable, and for a very brief moment in time Maryann had been a part of their crowd.

She hadn't been as fashionable or declared an

unrivaled beauty, but her wit and her family's connections had made her acceptable. Until that day when she had been required by Lady Sophie to publicly cut and humiliate Miss Anna Fielding.

Maryann had been unable to act in such an unkind and ruinous manner to the young girl, whose only misfortune had been for several gentlemen and society sheets to refer to her as the reigning beauty of the season. It hadn't mattered that those same people lifting her up had bemoaned the fact her family was merely genteel, her father only a captain in the royal navy with little connections.

Lady Sophie had been greatly insulted, and Miss Fielding was to bear the brunt of her displeasure. With a sigh, Maryann recalled the terrible distress she had felt when it was her, instead, whom they had publicly cut the following day in Hyde Park as they strolled down Rotten Row. Then the cruel whispers had started, calling her "a dowdy wallflower," or those referring to her as "plain," and then those calling her a "shrew with a viperish tongue."

They had all been orchestrated by Lady Sophie because Maryann had dared to act independently of their awful orders, and those in society keen to have the support of a duke's daughter had gladly wagged their tongues to make Maryann's life miserable.

She had wept at the loss of their supposed friendship, especially the bond she had believed she shared with Lady Justine. It was astonishing that they had once spent hours sharing dreams and confidences. Now Justine glared at her, and it was clear they suspected Maryann of playing a role in what had happened to Lady Sophie.

Why, she could not fathom, not when they had

made so many enemies with their thoughtless, banal cruelty. She lifted her chin and graced them with a small, mocking, yet indifferent smile.

A slight ripple through the crowd stole her attention from her former friends. It was Nicolas St. Ives, Marquess Rothbury. Maryann's heart fluttered uncomfortably; her cheeks grew warm. Logically she knew it was a reaction to his raw, physical appeal, but it distressed her senses to be so attracted to a libertine. Oftentimes she wondered if she was drawn to the dratted man simply because he appeared so improper.

It was the freedom he found in his reputation and scandalous pursuits she found compelling...*nothing* else.

Irritated that once again she joined the masses in ogling the man, she turned her back to him in time to see Lord Stamford leaving the ballroom.

Maryann sighed. So much for him asking her to dance. Perhaps what they needed to have between them was an honest, heartfelt conversation.

Taking a steady breath, she made after him, careful not to hurry and incite undue attention. Once in the hallway, she hesitated, uncertain as to the direction the earl had taken or even if she should follow the man.

It took her several minutes of entering different rooms before she came upon a small, intimate parlor nestled at the end of the prodigious hallway. She rapped her knuckles on the door, and once again no answer came forth. With a heavy sigh, she twisted the knob and stepped inside, only to falter.

A man and woman were entangled on the sofa by the fire. Loud, almost frightful noises came from the woman, who bounced with shocking vigor in the man's lap. Maryann was about to step back when the man lifted his head and stared right at her.

It was the earl, her supposed intended.

The shock of it was like an icy blast to her chest. Maryann struggled to take a breath and to move. The couple's actions were shocking. To her distress, the man cupped the woman's buttocks between his large hands and urged her to move even faster atop him, and she was moaning and begging him for something.

Anger and humiliation crawled through Maryann.

The shock of it had frozen her, but she lifted her eyes beyond their shoulders to the ormolu clock. The ticking sounded inordinately loud.

It felt like interminable minutes passed before she heard the girl's horrified gasp. And Maryann wondered if he had even removed his gaze from her. It was a matter of pride that she had not run away despite her revulsion. Finally, she lowered her gaze. The lady was young…perhaps even younger than Maryann, and she wasn't a guest at the ball but a worker in the household. The young maid was frantically trying to dress herself, while the earl remained reposed on the sofa, his mien uncaring and amused.

It galled her unspeakably that he was amused.

He gave the young girl some coin, which she tucked between her breasts before bobbing a quick curtsy. She rushed past Maryann, uncaring that she jostled a lady in her bid to escape. Maryann felt like such a child standing there still, gripping the knob.

"You've interrupted my pleasure," he said coolly, his gaze flickering over her dispassionately.

She stared at him, noting that he did not appear rumpled or undressed. He was even lazily drawing on a cheroot. *This* was the man who had offered for her. This was a man old enough to be her father…except he wasn't anything like her papa.

"Do you often dally with those who might be too afraid to lose their position if they resist your charms?" she asked with chilling acerbity.

His brow arched, and he took a deep draw of his cheroot before saying, "I take my pleasure wherever I want, whenever I desire it."

"Even if the lady is unwilling?"

His lips curved, and she was astonished at the sensuality in them and how much more handsome it made him. The earl did not look like a man to be two and fifty, with his lean, athletic physique and hair barely dotted with gray. "Oh, she was willing…they *all* are." *And you will be, too*, remained unspoken but somehow filled the air between them.

Such raw emotions filled Maryann that it left her shaky and breathless.

Over the last four years, she had formed incredible friendships with several other ladies who had inappropriately been given the sobriquet of wallflowers as well, and all of whom had been cruelly informed either by society or their families that they weren't "pretty, witty, wealthy, or well-connected enough" to take part in deciding their own fates. They must be used in bargains to bring gain to others and be happy about it.

When she had made her debut in society a few years ago, her hope had been to secure a husband to love. One who would love her just as much and proceed to build a large family together. Her other friends hungered to travel the world, learning other cultures, one of being a singer, another wanted to be a celebrated writer, another an inventor.

Such impossible and hopeless dreams.

Maryann had never before realized how improbable each of their successes actually would be to achieve.

A powerful agitation and dissatisfaction with life had urged Maryann to dare all of them to reach for those dreams, no matter the cost. Life was theirs to live only once, and it should count where it mattered the most—to their hearts and happiness. And damn everyone to hell who did not believe they deserved to reach for a contented life.

Yet when she lay awake at night in her bed, searching her heart for her dreams, all she found was emptiness and fright. Such terrible fear, for she no longer knew what she wanted and felt unmoored, a ship without an anchor drifting aimlessly on the wide-open sea.

She felt that very terror now, staring at the earl. Her family expected her to rest her future on *this* man and she of course should be grateful he would take a known wallflower to be his bride. Her heart pounded a furious rhythm. "There is a rumor you have a mistress," she whispered.

Humor lit in his dark brown eyes. "You are well informed for a lady of your background. I like that. It shows an inquiring mind and that I was not wrong about you."

She stared at him in muted shock, a desperate feeling of unreality creeping through her. It was a tidbit gleaned from a reluctant-to-gossip Crispin.

It felt naive of her, but she had to query, "I gather your dalliances, all of them, will cease once you are married?"

The earl's amusement grew even more pronounced. That man even had the temerity to chuckle. "Of course not. You are pretty enough to tempt me from time to time…but not enough to satisfy my urges, I'm afraid," he said. "I am a very base man, and I do not shy away from my carnal nature, nor will I apologize for it—to anyone."

She struggled with the urge to be mindful of her tongue, recalling her promise to her brother.

The earl stood, sauntered over to a small table which held a decanter of amber liquid. The earl poured the drink into two glasses and lifted one to her in offering. "A drink, Lady Maryann?"

Her chest rose on a ragged breath, and she tightened her fingers on the doorknob she had not realized she still held. If he had possessed some shred of decency, she could possibly have married him and tried to chase her dreams by his side. But what had he to recommend him save he was an earl? A wealthy one?

There was *nothing*. Nothing in him she could respect or esteem. He was a swine.

Unable to hold her tongue any longer, she scathingly asked, "Why did you offer for me if you have no interest in respecting and cherishing the woman you marry? If you have never attended a wedding before, *those* are the vows. It does you no credit that you would make your wife…your countess a laughingstock, a woman to be pitied and whispered about in society's drawing rooms with your salacious and unapologetic behavior! Not even servants may be saved from your lechery!"

He downed his drink in one go and set the glass on the table with a decisive *clink*. Then he strolled over to her, gripped her chin, and tilted her face to his. "I like intelligence in a woman. So many of you try to hide that behind bland smiles and insipid chatter."

She tried to withdraw her chin from his grasp, and

he tightened his fingers to the point of being painful. She stilled and he smiled.

"I overheard you a few months ago discussing a bill being debated in the commons with another friend. It was a rare thing seeing two ladies debating so spiritedly...and you shone brilliantly, your knowledge and insight alarmingly appealing. No one else was there to see it but I."

He turned her face a bit to the side with his hand. "I am a gentleman ready to settle down with a wife, and at that moment I decided you would do. Our offspring will not be vapid buffoons but ladies and gentlemen with keen wit and shrewdness."

As simply as that, her fate was decided as if she had no say in the matter. "Unfortunately, you will *never* do for me."

She tried once again to remove her chin from his grasp, but he held firm, and his eyes flashed a warning that made her freeze.

"How odd that you believe yourself to have a choice. The matter has already been agreed with your father."

He dipped his head, and her heart roared. Her first kiss would not be with this cretin. As his mouth made to brush hers, she wilted against him as if weakened.

She'd show him what a woman with keen wit could do.

Maryann felt the start of surprise run through his body, then he smiled, carnally and evidently pleased. He shifted, clearly meaning to cradle her closer to his body, and she lifted her leg swift and sure between his, just as her brother had taught her.

A choking sound slipped from his mouth, and he released her as if he had been burned. She had not brought him to his knees, but the corded muscles of his throat were on stark display, his eyes glittering with his ire. "I would not marry a dishonorable bounder who would keep a mistress with his wife, while bedding servants in his household and others."

She would have laughed at his slack-jawed expression if she were not so frightened and out of sorts. Maryann spun and hurried along the hallway to the ball, only to falter as his words reached her.

"I also like spirited. I am even more determined to have you, Lady Maryann, the pleasure I shall take in teaching you your place." His sigh echoed with licentiousness and pleasure at whatever he imagined.

Swallowing her revulsion, she made her way down the hallway and back to the ballroom. Before, she hadn't been certain how to extricate herself from this ridiculous union but now, she knew. That lady's room the marquess had surreptitiously climbed from would be confirmed as hers. Even if there was no truth in that statement.

Every prudent consideration of her position and her parents' expectations must be set aside. Misguided or not, this was happening.

She would ruin herself and let the chips land wherever they may.

The only question that needed answering was, *how do I let the polite world know that Nicolas St. Ives, Marquess Rothbury slipped from* my *room?*

CHAPTER FOUR

Nicolas was appalled at the rather astonishing degree to which he was aware of Lady Maryann. He decided it was because of that small curve to her lush, pretty mouth, the color of pink rosebuds. Her smile was alarmingly beautiful, and that sweet slant commanded his attention for several moments. It seemed mischievous…and naughtiness was never a thing associated with a reputed wallflower.

Her head was dipped in close conversation with a young lady he recognized as Lady Ophelia, a stunning creature who, for reasons beyond most gentlemen's comprehension, remained unwed. Nicolas was uncertain if her unmarried state had to do with Devlin Byrne, a man known in London's underworld for his ruthless shrewdness *and* also that he was possessive/protective of a certain songbird with a mysterious identity.

Nicolas suspected he might be one of only a few men in society to know the truth of her dual identity, which he had only discovered by chance. He had done nothing with the information. Devlin Byrne was not an enemy, and Nicolas suspected the fastest way to turn such a man into one would be to do anything that might threaten Lady Ophelia. Yet the lady seemed unaware that she had a protector in a man so dangerous and feared.

"Is it the ravishing Lady Ophelia who has you staring so raptly?" David, the Earl of Marsh, drawled as he came up beside Nicolas. "By God, she is rather fetching, isn't she? There is even a rumor that her father has increased her dowry to fifty thousand pounds, yet no one is offering."

Nicolas made no comment to that, but he kept the ladies in his line of vision as they made their way to the refreshment table.

"Is it her you are staring at?" David asked, resting his elbows on the balustrade and peering down to the crowded ballroom.

"No."

"Really?" A bored murmur. "Then who?"

The creature beside her, who had dared make a list with his name on it. *Allow St. Ives to ruin me.* Why in God's name that provocative wish had been haunting his thoughts was beyond Nicolas. What kind of ruination did she want? It had been a little over a week since that night in the gardens, yet the raw, sweaty dreams he'd had of her since only revealed the kind of ruin he wanted to deliver.

"Are you staring at the plain creature in the spectacles?"

"She is not plain."

David cast him a glance of surprise. "You *are* staring at her. *Why?*"

How befuddled his friend sounded, yet he made no protest as Nicolas descended the wide staircase. She hugged Lady Ophelia in farewell, then Lady Maryann met with another young lady before they headed out into the lantern-lit gardens. Ignoring the scandalized stares thrown in his direction, Nicolas allowed for a measure of stealth as he mapped her movements and followed behind her discreetly.

"Why are we following her?" David murmured from the side of his mouth.

"*I* am following her, and *you* are tagging along to be a thorn in my side."

David scoffed exasperatedly. "Fine, why are *you* following her?"

"She is the sister of Crispin Fitzwilliam."

His friend sucked in a harsh breath. "Have you ascertained that he was involved?"

The wolf, the dragon, scarred lips, and the black Dahlia, Nicolas silently mused, *I am coming for you all, but who are you, black Dahlia?*

Five men had destroyed something precious—The Stag with the Lily, The Wolf, Scarred Lips, The Dragon, and the Black Dahlia. All were monikers created by a girl who in her despair could only name them so in the letter she left behind.

Nicolas had already ruined the man Arianna referred to as "the stag with the white lily," a nobleman known in the *ton* and beloved as Viscount Barton.

And I promise the others will soon fall. Nicolas would never stop hunting until all the guilt and hatred in his heart had been appeased. He was playing the long game of revenge, methodically and mercilessly exacting his brand of justice. Nothing quick would do for those despicable blackguards. Their destruction must be profound, and there would be no rising from the ashes of their pain.

Nicolas knew all their identities except this black Dahlia. And that was the mystery which gnawed at him with relentless force. He closed his eyes, capturing Arianna's image, the one that had been fading from his memory no matter how much he desperately tried to get her to stay. Miss Arianna Burges…a friend, a girl whom he had loved with the reckless passion of youth, and one he had bitterly disappointed.

The eagle soars indifferent while the wolf betrays the dove.

The very first line she wrote in the letter she had left, before plunging into the raging river to her bitter death.

He stopped walking as the memories crept upon him like specters in the night, his heart thudding and sweat beading his upper lip, but he did not shy away from those ghosts. She deserved much more than that. While it was agony for him to recall how much he had failed her, what had it been like for her to be at the mercy of those much more powerful than her, physically and by the prestige of their birth? Men who only met with the likes of Arianna to take cruel advantage.

"Nicolas," David prodded at his silence. "Was Lord Crispin there?"

Nicolas still recalled the first time he'd seen Arianna. He and David had been playing by the lake when they spied her humming a song and picking flowers. They had only been lads of ten years, but that bright spring morning, they had both felt the blush of first love.

"I do not know as yet," Nicolas said, and resumed following Lady Maryann.

Silence fell between them as they wound their way through the small maze-like gardens. As she hurried farther into the alcove, she moved elegantly, her step light and gliding.

"Surely you do not think the girl had a hand in Arianna's misfortune?"

"Of course not."

"Strange," David said provokingly. "Methinks you are following this lady for an entirely different reason.

It is merely a coincidence she is Lord Crispin's sister. I declare I am rather eager to hear this incredible reason."

Ignoring his friend, Nicolas faltered in the shadows of the garden, close enough to see her curious pixie-like expression revealed by the glow of the lantern hanging in the tree above her head. He stared at her, distantly aware there was an increased pounding in his heart. Lady Maryann was not beautiful in the conventional sense, but she was most certainly not plain, as his friend implied.

She presented a *very* pretty picture with her large, inquisitive eyes, which were framed behind small wire-rimmed spectacles perfectly perched on the bridge of her pert nose. The slightest of dimples accentuated her chin. Nicolas admired the swell of her bosom, the narrowness of her waist, the pert lushness of her backside.

Her every move was an elegant glide across the lawn. And though she was not the beauty the *ton* revered, Lady Maryann wore sensuality like a second skin, unstudied and wholly natural. Her honeyed visage was unblemished and radiant, her hair a dark rich brown with streaks of russet red.

His gaze traced the swell of her bosom, encircled her waist, then went back up to her face. She made a breathtaking picture in her dark red gown, which flattered her shape exquisitely. The deep hem of lace on her dress fluttered seductively in the light breeze, accentuating the grace of her movements.

How in God's name did anyone think her a wall-flower?

A burst of heat blossomed over him, and he frowned. It was a long time since he had felt such an immediate attraction to a woman, if ever he truly had. Perhaps her challenging and bold nature increased her appeal. Nicolas had been so certain she hid in the dark at her parents' ball that night he appeared uninvited, but she hadn't given herself away. Her patience and lack of silly missish fear were admirable.

The two ladies' heads lowered close together, their girlish whispers stolen by the small stir of summer wind. Her friend finally leaned away, her eyes narrowed thoughtfully before she brightened and dramatically cried, "Oh, Maryann, only you would be so daring. I've heard of Lord Rothbury's sinful pursuits, but to climb into your chamber! Why, I cannot credit it!"

Nicolas froze. He had seen the silly piece in the scandal sheet this morning, and at the time it had merely amused his jaded senses. Every week there was something new to report on him, and he'd made no effort over the years to correct those wild assumptions. Some carried a smattering of truth, but most seemed invented simply to sell the noxious scandal-mongering pages. And in any case, they served his purposes. If the men he hunted thought him nothing but a feckless rake, they would never suspect he could be the man they were worrying about. There had been muttering over their failed investments, a few suspicions were aroused, but that couldn't be helped. They were not fools.

The lady covered her cheeks with her palm, as if to cool them. "Oh yes he did! *Very* wicked of him, I know, but there was nothing I could have done about it. He came, and he took what he wanted."

Nicolas's heart pounded even harder. *What in God's name is this?*

"Why, Maryann, whatever did he want?"

A fleeting smile touched her lips before it quickly

disappeared. "Oh, Fanny, I am not sure I am brave enough to say!"

Fanny affected the most charming mock swoon. "Did he...did he ravish you?"

"Yes, St. Ives," David muttered darkly beside him. "Whatever did you want to climb into an innocent's room! *Did* you ravish her?"

He did not bother to correct David. Nicolas stepped closer, careful to keep his footfalls light and indistinguishable from the soft rustles of the leaves and shrubs beneath the gentle wind. He was not the only interested observer of this little tête-à-tête. There were three ladies, more like nosy busybodies, a few feet away who were eavesdropping. Their eyes were wide, hands over their mouths, and he could all but feel their pleasure at the gossip they were overhearing.

Hell. He needed to stop the little liar before her fib led to consequences that would see her ruined.

She cocked her head in the direction of the listening ladies, a flash of a smile on her wide, lush lips before it disappeared. *Sweet Christ.* Nicolas stared transfixed by the vivid beauty of her smile and how she glowed in her loveliness.

Then a cold feeling swept through him as he recalled her list. The minx knew there were other people listening in on her conversation with her friend. Every word, all her dramatics and pauses were quite deliberate. Ah, this was what she wanted without a doubt. Only now Nicolas might face an angry father demanding he do the right thing.

What a fine show you are putting on. How convincing and calculating you are!

"Maryann," her friend cried. "I pray have some concern for my nerves. What did he do?"

"Oh, Fanny, I think…I think that libertine has some tendre for me!"

"Good God," David muttered, gripping his elbow and harshly whispering, "are you out of your damn mind?"

"I must have been," Nicolas said dryly, a throb of undeniable fascination going through him.

A pretty, clever little schemer, getting me to ruin you without even a touch between us.

The lady placed a hand over her heart and sighed. "He kissed me *most* thoroughly, I might add, and Fanny, it was scandalous, and decadent! He…he touched his tongue to mine," she said, sounding breathlessly horrified. "Then he hurriedly went back through the windows."

One of the eavesdropping ladies audibly gasped.

"Is someone there?" Lady Maryann called out, looking perfectly alarmed. "Oh no, I do hope no one overheard!"

The eavesdropping ladies turned around and hurried away, giggling. Nicolas already knew what would happen. They would happily impart to all listening ears that St. Ives had indeed climbed into the chamber of a lady of quality and lasciviously kissed her. The fact he had been in her room with her alone was enough to rain ruination on the girl's head. That "kiss" was icing on the cake.

It would start with a sly whisper that would soon become a roar, and his name would be on the lips of ladies as they met in their drawing room, and perhaps even the men as they dined and gambled at their clubs. They would wonder at his daring, and if he had stopped at a kiss. No one would believe a man as wicked and unprincipled as himself would leave her after just a kiss.

With merely a few words, this creature had linked their fates together.

She dashed around the fountain and peered in the direction where the ladies had hovered in time to see their skirts disappearing around the corner. A light, joyous laugh came from her—she clearly did not seem to mind the only path stretching before her was vilification by the *ton*. He would only get a few tongue clucks and an admonishing glance that might last for a couple days. After all, a rake will do what a rake will do—seduce and despoil virgins. But her...what recovery would there be for her?

His curiosity grew, and when David made to talk, Nicolas held up a hand, halting him. He did not want to miss anything. The more he saw, the more he would be able to break it apart, analyze, calculate the value to him, understand her motivations and exactly what he should do about it.

She whirled around to Fanny. "They have gone!"

Her friend fisted a hand on her rounded hips. "So you knew they were there?"

"Yes."

"Oh, Maryann, they fell right into your palm! Was this what you meant when you said your wicked plans included Nicolas St. Ives? I believe I had cautioned you against going down such a path!"

"This was not the initial plan, but I daresay it might work out very well indeed."

"I think you are playing a dangerous game. You do not know the manner of man he is—"

"What is there to know? He is a feckless rake who gambles and races recklessly. He associates with other useless gentlemen of society."

A dark wash of anticipation suffused Nicolas. *So,*

you think me useless? I'll take pleasure in rectifying that assumption, Lady Maryann.

"There is a rumor that he beds a different woman every night with no consistent lover or mistress," she continued, rolling her eyes. "There is something about him in the scandal sheets every week. So what is one more?"

"And if you are expected to marry him?"

"Marry the marquess?"

She said that with such astonishment, he could see entrapping him had never been a part of her plan.

"Papa would not allow that. His reputation is too diabolical."

"Maryann, the gossips will say he was in your room. *Alone.* Your parents—"

"I know," she said with an aching touch of regret. "I loathed the thought of hurting them with my actions, but I cannot marry Lord Stamford. I *cannot*, Fanny."

"Is he that awful?"

"*If* he had even an ounce of decency, I might have married him."

"I hope the rumors will be enough for him to end all talk of marriage with your father," Fanny said, reaching for Lady Maryann's hand to offer a supportive squeeze. "And I dearly hope the marquess will not be angry when he hears of it."

"St. Ives will lose nothing," she said a bit sadly, as if recognizing everything that she stood to lose—her reputation and her parents' trust. "When has society ever condemned a man for actions that can lead to a young lady's ruination? I daresay he will not even give a fig."

"I have never known you to lie to your parents. What will you tell them when they demand the truth of the matter?"

She snapped her fingers. "And that is the brilliant nature of my plan! I will tell the truth and deny that he ever visited my chamber. Papa cannot approach him and ask him to do the honorable thing. The man *is* innocent. The only way would be to work to stop the rumors, and though Papa is influential…the power of idle tongues is far superior. So I get what I want without really embroiling myself with any libertine!" She cast her friend a mirthful look. "Admit it…*I* am wickedly brilliant."

"Yes… you are," Nicolas murmured to himself with amusement and a pulse of fascination. "Clever indeed."

"Good God," David muttered. "Do you mean to say this lady is not known to you? That she deliberately used the reputation you have fostered over the years to achieve her own villainous end?"

Nicolas smiled. "Hardly villainous. Shrewd."

"You sound as if you admire her ridiculous plan."

"I cannot tell what I am feeling."

They watched as she and her friend looped their hands and strolled toward the eastern section of the lawns, their heads bent close together in conversation.

"This is a disaster," David said. "Surely you see that."

A warning tingle tightened the back of Nicolas's neck. In the distance, she released her friend to twirl, lifting her face to the sky. Her expression was that of one who had gained some sort of victory…freedom. That expression revealed a longing that was painful to witness.

What do you long for, my brave little minx? "How little do you know," he said softly.

"Her life is now in danger," David said tightly. "Do you see it as clearly as I do?"

"Perhaps." He truly did not want to think about the

far-reaching implications of her ruse. He had resolutely concentrated on seeking justice for Arianna, even at the cost of pursuing a family for himself. No distraction had been allowed. He had been ruthless, exacting, and disciplined.

And he had seen results. One of the men responsible for her death had been brought to justice, and another two were on the hook; he only needed to reel them in. He had aimed his vengeance where it would do the most damage: their reputations and wealth. Nicholas played the snake...the devil in their midst, without these idle sons of society understanding the true nature of the man they had let close.

He felt a stir of discomfort, too deep and unreachable from within him to properly understand its existence. But of one thing he was certain. This lady... this audacious woman who had been bold enough to use him for her end, he owed her *nothing*.

David slapped his hand against the bark of the tree. "There is no 'perhaps' about it. Did you not get the note Rhys sent you?"

Rhys Tremayne, the recently minted Viscount Montrose, was amongst the few men Nicolas called friend. Rhys was rumored to be part owner of a gambling hell, The Asylum, in the bowels of London. The man was a purveyor of secrets and dealt with the peddling of information on the black market. He had sent a note to Nicolas only a week ago, with a warning to be vigilant. "Yes, I got it."

"Rhys said a gentleman walked into The Asylum...a man whose identity was hidden, and he asked one question—what is *your* weakness. That says everything." David scowled. "You must admit the duke's suspicions have been aroused. What if he was the one asking after your downfall?"

James Wembley, the Duke of Farringdon—the dragon of Arianna's nightmare. Nicolas had already started his campaign to ruin the duke for his part in her pain, and the man was indeed suspicious.

David sighed most aggrievedly. "I feel as if you are not listening to me. If it is the duke, he cannot kill you; you are the Marquess of Rothbury. You may act like a feckless wastrel, but you have money and powerful connections. How would he dare? But your weakness would be the golden goose. And she…that damn *silly* chit, just announced to the world that you like and want her. *Sweet Christ*."

Nicolas tumbled it over in his head, ruthlessly analyzing the facts from all angles. "There is nothing to be done about it. We can only leave her to her own devices, then watch and see what happens."

David aimed at him a contemplative stare. "Perhaps you should work to dispel the rumors."

"*If* there is someone truly watching me, *that* would only confirm that she is important."

David sighed. "For years you have worked to ensure you name is never linked with anyone. You have taken no regular mistress or lover, avoiding all attachments until your…our work is over. And now…"

It wasn't really their work as David implied, though he too had loved Arianna. Though his friend showed a willingness to help Nicolas bring Arianna's attackers to justice, he had his reasons for keeping David at a careful distance from the entire affair.

Nicholas pushed aside the discontent worming through him. "The lady wants an engagement broken and simply used my name to do it. We have no associations. There is no reason for anyone to think she is important to me. She *is* nothing to me, and so it shall remain."

Yet the heavy feeling pressing into his gut grew in intensity. Should he warn her to be careful, or should he abandon her to whatever fate dropped at her feet? "Perhaps I should visit her father and offer for her hand," he muttered, amused with her imagined reaction. "That would teach her a lesson to be more careful in the future."

David sounded like he choked.

Nicolas cast him a sidelong glance. "Did a bug fly into your throat?"

His frown turned even blacker than before. "You should not jest about something so serious."

"The surest way to keep her safe is to have her close." He didn't like the eagerness that rose in him at that pronouncement. A man on his path of vengeance must walk alone. Known weaknesses were powerful tools in the hands of an enemy, and he could easily see how a woman of Lady Maryann's bold charm could be a man's soft spot.

But not mine. Attachments were not for him, not until he had banished the hatred and guilt from his heart.

The eagle soars indifferent while the wolf betrays the dove.

Taking down the wolf would be the most painful and challenging thing he would ever do. Nicolas didn't know if he had it in him to execute vengeance against the man he believed might be the wolf. It was a calculated risk, one with its own dangers.

Now was not the time to form attachments, false or otherwise.

CHAPTER FIVE

An hour after escaping the ball, Maryann was unable to fall into sleep. It felt a bit cowardly running from immediately facing the events she had set into motion. *Will it work?* was the question that had rattled in her thoughts during the carriage ride home. Lord Stamford had seemed so...almost frightening in his intensity. What would he do upon hearing the rumors? Surely he would be so incensed that he would cancel whatever negotiations had been started with her family.

If the earl and her parents proved stubborn, then Maryann supposed she would have to act in a far wickeder manner. Perhaps even kiss the damn marquess with witnesses about. Her belly went hot with need, causing Maryann to scowl. She wanted the marquess, and nothing seemed strong enough—certainly not his reputation—to make her stop wanting that dratted rake.

And how would she even achieve getting him to kiss her?

We must be daring and take what we need instead of waiting, wasting away on the shelves our families and society have placed us on.

How brave she had been when she had said those words to her friends. She felt none of that courage now, her stomach knotted with nerves at her daring. It was a bit terrifying to imagine herself subject to wagging tongues and drawing room discussions. Publicly, she had always held back her true nature, careful with every thought and deed since she had been reprimanded for being too opinionated. And now to plunge herself under the cruel optics of the *ton*…

By habit, she fixed the glasses perched so perfectly on her face, then padded from her room to the smaller library situated on the second floor. The best thing to do was read a book to calm her whirling thoughts.

It took a few minutes of searching the shelves before she decided on a title. Only Crispin would have bought such a book and slipped it on the bookshelves for her. Maryann adored gothic romances, the darker and scarier, the better. Her nerves feeling steadier, she hurried up the winding staircase to the third floor and to her bedchamber.

Twisting the knob, she stepped inside and closed the door behind her. She removed her spectacles, folded them, and placed them on her dressing table. She did not need them for reading, only for seeing those faraway images. It was more by habit they rested on her face for so long.

She padded over to the gas lamp, intending to brighten the room, and faltered. A strange feeling assailed Maryann, a cold prickling along her spine. Something…or someone lingered in the darkened chamber.

Maryann paused in the center of her room, raw fear and vulnerability cascading through her. Pressing the book across her chest, she waited, her heart thudding too painfully.

She couldn't say what gave her the impression that she was no longer alone. The fireplace burned low and the lamp had been turned down. Her bedroom was cast in more shadows than light.

"Is someone here?"

Feeling a bit childish, she turned slowly, peering at

the spot above her bed, beyond the billowing diaphanous pink canopy over her bedposts: the darkest corner in the room. The longer she peered, the more the shadows twisted and took form, mocking the bravery she tried to conjure. It was from there she felt the sensation of eyes…wickedly caressing over her body.

The wind kicked, and the thick blue and silver drapes billowed. Her throat closed, stealing her breath. The windows had been closed when she left earlier for the library. *Oh God!*

She inched toward her bedroom door, the shadows twisted, and a form seemed to move behind her bed toward the same direction. With a gasp, she dropped the book and rushed toward the mantel where a rapier was mounted. Maryann grabbed the hilt, lifting it from the sheath, and held it away from her, pointing at the ground.

Perhaps she should have tried to rush for the door, hoping to beat whoever lingered in the shadows. She was certain someone was there, and if it proved to be her imagination, she could laugh at herself later. It was better to be armed, and she was very skilled with rapiers and knives thanks to Uncle William and Crispin.

And what if your intruder has a pistol?

Pushing the thoughts from her frantic mind, she lifted the sword and balanced on her bare feet. "Show yourself, whoever you are! Gh-ghost or man!"

An odd choking noise, almost like stifled laughter, sounded in the air.

If someone did come out of the shadows, she would scream, though she feared that would be in vain. Her papa was at his club still, her mother asleep, and Crispin at the ball Maryann had left earlier with the excuse of a headache.

She sensed the movements before she saw them, and polished boots appeared at the bottom of her bed. Maryann didn't dare try to take a breath. In truth, it had been sucked right out of her. The silence in her chamber felt perilous. Those boots stepped forward, and Nicolas St. Ives, Marquess Rothbury appeared.

For several long moments, her mind blanked.

This man was dissolute, reckless, a gambler, a great participant of sensual debauchery, unprincipled and uncaring that he owned such a wicked reputation.

And he is here…in my bedchamber. Oh dear.

A heart-pounding awareness burned through her with fiery intensity. Even with the barely discernable light, she recognized those slashing cheekbones and the piercing brilliance of his golden-brown eyes that seemed to glitter under winged brows. A shadow of a beard accentuated the harsh sensuality of his cheekbones and the hard lines of his jaw.

Her stomach did a frightening flip. Maryann stared astonished, her hand lowering as if it had a will of its own, until the point of the rapier touched the soft carpet. "I… *You!*"

"Yes," he drawled darkly. "Me."

Good heavens! Maryann was unable to take her eyes off him, uncaring that she was speechlessly staring, belatedly realizing he, too, stared. Except his regard was predatory. To her dismay, her cheeks went frightfully hot, her throat and belly, too, an entirely unexpected and mortifying reaction.

The corner of his mouth hitched, but the eyes pinning her in place were unfathomable and watchful. She had never been this close to him before, and her pulse skittered alarmingly. Maryann drew a deep breath, trying to calm the wild pounding of her heart.

The sensation of his stare alone was like that of a hawk. The charming and ever-smiling rake was not present, and confusion rushed through her. She had observed him numerous times in the *ton*, unable to help the unwelcomed attraction she felt for someone so feckless.

He had never seemed so silent…so dangerous.

He was garbed in black trousers and jacket, with a blue waistcoat, and an expertly tied cravat. His raven hair was impeccably styled, curling softly at his nape. The man was unquestionably handsome, but that did not mean she should be admiring his male beauty when he had revealed himself to be a villain.

At a slight shift from him, his face was enveloped by the darkness. Though she could no longer discern his features, she *felt* his gaze in the erratic beat of her pulse and in the strange warmth fluttering low in her belly.

"Why are you here?" she demanded shakily.

He moved slowly, deliberately, almost leisurely toward her, and her heart kicked a furious rhythm.

She needed her wits about her, and it was crucial for her to appear unflappable. "You rogue," she said with a great deal of bravado, lifting the rapier to point at his chest. "How dare you break into my home and come into my chamber?"

Even more alarming, how did he know *this* was her bedchamber? The shocking audacity of the man dispossessed her of all rational thoughts. At the speed of a frightened horse, visions of true ruin, of being ravished by this libertine flashed in her thoughts.

"How positively astonishing. I do not believe you are afraid," he murmured provocatively.

"Is that what you expected? Hysteria?"

"At least a swoon and a mild attack of vapors," he said with a soft yet icy bite. "But here I am facing a racoon instead of a timid mouse."

A racoon? Though she had never seen one, Maryann had read about the creatures, knowing they could be small and fierce but were also considered pests. She narrowed her gaze at him. "I am well past the first bloom of youth; I think I am allowed the liberties of some eccentricities not normally credited to the female sex. That would be courage, if you are not of a mind to follow my arguments."

"How smart-mouthed you are," he said, his gaze intense on her lips.

Curious, she lifted her fingers to her chin. *Why is he staring at my mouth?*

To her utter shock, he lifted the silver-headed cane in his grip and withdrew his own blade. Did the man mean to cross swords with her? How utterly intriguing. Most gentlemen would be appalled and outraged that she would lift a rapier in their presence, thinking her unequal to the task and audacious for even thinking it.

Not you, though. There was an unmissable glint of intrigue in his eyes.

Her breath trembled on her lips, and a dangerous thrill burst in her heart; it took every lesson in discipline she'd ever had to remain composed.

Her reaction was unpardonable.

Pointing her weapon toward his knees, she mockingly saluted him. His gaze insolently caressed from her head to the tip of her toes, which she curled reflexively into the carpet. Conscious that she was only dressed in a nightgown with her hair tumbling down to her hips, Maryann tried to present a self-assured mien.

"Do you mean to skewer me, Lady Maryann?"

He knew her name. Of course he did! His presence in her chamber was not by mistake.

Before she could demand any more of what his presence meant, he lifted his sword and tapped it against hers, as if to say *lower your arms*. That *clink* echoed in the chamber.

"What are your intentions?" she said with a smile, unable to contain the reckless exhilaration busting inside. She flicked her rapier upward, light and graceful, then slashed downward, hoping to disarm him.

With impressive reflexes, he repelled her move, advancing forward with a lightning-quick attack that she dodged, then counterattacked. With agile speed and grace, he parried, and Maryann slid her bare feet across the carpet, attacking and defending in the tight circle he placed them.

Unable to help it, she chuckled softly, and his mouth twitched slightly.

The testing of each other's skills accomplished, he lowered his sword, and in the brilliance of his gaze, she saw something akin to admiration. Holding her sword in the en-garde position, she followed his lead, walking in a circle, assessing him as surely as he studied her. With a sense of bewilderment, she recognized that beneath her apprehension, there was a dark thrill to be sparring with him like this in her chamber.

Silly! For she did not know this man at all or what he wanted.

"You are impressive," he murmured, his voice low and considering.

She faltered and stared helplessly at him. No one had ever used such an appellation to describe her before, and with a curious frown, she resumed her slow dance, following him as he retreated. Or was it he who pressed forward and she in retreat? Whichever it was, their dance and lazy assessment of each other, swords held ready, felt remarkably intimate and yet perilous.

"What is one of London's most notorious rogues doing in my chamber?"

"Surely you meant to summon me," he said with lazy amusement and a far too carnal smile.

The rake!

"Did you not, Lady Maryann? With your clever little mouth?"

This could prove disastrous.

He must have heard the rumors, but even if he did, *that* truly did not explain his presence. Before she could recover from the astonishing alarm of that, he lunged. His moves were light, more testing her guard than rushing her with the strength evident in his frame. Somehow, she could sense the raw power and grittiness simmering beneath the facade of ease the marquess presented.

With a gasp, she nimbly defended against his terribly impressive and fast attacks, and to her utter shock, with a deft move she had never encountered before, he somehow managed to put his sword under the hilt of her rapier and tug so that it propelled from her grip and sailed in the air. And then he caught it! He did not stop there, and she gasped, stumbling back when he slashed toward her.

The man was mad!

Riiiip!

Then he stopped, backed away, and canted his head.

In a daze, Maryann lowered her eyes to the front of her nightgown. The marquess had slashed it open from the top of her thighs to her ankle. Her bare skin glowed creamy and pale in the room.

Her chest went so tight, she could scarcely breathe.

A hand fluttered to her mouth as she stared at him

with ill-concealed shock. Lowering her hand, she asked tremulously, "Should I fear for my virtue?"

The room suddenly seemed to be without air. His eyes darkened and his chest lifted on a deep yet silent breath as his gaze seemed frozen on her tumbled tresses.

This time, he smiled with his entire mouth. "Rakes are known to steal them."

She felt a primal and unfamiliar rush of physical awareness. Maryann glanced at the door behind her.

"Run," he murmured. "I have no problem chasing you."

Every wicked rumor she'd ever heard concerning this scoundrel rushed through her thoughts. She held still when he extended his rapier and used it to lift her hair from her shoulder. It rested against the silver blade like a curtain of burnished copper.

"Is your intention ruin?"

He flicked the blade, allowing her hair to slither off. "You've already done that on your own. Or did you think in the morning you would have some reputation left?"

She cleared her throat and gripped the front of her nightgown. "So…it's ravishment, then? Is that…is that why you're here?"

How it annoyed her that her voice came as a squeak and not with unruffled confidence.

He dealt her an arresting stare. "Ravishment?" The look in his eyes was curious and amused.

The amusement stung.

"No, Lady Maryann, I've no intention of ravishing you."

As if she would merely take the word of a celebrated libertine! Maryann spun and sprinted toward her door, uncaring that once she screamed, a man would truly be found in her chambers. And not just any man—*St. Ives*. Again!

Not that it mattered that the first instance had been fabricated. Her fingers brushed the doorknob, but then a fistful of her nightgown was grabbed, and she was yanked back.

To be so manhandled filled her with outrage. "How dare you! Release me at once!"

He whirled her around, then released her. Maryann peered up at him, her heart jerking too fast. Each breath sawed from her throat felt so painful. St. Ives placed a finger below her chin and yanked up her face. She bit back the whimper rising in her throat. How mortifying if he should hear it.

A clean, masculine scent assailed her senses. "What do you want?" she asked.

He leaned forward, his voice a purr of something lethal but also carnal. "You invited me, and I accepted."

The cat and the mouse.

That amused, provoking drawl lingered within her, and she cast another helpless glance at the door behind her, then faced him once more. "I…most certainly did not."

"Oh yes," he murmured, his eyes glinting with humor. "I recall distinctly that I *desperately* wanted to ravish these lips and simply couldn't help my wicked heart."

She cleared her throat, unnerved. "How…how could you possibly know what I said?"

Had they repeated her words exactly as she pronounced them? Maryann had hoped their sensibilities were too mortified by her lack of propriety to repeat her scandal verbatim.

"Is that truly your concern?"

She stepped back, and his finger slipped from her chin. *Thank heavens*. His touch felt...like strokes of flames over her skin, yet it also felt right. It might take her the rest of her life to figure out why she would ever think such a silly thing.

"I am going to scream," she said huskily. "It will bring all the servants here." A bluff, for everyone was below stairs in the servant quarters and would not likely hear her. Her mother always slept soundly after taking the tincture for her headache.

"Go ahead," he said smoothly.

Gritting her teeth, she thought of a counterattack to his slick assurance. "A few weeks ago, you were overheard at a garden party vowing to not wed before forty."

The scandal sheets had thought it so newsworthy, it had been mentioned by more than six different presses and for the entire week. It had left many maters disappointed, and also bolstered those determined to nab him to work their machinations harder.

One of those imperious brows arched. "Surely you will make a point soon."

"If you are caught in my chamber, you *will* be forced to marry me."

The provoking amusement around his mouth grew more pronounced. "I wonder how that end would be achieved."

Maryann's heart jolted. "Are you saying if you were to be discovered, you would refuse to marry me?"

"Of course. I am the one they call 'the daring and the wicked.'"

That was said with some derision, as if he found the *ton*'s penchant for monikers tiresome and uninspired.

For the first time since becoming aware of St. Ives, she wondered if more rested beneath the facade he presented to the *ton*.

Do you wear an armor like I do?

She delicately cleared her throat. "You've already heard the gossips naming me as the lady's chamber you climbed from at Lady Peregrine's house party."

His head lowered another fraction; his breath wafted against her lips. "The gossip you initiated. Very clever of you."

Oh God, we are standing so close. It was also exceedingly frightening that he hadn't just ignored the gossip but instead had broken into her home. What kind of gentleman did such a thing? *Silly, he is a libertine!* "I can explain why I did what I did, my lord."

"You wished to use my reputation to escape an engagement with Stamford."

She froze. "Yes."

He tipped an imaginary hat in her direction. "Well done. The earl might be offended enough to withdraw his offer."

With some amazement, she noted the marquess was not angry. Perhaps his tone was even tinged with admiration. "I hope so," Maryann said, watching the marquess carefully.

"Why do you wish to escape marriage to the earl? He is thought a decent sort."

"Only another libertine would think that man decent."

His lips twitched slightly before his expression smoothed. "Tell me."

This demand was hard and a bit intimidating. She saw nothing of the flirting charmer she had observed a few times at society events. This man…he was an enigma. He did not seem furious she had thought to use his reputation so callously, and a silent breath of relief escaped her. Maryann hoped a bit of honesty would keep him this indifferent to the notion. "I was given away to him, without any considerations to the kind of gentleman I'd hope to marry."

"Ah, so if you were consulted, you would have consented."

"No."

"Oh?"

"Perhaps if I had been courted," she said softly.

"A few poems, long walks, a carriage ride or two from Stamford would have been enough to turn your head?" he asked caustically.

As if he expected more from her. The idea was outrageous and laughable.

"It would have at least revealed to the earl that we do not suit."

"And how are you so certain of this unsuitability if you've not given him a chance?"

She held up three fingers, slowly lowering one after the other as she made her points. "Gentlemen of society do not like ordinary ladies, or ladies with opinions and a modicum of intelligence, and most certainly not ladies with simple but unbending expectations."

"You are intelligent...even shrewd, and I shall discover your expectations, but you are no ordinary lady," he said. "I am astonished you should believe it to be so."

Warmth fluttered through her heart that he would think her shrewd. And he said it with such admiration, too. "Of course I do not consider myself ordinary, but I daresay gentlemen of the *ton* do."

She flashed him a deliberate mocking glance from

beneath her lashes. "I am a blazing star that no gentleman has any notion what to do with. My wit skewers, my laugh enthralls, and they are daunted by my mouth. Should I continue?"

His expression shuttered. "You are not what I expected."

"Oh, what did you anticipate?"

"A mouse. But instead I found a lioness."

He robbed her of speech for precious moments. *A lioness*. A most particular compliment. The rake was determined to worm his way into her good graces, Maryann decided, almost fondly. "Better than a *racoon*!"

A quick flash of a smile from him had her looking away to regather her wits. "You were there, tonight, in the gardens," she said, assessing every nuance of his beautiful expression. It was an injustice for a man to be so handsome and yet rotten to the core. "That is how you know exactly what happened."

His head dipped ever so slightly, and she took that as confirmation. The charming scoundrel she glimpsed whenever she saw him in public settled over his face, causing an odd sense of fascination to blossom through her. The change was quicksilver fast, but somehow that dangerous aura melted away with effortless ease. This man was now the rogue, and the idea that he could have such a duality of nature sent a thrum of curiosity through her veins.

He shifted, and it was then she acknowledged how remarkably still he had been. He came closer, and the scent of him roused her senses alarmingly. Maryann instinctively stepped away until her back was flushed against the wall by the door. She stared at him helplessly, terribly aware that her thigh and legs were on display. Why were they conversing so intimately close?

"What are you doing?"

She loathed how breathless and nervous she sounded, and in response lifted her chin defiantly so she peered up at him. He placed the flat of each palm by her head, effectively caging and surrounding her with his bulk.

"You declared to the world that I ravished your lips thoroughly."

"I... Only two or three ladies overheard," she muttered.

Looking down at her, he arched one of his dark, slashing brows. "We both know there is an intrepid scandal sheet reporter burning the midnight lamp to ensure that story is run this week. Possibly even tomorrow. I've always not liked being accused of liberties I did not take. Surely I must rectify the matter."

"You are here to...to *kiss* me?"

"I've never kissed an innocent before."

She scoffed with a breath that trembled. "With all the ungovernable debaucheries laid at your feet, I highly doubt that sentiment."

"I've never kissed a lady who didn't want to be kissed."

She believed him, but Maryann wasn't about to reveal that in the dark of her room, she had thought about kissing this rogue more than once. His head dipped, and Maryann felt certain she was about to faint. She placed the flat of her palm over her lips to protect them from his ravishment. A gleam, one of amusement, stole into his eyes, and he pressed his lips to her knuckles. His lips felt like the softest brush of a butterfly's wings against her flesh. Her lashes briefly fluttered closed at the feel of his mouth on her fingers.

It wasn't a kiss…but her knees weakened.

Silly, silly knees.

"How interesting that you're not skewering me with this clever mouth of yours."

Her breath softly hitched. He had perceived that she was not as indifferent to him as she'd like him to believe. They stared at each other through the space between her fingers. Maryann wondered if his heart raced as fast as hers did, or was this a game to him? A flirtation that only amused him?

A quick flick of his tongue, and he licked between the vee of her fingers. A sweet, wicked ache trembled low in her belly, and Maryann's entire body blushed hot. For the breath of a moment, her gaze locked with his. The eyes watching her were hard and sharply intelligent.

Noting her reaction, his hard, sensual mouth slowly curved.

"You want me to kiss you," the devil murmured.

"I once wanted a pet skunk, too."

The marquess chuckled, and she couldn't suppress a dismaying ache of want.

His head shifted to the side, and he pressed his diabolical mouth right next to her smallest finger, at the corner of her mouth, then bit down. The slow nip against her mouth was shocking and sudden and shatteringly erotic.

"You scoundrel!" she gasped, hating how husky her voice sounded. Hating how her heart pounded. Hating how she trembled infinitesimally.

She only needed to lower her hand and turn her head the smallest of fractions, and their mouths would meet. Her entire awareness became centered around the featherlight pressure of his lips at the corner of her mouth. Maryann could feel his heartbeat in the space between them—or was it hers?

He was lacking in morals and propriety...but he was so tempting to her senses. What if she could do all the things she secretly dreamed of doing? Like kissing this rogue. She stood on the precipice of madness...of feeling something other than a vague hope, yet she did not move her head that slight inch that was needed to taste his mouth.

Before she could gather her wits and push him away, he lifted his head. The marquess kept his eyes closed for several moments before peering down at her.

"In the coming days, if anything odd should happen to you, you will let me know right away."

The shift in his mood and conversation rattled her for a moment. *How mercurial you are.* "Anything odd? Whatever do you mean?"

"You were reckless enough to link our names together. So now...my friends are your friends."

"I dearly hope not," she said with a scoff. "I assure you my intention was never to importune upon your undesirable connections."

He laughed, the sound rough yet so charming. "And my enemies are now your enemies," he murmured, staring at her with an indefinable expression.

There was a flash of an unfathomable emotion in his gaze when he said that, and despite the bemused smile above his sensual lips, he was most assuredly serious.

"Enemies?"

"Yes."

"I do not understand."

"You were happy to use my name to escape an engagement, so you will accept the consequences that come with the ruse."

Good heavens. "Consequences such as you breaking into my room, scaring me out of my wits...and anticipating odd occurrences in my life?"

"Yes."

"You are a madman," she said faintly.

"There is more."

"Surely not," she said with a sarcastic bite.

"You will still owe me a kiss."

A flash of heat went through her. It appalled her, knowing he was not the man for her, that she could still be so drawn to him. "I owe you *nothing* of the sort."

His chest rumbled with a low, primitive sound, drawing a startled gasp from her.

Palpable tension infused his frame. "Do you want me to take it now?"

Take it? How crude, unflattering, and unromantic. But also, raw, honest, and real. A surge of wild heat flamed between her thighs, and her heart quickened. "I... No!"

"Is this all you wanted of me, to use my reputation?"

The low roughness of his voice and his unexpected intensity had the strangest sensation twisting low in her belly. Maryann had never felt it before, and it rattled her nerves. "Yes."

"What about this?"

He dipped into his pocket and produced a wrinkled paper. He flicked it open and she recognized... It was her list! Mortification struck her like lightning. She snatched it from him and crumpled it in her fist, the memory of writing about wanting his kiss making her wish she were the fainting sort. A swoon into oblivion would do right about now.

"Where did you get this?" she whispered, so very aware if she leaned in only slightly, and tipped, their mouths would meet.

"You dropped it in the gardens at our first meeting."

She stared at him, her breathing ragged. He reached out and gently encircled her throat, his thumb rubbing a soothing motion over her racing pulse. The touch was dominant, possessive, and sent a new wave of shock and heat hurtling through her senses. Maryann's lips parted. "It was really *you* that night...the man in the mask."

He seemed fascinated with the hand he held to her throat. His touch was tender, but somehow, she felt the power in it.

"I'll be seeing you around, Lady Maryann."

Her heart jerked, and she made no reply. He released her and whirled around, his coat swirling at his ankles. Then he dipped and went through her windows, closing them from the outside.

Several minutes passed, and Maryann did not move from where she leaned against the wall, quite aware her heart had not settled. She kept waiting for the man to reappear. Hurrying to the window, she closed the latch and rested her forehead against the cool pane.

Oh God, what have I done?

CHAPTER SIX

Nicolas bit his knuckles through his gloves until they ached. Not even that pain stopped the desire stirring to life with violent force. Hovering in the dark gardens of Lady Maryann's home, he peered up, watching her silhouette at the windows as she looked down upon where he lingered. His intentions had been for her to understand that there might be danger in associating with him, and that she should be careful. Nothing more.

So then how had that devolved into him staring at her like a hungry predator as she entered her room, then sparring with her, to then convincing himself not to toss her on the bed and have his carnal and oh-so-wicked way with her?

So it's ravishment, then?

He closed his eyes against the memory of that husky whisper. The heat in her eyes as she stared at him had affected his senses most profoundly. And it shocked Nicolas, this unanticipated interest on his part. Lady Maryann had wanted him to kiss her, but beyond the curious arousal in her eyes, there had also been fright, and that awareness had leashed his as nothing else could.

She moved away from the window, and he let out the breath he'd been holding. Moving with efficient stealth, he walked away and jumped over the side gate, lingering in the shadows cast by the small trees and hedges before strolling down the streets.

"Her damn mouth needs to be outlawed," he muttered, thoroughly irritated with his attraction. And her eyes, bloody hell, they were the finest he'd ever seen. Golden brown flecked with sparking green at the center. "And why is she so fearless?"

When she had realized someone lingered in the dark, she hadn't screamed or fainted, which he truly expected. It had intrigued him that she went for a weapon when it shouldn't have, given the night with the shovel. Her skill with a rapier was greater than that of most gentlemen he knew, and her mettle might even be tougher. The brilliant splash of her unbound hair had captivated him, and even the peek of bare feet and dainty toes had tied him in knots.

He had deliberately acted the scoundrel, slashing open her nightgown, and even then the damn woman hadn't fainted away. Her fresh, artless loveliness would tempt any man, yet based on the little digging he had done, she was often overlooked. "Damn fools."

How could anyone not notice her? Yet Nicolas had done so for years. According to David, Lady Maryann had been out in society for the last four seasons. If not for that night in the gardens, would Nicolas have even noticed her?

He might never know, and it should not matter. In another place, another time, she might have been a welcome diversion. They would not be acquaintances, friends, or lovers. Especially if her brother was the black Dahlia, that would mean he was one of the men who had hurt Arianna. And Nicolas would irrevocably ruin him should it be proved true—the men who violated her could not be redeemed, and everyone would pay for their crimes. If her brother became his enemy, then Lady Maryann would indirectly become his enemy.

Arianna. It was hard to recall the shape of her face,

the sound of her voice, or how she had tasted. They had kissed several times, but he had prevented himself from being callous. He was the son of a powerful marquess and she the daughter of servants. Their match would never have been accepted, and he'd promised himself to not ruin her.

Yet in a different way, he had.

The eagle soars indifferently while the wolf betrays…

He was the eagle. That was how she'd always seen him and had joked about it often enough. She had believed him indifferent to her pain and died believing those blackguards were his friends, and that they'd had his approval to debauch her against her will.

And why wouldn't she have believed it? When Arianna had confessed her love, he had looked down his damned aristocratic nose and reminded her she was the daughter of servants and it was his duty to marry someone of the right station. He'd admitted his budding love but told her they could not marry. The shame, pain, and crushed dreams in her eyes had almost felled him.

He often wondered if those who had never felt its sting understood the absolute power of guilt. There were days its claws and talons ripped into his gut and tore him apart. She had been his friend, a girl he loved, and he had not been there in her greatest time of need. Five young men from the finest families in the aristocracy had ruined her purity with rank callousness, and unable to bear the pain and shame of her situation, she had flung herself into the river.

Nicolas entered the parked carriage which had been ordered to linger several houses down from Lady Maryann's. He rapped on the roof, and the coachman urged the horses into a trot, taking him to Mayfair and the home of Viscount Humber, a most distinguished gentleman and one of society's great orators of the House of Lords.

It was after midnight, but a careful analysis of the man's habits for the past month indicated he would be in his study, reading scientific reports. Once again, Nicolas's coachman stopped the equipage a number of houses down, and he alighted. He turned up the collar of his coat against the unusually brisk wind, gripped his silver-handled cane, and strolled toward the viscount's house.

With little effort, Nicolas broke into the man's home through the kitchens and silently made his way up the servants' stairs to the lower floors. With the information he'd obtained from a chambermaid he had bribed, Nicolas quickly found the man's study.

A sliver of orange light peeked from beneath the large oak door. A careful test of the lock, and it turned in his hand. Nicolas entered silently, braced for the possibility of alarming the man. Predictably, the viscount was at his desk, several lit tapers close to him as he read from a book and at times made jottings in a ledger. The man was so engrossed in his task, he did not hear or sense Nicolas as he padded over to the bookshelf, the darkest corner of the room.

Nicolas waited for his presence to be felt, and after a few minutes, a humorless smile curved his lips. "Humber," he said quietly.

The viscount dropped the book and half rose out of his chair. "Is someone there?"

Staying ensconced in the shadows, Nicolas retrieved the rolled sheaf of papers tied with a dark ribbon from his pockets, then with precision he tossed it to land on the man's desk.

"What is the meaning of this?" the viscount

snapped, moving swiftly around his desk and grabbing up the papers and setting them atop his desk. "Who are you?"

"A messenger. I mean no harm."

"Yet you broke into my home," Humber snapped, a scowl darkening his features.

"Lord Humber, you are known as an upright man... who is just and abhors reprehensible people, especially if their crimes are vile."

The viscount remained still for an inordinate amount of time, his chest lifting on his rapid breathing, staring into the shadows. "What is this about?"

"Another rumor says that you adore your daughter and are not ashamed to admit she is the apple of your eye. You've betrothed her to a man most vile."

The viscount curled one of his hands into a tight fist at his side. "Who are you?"

"A most concerned party."

"A *friend* does not approach me in this villainous and secretive manner."

"I did not claim friendship, but I am not your enemy, either. It is best for the both of us that my identity remains hidden. I swear upon my honor, I mean you and your household no harm."

The viscount seemed to struggle for a few moments before he swiped the cylindrical roll off the table and impatiently ripped off the ribbon. He straightened the papers against the desk and bent over them, reading the information presented. Nicolas patiently waited for the man to absorb the information.

"What is this?" the viscount asked with dawning outrage.

"Your daughter's betrothed frequents a particular house in Soho Square."

Humber straightened. "I do not believe this!"

The duke had recently completed the arrangements with Viscount Humber for his daughter's hand in marriage. The girl had a dowry of fifty thousand pounds, plus two unentailed estates and shares in a copper mine. Farringdon had been pleased with the match, given his financial straits, and bragged in the clubs he would soon be flush in the pockets. The viscount was equally pleased his daughter would marry into such a powerful family.

Dirty secrets that had the potential to bring scandal and ignominy to a family had the power to crumble even the most sought-after alliance.

"That information was carefully collected over the course of eight months," Nicolas murmured. "I made no mistake. The duke has a penchant for depravity and that brothel in Soho caters to his every whim. He also hurts those under his protection without regret."

Lord Humber's fingers tightened on the paper. "This report says he has foisted a bastard on a young maid in his home before running her away."

"To suffer a life of poverty and misery. The girl was only fifteen."

If Nicolas hadn't kept such a keen watch on the duke, he wouldn't have been able to assist the girl in her darkest hour of need. That young girl had been returned to her family in Cornwall with a draft of two thousand pounds, a fortune she'd hardly known what to do with. But her relief had been palpable, and Nicolas had witnessed the despair lift from her shoulders as hope had shone in her eyes. When she had impetuously flung herself into his arms and hugged him, he had just stood there, but inside, complex emotions had tumbled through him in unrelenting waves.

The duke hadn't lost a night's sleep and had simply moved on to his next pretty prey. And Nicolas's revulsion and need for vengeance had deepened.

The viscount looked away into the fire.

Nicolas shifted a bit closer. "While not uncommon for some men to seduce dependents in their household, your daughter would be the duchess of a man who will dally indiscriminately right under her nose and bring her shame and embarrassment."

The viscount grabbed up another sheet, reading the words. Humber's heavy sigh echoed in the library. "He vowed to me to end all his dalliances. He has given his mistress her *conge*."

Nicolas scoffed. "How bitterly disappointed you must feel to know he has only moved her from town to Bath. The duke has *no* honor."

The viscount's gaze swung to the very spot he stood.

"And what do you gain from bringing this to my attention?"

Another step closer to destroying everything the duke valued. "What does it matter?"

"I'll not be another man's sword!" Lord Humber growled, fisting his hands at his side, uncaring he crumpled the paper. "If you think to manipulate me, you are wrong. My daughter will be a duchess, and that makes her happy. There is nothing more to it."

"Act in haste…and greed, you shall surely repent in leisure."

Nicolas whirled around and made his way from the library, uncaring the man had full view of his retreating back. His dark hair and black coat would not reveal much.

"What did the duke do to you?" Humber demanded gruffly.

Nicolas paused with his hand on the door.

"He stole the life of a young girl who mattered to me." Then he opened the door and slipped away from the viscount's town house.

His work for the night was not done. From what he knew from studying the viscount, the man would not be able to sign his precious daughter over to the duke. Nor would Humber sleep on the matter. Despite his brilliance in parliament, the man was driven by his emotions, perhaps the very reason he was able to sway so many to his side of whichever bill he supported. His emotions and passions were effortlessly conveyed and felt.

That very emotion driving the viscount would work in Nicolas's favor.

• • •

Nicolas took a deep breath of the chilled night air. He was headed to the Asylum, a most notorious gaming hell, and there he would wait for the show to begin.

His thoughts lingered on Lady Maryann, and he wondered what she had done after he left her chambers. It was an entirely new experience for him, thinking about a lady this often. With a soft chuckle, he shook his head, for he anticipated the next time they would cross wits.

What will you do when you see me again?

Nicolas strolled for several minutes to where his coachman waited with his carriage. Less than an hour later, he hopped down from the equipage and strolled toward a large three-story brick building that had two men standing outside by the door. A light rain fell, and a few carriages queued near a fog-shrouded gas lamp.

The men recognized him and, without asking any questions, opened the door, allowing him entry.

Nicolas waded through a thick crowd, the sounds of women laughing, the dice slapping against a table, the scent of tobacco, curls of smoke twisting in the air. He inhaled deeply, always astonished that this was a place he felt comfortable. A place that homed a truly disreputable group, men of such ruthlessness, one had to learn to tread carefully or face the possibility of losing their life.

Except Nicolas hadn't learned to tread carefully and bow to their underground power—he had made himself to be cunning and ruthless in order to earn their respect. There were days he felt like he did not know himself. His feelings and thoughts were always hidden behind a wall of charming affability and rakishness, and there were times he felt restless and dissatisfied.

François de La Rochefoucauld wrote that man was so accustomed to disguising themselves to others—their fears, needs, wants, desires—that in the end, man became disguised to themselves. Nicolas had pondered that very complexity of his nature a few times. Who was he? He often lay in the dark and stared sightlessly at his ceiling, wondering why he felt so unrooted.

Was he the rake, the charming libertine who loved to seduce women, drink, race recklessly, and gamble? Or was he the man Riordan O'Malley called Hawk, someone believed to be just as dangerous as the owner of the Asylum, a man who had killed while dueling and whenever provoked to act in defense of his self?

"My Lord Rothbury," a voice purred. "You are the very man I wished to see."

It was Madame Salome herself draped in a scandalous gown of flimsy green silk, her mass of vibrant red hair tumbling over her shoulders. Her gown clung to her dazzling form, accentuating and displaying what lay beneath. The lady had a reputation of arranging discreet trysts, allowing women and gentlemen of high society to indulge in experiences under the banner of secrecy. She gambled often at the Asylum and was rumored to have a debt of over fifteen thousand pounds, yet O'Malley had not called her in vowels.

"Salome," Nicolas said by way of greeting, a slight dip of his head acknowledging her interest. "How may I be of service to you?"

She laughed, light and tinkling. "On your knees, preferably. I am restless tonight, and I do not believe I've had you yet."

He stared at that charming smile, oddly unmoved. The woman was beautiful and intimately knew of her allure. He admired her confidence and even her cunning, for she was a lady protected by some of the most powerful lords of society—those belonging to the *ton* and those of the underworld.

Hunger stirred Nicolas's veins, but it was not for this woman. All his thoughts and attention were with another lady. One who probably would skewer him if he truly tried to kiss her. It should be alarming, the degree to which Lady Maryann compelled his senses.

"I am flattered," he said with a slow smile to lessen the sting to her vanity. "Regrettably, I must decline."

Her light blue eyes flared wide, and it was clear the lady was not accustomed to rejection.

"You are horridly disobliging," she said with a pout meant to entice. "Could it be the rumors *are* true? That you've formed an attachment with some naive little thing?"

It did not surprise him that gossip had already made

its way to this particular gambling den. The owners traded in information on the black market where the currency of secrets was more powerful than money itself. Everyone who visited the Asylum told of what they knew to see if they could gain some value from the knowledge they provided.

"If only they were," he said calmly. "Either way, I do not give a damn about said hearsay."

"How disagreeable of you." A calculating glint entered her eyes. "I have never heard you deny a rumor. Is the marquess protesting too much?"

Nicolas smiled but made no reply. Yet he perceived the threat in her probe. *Bloody hell.* Who else was actively wondering how important Lady Maryann was to him?

He walked past Salome, and he could feel her stare boring into his back. Perhaps she worked with Farringdon, the very duke Nicolas was knocking down a peg tonight.

It would explain her sudden interest, and there had been a rumor some months ago that they were lovers. Perhaps her task had been to seduce Nicolas and ferret out the truth. Or a weakness he was sure to have. Either way, he would not allow her to distract him from his purpose, but he would keep discreet tabs on her.

And most importantly, he would hire two of O'Malley's men who were former runners to discreetly watch over Lady Maryann and protect her, should the need arise. It was better to be safe than regretful. And the idea of anything happening to her was…truly unthinkable.

Nicolas stopped at the railing on the upper bowers, peering into the crowd of dancers as they twirled to the waltz. The ballroom was as elegant as those found in the best town houses in London, possibly even grander. All the women on the floor wore decadent masks to hide their identity from scandal, and in the arms of the men they twirled with, they were far bolder and more scandalous than ladies of the demimonde.

Nicolas spied Farringdon sitting at a table in a corner, conversing with the owner of Asylum, Riordan O'Malley. The duke appeared agitated, and he glanced over his shoulders several times, rubbing the back of his neck, and other times tugging at his cravat.

"He is getting desperate," David said, coming to stand beside Nicolas. "Someone has gone around and bought up all his debts and vowels. It is delightfully diabolical of you to have the bankers and merchants call them in at the same time. He is certainly feeling the pressure. And then—"

"I do not need a blow by blow for what I have done." Nicolas had methodically planned and executed it all. Though he quickly relayed the placket of information he had left for Viscount Humber.

David sent him a look of black admiration. "What did you trade to get the information from the broker that the duke likes to play with his own sex?"

Nicolas had obtained that with careful patience and by following the duke for months. But he did not reveal his hand to David, despite the man being his longest friend. Nicolas ignored him.

"By word, man, are you really not going to say?" David asked crossly.

"Ah, the show is about to start," Nicolas murmured.

Viscount Humber strode into the bowel of the den, his lips curved in disdain as he glanced around the decadent halls of the gambling club. When he spied the duke, he narrowed his eyes and marched over to him.

The duke glanced up, jumped to his feet, and met the man in the middle of the floor. The viscount gestured furiously, and whatever he said had the duke paling.

The viscount turned around and walked away stiffly. Farringdon stood there, his hands clenched at his sides, his expression one of unchecked rage.

"I believe the alliance between the families has been dealt a blow," David said, gripping the railing. "Are you satisfied?"

"Not even close," Nicolas murmured.

With each of Arianna's violators he brought down, there was never a feeling of satisfaction. In truth, the hollowness in his gut seemed to expand, wanting to fill every crevice of his soul. The hatred did not ease, and the guilt did not, either.

She was dead…and even when they paid, she would still be so.

He watched as the duke swept his hand and sent the glasses and the decanter of whiskey on the closest table shattering to the ground, then he collected his coat and hat and strode from the club.

"I hear that Viscount Weychell is already squirming on the hook," David said, inhaling deeply.

Viscount Weychell—the one Arianna had called Scarred Lips. Nicolas made no reply but gripped the railing until his fingers ached.

David sighed. "They have paid dearly; it feels almost frightening to know the end is near. There will be a day soon when every man who took part in her demise feels only regret and shame."

Silence fell between them.

"Do you remember the way she used to laugh?" David asked softly. "Her entire face would light up, and her mouth would be wide open."

No. The memory of her features had long faded and so had the sound of her voice. It was the conversations Nicolas recalled—those endless talks of dreams, hopes, and the future. "You normally teased her that she would catch flies with her laugh," he said gruffly, an ache rising in his throat.

David chuckled. "I've missed her every day for the last ten years, our little faerie dove."

The name they had given her when she had only been a girl of eight and they silly lads of ten years.

The eagle soars indifferently while the wolf betrays the dove...

"Did you know what would happen to her?" Nicolas asked softly.

David stumbled away from him, something wild and raw appearing in his dark gray eyes. "What did you just say to me?"

"You heard me."

David scrubbed a hand over his face. "I will forget that you asked me that before I plant a facer on you. I *loved*...I loved her and wanted her for myself. You know this...you know how much I loved Arianna."

The older they had become, the more her gentle attentions shifted to Nicolas, even though they had both pursued her. It was one of the reasons he had turned to David when he started his pathway in seeking retribution for the awful wrongs done against a girl they had both loved. But Nicolas could never forget her joy in the games they played as children by the lake and in the glen—she was the faerie, other times the dove, he was the eagle...and David the wolf.

The eagle soars indifferently while the wolf betrays the dove...

"I am heading home," Nicolas said with a sigh,

rubbing the back of his neck. Unexpectedly, he felt weary. As if he would sleep for a full day and hoped nothing haunted him.

"Have you ever given thoughts to what you will do when this is all over?" David asked. "I am thinking to make myself available on the marriage mart."

Nicolas dropped his hand and faced his friend. "You, *marry*?"

"I know, I can hardly believe it myself," David said dryly, his gaze watchful upon Nicolas. "I am twenty-eight. I've tupped enough. Time to give the old ball and chain a go."

Nicolas had lived so long in the pain and anguish of loss and guilt, in the need for vengeance, that he had not given a thought to the future. Not even when his mother had urged him to find a lady of quality and settle down had he been diverted from his purpose.

The dowager marchioness was aghast at his reputation, and at least every three months, sent him a letter beseeching him to mend his wild, wicked ways by selecting a fine girl of quality to marry.

Because in the *ton*, marriages solved everything.

Nicolas had allowed no distraction and no weaknesses since those he hunted had enough power to cause him considerable loss if they ever discovered him.

As if to mock him, a wide-eyed stare behind round spectacles swam in his thoughts. He ruthlessly suppressed her image and the arousal she had stirred to life. It was a delicate balance, but one he had maintained for years, and he would not misplace his footing now. "Whenever this is over, I am leaving England for a couple of years."

"Leave? And go where?"

"Sailing."

"That's it? Sailing?"

"Yes." That was one of the only pastimes he allowed himself. Every now and then, he would head to Dover, take out his yacht, and sail, feeling the wind behind him, the sun or rain on his face, and an inexplicable sense of freedom hovering on the horizon.

"You are a madman," David said with a laugh.

Nicolas smiled. "Miss me, will you?"

David snorted. Nicolas laughed and slapped his friend on the shoulder and then made his way out from the revelry and enticement of the club. It had been an unending day and an even longer night. He wanted to go home and fall into bed. And he wanted a deep sleep, one undisturbed by memory or guilt or one of the most painful things he would ever have to do—destroy the wolf.

CHAPTER SEVEN

The rumor would have started last night and spilled into society like fire on dry kindling. It was early yet, but those who had taken their obligatory stroll to be seen in Hyde Park would have stopped to gossip, and afternoon calls would be made scandalously early in drawing rooms to spread this latest *ondit*.

The bedchamber Nicolas St. Ives, Marquess of Rothbury had been seen sneaking from *was* that of Lady Maryann, a desperate wallflower, the daughter of the Earl and Countess of Musgrove.

"I am silly—no one would be that bold," she said to herself as she hovered in the hallway leading to the dining room. "More likely they will say St. Ives's mysterious lady is 'one Lady M, daughter to the earl of M.'"

Then the *ton* would use that affirmation along with the whispers at the ball and drawing room to condemn her.

Squaring her shoulders, lifting her chin, she entered the dining room. Her father, mother, and brother were already seated and eating. From the lack of laughing and talking, Maryann gathered they were already aware of the rumors. Her mother always took an early morning ride in Hyde Park, and many would have been only too happy to drop their sly hints and suppositions.

Her mother's light green eyes lit up in reserved welcome. She still retained a youthful bloom in her cheeks, and often dyed her hair to cover the smattering of gray that would otherwise appear at her temples.

Her father sometimes remarked on how her mother retained her slender, elegant carriage despite having birthed two children.

Going to the side table laden with food, Maryann selected a plate and filled it with sweet buns and slices of succulent ham. Everyone watched as she took her place by the table, and to her shame she could not meet their eyes. She reached for a bun and bit into it instead, savoring the honeyed and cinnamon flavor bursting on her tongue.

Her papa cleared his throat, and she lifted her gaze to look at him.

His was more curious than angry. "It seems you are also aware of this rumor going about."

"Yes, Papa." *I started it.* She closed her eyes tightly, hating that there was an ache of tears in her throat and behind her eyes.

"Why do you appear so out of sorts?" he demanded gruffly.

"Because I brought scrutiny to our names," she said, a hitch in her voice.

Anger flared in her father's eyes. "I know you acted with admirable conduct. It is this blackguard, Rothbury, who had the nerve to enter your chamber and ruin your reputation! I can only imagine what he did, that bloody bas—"

"Philip," her mother gasped, cutting off whatever improper word her husband was about to say.

"He did nothing, Papa," Maryann hurriedly said. "This is only a rumor."

The earl took a steady breath. "The marquess's actions will not be allowed to go unanswered. I will visit him and demand that he comes up to scratch."

Alarm scythed through her heart. "Papa!"

"I will not have that…that scoundrel marry my daughter!" her mother cried, staring at her husband in horror.

"Then he will meet me over dueling pistols."

Maryann almost fainted. "He did not climb into my room, Papa! It is just a baseless rumor. There is no truth in it."

Relief lit her father's eyes, and with a sense of shock, she realized he was worried that she had been ravished. The marquess's reputation was that dastardly. And of course, that was too much of a delicate conversation to have with her.

"He…Lord Rothbury was never in my chamber." And curse it, she blushed, recalling every provocative and provoking instance of the man actually being in her room last night.

Her father's eyes sharpened, and her mother appeared ready to swoon.

"Good heavens," the countess breathed. "This…this man, really…he…I…"

"No, Mama, the rumors you are hearing…they are baseless. He did not steal into my chamber at Lady Peregrine's house party. I spent most of my time with Ophelia."

"We should never have sent you," the countess moaned, her eyes tearing up. She cast a wrathful glance at Crispin, who seemed silenced with shock. "You were to have chaperoned your sister!"

"Even in her bedchamber, Mama?" her brother demanded in a choked whisper. "The marquess is reputed to be a crack shot, but I do not care! I will visit his club tonight and demand—"

"Stop!" Maryann cried. "There will be no duels or talks of duels because Lord Rothbury did not steal into my chamber! I…I started the rumor."

Dear God. Her entire face flamed once again, and she wanted to slide under the table at her unguarded reaction.

The countess paled and simply stared at her. Her mama had a reputation of being very haughty and concerned with rules and propriety. Regret clutched at Maryann's throat for the discomfort she was about to cause her family.

Her mother leaned back in her chair, her fork clattering to the table. Silence fell, and Maryann gazed at them miserably. Despite planning to mislead them, she could not hold her silence, not when they were talking of duels and marriage within the same breath. Not when she knew of her brother's fierce protective instincts when it came to her. Maryann had thought they would have accepted her explanation that it was simply a rumor, but it wasn't so.

Despite everything, her parents had taught them to always rely and trust in each other. It had been one of the reasons their decision to marry her off without considering her opinion had shredded her heart so much and had seen her crying for several nights before deciding to rescue herself.

"*You* started the rumor," her father repeated flatly, lowering his knife and fork.

Her lips trembled, and she bit the inside of her bottom lip to gather her composure. "Yes."

"But you are blushing. If he did not ravish—" Her mother closed her eyes as if unable to finish the very thought.

Maryann clasped her fingers together on her lap. With admitting her part in her own scandal, hopefully they might send her to their country home in

Hertfordshire for the next few months. That way she would have little chance of ever encountering the earl and any courtship on his part. Maryann reminded herself the most important part of her plan was for the rumor to be out in the *ton*.

"What could have possessed you to conduct yourself in such an odious manner?" her mother demanded sharply.

"I was desperate, Mama."

"So desperate you invited this man to your chamber? Have you irrevocably lost all sense of who you are and your position within society?"

She almost groaned. "The scandal sheets reported a sighting of Lord Rothbury climbing from someone else's windows. I…deliberately said within the earshot of a few ladies that it was my chamber he escaped from. There was no ravishment, Mama. No one climbed into my chamber at Lady Peregrine's house party. I vow it."

The varying degree of dawning shock indicated they finally believed her.

"Maryann," her mother cried, her color heightened. "What a dreadful scheme!"

She was painfully aware of the cold disappointment emanating from her father and Crispin's shock.

She lifted her chin. "A scheme I had to undertake because my family dismisses my hopes. I anticipated that Lord Stamford would hear the rumors and decide I would not do for his bride. I cannot conceive of anything worse than being his wife."

"You silly, provoking girl," her mother said, her eyes flashing with anger. "You are three and twenty and have had no offers! In a few months you will be four and twenty!"

"I would rather be called a spinster than Countess Stamford," she replied firmly, a lump growing in her throat.

"I see," her father said, his tone grave.

It was hard for her to hold his stare, but she stalwartly fought and did. "Papa, I tried to tell you several times. You ignored my hopes as if I were of little consequence to you. And *you* taught me I should always fight for the dreams in my heart."

Her father regarded her curiously for a moment. "So it is my fault for being over-indulgent," he said with a chilling bite.

"Papa—"

"It is my job to see that you do not end up an old spinster."

"This is ridiculous," she said softly.

Her mother sent her a swift glance of rebuke. One did not question the earl, but followed his orders, for as her mother often reiterated, he knew what was best for this family.

"I beg your pardon, young lady?" he demanded quietly.

Her father had that way about him. He did not shout or get angry. In truth, she could not ever recall him displaying an excess of emotions or even the bare minimum. It had always astonished her that Mama often said their courtship had been sweet and romantic.

"Papa, I am only three and twenty. Surely I can wait a few more years for marriage."

"And if no one offered for you in the bloom of youth, who would come up to scratch for you this season or a few years from now? I did my duty, and you will be a countess."

"An unhappy one?"

In a rare show of temper, he lowered his cup with a soft *clink*. "I've ensured someone will have you, and by God that will be the end of this obstinacy from you!"

Unexpectedly, she could not seem to catch her breath or stop the tears from burning her eyes. Her throat felt cramped, as though a noose were closing around it. "So it is because you pity me, Papa, that you've arranged my marriage to a man whom I do not know? A man I could not possibly grow to love? A man who would not value me or my opinions? I have no wish to marry Lord Stamford."

In a rare show of discord, her mama lifted her chin and said, "Perhaps we should allow for—"

"Our daughter will marry the man who offered for her," he said, reaching for the pressed newspaper.

"Why?" Maryann demanded, her voice raw. When her question was ignored as if she were an irritant, she curled her fist below the table. "I have no wish to marry, so why must I do so?" she stubbornly asked again. Mama shook her head, cautioning her, but Maryann did not want to hold her tongue, even if Papa were to punish her for challenging his authority. Her hands were shaking. "Papa, if you love me as you say you do, please consider my happiness."

He lowered the paper and sent her a frown. Of course this would all be an oddity. She had been raised with the notion that his words were absolute law, and she had never challenged him. Not even her brother dared.

"I *cannot* marry a man who does not care for me and has only shown he is brutish and unkind, paying little regard to my thoughts and preferences."

The silence felt painful and unnatural.

Her father's stare grew curious, as if he saw her for

the very first time in her three and twenty years. The last instance they had walked in the apple orchard as she regaled him with stories she had read had been years ago. Since her societal debut, they hadn't been as close as during her childhood.

It was as if she turned sixteen and was no longer a daughter but had been handed over to her mother to be altered into a wife—someone who no longer greeted her father with hugs but polite curtsies, someone who could no longer steal into the apple tree on a branch and read, but must stay indoors and practice the elegances of ladylike walking. Their long conversations by the fire in the library had stopped, and he no longer took her for morning rides and archery as he did with Crispin. So many things had changed, and her life had become how to be a proper wife to whichever gentleman accorded her the honor.

Only Crispin had remained constant, and she loved him dearly for it.

But now their father stared at her in a searching manner he had not ever turned on her brother.

"And how has Lord Stamford ignored your preferences?" her father asked.

Tentative hope stirred inside, and Maryann tried to not stare at her mother's flat and disapproving mouth.

"Well, young lady?"

She held her papa's stare. Maryann couldn't bear talking about what she'd witnessed. The mere memory alone was mortifying. "He…" Her face heated. "He attempted to kiss me when I did not want him to." Still uncomfortable to speak about, but it seemed the lesser of the two humiliating encounters.

Her father merely stared, as if trying to understand the creature speaking before him. Maryann almost squirmed under his attention. This was clearly not going to work. They had made their minds up and would not budge. She had only one throw of the dice left that she could try.

Her father folded his paper. "It is the way of courtship for a suitor to steal kisses. Stamford is clearly passionate and not one to hide his feelings. Is that the reason to rebuff a man who seems to be earnestly seeking your hand in marriage? When no other path to marriage stands before you?"

She smoothed back an errant lock of her hair that escaped the loose chignon. "May I speak with frankness, Papa?"

"You may."

"Like many gentlemen before him, the earl does not see me as a person with thoughts and opinions of my own." The memory of how he had gripped her chin and his cold mockery crowded her thoughts, and she forcefully shoved them aside.

"There is one more matter. I, er...came across him at the Metcalfs' ball." Maryann paused, embarrassed at what she had to say, then blurted out, "He was in a *very* intimate act with one of the maids. He was unabashed by my presence and bluntly informed me that he had no intention of changing his ways after we married."

The countess choked swallowing some tea, looking too shocked to say anything either to rebuke Maryann or to criticize Stamford. The earl's lips had flattened, but he also did not rebuke the earl's conduct.

Maryann tried again in a more conciliatory tone. "Do you know that I am called a wallflower by almost everyone in the *ton*? I've had four seasons because you insist on parading me to the gentlemen of society as if I am a horse that needs to be taken off your hands, then given to another for breeding."

Her mother fixed a gimlet stare on her. "Maryann! Such crudeness is unbecoming!"

She lifted her chin. "Each season grows more tedious than the last. The gentlemen of the *ton* do not find in me a favorable match to marry, despite my rumored dowry of fifty thousand pounds. And Papa, *I* do not find *them* favorable."

Her father stared at her thoughtfully for long seconds, then he said, "Continue."

Her mother made to protest, but he reached for her hand and brought her knuckles to his mouth in a brief kiss.

"Papa, the only option you have been giving me is marriage to a man who has been speaking to you of an alliance for over three months. Yet in that time, he has not made any attempt to court me. There is no kindness in his eyes. There is no gentleness in his touch, no sincerity in his conversations. For many years, you spoke to me of my worth and how much you cherished me. Yet you want to give me to a man who does not hold me in the same regard and worth that you taught me. If I cannot have at least that in a union, why must I submit to it? Surely, I was not educated and encouraged to dream, and then be told I am only fit to be a bride?"

Her mother looked ready to swoon, and Crispin stared at her as if she had grown horns. Only her papa remained unflappable, and Maryann knew it was he she needed to convince.

"Then what do you desire, if not to marry and have a home of your own?"

The question so startled her, she flustered for a few moments. "I do not know as yet, Papa."

A black scowl formed across his brow. "Maryann…"

"I do not discount ever having a family of my own, Papa. But as to what else life has to offer, how can I expect to know it when I was never given the freedom to dare to think there might be more beyond the constraints of your expectations?"

She swiped at the tears she hadn't realized spilled on her cheeks. "Please, Papa. If I have that freedom, perhaps I might find what my heart truly desires."

Her father remained contemplative for several moments. "We will withhold announcing the engagement for a few weeks."

She tried to stand and go to him, but relief made her knees wobble. "Thank you, Papa."

"You have until we retire to the country in October to find what it is you seek."

Oh God, that was only three months. "And if I do not find it?"

"You will marry Stamford."

A raw gasp escaped her.

"And what if I should find it?" she asked hoarsely.

"Once I approve, you will be allowed to reach for whatever it is."

It was more than she had expected but less that what she had hoped for.

"The countess and I will deal with the current gossip. Should it prove unmanageable, arrangements will be made for you to travel to Hertfordshire until it settles down. Crispin will accompany you while your mother and I remain in Town."

Her father was a powerful man in the *ton*; if he could squash the rumors, they would fade away like ashes in the wind within a couple weeks. A hard lump formed in her throat. "Yes, Papa."

She had always known the power of her ruse would be a momentary shock wave that would cause enough ripples in society to influence Stamford's actions. She'd once overheard her brother remark that a gentleman would not wish to marry a lady suspected of dallying with another gentleman. And everyone knew the marquess was a right rogue, the worst of the lot when it came to debauching innocent misses.

That was the whisper about for the last few seasons, and surely Stamford had heard them. Would he show up this morning, honor insulted, and withdraw his ridiculous offer?

"Papa...what if Lord Stamford should hear the gossips and withdraw his offer?" She ardently prayed he would.

Her father's expression shuttered. "He won't."

"But you cannot be so certain that—"

"He won't."

All appetite killed, Maryann excused herself, pushed back her chair, and walked away. A cold, heavy disquiet settled on her shoulders. How certain her father seemed, as if there was more to the matter.

With a sense of dread, Maryann wondered whether her father still possessed every intention of pushing through that alliance. With a deep breath, she accepted the truth—he had no intention of allowing her to escape marriage to Stamford, and whatever she wanted to pursue would be denied.

How could you, Papa?

CHAPTER EIGHT

Maryann reposed on a chaise longue in her personal parlor, working on delicate stitching for her embroidery. She had taken a tray in the parlor, too engrossed in completing her design of a chaffinch to join the family in the formal dining room. She wanted breathing room away from their heavy press of disappointment, and the hurt she felt that they still continued to ignore her heart's wishes.

The last few days had been emotionally tiring. Her mother had not berated her as expected, but the countess's eyes had been dark with disappointment, and that had hurt Maryann's heart more than a deserved tongue lashing. Crispin continually demanded to know if she wanted to start a scandal from which they might never recover. He scolded her most fiercely, blaming himself for her outrageous conduct. If not for his overindulgence, could she dream of being so boldly rebellious?

She had often heard the tale that as a babe she cried often, a misery not even her nursemaid could soothe. Only when Crispin took her into his arms was she soothed. A young boy of only four years at her birth, he had taken to his role as her protective older brother rather fastidiously. It had been mutual love, and never had he been angry with her as he had been this morning.

Growing up, she'd wanted to be a part of her brother's life simply because she loved him. For every rambunctious adventure he went on—the riding, the hunting, the fencing—she had pleaded to go with him. And because Crispin loved her in return, he had made room for her in his life. So many days, weeks, months he had snuck her from the school room and from under the noses of strict governesses to partake in his misadventures.

She had learned to change her own clothes, to dress in breeches and shirts without their parents getting wind of what they had been up to. She had learned to ride astride, how to perfectly handle a bow and arrow, and how to fence. Crispin had finally balked when she asked him to travel with her to a gambling hell, and she hadn't the heart to press the matter after seeing his distress. Maryann had decided in some matter, it was best to retain her ladylike demeanor.

It was a few minutes before nine p.m. that she placed the cambric in her embroidery box and made her way to her chamber. *He wouldn't dare, would he?* was the thought that rolled through Maryann's awareness as she choked on her gasp, whirling around to ensure her lady maid did not enter the room.

"I won't be needing you tonight, Susie," Maryann said, annoyed with how breathless and nervous she sounded. Her heart thrummed in both panic and pleasure. The former, she understood. The latter, utter madness.

"Milady?"

"Yes," she said with a firm smile. "I believe I shall manage on my own tonight. You should continue reading that book I loaned you."

Susie flushed. "I am still fumbling over some of the words, milady," she said, her voice rich with pride.

"Then write them down, and in the morning we shall discuss them."

Susie bobbed, turned around, and hurried down the hallway, a jaunt in her step. Maryann closed the door, resting her forehead on it briefly. She was shocked to realize she was trembling.

Taking a steadying breath, Maryann whirled to face the marquess, who seemed to have dragged an armchair to the window, and now reposed in it, one of his knees crossed atop the other.

"Am I to play your maid tonight, Lady Maryann?" A deliberate pause, which felt fraught. "It would delight me, of course."

She choked on air. "What are you doing here, Lord Rothbury? My maid almost discovered you."

A lazy smile curved his mouth, and she flushed for even noting its sensuality.

"I am certain you would have some reasonable explanation."

"Of having a man in my bedroom at…" She glanced at the ormolu clock on the mantel. "At nine in…at *any* hour in the day?"

"I miscalculated your routine. If you are not at some social event, you would normally come into your bedroom at about eight and prepare for bed. Since I arrived only fifteen minutes ago, I assumed that routine was already done."

"You know my routine?" she asked faintly.

"How else might I ensure your safety?"

She rolled her eyes. "There is no threat to my safety; you are using it as an excuse to be a libertine."

"Oh!" he said with mock affront, pressing a hand over his heart. "I am too wounded to find a witty remark. This round to you, my little racoon."

Maryann refused to dignify his outrageousness with an answer.

"Did anything out of the ordinary happen to you today?"

"No, why would it?" she asked. "Your invisible *enemies*?"

"Not even on your walk this afternoon with Miss Nelson? She seemed out of sorts."

"Were you there?"

He closed the book with a snap. "No."

Yet he knew of her stroll with another friend, and that dear Charlotte had been upset. There was a rumor the Marquess of Sands had eloped, and the news distressed her friend, who was secretly in love with Lord Sands. That story and Maryann's scandal seemed to vie for equal attention in the fickle hearts of the gossipmonger. "Nothing happened that would concern you, my lord."

"And what made you curse upon leaving the lending library?"

Maryann glared at him. She suspected the man before her might be aware of everything she did since waking, and Maryann was decidedly unsure what to think about that. Clearly he had bribed a servant in her household for information. "There is a great possibility *you* are the danger, my lord."

His teeth flashed, and her heart lurched at the beauty of his smile.

"I assure you, my lady, you are always safe with me."

Did she imagine the emphasis on "my lady"? Maryann leaned against her door, feeling that, should she step closer, the very air between them would be altered.

His stunning golden eyes entrapped her attention. "So, you've been teaching your lady maid to read."

"I…" She blew out a sharp breath, rattled by the quick change in conversation. "Yes."

"Not many people care about their servants enough to use their time to educate them."

She returned his regard, and when he arched a brow, Maryann pertly said, "Was there a question?"

"I am merely curious…about you."

This he said with a frown, as if he was baffled by his own admission.

Maryann found it most difficult to break the potent hold of his very direct regard. He stared at her as if unraveling a mystery. A tight, hungry feeling was trapped somewhere inside her, and being secreted in her chamber with the marquess made her yearn to just be.

"Susie always sees me reading, and she was very curious as to how I found such enjoyment in the written word," Maryann said softly. "She is very uncomplaining with my determined efforts to see her reading a book on her own by the end of the year."

Maryann did not say that she had moved from having one student to now having four, the youngest being a sweet girl of twelve who served as a scullery maid.

"And I am also very different from these other ladies you seem so intimately acquainted with."

"That I can tell."

Her mouth curved a bit, but she bit inside her lips to stop the smile. Perhaps he did not mean it as a compliment.

"What is your most rousing read?" He turned over a small volume in his hand. "I dearly hope it is not this."

She laughed. "Whenever I am curious about something, I find if there is a book with the subject and read."

"So, you are interested in the mating habits of sheep?"

Maryann turned the lock with a soft *snick*, and mocking yet sensual delight suffused his features. The man was extravagantly handsome.

"I only closed it because I would hate for anyone to discover you here," she snapped. "If society knew how easy it was for a libertine to break into their daughters' chambers, every mother would have found a way to build iron bars over the windows by now."

Maryann sauntered over to the sofa and sank gracefully into its softness.

"I am certain you did not break into my room once again to question my reading tastes," she said pertly. "And nothing strange happened to me. I daresay if you should tell me what I am supposed to look out for, I could inform you better?"

"There is no reason for you to be involved more than necessary. The entire scheme might eventually reveal that I am merely overcautious," he said, a sardonic look in his eyes.

"Do recall that my parents are diligently crushing those rumors I started. It is very unlikely anyone might believe we have a tendre."

He said nothing to this.

"How did you get inside?" she whispered.

He spread the fingers of one lean, elegant hand. "I picked the locks."

She had thought a servant let him in, the very one he learned her routine from. "Of course that skill is a part of your repertoire. How…how did you learn it?" For she was considerably curious about the enigmatic man before her.

"From one of the greatest thieves to roam the streets of Paris."

"Paris?"

"Hmm, we did not stay there long once we found each other."

"And how exactly did you find each other?"

"I rescued him from the night's watch. Seems he had broken into a home occupied by soldiers and stolen some bread. He was only thirteen years old."

Her heart squeezed violently. "How did you rescue him?"

The marquess canted his head, and a faraway look entered his eyes. There was such strength of purpose etched into his face. "A clash of steel that thankfully did not last long. Then the good lad and I fled to the countryside, Rodez in Aveyron where I have a modest home."

He leaned over and plucked another book from the pile she had left on her windowsill, her favorite spot to repose and read. "Ah, my sisters are always asking me to buy these for them."

Her cheeks warmed, for it was a gothic romance. "You have sisters?"

"Hmm, two delightful hellions," he said rather fondly. "Is it safe for me to purchase a copy and send to them?"

Maryann cleared her throat delicately. "There is an extremely passionate kiss somewhere in there. Are they old enough to read about that?"

His lips twitched briefly. "They would cry and whine and tell me they are, but clearly they are not."

They stared at each other, and Maryann did her best to remain unflappable. The entire situation was so unusual. "How old are they, your sisters?"

"Thirteen. They are twins. A late surprise for my parents."

The echoes of affection lingered in his tone and rendered him so much more approachable.

"Have you not satisfied yourself that I am safe and nothing odd happened?"

"Yes."

"Yet you are still here in my chamber."

"As soon as I borrow a book, I shall leave. You have an eclectic reading taste. It is impressive."

Maryann felt the warm admiration of his tone all the way to the pit of her stomach. "What…what do you like to read?"

"Why do you sound so surprised that I do?"

She lifted a shoulder in an inelegant shrug. "Well, you *are* supposed to be a rake."

"Ah, and we are creatures who cannot read?"

"Hmm, too busy with debauchery. Wherever would you find the time or the inclination?"

His wry chuckle quickened her pulse. They were reaching quite another level of intimacy with their conversation.

"I like William Wordsworth and E. T. A. Hoffmann. I've never told anyone that before, so guard the knowledge with your life." Slipping her gothic romance book into his pocket, he said, "I will borrow this book and read it for myself. You are blushing so delightfully, that means I made the right choice."

Maryann rolled her eyes. "If that is your desire, am I able to stop you?"

His slow smile made her heart beat suddenly faster, for he surveyed her with disturbing intensity with those brilliant eyes. "No, I suppose you cannot, but I would not take it without your permission."

"Are we still talking about the book?" she murmured.

His eyes darkened. The marquess seemed riveted. Unexpectedly he stood, bowed, and shoved open her window and went through it. A breath escaped Maryann in a rush. Her heart raced in earnest. Would he truly visit her often to ascertain she was safe? She really did not know what to make of him, but a keen awareness lingered that he excited her unbearably.

• • •

Visit three was the very next day. This time he traveled with a card pack and invited her to play piquet with him. When she bemusedly said she did not know how, he lowered himself to the carpet by the sofa and with an enigmatic wave of his hand invited her to sit. Maryann toed off her slippers and joined him.

"Why are you here again?" she demanded, despite anticipating his presence. *Oh, why do I like you so?*

"I told you the consequences of linking our names together."

"So, this is you checking in on my safety?"

"Most assuredly."

"I do not believe you."

"Then why do you think I came?"

She arched a brow. "For my charming company, of course."

Something wary flashed in his gaze, as if she had hinted at a truth yet not acknowledged by him. Her heart stuttered, and she remained silent for a long time.

Maryann wondered if he was lonely, then felt bewildered by her supposition. At the balls she'd seen the marquess at, he was always surrounded by a bevy of lady admirers. Even the young bucks seemed like they desired to emulate the marquess. But perhaps he had no genuine friendship with his admirers?

"What are you thinking about?" he asked, staring at her too intently.

"Exactly how I am going to talk about you in my diary."

"Your diary?" This seemed to surprised him.

"Of course," she drawled. "Most ladies do have one. It is a place where we are allowed to express ourselves freely, you know."

A glint entered his eyes, one of relish perhaps. "I wonder what secret longings are on those pages."

"None you'll ever be privy to," she said pertly, fighting a blush, for she had wondered on those pages what it would be like to have the attentions of this dratted rake.

He leaned in slightly and gave her a decidedly wolfish yet sensual smile. "Is that a challenge, Lady Maryann?"

That outrageous, inexplicable desire to kiss him filled her once more.

Considerably shaken, she shifted away so he could not see her expression of want. "Are we to play piquet or not?"

Devilry danced in his eyes. "Let's play."

After almost an hour of the game, his stomach rumbled, and his sheepish smile made him seem so much more approachable, and not the dangerously mysterious stranger or charming rake who made her pulse trip with alarm.

Maryann rang for a maidservant and asked for a tray of leftovers from their dinner, delicious slices of roast ham, beef, and asparagus in cream sauce, to be sent to her room on a tray. The maid might have thought it odd she had collected it in the hall but wisely made no comment. They sat there on the carpet, the tray to one side as they both ate from the array of delicacies and continued their game.

• • •

Visit four, Maryann pled a headache and did not attend Lady Gladstone's soiree. After dinner, she raced up the stairs and flung her door open. Disappointment pressed in on her gut, for the marquess wasn't in the chair by the window.

Maryann went over to her vanity, sat, and slowly unpinned her hair, intending to ring the bell for her lady maid. It was then she felt the profound power of his stare and whirled around to see him lounging on her bed.

"You are unpardonable," she gasped.

"More like tired," he replied, a twinkle in his eyes. "Did anything out of the ordinary happen today?"

A thrill went through her. "*If* you truly have some-one watching me, Lord Rothbury, you know this already." He hadn't come to check on her safety; it was an excuse. And God help her, Maryann was almost afraid to wonder what it meant.

"Perhaps I missed you," he said with lazy amuse-ment.

Yet there was a most astonishing flush along his jawline. He shifted, casting himself perfectly in the shadows.

You are hiding from me.

She scoffed, even as her heart raced. "Do you know how outrageous it is for you to sneak into my room once more?"

"I *was* exceedingly careful." He propped a pillow

behind him and the headboard. "Why did you stop?"

She became aware her fingers were still frozen on a pin in her hair.

"I have never seen hair so beautiful. The dark russet fire of sunset."

Maryann was silent for a few breaths. "It is brown," she said, staring at him, an inexplicable feeling stirring inside.

"Let me see it unpinned."

That provocative urging set her heart into an alarmed start.

"Absolutely not." And for good measure Maryann repinned her tresses even tighter than before.

The man only smiled, stood, and stumbled slightly. It was then she noted the dark shadows of exhaustion beneath his eyes. "How long have you been awake?"

"Since I last saw you."

"I will allow you three hours of sleep."

Now he faltered into stillness. "Here?"

"Yes."

"Living dangerously, I see," he drawled teasingly but tumbled into the bed. "I might need a bedtime story." The marquess patted the mattress beside him. "I will not object if you wish to sleep as well."

The scoundrel!

Maryann stood and plucked a book from the small pile on the table. "How apropos. The mating habits of sheep."

He laughed, then a second later his deep breathing echoed in the room. She walked over and peered down at him, charmed at how boyishly handsome he appeared in sleep. *Almost vulnerable.*

No doubt he had spent a full day carousing and was deeply exhausted, but why had he still insisted on visiting her?

"I cannot pretend to understand what drives your interest in me," she whispered in the stillness of the room.

Maryann eventually fell asleep on the sofa, but when she stirred some hours later, she was in her bed and the marquess gone.

. . .

A few days later, as she woke, Maryann sat before her small writing table and poured her emotions and thoughts onto the pages of her journal.

Dearest Diary,
I am beginning to wonder if it is possible to form a friendship with one of London's most notorious rakes.

Maryann paused writing and closed her eyes. *Friendship? Oh, what am I thinking?*

The marquess has stolen into my chambers on five occasions. He never stays long, and I do not believe in the reason he gives for being so improper. Nor do I understand why I indulge his actions. And I do, for I increasingly look forward to his visits.
It has been a week since I last saw him, and my silly curiosity wonders why he has stopped visiting me. There are times I feel his stare from across a busy street but when I look, no one is there. I saw him once this week, on High Holborn, and I maintained a respectable distance, fearing all of society would see my fascination. Fearing he would see it. The marquess watched me discreetly, the curve to his lips provoking, and his gaze

*stroked against my skin, a delightful caress that I know
is not real.*

That man is unequivocally intrigued by my mouth.

*I think perhaps that night he visited me, I woke to
find my nightcap missing and my hair spread across
my pillows. I should have been startled, but I was
everything but. Instead I wondered how long he had
stayed, wondered if he had watched me sleep as I had
watched him, wondered if he too dreams of kissing me.
Something unknown quivered through me, hot and
startling. What are these feelings I cannot say, for I've
never encountered them before, though they felt
remarkably like how desire is supposed to be.*

Maryann lowered the quill and closed her diary. Just
thinking about the marquess made her entire body
grow warm and flushed. Since that fateful night she had
spread the rumors, Maryann hadn't been to another
ball. Her parents forbade it, hoping her absence would
urge society to forget. To her regret, her parents were
using their influence to squash all murmurings linking
her name with the marquess. Tonight, she would be
attending a ball, a test to see if they had successfully
undone the damage she'd willfully casted upon her
reputation.

And her mother had sternly warned Maryann to
ignored Nicolas St. Ives, Marquess Rothbury at all
cost. Maryann closed her eyes, hoping that the curious
hunger she felt growing inside did not lead her to ruination…or something far worse.

CHAPTER NINE

Almost three weeks after the first night the marquess stole into her chamber, Maryann stood on the terraced balcony of Lady Trembly's home, escaping the stifling heat of the overly crowded ballroom. She lifted her hand to her mouth to hide an indelicate yawn. Maryann felt a bit weary and wished she were at home snuggled in bed reading or working on her latest embroidery. The late summer day had been unusually dreary and overcast, and she had spent the day indoors, canceling a shopping date she had with her friend Ophelia.

This midnight ball was her second affair this week, the first a picnic at Hyde Park. Maryann had tried to escape attending this ball, hating the very idea of encountering Lord Stamford without a new plan. The countess insisted the first step in proving the rumors untrue was to make a united show to the *ton*. They were all at the ball, even her father, who spent most of his evenings at White's with his cronies, a glass of brandy, and their political debates.

There was a faint stir when they had entered, but their hostess had hurriedly greeted them, signaling her belief in the Fitzwilliams' impeachable reputation. Once in the ballroom, a few sly speculative whispers had reached their ears, but her mother acted as if those persons were ants below her heels. Maryann had danced three times, once with her father and twice with Crispin.

Lady Sophie stood in a circle of admirers, her humiliating spectacle of a few weeks prior forgotten.

Or no one dared mention it when her brother, the duke, attended the same event. Old gossips were quickly forgotten in lieu of new gossips, and tonight it was Maryann's name on those wagging tongues. Maryann suspected it was her scandal which had forced the duke's sister to attend. It would not do for her to stay at home and gloat at another's downfall. That must be done in person.

It was Lady Sophie and her coterie sauntering in Maryann's direction with malice on their faces which prompted her to seek fresh air on the balcony.

They had not witnessed her escape, and she reminded herself that she was not running or cowering away. "There are other days to fight," she whispered.

With a heavy sigh, she lifted her face to the sky, pleased to see a few stars out. Knowing that her family was disappointed in her hurt. She had told Crispin earlier it was that same disappointment she had endured when they had plotted her future without a single say-so from her.

The feel of eyes on her body had her scanning the crowded ballroom. A gasp stifled in her throat when she spied Stamford by a potted plant. The manner in which he stared at her was decidedly outrageous; he did it boldly, and quite uncaring that people might see and speculate. His insolent inspection was enough to create another scandal.

Horror darted through her when he started to discreetly move toward her. If she hadn't been watching him, it would have slipped her notice. With a stifled curse, she hurriedly slipped inside the ballroom, scanning the crush for her mother or even Crispin.

Her brother danced the waltz with a young lady she did not recognize, and she did not see her mother or father. Now that she was in the thick of the crowd, she stayed on the sidelines watching the twirling couples. How graceful and charming they all appeared.

"Lady Maryann," Lord Stamford greeted, coming to stand before her.

She dipped into a quick curtsy. "Lord Stamford."

"Business had taken me to Derbyshire for a few days, but now that I am back in town, I feel we should have a private chat that is long overdue. Might I ask you to join me on the terrace?" he said with a mocking smile. "You will go first and then I will follow, discreetly of course."

She smiled up at him, and he sucked in a sharp breath, looking decidedly startled.

"Denied," she said sweetly.

"I beg your pardon?"

"You truly did not anticipate my refusal? How *arrogant*."

A warning flashed in his eyes, one she chose to ignore.

"Then I will claim your hand in the next waltz."

"The next set is not a waltz," she said, not liking the idea of being in his arms.

With another mocking smile, he dipped into a bow and made his way over to the twenty-piece orchestra set. Maryann did not wait to see what he would do. She spun around and waded through the throng toward escape. She was intimately familiar with the town home of Lady Trembly, after visiting so often with her mama.

Once in the hallway, she rushed to the curved stairs and made her way to the second floor and tested the first door she came upon. It was a quaint little sitting area, with a long sash window that opened onto a terrace. The moon provided her with enough light for her to navigate outside to the balcony.

Laughing voices reached her and she peered down into side gardens lit by a few lanterns.

The Marquess of Rothbury.

His back was turned to her, so perhaps she was mistaken, but the wild beat of her heart told her she wasn't. The man shifted, and a soft breath escaped her. It was indeed the marquess in the gardens, smoking. For a brief, outrageous second, her heart soared.

As she stared at his dark masculine beauty, longing halted her breath, and for the first time, she wished she had kissed him that night he broke into her room. And perhaps every time after that.

She lifted slightly shaky fingers to her mouth. The attraction she felt for the scoundrel was so frightful and improper, but worse was that she had no notion of how to get rid of it. She wondered if she would have seen St. Ives with another woman, would he have been as vulgar as Stamford about it? It would be expected of such a rake, but even the thought of him so carnally with another woman annoyed her. She had no claim on him. No right at all to be jealous. However, she thought somehow that he would not be sordid and indiscreet in his affairs.

What would it taste like to be kissed at last…and by you?

The three gentlemen the marquess stood with spoke low but laughed uproariously at whatever quip they shared. She wondered if they noted that though he smiled, he did not truly take part in their merriment. As she suspected since the night he had climbed into her room, there was more to the man than what he presented to the world.

Tonight, he was dressed in unrelenting black, save

for the bright purple waistcoat he wore. If he had been trying to appear a dandy, in her eyes he failed. He was such a unique combination of casual power and refined elegance.

A fourth gentleman joined them, and she stiffened, gripping the end of the iron railing. The man dragged a girl with him, and despite that she seemed frightened and quite unwilling, he prodded her ahead.

"And who is this little morsel?" St. Ives drawled, removing the cheroot from between his lips.

His tone suggested debauchery lingered in his thoughts, and from the guffaws of his friends, they agreed. Maryann frowned, for it did not ring true to what she had come to know of his character.

"This is the governess, Miss Laura! I found her peeking inside the ballroom. Seems she would like a spot of fun," the Duke of Farringdon drawled.

The man was Lady Sophie's brother, but Maryann had not thought him so lacking in morals and honor. The girl was clearly frightened out of her wits! Then to Maryann's shock, the duke drew the girl to him and nuzzled her neck. The young girl pushed him away and lurched back, until she encountered another bounder. This time she recognized Viscount Weychell, the son of Lord Tremelle. How dare they?

"Governesses are particularly tasty, but she's not pretty enough to tempt me; I daresay you should let her back inside," Lord Rothbury said blandly.

The young girl threw the marquess a grateful look before her face crumpled.

"Are you mad?" the man currently holding her, Viscount Weychell, demanded. "She is a lovely piece of flesh. We should be able to have some fun in that secluded spot over there."

"Ah, I thought you had a more discriminating palate," Rothbury said with a measure of arrogance and disgust. "But what can one expect?"

The viscount stiffened, his features creasing in a black scowl. "What do you mean by that, Rothbury?"

He wore a carefully cultivated expression of restless boredom. "A young governess? If you want women of varied expertise, there is a place I can take you to in Soho."

"And if it is her we want?" the viscount demanded belligerently, while the other two silently watched.

"It would be remiss of me to allow my friends to act foolhardy and not tell them. She is an employee in the earl's household. He would not look favorably on your actions tonight."

"She wouldn't dare tell," the man who had brought her outside said. "Who would want to admit to dallying with their lord's guests?"

The girl started crying, and St. Ives snorted in affected disgust.

"I am not attracted to her mousiness. Are *you*?" he asked with such exaggerated astonishment, the viscount tugged uncomfortably at his cravat.

Maryann realized he wanted the girl safely away from the degenerate lot but had gone about it in this fashion. *Why*? Why not rebuke them for their improper conduct and whisk her away? Was it because he was outnumbered?

What are your reasons, St. Ives?

After much muttering, they released the girl, St. Ives passing her a handkerchief plucked from his pocket. Maryann strained to hear what he said to the young girl but missed it. She, however, bobbed her head, skirted around the men, and hurried inside.

"Do we head to Soho, then?" one of the men asked, smacking his lips.

"After supper, I cannot swive on an empty belly."

They laughed and made their way in, all except the marquess. The tip of the cheroot flared orange as he dragged the taste and scent into his lungs. She should make haste and return to the ball, but she found herself resting her gloved elbows on the railing and studying him.

"Did you enjoy the show?" he asked, taking another drag.

She leaned over to see who had come outside and frowned when she saw no one. To her surprise, he turned around and looked right at her. She sucked in an audible breath and gripped the railing. "I was not aware my presence was felt."

The very faintest of smiles creased his mouth. "I might be going mad, because it was as if I tasted you on the air—apples and peaches with a hint of cinnamon."

She ignored that provocative drawl and said, "As to the show you referred, I was singularly unimpressed. You keep ghastly company."

He pressed a hand over his chest. "Even with my heroics?"

"They were more the acts of a bounder. If you had raised a fist and given them a facer each, then I could salute you, my lord."

"How violent you are," he mused, that smile again teasing his mouth. "I like your fierceness."

"You silver-tongued devil," she murmured with mock gratitude. "It is what we racoons are known for."

He smiled and sauntered in her direction.

The door behind her rattled, and she whirled around.

"Lady Maryann?"

The solid oak muffled the voice, yet still an undeniable foreboding filled her body. Maryann contained her gasp when the door opened.

"Lady Maryann," the voice called with that mocking lilt.

It was Stamford! How had he found her here? She turned around, rapidly thinking. It would not do for him to find her in such a secluded place.

"What is it?" the marquess demanded, his expression hardening.

She shook her head wordlessly.

His gaze narrowed, and it alarmed her how lethal he suddenly appeared. "I can see the panic on your face. Stay there. I will make my way to you."

"No," she whispered furiously. That would be an even worse scandal, the possibility of being caught with two men in a secluded room. And yet...instinctive knowledge filled her. Stamford meant to compromise her.

"Catch me!" And without overthinking the matter, she slung one of her legs over the railing, then another.

"And allow you to flatten me to the ground?" he asked drily.

"A disagreeable prospect, I agree, but what am I to do?"

"Reach for the trellis to your left," St. Ives commanded, walking closer to the balcony.

She did and gripped it, feeling with her foot for the vines that would give her purchase. Maryann found it and started to climb down, grateful for all the misadventures she'd had over the years with Crispin. The overflowing vines seemed to come alive, scratching at her arms and pulling at her clothes and hair.

Holding on for dear life, she made to step down again and slipped. She closed her eyes tightly, swallowing the rising scream as she plummeted to the ground, placing her trust in the scoundrel beneath her. The very one who might ignore her, since he did not want to be flattened.

With a soft grunt, she landed in his arms and against his chest.

"I've got you," he said, his mouth a dark murmur at her temple.

Maryann was terribly aware that she was held perfectly in the marquess's arms. Though his touch was through layers of gown and petticoats, she felt him like a searing brand. "You may put me down."

"Must I? I like the weight of you in my arms. It rouses certain fantasies to life. Shall I tell you of them?"

She pinched his shoulder with great force through his jacket. "You are unpardonable!"

The cynicism left his countenance, but in his half-closed eyes lingered a gleam far more alarming. "I'll take pleasure in taming you, Lady Maryann."

"You are odiously provoking," she gasped in a suffocated voice.

He caught her about the waist and swung her lightly down to her feet.

"You still like me—I can tell."

Maryann hurriedly stepped back a few paces. Her hands were no longer quite steady as she smoothed the front of her gown. She remained where she was, carefully eyeing him, attempting to swallow down the impulse to retreat inside. It affected Maryann that he rattled her nerves so easily.

An awfully intense sensation twisted low in her

stomach when he rested a strong, powerful arm about her waist, and stepped in a pocket of shadow.

"My lord—" she started to protest at the intimate way he held her body against his.

He lightly pinched her chin. "Shh."

She was unequivocally flustered. And it was then she heard the footsteps above. The earl had come out onto the balcony. A quick peek upward revealed a dark shadow, the clear outline of a man, leaning against the iron railing and looking down. Reflexively she gripped the lapels of St. Ives's jacket, her heart pounding.

Wariness rolled down her spine in a chilly wave. "Why is he so persistent?" she whispered. "I cannot understand it."

"Sometimes racoons are highly coveted."

Maryann glared at him, barely able to discern the flash of teeth in the darkness. With each inhalation, his masculine scent seemed to trap in her lungs. A strange, darting heat pooled low in her stomach, and to Maryann's annoyance, she very much liked the feel of his body pressed against hers. They fit. The top of her head brushed against his chin, and she swore the man smelled her hair.

She made to lift up her head, and his hands tightened on her hips, arresting her movement. She slowly became aware that his heart was pounding, and she could feel its thud in the space between them. Uncertainty rippled through her at the provocative embrace...at the closeness...at the tripping of her heart...

At the butterflies in her stomach.

The heat of his body surrounded her. "Don't move," he whispered. "We are now one with the shadows; any sudden movement might give away our presence."

A tremor traveled through her and vibrated against his chest. A lengthy, tension-filled silence stretched between them. A minute or two perhaps passed with no words between them, just a dizzying awareness of his closeness and how improper their entire encounter was.

"Is he still there?" she asked huskily.

"Hmm."

"What is he doing?"

"I don't know."

"Aren't you looking?"

"No."

She let out an exasperated huff. "Why not?"

"I am too busy staring at you."

The diabolical fiend. "If you are minded to be wicked, I implore you to try your wiles on someone else." The marquess was notorious for his womanizing exploits, and she was not about to become one of his amusements. It even astonished her that she would be, not when he had so many eager girls for his salacious attentions.

He smiled, and suddenly it was unbearably tempting to press her mouth to his. Annoyed with herself for having the desire, Maryann twisted and glanced up. "You fiend! Lord Stamford is no longer there!"

Before Lord Rothbury could reply, she balled her fist and punched him in the gut. It was as if she'd slapped a rock, and it was her hand that throbbed. With a huff, she sidestepped him with the intent to rush back inside before she was discovered.

Gentle hands clasped her waist, lifted her, and placed her back in the pocket of the shadows. Maryann was so astonished at his audacity, she spluttered.

"Sheathe your claws, little racoon; your hair is a

mess, and you have twigs and leaves all over your clothes."

Oh! A warm, melting sensation flowed through her. "Thank you."

"Hmm."

He unerringly found the few twigs and removed them in silence. His gloved finger brushed her nape and that warm feeling muted to pure heat. She did not understand her reaction to the man, and she wondered if he felt anything at all.

A lone finger caressed her spine up to the exposed part of her neck. When had he taken off his gloves?

"You have the most delightful skin. So unbelievably soft."

"I gather this is a marriage proposal, since you want the privilege to touch what is not yours?" she asked with some amusement, unable to be annoyed with his impertinence, not when he made her heart race in such a recklessly curious way. There was an inexplicable part of her unbearably tempted by the marquess.

He made a rough choking sound.

"A feverish aversion to matrimony, I see," she said lightly. "Yet here we are, alone and enshrouded in darkness."

"Mothers do warn their daughters from slipping away with me to dark corners, a message that seemed to miss you."

When she stiffened, he chuckled.

"And in the same breath, they tirelessly plot how to trap you into marriage," she drawled. "I cannot fathom what is the charm."

"It seems the title and my wealth are enough to overlook the dastardliness."

A curious hunger rushed through her. "It is

rumored ladies fall into your bed with just a smile from you, and you've left countless broken hearts behind."

"It is a lovely smile," he said drolly. "Very hard to resist."

"Oh, it is more than lovely. Beautiful I would say, devilishly unfair."

A hitch in his breath sounded, and it gladdened her that she had rattled a man so self-assured.

"I've never had a lady flatter my vanity so shamelessly," he murmured.

Maryann snorted indelicately. "*I* am not one of those women silly enough to fall rapturously in love with you because you bared your teeth."

"You exaggerate my abilities."

Laughter and something unfathomably dark lurked in his tone. A warning that she played in a league she did not belong in slithered down her spine. "I was more in despair of those ladies' mettle."

Provocative silence fell between them, and Maryann peered up in the dark, trying to discern his expression.

"Did Stamford cancel the marriage offer?" he asked abruptly.

There was an undecipherable emotion in his voice.

"No."

"It has been several days since you started the rumors."

"Perhaps he only heard them tonight and chased me to offer his reprimand," she replied lightly, though she felt uncertain about the earl's reasoning.

"If he meant to act with honor, he would meet with your parents."

"I..." The earl had somehow known she had escaped to the small parlor and had attempted to enter knowing she was alone without a chaperone. "I cannot fathom his intentions."

The shadows made it hard to decipher his expression fully, but she suspected he stared at her with maddening deliberation. "A liberal experience with debauchery lets me know when another is set upon it. Be incredibly careful in his presence—take care to never be alone with him."

"Thank you," she said softly, perplexed by the warmth streaking through her veins.

"Were your parents successful in squashing our scandal?"

Our scandal. "They are trying rather fiercely."

"Your reckless ploy failed."

"I fear my father means to marry me to the earl at all cost. Papa gave me a few weeks more of freedom, but after that I am certain it is expected I will fall in line like a biddable daughter."

"Will you?"

"I do not wish to hurt my parents, for I love them, but if Papa still insists I marry Stamford, I *cannot* do as he commands."

"Ah, so you need to be wickeder?"

"You sound as if you approve."

"Wholeheartedly."

Her belly did a frightening flip. *The devil!*

"Perhaps you should start another scandal," he murmured.

Maryann smiled. "I *should*, though I would most certainly be banished to the country immediately. That would make it harder for you to sneak into my rooms."

"Ah, is that censure I hear for not visiting you for the past week, Lady Maryann? Why, I do believe you missed me."

Before she could make a witty retort, he walked away without bidding her adieu. She stared wistfully after him, heart jerking when he stopped. Maryann waited in the shadows until he turned around. She should hurry away in the opposite direction—common sense had to prevail, and being here with him was inarguably reckless. Yet her feet remained rooted as if they had a will of their own.

He took a step closer to her but remained in the light cast from the lantern strung above him. "History shows us that real change is accepted *after* a rebellion. You have a bit of rebel in you; do not let others' expectations stifle you. While it is expected a daughter should always obey her father, if you wish for that perception to change…"

"I suppose I must rebel," she said, her tone rich with amusement.

Another step. "Your ferocity *can* be charming; I am sure you've been told."

He so shocked Maryann, she laughed before covering her mouth. He thought her rebellious…and *that* was charming.

"Perhaps I might ask you to reserve a dance for me before going in to supper?"

A dance. "With *you*?" she asked, genuinely shocked…and thrilled.

His head dipped slightly, as if to hide the intensity of his expression. "Imagine the wicked scandal of that. Lord Stamford might call me out then and there." His eyes were a piercing gold shadowed by rich, dark eyebrows, and this near, she could see the devilishness that lurked within. He touched the tip of her nose with a finger. "More biting discourse with you would also be a welcome diversion from the tedium of the evening."

Maryann stared at him, trying to gather her scattered wits. To dance with *this* marquess would be inviting ruin in a manner that was most profound. And why would he even help her?

A welcome diversion. "Are you by chance amusing yourself with a flirtation, with *me*?"

Another step closer. "I see you find humor in the notion."

Maryann had reached the age of practicality, and she no longer indulged in silly dreams. Yet peering up at him, barely able to discern his expression, she felt a surge of hunger so painful, she felt mortified. "I've never flirted with a gentleman before," she said musingly, "but then you are no gentleman, are you?"

"No, I suppose not."

A rake, a libertine, and a dangerous hellraiser—all the names she'd heard whispered about him. "I am not the sort of lady men of the *ton* flirt with, that I am certain you know."

"I don't," he said a bit abruptly, before once more stepping into the shadows of the trees which hid them from any prying eyes. The marquess leaned into her—uncomfortably, yet thrillingly close. "I thought you were a blazing star that no gentleman has any notion what to do with."

"Yes, the buffoons," she murmured, startled at how provocative she sounded.

That finger gently trailed from her nose down to rest against her lips. "*I* know what to do with every inch of you, Lady Maryann."

She was scandalized and a little bit frightened by the primal sensations stirring violently to life.

Violent delights have violent ends…

Maryann felt quite unequal to crossing wits with the

marquess. She breathed in deeply, slowly, and exhaled on a long sigh. "You are very tempting," she said huskily.

Their conversation had become remarkably intimate, and the air felt fraught with peril. She wondered at the madness of still being this close to him. Maryann understood right at that moment, being here with a man like Nicolas St. Ives, was her own choice of rebellion—against her parents, society, and even the cage of proper conduct she had placed herself. She was here because she liked him, more than she should ever allow. "I think it is best if I never dance with you, your lordship."

But I am so very tempted.

A finger came up and lightly brushed at the curls of her temple. "I am wounded."

A desperate flutter wormed its way through her heart. "You are dangerous." This man was a threat to her virtue, her sensibilities, and her heart.

"Never to you," he reassured, sounding earnest and bemused in the same breath. "Everyone else but you."

Maryann couldn't suppress the inexplicable yearning for impossible dreams that surged through her heart. She averted her eyes before saying, "As if I should be swayed by nonsensical flattery that was learned by rote by a man such as yourself." But her silly heart shook at the fervent and impossible promise. "I daresay there are many other ladies who will be thrilled to be your amusement."

He regarded her with an air of cynical amusement. "Acquit me from such a capricious intention," he said, pressing a hand over his heart. "I am always terribly *serious* about seduction."

The very air between them felt altered. Yet there

was a vein of self-deprecation in his tone, as if he silently mocked himself. Maryann was alarmed at the ease at which they moved from flirtation to seduction.

Before she could retort, he said, "And if I should ask you to dance?"

Everything urged her to say yes, for surely that would feed the gossip mill even more. "Bite your tongue," she said in mock horror. "That would send those with loose tongues into a tizzy."

He placed a finger under her chin and tilted her face toward the soft glow of light, searching her expression. "I am glad it is not an aversion to being in my arms that caused you to recoil so."

She smiled and arched a brow. "And weren't you worried our close association might alert your very mysterious enemies?"

He lifted a shoulder in a shrug, but something undecipherable flashed in his gaze.

"Ah, so sneaking into my rooms *was* really because you missed my company."

His eyes darkened. "I am beginning to suspect myself. How astonishing, hmm? The rake and the wallflower."

The pitter patter of her heart made her feel decidedly flushed. "So I am safe, then," she murmured, concentrating on the vague enemies he thought he was protecting her from.

"Alas, I might have been overzealous. Nary a stub to your pretty toes. Perhaps a rogue might be allowed to climb into a lady's chamber, ravish her most *thoroughly*, and no one think it odd."

"There was no ravishment," Maryann said with a scoff. *Not yet.*

It was as if his voice caressed against her mind, so

implicit were the unspoken words, that unexpectedly, she felt out of her depths and retreated warily. Nicolas lowered his arms. Thankfully, he did not advance, and she needed that space to think, to clear him from her awareness. She stepped back until she whirled around and hurried away. It felt silly but so *very* necessary.

"Run. It makes no difference."

She stumbled and glanced behind her but could not make out his shape in the shadows where they had lingered.

Run. It makes no difference. Had he really said those words with such throbbing intent? With a sense of shock, Maryann realized it wasn't fear she felt at the notion of the marquess chasing her—it was reckless, heady anticipation.

CHAPTER TEN

Maryann was unable to dismiss the ache of longing as she stared at the couples twirling with gaiety about the dance floor. She tapped her feet to the beat of the violins, humming the music beneath her breath.

Her mother hurried over to her, her cheeks a bit pink from exertion.

"Well," she said, unfurling her fan. "I had the most amiable conversation with Lord Stamford just now. He will be coming over to lead you into the quadrille, then he will join you for the supper waltz. I have arranged with the hostess for you to be seated beside him at the supper table."

Maryann pressed a hand to her stomach, as if that would soothe the knots of anxiety twisting through her. "Mama. Papa has said—"

Her mother's eyes flashed a warning. "Pish! It is not the men who decide these things. Mothers know how important it is for their daughters to make a good match."

Maryann's heart hammered against her breastbone. "Were you forced to marry Papa?"

"Maryann—"

"Were you, Mother?" she demanded crisply. "Because I recall growing up that Papa used to tease many smiles from you, dance with you in the hallways, and have long picnics on the lawns. You stared at him with tenderness in your gaze…you *still* do."

Her mother glanced away, staring at the couples dancing silently for a long time. "Your father and I are a different matter, and your rebellious attitude is becoming tiresome."

The dance ended, and the orchestra struck up another song right away. The sound of the waltz floated on the air, dancers making their way to the floor. Lord Stamford started walking over to her, and Maryann swallowed down the anger clawing through her throat.

"Lady Musgrove," Lord Stamford said, smiling in greeting. "Lady Maryann, thank you for honoring me with this dance."

"I do not recall agreeing to it," she said coolly.

Her mother stiffened, and the earl's gaze narrowed in warning.

"Yet you will allow me to escort you to the floor. Now."

She cast a quick glance at her mother, who did not seem inclined to take issue with the arrogant, proprietary way he spoke to her daughter.

"Ah," a voice drawled with careless charm. "There you are, Lady Maryann. I got lost in the crush trying to find you to claim my dance! I am most relieved I have found you, my lady." The marquess placed emphasis on the word "my" as he bent over her hand.

A garbled sound came from her mother's throat, as if she swallowed a bug, and Stamford faltered into stillness, his eyes cold and cutting into the marquess.

Maryann turned to him, and his eyes were alight with devilry, a smile curling his beautiful mouth with his hand held out to her. Surely he knew she could not take his hand in hers. It would create more gossip if she snubbed Lord Stamford and danced with the marquess.

If she was so bold and publicly danced with this man, the story would make the rounds of the drawing rooms. It would be considered proven that he had taken liberties with her and occupied her bed. For her to be seen in his arms would be a confirmation of every licentious whisper circling about.

Maryann had wanted mere gossiped speculation, not for the *ton* to crow about their affair as irrevocable fact. For if they believed they had such proof, her reputation would be so besmirched, she would not be received in any drawing rooms or be invited to any balls. Even though her father was the formidable Lord Musgrove. Even her dear friends would be forced to cut her off for fear of being associated with her wantonness.

When the marquess did not lower his hand but patiently waited, a wave of murmurs swept through nearby onlookers.

"Maryann—" her mother began furiously, before unfurling her fan and waving it vigorously.

"Oh my," someone affected in a deliberately loud whisper. "There might be some truth to the rumors after all!"

Her mother's face mottled, and a flash of fury lit in Lord Stamford's eyes.

The marquess's expression was faintly amused, a dare evident in his golden eyes.

"The waltz has already started," she murmured.

From the mocking glint in his eyes, he knew exactly how outrageous his actions were. A startled laugh escaped before she choked back the sound. Her mother looked ready to collapse, and Crispin had abandoned his post by a potted plant and was walking over.

Cut him, Crispin mouthed.

The refusal hovered on her lips, but she straightened her back and smiled. Then Maryann held out her hand to Lord Rothbury and allowed a notorious libertine to sweep her into the waltz. She stared at no one but him and worked to keep the smile off her face even though her heart pounded so.

His lips curved ever so slightly. "Ah, my little rebel, how does it feel?"

"To shock the *ton*, distress my mother, and possibly unalterably ruin myself?"

"You think all that will happen from this one dance?"

"Your reputation precedes you."

"Hopefully, you'll be free of Stamford. I saw the distaste on your face when he approached you."

He swung her into a wide arc with stunning grace before drawing her too close for the sticklers.

"And is that why you did it?" she murmured. "To help me escape him?"

"Isn't that what you wanted?"

They twirled across the ballroom, and Maryann could feel the eyes of the crowd directed at them. "This is my first dance in over three years not with my family," she said, sliding her elbow against his, then spun to meet him back again in this very intricate and very sensual dance.

"I've never danced at a society ball before."

Her breath hitched. "Is that true?"

"Yes."

"Oh my, this scandal will be heard even in the country." Everyone would ceaselessly speculate why the marquess chose to dance with her of all the other ladies and debutantes. "Thank you," she whispered.

"My pleasure."

Maryann was unable to take her eyes from his. "Are we friends, my lord?"

Their gazed locked, as if they were unaware of their audience.

"Of course not."

Her heart jolted and skipped a beat. "Then why—"

His lashes lowered, hiding his expression for a moment. "It suits my reputation to be seen as indifferent to their narrow-mindedness…"

And they said nothing more as they twirled to the rousing strains of the orchestra until the dance ended. The marquess escorted her to her mother in silence, and he bowed to the countess, who only stared at him frostily.

Stamford was nowhere to be found, and for the first time in months, Maryann's heart felt a bit lighter.

• • •

"Ah, a woman's view on politics—it is to be expected that it would have little to no form with any true understanding," Nicolas murmured, wanting to stab himself for even saying such bloody nonsense.

Lady Maryann flushed, and the gaze that looked at him was wounded, before her incredibly long lashes lowered, shuttering her emotions. Her delicate fingers climbed and pushed the spectacles up her pert nose before she took up her fork and resumed eating the succulently prepared lamb.

That's right, my little racoon, he silently encouraged, *treat us like the ants we are.*

A few of the men who had overheard laughed, and one even said, "Hear, hear, the place of ladies is in the home, and if not to give opinions on balls or the nursery, a lady's mouth should be closed at all times."

A general murmur of assent swept their end of the splendidly lavish dining table and Lord Crispin's face darkened with his ire. Lady Musgrove had given her excuses earlier and departed the ball, no doubt overwhelmed by the chattering which erupted once he had returned her daughter to her side.

Whispers of how nefarious he was for stealing a kiss from Lady Maryann had flown from many lips. Some had been titillated at his audacity for dancing so publicly with her, and someone had dared to remark how terrible it must have been for him to kiss such a plain wallflower.

She'd handled herself admirably and ignored those determined to gossip. Her chin had been lifted high, a mocking smile on her sweet lips, as if to say, *I dared, come what may*. Lord Stamford had watched her, his face inscrutable, but in his eyes there had been a promise of punishment. Nicolas prayed he had been mistaken.

Lady Maryann had also received many envious stares from ladies who had set their caps for him over the seasons. Of course, she had seemed oblivious. Nicolas hoped he hadn't been reckless in his need to feel her in his arms, and to help her escape the attachment her parents pushed against her wishes. While chatting with her in the gardens, he'd silently acknowledged how careful he had become, seeing the possibility of danger in everything. Not even his sisters Nicolas allowed to visit him in London, and he had men who discreetly kept a careful watch on his family, despite the fact that no threat had ever presented itself. Nicolas preferred to be overly cautious than regretful with loss.

Then when his walk with vengeance was over…then and only then would he live without restraint.

He glanced at her, and from the stiffness of her shoulders he could tell that she was upset and bravely masking her hurt. Lady Maryann had offered her opinion on a bill that had passed in the commons and would be debated by the lords at the next sitting of parliament. Her insight had impressed him and rendered those within earshot silent. He hoped he masked his admiration and so had delivered his cutting remark.

He'd wounded her pride grievously, but he would not apologize for it, since it was in keeping with the person he wanted to be before these people — the careless rake who had no true attachment. If before they thought the rumors and dance had meaning, now they would be forced to reassess their perception. If to Lady Maryann's detriment, Nicolas had dismissed a lurking threat too soon, now that hidden danger would think it had been a mere dance, nothing more.

Forgive me, but I must always be a step ahead.

One of the men responsible for breaking Arianna sat at the supper table with them: Viscount Weychell, heir to a most prestigious earldom. The duke had left earlier with his cronies and had invited Nicolas to join them at some new haunt they had discovered. He had declined, a surprise even to himself. He did not normally allow the opportunity to be close enough to the duke to pass him by, it was a chance to observe and patiently watch so Nicolas could learn all the duke's picadilloes.

The Duke of Farringdon had become more careful and paranoid of late, mumbling to all who would listen that he was being watched and followed, and that someone was out to ruin his investments and reputation. Both Viscount Weychell and the duke had reasons to be more careful. They had the proof of one of their chummiest cronies fleeing England to Italy to escape his debts and crumbling reputation.

That man, Viscount Barton, had been the first to fall to Nicolas's scheme. In the letter Arianna left behind, she had detailed clues about each of her villains, for she had not known their identities. How could she? They moved in elevated circles she had only entered in her dreams and hopes. She had mentioned Barton's coat of arms—a stag with a flower between its teeth—and that was how Nicolas had found the man and assuaged a bit of the rage in his heart.

The stag with the lily in its mouth was the most brutal, for it was that one who taught me that fear and pain lie in a touch.

Closing his eyes against the broken whisper in which he heard the tone of her letters, he lifted the glass of wine and emptied it, wishing they had served something stronger.

It was surprising that Farringdon had been savvy enough to start suspecting Nicolas of not being what he presented to the world. His scheme possessed a crack in its design, and he must find it and fix it posthaste.

While they had smoked earlier in the gardens, Farringdon made several tasteless and ribald jokes in regard to the rumors circulating about the ballroom.

"Is the cunny of a wallflower any different than a lady of varied experience? I imagine Lady Maryann has been grateful for your attention. Perhaps I might take a turn when you are through amusing yourself."

It had taken acute willpower not to smash the duke's teeth in.

"You speak of a lady who could be your sister. Show some discretion," Nicolas had coolly warned.

"You defend her so readily, Rothbury. Do you plan to court her then? How prettily she smiled up at you

when dancing. I cannot recall you ever dancing with a bit of quality before. Do you recall it, Weychell?"

The viscount had looked between them anxiously, a frown splitting his brow, his blue eyes worried and silently questioning.

"Court her? Don't be stupid," Nicolas had said with a mock shudder, pulling on his cheroot. *"With my reputation, dancing with her wasn't a good thing. I had my reasons."*

"Which are?" the duke had demanded.

"My own," Nicolas had replied with a deliberately carnal smile.

Though Farringdon had laughed and slapped Nicolas's shoulders, his gaze had been shrewd and assessing as he watched Nicolas's expression.

Judging to see if Lady Maryann mattered.

Judging to see if she could become a pawn.

Judging to see if Nicolas's coveted weakness had been uncovered.

Very reckless of the duke, as if Nicolas would ever allow a woman to become so important she was a weakness. Laughable really. They did not truly know him.

Except…he rubbed the spot above his heart, which damn well ached with hunger.

His cutting tone just now might serve to distract the duke from whatever nonsense he'd been thinking. Nicolas closed his eyes, battling the raw feelings stirring inside. He couldn't explain it, but *this* he did not want. He did not want to use Lady Maryann for any purpose. He did not want her ruined even if it might help her plans. He did not want her cut from her society and friends. *Bloody hell.*

Lady Vivienne, a widowed viscountess for a number

of years, briefly touched his arm to garner his attention. She pursed her lips and graced him with a sexually charged smile. "Many of us ladies would never do something so gauche as to attempt to tread in a man's world and give an opinion on politics. It is just not done and so very unflattering to a lady."

She leaned in intimately close and suggestively purred, "I do not fully agree with Lord Prendergast; there *are* some wicked reasons a lady might open her mouth. It's been an age since I've indulged, and I've heard you are *excessively* naughty."

Nicolas examined the anticipation in her eyes, suppressed his ire, and replied with a modicum of civility.

"Not tonight, I'm afraid," he murmured, once again surprised at himself, for the widow was an exceptionally beautiful woman many had tried to woo to be their mistress.

She had rejected everyone, including David, and here she was offering Nicolas a night of debauchery. And he was decidedly uninterested. The woman he wanted splayed wide underneath him, legs high around his waist while that lush mouth begged him for relief from the agonizing pleasure he would give her had not looked at him since his cutting remark. The awareness of his singular lascivious *and* inappropriate thought had him stiffening. *Hell.*

Earlier, Nicolas discovered he quite enjoyed playing the rake with her, delighting in her quick wit and replies to his banter. He had found himself wanting to know so much more about her than the snippets gleaned whenever he stole into her chambers, and the desire had flummoxed him.

But tonight, when she smiled up at him, Nicolas felt like he was given the key to a secret kingdom—he only had to reach for her and everything he'd never known was missing from his life revealed itself. Through Maryann.

All that from a damn smile.

But to be so provocatively carnal in his thoughts toward the lady would not do.

Run. It makes no difference, he'd taunted, desperate to drag her into his arms and ravish that delightful mouth.

It was that feeling of desperation that had allowed him to draw back on the impulse and allowed the fires of passion stirring to life to die an unceremonious death. The only thing he should be desperate to do was complete his retribution.

Only that.

The viscountess arched a brow in affected dismay. "You are distracted."

"I was never engaged."

She pouted. "Are you minded to be disagreeable?"

His gaze cut to Lady Maryann before he controlled the impulse.

A curiously thoughtful expression settled on her face. "How astonishing…you are attracted to the *mouse*," she said with feigned amusement. "I had thought it so odd you would dance with such a wallflower."

A mouse. If they only knew the fire that rested below the facade Lady Maryann showed the world. Perhaps they *did* know, which was why they hurried to give her the sobriquet of wallflower, hoping it would dim her piquant prettiness and vivacity.

Tonight, she presented a lovely picture, with her lustrous hair piled on her head, exposing the graceful curve of her neck, with curls kissing along her forehead. Her slender, willowy build was draped in an elegant dress of cerulean blue. The off-the-shoulder bodice revealed Maryann's unblemished shoulders, accentuating the fullness of her bosom and slenderness of her waist. Her prettiness was sublime. And one had to be blind to miss it.

"Spitefulness does not become you, Viscountess," he drawled.

Outrage flared in her eyes, and her lips flattened.

"Keep your claws away from the lady."

She sniffed, an air of offended dignity settling about her. He almost laughed at the hypocrisy.

"And if I do not?" the viscountess said tightly.

"My retaliation will be felt for years to come."

Shock bloomed in her eyes, and he cursed himself silently and virulently. He allowed a carnal smile to curve his mouth and the viscountess flushed, her eyes darkening. "When I am done with her, then you can do what you will."

"Oh, you are very wicked. She *is* an innocent or isn't she?" The viscountess leaned in. "Whatever happened when you climbed into her chamber?"

"Are the rest of us to be privy to the conversation?" David asked archly in a timely intervention.

The conversation continued to flow at his end of the table, and he tried his absolute best not to allow his gaze to linger on her. Her vibrancy, her lush prettiness, that heart-bewitching smile seemed diminished. Or perhaps contained. She pushed back her chair and offered a small smile to their hostess at the end of the long table.

The viscountess said something to him that he missed, for Lady Maryann leaving the table snagged his awareness. Though Nicolas stared at David, he was very conscious of her walking past his chair and heading in the direction of the ballroom.

It was strange that he could not rid himself of the aching, perplexing desire to want to know her. Earlier in the shadows of the gardens, he had felt different, that the darkness that clung to him, the hatred that blackened his heart had vanished. It had been replaced with something unknown, but it felt warm and curious.

With every word they exchanged in conversation, something in him shifted, reshaped, and whatever that was, it surged to life whenever he spied her. He felt it in his heartbeat, that brief, alarming way it would stutter at his first sight of her before settling in a normal rhythm.

It made no sense to Nicolas. *What was it about her?* Certainly, she was very clever and amusing, with a wit and fierceness that bordered on scandalous. He liked that about her. That didn't warrant his current preoccupation.

He excused himself several minutes later and made his way outside into the gardens, where he had a perfect view of the inside of the ballroom. She wasn't there. Footsteps sounded behind him, and he did not have to turn to know it was David.

"Let it go," his friend said, coming to a halt beside him.

Nicolas allowed his lips to curve in a humorless smile. "I am at a loss as to what you refer."

"You left shortly after Lady Maryann," David said mildly.

"You mistake the matter; I simply needed fresh air."

David cocked an eyebrow. "For years I've lamented your brooding inscrutability, and just now I could tell that you were chasing after her. I do not understand it."

Neither do I. But Nicolas did not give a voice to those sentiments.

David offered him a cheroot, which he took. "Did you not just meet her? Or is there more to the story you are not telling me? Is she a past acquaintance?"

"She really is nothing to me. You are giving more thought to it than what is warranted. I feel regret for embarrassing a lady tonight, nothing more."

David sighed. "I understand why you did it. Anyone at that table could see the hurt in her eyes. If you cared about her, you would not have put it there. The enemy, *if* they were watching, will think she is nothing to you. And she should be nothing to you."

He regarded his friend with interest. "I give her no importance. I am curious to why you are doing so."

"Then why are you searching the ballroom for her?"

"Do not presume to know my thoughts." It shocked Nicolas to even think he could be obvious in his reactions. He had spent so many years mastering his emotions to be the finest actor the *ton* had ever seen.

"I am heading to White's; do you accompany me? There are several wagers I want to take part in. Farringdon and Beswick will meet us there."

He clapped David on the shoulder. "Another time. I have business to attend."

And that business included the very "friends" David mentioned. Instead of calling for the carriage he traveled in, Nicolas made his way on foot until he spied a hackney, which he hailed. Hopping into the coach, he ordered the coachman to take him to the edge of Covent Gardens, where he would meet Rhys Tremayne, Viscount Montrose, the man the underworld knew as the Broker.

Montrose was a decent sort, even if he kept away from the underworld more often of late, since he married his young and very ravishing duchess. The man had been lucky in love, and Nicolas astonished himself a few times by feeling envy at the man's state of contentment.

Hazel eyes, a really poor description for Lady Maryann's lovely eyes of brown flecked with vibrant green swam in his thoughts. They didn't glow with mischief and daring but with hurt. It confounded him that it mattered that he had wounded her. He should not care, since he made no allowance for anything outside of his current purpose. Nicolas had been extraordinarily selfish in his desire for vengeance. Even his father he had distanced himself from for a number of years until he had fallen ill. Only then had he returned to his side, hoping to mend the hurt of the past.

"She is nothing but a lightskirt, a thing for your amusement. What does it matter that a few gentlemen took their pleasure with her?"

He loathed that those words from his father, which had been a mild rebuke in a tone of amusement, had been interred in his memory. His father's blithe dismal of the rage he felt for the atrocity visited upon Arianna always lingered under the hardened surface of his heart. When he'd discovered her death and what led to it, the person Nicolas went to had been his father. And the man he admired most in the world for his honor had dismissed the facts that she had been cruelly used.

His father's honor only extended to those of similar ilk—aristocratic families. Miss Arianna Burges had been the daughter of servants. Insignificant. Even the magistrate had lost his interest in the case after he discovered her origins. The man had put on a show, but Nicolas had named those he suspected, and the man hadn't the balls to question the sons of earls and dukes.

Nicolas had then met with those in Bow Street himself, demanding justice for her. There had been none to be had. No one was willing to ruffle the feathers of such powerful men and their families. Not even the law.

He'd had a terrible row with his father when Nicolas's persistence had been discovered.

"Do you wish to humiliate and antagonize powerful men for that bit of a lightskirt?" his father had roared, angered enough to draw a rapier and point the tip against his son's chest. *"Do you wish to embroil some of the most prominent families in a scandal, compromise the reputation and personal liberties of their sons? I am ashamed of you!"*

He had stared at his father's heaving chest for several moments and had quietly said, *"I am ashamed you are my father."*

The very next day he had run to Paris and drowned his sorrows in drink, a steady, reckless hate growing in his heart. There he had lived through the revolution, the terrors of the Committee of Public Safety and the horrors of Emperor Napoleon's bid to conquer Europe. He had fought precisely six duels, all defending women who had no one to right the wrongs done to them, until he had been compelled to return to England with one thought driving him. Arianna's pain and death would not be in vain, while those responsible laughed and made merry as if they had not stolen something precious.

The hackney rumbled to a stop, and he alighted into a crowd of people in the streets heading to the entrance of the gardens. He spied the large frame of Montrose hovering in the shadows, almost unrecognizable unless a man was used to seeking danger when it was not obviously presented.

Nicolas made his way over to his friend and stood beside him.

"Farringdon holds scandals and secrets on many in society. He uses the information to shamelessly bribe and blackmail those he wants under his power. He even has a file on Viscount Weychell."

That surprised Nicolas. The two were thick as thieves, their debauchery and dishonor a shared affinity.

Viscount Weychell— *Blond hair and blue eyes with a scar splitting his lower lip. He laughed through my screams, tis a sound I shall remember on my way to hell, for I am no longer worthy of heaven.*

This man was almost within Nicolas's grasp. He had enough to embarrass him, perhaps, but he wanted the icing that would let the man feel his punishment for years to come.

"Farringdon…" *The dragon wings spread wide, a rose of coronet upon its head…how merciless this dragon was, tempting me with chances of escape only to catch me again when I tasted freedom.*

He ignored the haunting whisper of Arianna's voice and said, "The Duke is suspicious of me."

"It wasn't he who asked me about your secrets," the Broker murmured.

The duke was indolent and spendthrift, and the dragon in Arianna's letter. Farringdon shamelessly importuned on his late father's connections, which had made him a powerful man in his own right. He had genuinely believed him to be the one questioning Nicolas's motives in their lives. "Viscount Weychell?"

"No."

Rhys had a reputation of protecting anyone who came to him to trade information. Though he and Nicolas had been friends for some years, Rhys would not betray any link within his network.

"That is interesting," Nicolas said. "Someone else has placed themselves on my board. Someone I did not account for."

"Be careful, my friend."

A warning. Disquiet sat heavy in his gut and with a jolt, he realized it was not for himself. "You believe this person is dangerous to me."

"Very."

"That means he is powerful. Even more so than I?"

Rhys sent him a chiding look, and Nicolas opened his arms wide as if to imply the query was innocent. But the knot in his gut drew even tighter. Whoever wanted to know his weakness was connected and powerful.

Who have I offended?

"What must I know about Weychell?" Nicolas asked, driving to the heart of why he had met Rhys. Nicolas had paid handsomely for the underworld to be on the lookout for anything in regard to the men he would bring down.

"There are whispers he might be leaving England soon and may not return for some time."

Bloody hell. "Is it a certainty?"

"It is just a whisper."

The fact that it existed was cause for worry, though. "Thank you, Montrose."

"Our word is our business," Rhys murmured calmly.

They shook hands, and Nicolas walked away. He needed to move a bit faster. It was important that he procured whatever Farringdon had on Weychell. Montrose would not sell the information to more than one buyer—honor among blackguards and devils.

"If she is important, cast a net around her," Montrose said, some distance away.

Ice formed in Nicolas's veins, and he faltered into stillness. "If who is important?" he asked with dangerous restraint.

Rhys's chuckle was filled with mocking amusement. "You stopped, my friend...you stopped."

And Nicolas supposed the theory was that if the lady were insignificant, he would have kept walking. "You are a friend...aren't you?" Nicolas drawled, unable to do anything about the dark throb of warning in his voice.

"Definitely a friend," Rhys said, coming up beside him. "And I will keep it in mind that she means something to you."

"She does not," he said flatly. "I barely know the chit."

His friend melted away in the dark, his low, mocking laugh lingering in the air.

It was Rhys's turn to stop when Nicolas asked, "Did he ask you about her?"

He closed his eyes, hating the fact that he asked, for it confirmed a belief that he himself did not understand.

He...the shadow that might prove to be Nicolas's most dangerous adversary in the long game he played.

Rhys did not answer for several moments, then he replied, "He was most interested."

The shadows swallowed him, and Nicolas took a deep breath to calm the sudden pounding of his heart.

You little fool, how recklessly you linked our fates and I danced with you tonight.

He took a hackney from Covent Garden to Berkeley Square and exited the equipage a few houses down from her home. Gripping his cane, he made his way in the shadows of the gas lamp of her home. He waited a few beats before crossing the streets and climbing over the side gate, walking with careful stealth around to the gardens that faced her windows. Standing there, he peered up. There was a light in her room, and she sat at the open windows, her chin resting on her drawn-up knees, staring out into the night.

Her glorious hair was unbound, a few long curls waving in the gentle wind. She looked wildly desirable and forlorn. Nicolas stared at her, perfectly hidden in the dark of her gardens. He was almost tempted to climb the trellis to her small balcony. Would she scream? Slap him?

No, she would be dignified in her hurt. He blew out a low breath. How presumptuous of him to even dare think his remark had been enough to cause her injury. Lady Maryann had exerted no effort to captivate him, yet he was unwillingly entranced.

"I know you are there," she said so softly, he wondered if he imagined it.

How had she known? Was it the same for her, that her skin burned with awareness at their proximity? Nonsense, but deep inside, something purred. The need stirring to life felt unusual, foreign, and it shook him to the core. It made no earthly sense that his resistance to her allure was so fragile.

He was not a man to be entangled with matters of the heart or of the flesh. He'd only taken four lovers in the years he'd spent abroad, all Parisian actresses, and only a few since he returned to England. Each connection had been a momentary burst of pleasure; all had been easily obtained and relinquished with greater ease. He had formed no attachment, and he hungered for none. His mistress these last two years had been a deeper dive into vengeance, understanding its complexity and becoming the man it required.

Building a reputation such as he had did not happened overnight, but by layer of deceptive layer infused with a healthy dollop of cunning.

His heart jolted, and with a sense of shock, he realized he'd not taken a lover in about six months, and whom Nicolas truly couldn't remember. All the debauchery done in the most exclusive whorehouse to bestow him the moniker "the daring and the wicked" had been a part of his machinations. Those women had been paid handsomely to ignore him as he paced their boudoir and mentally calculated his next steps. Only when his need had been great did he tumble with one into true debauchery that would last the evening.

"Why did you come?"

"Did I place that wounded look in your eyes?"

She lowered her gaze briefly, and he detected the gentle shudder as it worked through her slender frame. She looked so young and innocent, her lashes long and thick against her pale skin. Her eyes opened, and a faint hauteur settled on her face. "How arrogant to think you would have such power," she said with a smile of disdain.

That curve of her mouth was meant to mock, but the irresistible pull of its latent sensuality had his breath hitching in his throat. The part of him that he had silenced in his drive for vengeance stirred and stretched.

"I am sorry," he said gruffly, unable to offer anything else. "I am so damned sorry."

CHAPTER ELEVEN

Maryann inhaled at the flutter of warm sensations that erupted in her stomach and her heartbeat quickened uncomfortably. A dart of awareness prickled along her skin, as if she had summoned the devil who tormented her thoughts. It was inexplicable, but she had known he lingered in the dark. She had felt him in the sudden throbbing of her pulse, in that warm, unexplained ache low in her belly.

I am sorry.

She peered down at him, and even with the half-moon out, the marquess was nothing but shades of black and gray. Yet at times, she fancied the brilliance of his eyes cut through the shroud. The marquess seemed different tonight, more like how he had appeared the first night he stole into her chamber. A tension lingered around him, something fierce and inexplicable, and she could feel it.

His hand was clenched tightly over a silver-headed cane, and the gaze staring up at her was unwavering. The yearning she felt at the sight of him overwhelmed and infuriated her in equal measure. To long for a man who had insulted her was unpardonable.

"Why did you say it?" *After our dance had been so incredible.*

"There was someone at the table…I did not want that person to believe you important to me."

"Even without your boorish tongue, I cannot imagine why anyone would think such a thing."

Mine enemies are now your enemies…

Her stomach went hollow. The marquess once again hinted of his secrets.

Somewhere downstairs, a servant turned on a gas lamp or perhaps several, and the light beamed out into the garden and tenderly washed against his rigid jawline and flat unsmiling mouth. She watched him with a terrible fascination, unable to take her eyes off his expression of almost cruel insouciance.

"You wear two faces," she said in wonderment, resting her chin on her palms, never taking her stare from his. "The height of cleverness is to be able to conceal it." And to Maryann's mind, the marquess was very clever indeed.

He jolted a bit, a quick frown slashing his brows before his expression once again smoothed.

"It is very interesting to hear a lady quote Roche-foucauld."

She smiled. "Many would not know that I did."

He stared at her with a guarded watchfulness and chilling civility. To where had the charming and flirty rake disappeared?

The sky rumbled, and the wild, earthy scent of raindrops assailed her nostrils. "It will rain quite soon."

"Is that an invitation to come up to your chamber?"

She had to fight down the thrill of anticipation those words gave her, even when said so blandly. "No."

There it was, the slightest shift in his posture, but that dangerous air blew away like ashes in the wind. How did he do it? And it was most certainly not the trick of the meager light upon his countenance. She suspected then, if he revealed his true nature, his presence and vitality would fill the room, it would intimidate, and it would seduce. Now the *ton* looked at him as a feckless son, and also a charming rake many maters would still offer up their daughters to wed.

Should he show this other side, how would they greet him? Respect? Fear? Anger that he'd been duplicitous for so long? She wanted to converse with him, but not here in her chambers. Maryann wasn't so foolish, and she understood he presented a threat to her virtue simply because she wanted his kisses.

Another rumble of thunder, and a slight misty drizzle started. She reached out her palm and caught a few drops in her hands, loving the cool feel of water against her skin. Acting on impulse, she thrust her head out and turned her face up to the sky, laughing as the rain fell tenderly against her forehead and cheeks.

"Fucking hell!"

The raw, crude words shocked her, so she froze. Hurriedly drawing her head inside, she gripped the edges of her windows and looked down. He was no longer standing in the gardens. The scream died in her throat when the marquess suddenly vaulted over the railing and landed on her small balcony.

She stared at him in stupefied amazement. Before she could react, he dropped onto his knees and his hands found her throat in a clasp that was tender yet provocatively intimidating. His eyes were dark and heavy-lidded, his jawline flushed red. This close, she could see the different striations of gold in his eyes, the rain on his brow and the bridge of his nose…

The hunger in his eyes.

Maryann felt beguiled by the unknown expression tightening across his sharply slanted cheekbones. It struck her then with the force of lightning. He wanted *her*. This was not a game or mild flirtation.

She felt flushed, shivering, light-headed. Silly and

empowered in the same breath. A gentleman had *never* wanted her before. No one had ever shown her that she could even be seen as desirable, and here was a proclaimed rakehell, a reputed connoisseur of beautiful women who indulged in all manner of wantonness, staring at her as if he felt compelled.

As if she were beautiful.

Was it that she presented as a novelty?

"I…I…Nicolas," she stuttered. "I…I need to think…"

"You are making me lose control," he hissed. "I must not be *here*, with you."

"Do not blame me for your lack of self-restraint," she gasped. "Just admit it…that you feel the same way I do." The boldness of her vague confession left her breathless.

He leaned in unexpectedly, took her lower lip between his teeth, and bit down sharply. As if to punish her for making him lose control. She sucked in a harsh breath at the arrow of need that shot through her, striking deep in her belly, and ending in an aching pulse between her legs. "Why did you bite me?"

"Rakes do that," he said dangerously.

Oh!

He pressed his lips to the corner of her mouth, and asked against her flesh, "Are you frightened?"

Yes. "No."

"You hold my stare so fiercely, an undeniable fire in your gaze." His thumb moved in a firm caress across her cheek. "I want to touch that fire, and I can only do that by possessing you."

"And who are you?" she murmured. "Surely not the rake. That man is a charmer who would seduce me with empty flattery and false promises."

"I have none of that to give."

That tormenting thumb swiped over her lip, almost bruising and then gently. Ripples of warmth ghosted over her skin, chilled from the pattering rain.

"Have you ever had a man?" he asked.

Her heart almost exploded from her chest. She couldn't be sure she had grasped his meaning correctly. "Have I ever had a man do what?"

Regret flared in his eyes before his expression shuttered.

"You want me," she whispered, "to be wicked with you." And he had been trying to ascertain her experience with wantonness. *"Oh!"* she said softly.

A half groan issued from him before he swallowed it down.

"I do not dally with innocents, even if they have the temperaments of racoons."

He stirred something inside her that was wanton, unrecognizable. "Ah, so that is what you want from me, a mere dalliance, you *cad*." Her voice was whisper soft, flirty, with no sting at all behind her words.

His eyes were no longer inscrutable, but intense and hungry.

Kiss me, she silently implored.

When he made no move, it was her turn to lean in and bite his lower lip. The raindrops on his mouth settled onto her tongue, and with it a taste of dark fire and whiskey.

His hands slipped from her throat as if he had been burned. Breathlessly, her heart slamming against her chest, she used her finger to trail a raindrop along the bridge of his nose. "Racoons do that," she whispered.

His chest lifted on a deep breath. Unexpectedly he

leaned in and pressed a kiss to her temple. "Close your windows."

Then he released her, slowly stood, turned, and launched over the balustrade. With a gasp, she thrust forward, wondering if the damn bacon-brained man had leaped to his death. But then she sensed him and looked up to see him walking along the path that would lead him to the streets.

She leaned away from the window and closed it gently. The Marquess of Rothbury wanted her.

And, from the struggle she saw in his eyes, quite desperately.

"You are no rake," she said into the night, a smile on her lips.

He had shown admirable restraint. The marquess had acted like a gentleman.

Then she recalled the hot brand of his possessive touch encircling her throat, the bite on her lips, which still throbbed.

In his own unique way, he had been a gentleman.

"I want you, too," she whispered, testing the words aloud.

Maryann rested her forehead against the cool window, silently listening to the pitter patter of rain outside.

"We must be daring and take what we need instead of waiting."

The words she had used to enflame her other friends teased her, nay tormented Maryann, prodding her to take what she wanted.

"And damn it all to hell," she cursed, satisfied she had done so.

And what she wanted was Nicolas St. Ives, Marquess of Rothbury—the charming rake and the unfathomable man she sensed lurking within.

"I want you," she said, closing her eyes, pressing trembling fingers to her lips, "and I am going to have you."

. . .

Almost a week after he lost his senses in Berkeley Square kneeled atop a particular balcony, Nicolas slipped inside the Duke of Farringdon's lavish home in Grosvenor Square, a little past midnight. The house was silent. The duke and his sister should be on their way in a carriage to the Duchess Hardcastle's midnight ball. A ball given by the young duchess was rare, and invitations were selective and highly coveted. Nicolas had known Farringdon wouldn't let the opportunity pass by to rub shoulders socially with the young duchess or her husband, for an hour or two, even if his usual appointment at a house in Soho Square was planned for tonight.

Nicolas padded down the prodigious hallway, careful to move with stealth and not alert any of the servants below stairs. Knowing his dire straits and that it would embarrass him, Farringdon hardly entertained. Nicolas had only been over to the duke's town house once for drinking and a private game of cards, but he cut through the dark without any mishap.

At the end of the hallway, he came upon the duke's study and entered carefully. The room was dark, save for a low fire burning in the grate and a single taper on the mantel. Nicolas searched the room thoroughly, and it was not long before he found the papers he sought in the third drawer in the man's large oak desk. It was the report O'Malley had traded to Farringdon.

How arrogant. The duke did not even imagine someone would dare to break into his home. Nicolas padded to the mantel, held the papers under the candlelight, and read.

There was not much there. Weychell had two bastards, age two and five, with a mistress hidden away in Cornwall. Uncommon knowledge, but one Nicolas would not use. Children should not suffer for the misguided deeds of their parents. And once he took the viscount off the board, Nicolas would have to make a generous provision for them.

He read the second sheet, which detailed his creditors and gambling debts to the tune of twenty thousand pounds. And then the final page hinted that during the war, Weychell had been a close friend with a man who had been a general in Emperor Napoleon's army. And from the detailed outline—houses that were let, a chateau, and monies and jewelry sent abroad, this general was more than a close friend. There was a speculation that Weychell might have acted as a spy for the general.

Treason.

A dark hum of pleasure blasted through him. Nicolas filed the information away and returned the papers exactly as he found them. Then he made his way from the library, only to duck inside another room as a strident female voice came down the hallway with the sound of rapid feet.

Peeking through the space he left by not closing the door fully, he watched the duke's ravishing sister, Lady Sophie, make her way up the stairs while a gentleman lingered, waiting for her. She came back down a few minutes later and handed him a case, which he opened.

"You are a study in recklessness, aren't you?" the

man murmured, taking out a necklace of glittering rubies to clasp around her throat.

"I had to come back for them when my brother left the ball."

"Perhaps you should tell him that you have them and stop this mad dash home whenever he leaves a ball for them."

"Darling, I cannot let him know. He will pawn them."

"Is it that bad?"

"I fear it is, and he tried to keep it from me. He is furious the match fell through with that heiress. But he is a duke, you know. Another is bound to come along soon."

They headed outside, and he padded behind them at a careful distance, listening to their conversation, storing whatever he deemed to be valuable information. A warble sounded on the night air, a signal by David. Nicolas hurried down the servants' stairs and through the kitchens to meet him by the hedge of small trees and shrubs. They were perfectly hidden in the dark.

"Did you find anything?" David asked.

"Nothing incriminating." Nicolas always played his cards close to his chest, and he did not regret it. It always paid to be cautious.

"A waste," David said with a sigh. "When I saw the return of the lady and her companion, I started warbling like a madman. What are you doing?"

"I want to hear what they are saying."

They were still standing by the steps instead of making their way to the parked carriage, and it seemed as if they argued. Nicolas bent low and walked along the path leading up to the couple, staying stooped so they had no chance of spying him.

"Isn't that taking it a bit too far?" her companion said in a low voice, casting a careful glance at the waiting coach. "Sophie, my darling, perhaps we should—"

"No!" a strident, and a bit shrill tone rejoined.

"Be careful," he snapped. "We do not want anyone hearing this conversation, even if they are just servants. We know they spread gossip quicker than fire to dry grass!"

She grabbed his arm and took him around to the side of the house toward the private garden area.

Nicolas deftly followed, conscious of David close on his heels. Stopping in the shadows of the alcove, he watched the female pacing back and forth by the fountain of Neptune.

The lady took a deep breath. "I want Lady Maryann *ruined*. And I want it done tonight."

It seemed she had discovered the author of her misfortune. Everything inside Nicolas went quiet.

David cast him a dark, amused glance. "I thought her nothing?"

He made no reply but held up his hand for silence. It was important to hear every word exchanged between the pair.

"How can you be so certain it was Lady Maryann who set those critters loose?"

The man with her was unfamiliar to Nicolas, which possibly meant he did not haunt the seedier and darker hells of London, nor was he a frequent guest in ballrooms. Yet the man seemed familiar.

The lady scoffed. "Who else would dare?"

"Lady Maryann is so quiet. She does not seem the sort—"

She rounded on her companion. "Are you defending her?"

"No, my darling, I am trying to be practical."

"It must have been her. It was her mother's ball."

"That does not mean—"

"It was *her*. And if you mean to be a part of my brother's business venture in the future, you will avail yourself to do what needs to be done. And this is also to your benefit. Did you not say you needed to marry an heiress?"

"I do need an heiress."

"Then take her. I've outlined a plan—keep to it and we shall both get what we want. After the scandal of being caught half naked in your arms, her father surely will insist you marry her to render her respectable." Lady Sophie smiled, her satisfaction at her plan evident. "I will relish her humiliation. And you must ensure she is in a state of *déshabille* when you are discovered."

"She might not be persuasive to my seduction."

Nicolas would take pleasure in killing this stranger.

Sophia smiled, and even from where he stood, Nicolas saw the malice in it.

"I am certain there are methods to ensure her compliance. Must I think of everything for you? I want her humiliation to be profound. I would urge you to treat her in a manner as you did that governess."

"How did you know about that?" he demanded tightly, clenching his fists at his sides. "And it is not what you think."

She wagged her finger. "You know the reason your father sent you to France. Don't be facetious."

Ice congealed inside Nicolas's chest. How did they dare? The lady seemed to be aware that her brother collected others' dirty secrets and availed herself to them without shame. Though the gentleman seemed discomfited, he took a deep breath. "Are you certain her dowry is fifty thousand pounds?"

"Everyone knows it," she said smugly. "And there is no need to look as if you lost anything. You'll be doing her a favor at the end of the day. She'll be married *finally*. Her father would never dare turn you down afterward."

Then she whirled away and hurried toward the front of the town house to the waiting carriage. The man took a deep breath and trailed behind her. Nicolas watched as they climbed into the conveyance and rattled away.

"Do you know the identity of that man?"

David hesitated. "He is recently back from abroad, about four months now to claim his inheritance. He is Viscount Talbot. A good sport and decent sort."

"Our notion of decent differs. How disappointing."

David cast him a fierce scowl. "Bloody hell, man! I am sure you've heard the rumor calling Lady Maryann a wallflower. Not a flattering moniker at all. At least his intentions are not all dastardly, and the plan *is* to marry her. Letting the chips land where they fall would be doing a chit with her unfavorable offerings a good deed."

The thought of Lady Maryann hurt, humiliated, and forced to marry a man of such despicable honor had the strangest, gut-wrenching effect on him. "They plan to irrevocably ruin her," Nicolas said coldly.

"*Is* it ruination?" David asked pragmatically.

"You're right, such a pretty word for what they intend. Rape is what it is."

David flinched. "The man is reputed to be a skilled lover. I am more than certain he will be very persuasive, and she will succumb to his seductive wiles. I urge you to recall the lady will be married to a respectable title. And she will be safe from those who might be wondering if she is important to you."

Nicolas walked away, lightly jumping over the wrought-iron fence, his great cloak swirling around his boots. David silently kept pace and cursed under his breath when Nicolas turned right onto Russell Street instead of left.

"Have you lost your senses? You are going to the duchess's?"

He did not slow his strides. "What of it?"

"I cannot conceive that you should attend," David said tightly. "You are not dressed for the occasion and as such, your presence will stir unnecessary attention and speculation."

"Your company is not required," Nicolas said, coolly dismissive.

"What is it about her?" David ground out, grabbing on to Nicolas's arm. "We have a plan tonight to reel in Weychell on our hook. One of the men who hurt our Arianna. And yet you are running to save this girl…this girl who is *nothing*?"

"You are comfortable with an innocent being shredded?"

David grimaced. "She'll be respectably married to Talbot after."

The ice in Nicolas's gut grew cold enough to encompass his entire being.

"Do not look at me like that," David snapped, appearing wary.

"And how is that?" Nicolas murmured icily, doing nothing to temper the dangerous feeling clawing up inside him.

"You are spending too much time watching her, protecting her from a force that might not be there," David hissed, scrubbing a hand over his face.

"How do you know how much time I spend watching her?"

David scoffed. "I noticed!"

Something lethal trembled through Nicolas. "Only if *you've* been watching her."

The wolf betrays…

"Bloody hell, man, do you see how you are looking at me? For a bit of skirt, you—"

"For a bit of what?"

David faltered, then looked away from him before meeting his eyes once more. "I hate to see your distraction when now is the time you should be more determined. We are almost at the end, Nicolas. The end…after ten long years. I *know* how calculating you are…how shrewd and ruthless, so she must serve a purpose for you, I can tell, *but* she is just one piece on your board. A pawn. Do not lose sight of everything for a bloody insignificant pawn."

The silence that fell between them felt brittle.

"I will meet you at the Asylum in a couple of hours," Nicolas said flatly, whirled around, and headed to the duchess's ball.

Is that what you are to me, Lady Maryann…a pawn?

There was merit in David's argument. Her marriage would make her safe if the danger he perceived truly lingered in the shadows. Yet acute distaste filled him for the duke's sister and her cohort. The very idea that they would be so underhanded urged him to teach them a lesson they would not forget anytime soon—or ever.

Lady Maryann deserved a choice, always. It was that

simple for him.

Except it is more.

He could feel it, simmering low and brutal in his gut, waiting to burst free should he let it. A sharp hiss escaped him, and he ruthlessly disciplined all the fire of lust and strange emotions twisting inside him. This was simply a good deed he would do for any lady in trouble.

As if to mock his will, her light brown and green-flecked eyes swam into his thoughts. That remarkably ravishing smile she owned, and her clever tongue and defiant will. That sharp, retaliatory bite on his mouth.

Racoons do that.

He wanted her, more than he'd ever wanted another soul. Perhaps if he should kiss her, even once, he would find there was nothing remarkable there and she would simply disappear from his thoughts and waking dreams. Yet he did not want to risk kissing her or being too close, not when her brother might be his enemy.

The best way to let her disappear is to let her marry, his conscience taunted. *Let Talbot seduce her to his bed.*

The feelings that scythed through Nicolas's heart were so unfamiliar and ridiculous that they took several befuddling moments to register to his senses — raw, primal possessiveness and protectiveness. If he were an uncivilized creature, he would have been screaming "*she's mine*".

Nicolas felt…unnerved.

He took a slow, deep breath, steadying himself against the unfamiliar emotions, and moved through the night, silent and set on his current goal — to save Lady Maryann from a spoiled debutante's merciless plot.

He rubbed the back of his neck, admitting with a

silent snarl that it served his purpose to think he was running to rescue her. The truth of the matter was it would be more likely that he would be saving them from *her* wrath and rapier.

God, he hoped so, for if Talbot touched her, the man would lose the hand with which he created the offense.

CHAPTER TWELVE

Another day of endless rounds of social calls, another night of attending a ball where Maryann stood on the sidelines with her mother indulgently looking on, content in her delusion that her daughter's reputation had not suffered a blow. Maryann had refused to attend, but Crispin had begged her to cease aggravating their mother's nerves, and Maryann had relented. Attending a ball did not mean acceptance of a marriage offer.

Maryann would give it an hour before pleading a headache and making her way home. Several dancing couples glided the intricate steps of a minuet, others reposed on chaise longues, while others stood drinking champagne and laughing. She watched Crispin's graceful form as he moved with his current partner, Miss Lydia Moncrieff, who peered up at him with her heart on her sleeves.

That tender look of longing brought a hot lump to Maryann's throat. Merely existing these days was proving itself a tiresome business, a notion which filled her with guilt. She had many blessings to be thankful for, but Maryann couldn't escape anymore that she lived a life she found unbearable.

"I am not content with my lot. I cannot believe any of you are happy with your situation. We must be daring and take what we need instead of waiting, wasting away on the shelves our family and society have placed us on."

The very impassioned words she had flung at her

group of friends now haunted her, taunting her earlier confidence that she could direct the outcome of her happiness. Her one daring moment had been to claim a ruination that did not belong to her, and these last few weeks she had witnessed the power of her mother and father working to squash those rumors. That ball where Nicolas danced with her should have been the icing on the cake. And the scandal sheet that thought it worth a mention would have been adding ice cream to the decadent bowl.

Instead, despite every provocation, her parents wielded their influence with notable lords and ladies in the *ton*, to show the world all of Maryann's missteps were simply charming eccentricities. But whereas before she had faded into the background, tonight when she entered Lady Vidal's brightly lit ballroom, many had stared, fans had lifted to mouths, and the whispers were rabid.

Those in the ballroom seemed to be unsure how to interact with her. Surprisingly, a few sighs of envy from ladies had been aimed at Maryann, but there had also been cutting speculations. Even a few ladies who usually ignored her presence engaged her in brief conversation. Maryann wasn't certain if that was due to her parents' influence, or if dancing with the marquess had done the opposite: given her a stamp of approval that she was sought after…perhaps elusive.

Her society was so changeable, it was ridiculous.

What else must I do?

She opened her fan, waving it gently to and fro, wishing she were anywhere but here. None of her friends seemed to be in attendance, and she wondered why Charlotte had not come tonight after promising it.

I must remember to call upon her tomorrow.

A nameless agitation was upon Maryann, and it had nothing to do with the very direct and ungentlemanly stare from Lord Stamford. How surprising that he was at almost every ball she attended, when he had been conspicuously absent the last few seasons.

Maryann vowed to refuse him should he approach her for any dances.

To the earl's credit, he did not approach her, and she wondered at his restraint. Perhaps after his failure to compromise her, he had moved on to another lady. Quite wishful thinking on her part, for though he must have heard the wicked rumors, he did not break the alliance.

"Excuse me, my lady," someone at her elbow said.

She turned to see a hovering footman. He held out a folded note to her. "Your friend bid me to deliver this to you."

With a frown, she took it from him, unfolding the paper.

Maryann, the most dreadful thing has happened. I need you to come to me discreetly in the glass house. Please hurry. Ophelia.

Maryann's heart jerked with dread. The inelegant scrawl did not look like it belonged to Ophelia, unless she had written it in haste. Maryann hesitated, and glanced around. No one watched her. Somehow the note felt grave. She hadn't seen her friend earlier, but Ophelia always attended balls notoriously late.

Snapping the fan closed, Maryann hurried from the ballroom and down the long hallway that led to the conservatory from inside. She wouldn't hurtle recklessly inside but try and see that it was indeed Ophelia waiting before she entered. Maryann increased her pace, terribly worried something dastardly might have happened to her friend.

Suddenly, someone reached out from in the shadows and grabbed her hand. With a gasp of alarm, she whirled, lifting her fan.

"Call for your carriage and leave the ball immediately."

Rothbury!

She had not seen him since that night on her balcony, and her heart sang with a peculiar thrill. Maryann tried to tug her hand from his, but his clasp was unyielding. "Why do you make such a demand without an explanation? What has happened?"

Instead of answering, he tugged her to keep pace with him as they moved toward the glass house. And more shadows. At that awareness she pulled her hands from his with a sharp tug, and he reacted by putting his hand around her waist fully and whirling with her, so she was pressed against the wall and in complete darkness.

"What are you doing?" she gasped.

Maryann stared up at him, trying to decipher his expression, confounded with the unexpected sensations coursing through her body. "Why must we always meet in the shadows?"

"The note you got just now was not from your friend."

Maryann froze, her heart jerking an uneven beat. "How…how did you know she asked me to meet her in the conservatory?"

He touched her cheek with a finger, surprisingly bare of a glove. Then he lowered that tormenting finger to touch the fullness of her mouth before dropping his hand and stepping back. His caress had been so fleeting…so careless, as if he often stroked the tip of his fingers along the curve of a lady's cheek and then brushed it against the fullness of her mouth.

The sheer agony of wanting this man was…exquisite. "Do you act in such a wicked manner with *all* the ladies of your acquaintance?"

She had to know. Not that she wanted to be special in any way, but to be forearmed with an understanding of his behavior was to be forewarned. And would perhaps stop the foolish dreams she had taken around with her for the past few days.

"Wicked?" A rough, low chuckle that was as fleeting as that touch echoed between them. "You are truly an innocent bit, aren't you?"

She frowned. "I…"

"There is no time for chatter. Go, call for your carriage."

"Call for my carriage?" she repeated, considerably astonished. "Why are you ordering me about in this fashion? I am to meet my friend."

"She is not awaiting you," he said tersely.

"Why should I take your words it is not so?"

Maryann felt when he stiffened.

"If you wish to continue against my better advice, I will not stop you."

She did not like how chilling and dismissive he sounded. Not that she expected anything from this man.

Did you miss me? she wanted to ask him against her better judgment. He had shown no marked attention that was positive. That she should wonder at his intentions at this point sparked her temper—more at herself than anything else. Maryann skirted around him.

"There is a man waiting for you there. Since your dowry is fifty thousand pounds, the plan is to see that you are well and truly compromised, to see you divested of your virtue if necessary…and then be discovered."

The arrow that pierced her heart then had her pressing a hand to her chest. Her entire body felt cold. "To steal my virtue?" she asked faintly.

"To rape you," he hissed, as if angered by the slow comprehension of the plot against her.

The words were like a rope around her throat, and she struggled to get her thoughts out. "Ophelia would *never—*"

"The design is not that of your friend. Her name was simply used to assure your participation."

Maryann stared at him wordlessly, painfully aware that someone who had planned to…to compromise her most foully waited for her. Still, the very notion of what he claimed bordered on ridiculous and the mischief of some silly person who surely did not know Maryann's strength or her papa's consequences. Such a dishonor would never net them a marriage. "I…I have no enemies."

He sent her a look of such incredulity, she blushed.

"Naive," he murmured low, but she caught it.

There was something different about him in this moment that scared her a bit, though what it was she could not say. It was just present.

"Leave. I will take care of this matter."

That promise jolted her.

"I will come with you," she said. "I must…I must know the identity of the man who would do me harm, at least."

He stared at her, his expression becoming chilled. She took an instinctive step back, made uncomfortable by the iciness of his mien.

"Viscount Talbot waits for you."

The last man she had expected him to name. "I…"

"Do not let me tell you again to leave this ball, Lady Maryann."

She did not like him at all like this. Hating that she felt uncertain, she walked away. Once at the end of the corridor, she glanced over her shoulder to note he watched her with the stillness of a hawk.

Why did you come to warn me, and how did you know of their scheme?

Breaking the stare, she rounded the corner and stopped. Biting at her lower lip, she flushed against the wall, then carefully peeked toward where she had left him. His shadow disappeared toward the steps leading to the conservatory, and grabbing the edges of her gown, she ran after him. Surely he really did not believe she would meekly obey him. And it was not that she doubted his shocking call of villainy waiting for her, but she wanted to see the evidence of it for herself, in the hopes that she was not being deceived by some forces she did not understand.

He had left the conservatory door unlocked, and she slipped in, grateful the room was in more darkness than light. Her heart pounding, she stopped, tucking herself away in the slim shadows made by the potted plants and begonias.

"Who the blazes are you?" a voice she recognized as Viscount Talbot demanded.

Her heart sank, and a heavy weight pressed against her belly. The man was a friend of Crispin and he was known to her. Why would he partake in a scheme so ugly?

"The lady you are expecting will not be coming," the marquess said. "I suggest you find another lady to fix the problem of your empty coffers."

"I do not know what you are babbling about, Rothbury. I suggest you—"

"I know the full of it, the plans you made with Lady Sophie."

A shocked wheezing sound came from the viscount's throat.

"It is useless to feign ignorance with me," St. Ives said mildly.

They could have been discussing the light patter of rain against the glass of the conservatory.

She frowned at the import of St. Ives's words. *Lady Sophie.* Maryann should have guessed it was that bully ruffian.

By the large potted plant in the corner, she peeked to see what was happening. The viscount waited, his posture one of stiff tension, with a note clutched in his fist. He tugged at his cravat, and even with the low light from the burner and the fireplace, Maryann detected the sheen of sweat above his brow.

St. Ives leaned casually against a table which held a pair of pruning shears and a clay pot.

"Are you here to issue a private challenge?" Talbot demanded tightly.

Maryann gasped. *A duel?* What was it with these gentlemen solving problems over the brace of pistols or a clash of swords? They were ridiculous in the extreme!

"Do not be foolish," St. Ives said bitingly. "I leave such things to the purview of the lady's family. And since they are very much in the dark about this matter, it is unlikely you will be facing a pistol at the crack of dawn."

"What business is it of yours, then?"

"Indeed, I have asked myself the same question."

He sounded bemused. "But then how could I ignore the dastardly act you have planned for her? Planned for any young lady?"

"You will mind your own—"

With a swiftness she could barely track, the marquess grabbed the pruning shears, opened them, and fitted the vee perfectly at the front of Viscount Talbot's neck. Maryann instinctively stepped forward, the violence of the marquess's action shocking her into almost fainting. The move placed him in the light, every nuance of his face evident for her to observe.

He was unjustly, unfairly handsome, his classical profile turned saturnine only by the cold in his eyes. She did not doubt that he could or would inflict damage of death to the viscount. Unusually, he was dressed in clothes far too casual for a ball. He had been somewhere else when he learned of the ruse. *And he rushed here to warn me...to protect me.* The shattering realization had one of her hands fluttering to rest above her heart.

"Rothbury! What in God's name are you doing?" the Viscount's voice trembled something fierce. "Do you mean to murder me?"

A harsh silence fell. The longer the marquess stared, the more the mask of affable geniality and charming rake slipped to reveal someone unquestionably dangerous.

"I am considering it, Talbot; I am considering it." The shade cast about him rendered him in a light she had never seen before—a dark protective force with wings of shadows and cunning golden eyes.

And with a flash of insight, she realized the charming rake and amusing libertine was truly not Nicolas St. Ives. He was also the hard, dangerous man in front of the viscount.

"Please, Rothbury, I heard the rumors that you fancied her, but since you made no offer, I did not think—"

Talbot's words became a gurgle of fear when the pruning shears shifted.

"I will only say this once. Lady Maryann is under my protection."

For a wild moment, she could not breathe, and it was as if her feet had a will of their own as they tugged her closer. She hugged the shadows, watching him as he kept his piercing...and most certainly frightening... regard on Viscount Talbot.

"In simple terms, that means I will *absolutely* kill you should harm befall her by your hands or those of Lady Sophie."

Talbot believed him, for the man's entire body shook. Maryann was caught between revulsion and admiration. That no one foresaw the danger that was Nicolas St. Ives amazed and alarmed her in equal measure. He was something that lingered in the dark, waiting for the right opportunity to strike.

Who are you?

As if he heard her silent whisper in the darkness, his head turned, and those brilliant eyes pinned her in place. Certainly, he could not see her...could he? Maryann swallowed, walking backward ever so silently, toward the deeper shadows.

He lowered the shears from around the man's neck. "Get out."

The viscount hurried in her direction, and she pressed up against the plant.

"Not that way," St. Ives said.

Talbot spun around and went through the doors

that led him on the outside path into the rain. Maryann silently hoped the marquess would go that way, too, but he remained still, staring in the direction of her potted plant.

She turned around and attempted to stealthily walk back the way she had come. The echoes of his steps behind her felt deliberate. Hating how harshly she breathed, she paused, and leaned her back into the wall, hoping the shadows were impenetrable, and he would not make out the color of her icy-blue ballgown.

She did not want him to know that she had seen the ruthless man beneath the careless facade he presented to the world. She did not fully understand the desire, only knowing that she must act upon it.

Oh God. He did not walk past her and depart the conservatory. He stopped. The face that stared toward her held a hint of merciless mockery, his lips flat and unsmiling, and his eyes…she had never seen them so unfathomable. He shifted, and then he, too, was cloaked in darkness. Very slowly, the dancing shadows reached across the space between them and cupped her face.

Maryann trembled.

His thumb traced her cheekbone. That hand disappeared, and a harsh breath sawed from her throat. Yet she did not move, nor did she speak. Maryann couldn't imagine leaving now. She didn't *want* to leave.

A warm touch to her bottom lip. Her lips parted and her chest lifted on a deep breath. Shock bloomed through her when he slid a finger into her mouth.

"We will have to be wicked, improper, and terribly scandalous."

The words she had said to her friends echoed in her thoughts and settled low and hot in her belly. Wicked…

improper…scandalous. Maryann could not say why she did it, but she stroked her tongue over his intruding finger, and the first sound rode the air and settled between them. A groan. Low and hungry.

But it also sounded like a warning.

His finger slipped from her mouth, and she strained to see him in the dark. His figure was just a vague outline of power and strength. The presence surrounding her at once intimidated her, for he was ruthless enough to kill a man without hesitation, but she was also reassured, for he was undeniably protective of her.

Why? A question she wanted answered, but also feared knowing. His attentions and the feelings he elicited in her might once again rouse dreams she had long buried and no longer wanted as a part of her future. And it was also nonsensical to entangle any dreams and wants she might have with *this* man. He was a stranger…a complex one, whom she might never understand. Maryann must never delude herself as to his reasons for warning her.

And despite knowing that…inside she felt warmed… Cherished.

A sob at her foolishness hitched in her throat. Her heart would not listen. The shadow shifted, and with a sense of shock, she realized he had knelt. His gloveless hand encircled her ankles and started to slide her gown up her shins, exposing her stocking-clad legs.

"Rothbury!" she gasped, her entire body trembling. "Yes!"

"Nicolas," came his dark murmur. "Let me hear it on your lips."

"Nicholas," she said on a husky whisper, aware that her dress was now above her knees.

She felt when he leaned in, and his lips unerringly

found the soft spot of her inner thigh not covered by her stockings and garters.

A shameful, wanton curiosity burned hot and frightful in her veins.

This is not what I meant when I said to be wicked and take what we want. Because Maryann did not desire a lover…

Did she?

His tongue as it stroked over her skin was a searing lash of heat. The feel of his mouth on such a vulnerable place set her heart into a frenetic gallop, her awareness of him heightening to a physically painful degree. How remarkable her skin could be this sensitized! His tongue lashed against that spot once more, and she made a small helpless sound of need… of desire.

Was that what this was—this flushed sensation stealing over her entire body and settling low in her belly? Her nipples ached, and each breath made the fabric of her gown rasp against them, further agitating the sensation.

She tried to deny the hunger sweeping through her body, fearing the reckless need it inspired, but then he gently sank his teeth into that spot on her thigh, and she whimpered, "Nicolas," as he sucked at her flesh at first harshly and then tenderly.

When he released her skin, he stroked that spot with his tongue, a glide meant to soothe. All thoughts scattered when he kissed a spot higher on her thighs. It was such a soft caress, yet her lashes fluttered closed, and she savored the hot brand of his lips to her skin.

He kept going up with his kisses.

"Nicolas?" she cried softly.

His mouth left her body, but she could feel him

staring at a part of her no one had ever seen. The darkness of the conservatory pressed in on them, cocooning them in intimacy and secrecy to just be. Maryann swore he could see every bit of her in the dark and through her drawers.

He pressed his nose against her and inhaled her womanly scent. Her cheeks burned with alarm and aroused mortification and she was grateful for the dark. The feeling of his teeth against her mons was shockingly, overwhelmingly intense. It was also *more*. The feeling was evocative, and delicious tremors went down her back.

There was a sharp tug and her drawers parted, exposing her sex to the air. "You're the devil," she gasped, her fingers twisting tight in his hair.

"I know," he murmured. Then he licked against her sex.

She slapped a hand over her mouth to stifled her scream. This…this was *indecent*. And so, so pleasurable.

He nudged her legs apart wider, then wider still, forcing her legs to accommodate the width of his shoulders. With a sense of aroused alarm, Maryann realized he was lifting one of her legs and draping it over one of his shoulders, the edge of her dancing shoe resting against his back.

Then he licked her again. This time slower. As if he savored her. This time his tongue dragged against her nub, striking it with raw pleasure. Hot flames curled through her and the jolting sensations were so powerful, she quaked.

Maryann sobbed, collapsing against the wall.

"I have you," he murmured, his voice vibrating against her mons. Then he went back to that nub and licked it again and again and again.

Something awful tightened low in her belly, a sensation Maryann never dreamed a body could be capable of withholding. It did not expand out but contracted, coiling into a tight ball of heat low in her belly and at that bundle of nerves he tormented.

Her thighs started to shake, and one of his large hands grabbed her hips and tugged her to his mouth. As if she could escape. To her back was the unyielding wall and at her front, his strength and devastating tongue.

"Nicolas, please!" she cried, not knowing what she demanded.

She gripped his hair, thrusting her fingers through his strands. Maryann couldn't tell if she did this to hold him to her or to yank his head back to get an ease from the unrelenting pleasure he assaulted her senses with, and he made a guttural noise in his throat, low and approving. Then he closed his lips over her nub and sucked.

She screamed. A thin, high wail that echoed in the conservatory. A surge of agonizing pleasure tightened low in her belly, so hot and uncomfortable, desperate and straining. Her thighs trembled fiercely as that tight coil within her snapped and blossomed through her body in shuddering waves of delight.

Oh God, she was mortifyingly wet. She could feel it along the folds of her sex and thighs. Maryann thought with the release of that agonizing pleasure, his tormenting tongue would have eased. But it did not, and her throat felt raw with the effort to not scream when he once again changed the dance of his tongue.

"Nicolas! Oh God, please, Nicolas," she gasped huskily, arching involuntary, pushing against his mouth until the devastating pleasure became a raging tempest, stripping her of shyness and uncertainty. She could feel her heart racing, the heat surging in her veins.

Maryann sobbed. She gripped his hair so tight he might own to a bald spot later on. Her head fell back against the wall as she gasped for breath with each flick of his tongue, each nibble of his teeth pushing her closer to devastation. And then it was there, and Maryann swore she went flying from her body as pleasure took her apart. She raised trembling fingers to her cheeks, shocked to find them wet with tears. The pleasure had been that excruciating.

Her leg was gently lowered, her dress, too. Then he rose in the dark, hitching that leg that had been over his shoulder at his hips, cradling his weight between her legs. Maryann wondered at the hard bulge she felt at the front of his trousers.

"I am so damn tempted," he said roughly. "You are so soft and hot against me. So *wet*."

Her face heated.

He reached between them with a hand, his knuckles brushing butterfly soft over the folds of her sex.

"Even with this wetness, I can tell that you would grip me tight," he murmured.

To her chagrin, she felt another blush steal up her cheeks. Maryann was ever so grateful of the darkness in the conservatory.

"I am holding on by a damn thread," he hissed, removing his hand from his obvious source of temptation. He buried his face in her throat, and she dazedly realized his body shook.

"Nicolas," she whispered, a feeling of awe sweeping through her. "You tremble." *I made you tremble*.

"So do you."

And it was then she realized her body also quaked and her breath puffed from her fast and unsteady. She twined her hand around his neck, holding him close.

His head lifted from her throat.

"Breathe, Maryann," he whispered at the corner of her mouth.

The air left Maryann's lungs in a harsh rush.

"I frightened you."

No...*yes*. She could not speak. *I frightened myself.*

The soft folds between her thighs were tender, sensitive...achy and needy. Except she had no notion what more her body could possibly be wanting. At her lingering silence, he pressed a kiss to her brow, down her nose, and then lightly across her lips.

It wasn't a kiss, but it shattered her. His head dipped even lower, and the marquess once again buried his nose in her neck, inhaling her scent, and her heart tripped inside her chest and then squeezed.

"It is not safe to be here with me."

"I have never felt safer," she whispered, unerringly kissing the top of his head. "You do not kiss my mouth." *That* she had not intended to say.

"No."

"Why not?"

"If I should taste you...I won't stop."

"Didn't you already just *taste* me?"

His raw curse had her blushing.

"Your mouth is a particular weakness of mine. If I should kiss you...feel your lips against mine, I will sheathe you on my cock right here and I will not tup you with the gentleness and consideration you deserve."

Maryann assumed that meant ravishment. Her chest rose and fell on an unsteady breath. "And is that a bad thing?"

They both stilled, for he clearly understood she was asking after his intentions.

His voice throbbed with a dark undertone of carnal warning. "That is a most dangerous thing."

She closed her eyes against the ache his words roused. Should he kiss her, he would not stop, and he was not likely to offer marriage after. And even knowing that, Maryann had the most appalling and maddeningly tempting urge to grip his hair, lift his head, and kiss him without any thoughts to the consequences.

"Then let me go," she whispered.

He jerked back as if something burned him.

"Go home," he breathed roughly.

She smoothed the front of her gown with still-shaking fingers. "I will go back to the ballroom and let Lady Sophie see that she failed in her disgusting plans."

He pulled her roughly, almost violently, into his embrace. "Maryann?"

"Yes," she gasped, so very aware of their bodies pressed together.

"Do not test me. Go home."

In this moment, Maryann found him terribly frightening *and* compelling. Her lips parted, but no words would come. "I…"

"I do not wish to kill Talbot. And if you return to that ball and that spoilt rotten little witch sees that you escaped her machinations, she will blackmail Talbot into acting foolishly."

He cupped the back of her head with one of his hands and pressed his cheek against her temple. "And if he even breathes in your direction, I will kill him. Do you understand? I have a veritable passion for retribution."

"Yes," she said faintly.

"Now go."

And Maryann did, very conscious of the empty ache low in her belly and the silly, ridiculous smile on her face.

CHAPTER THIRTEEN

A soft noise in her chamber urged Maryann to stir lazily among the pillows, rolling over with an indelicate yawn. Her maid tugged the heavy drapes open, pouring sunshine into the chamber. With a low moan, she lifted an elbow across her eyes.

"Mornin', milady, the countess wishes you below stairs right away."

Still feeling exhausted, Maryann rubbed the sleep from her eyes and turned over in the bed. A peek at the clock on the mantel revealed it to be afternoon. With a gasp she lurched upright. "Have Lady Ophelia and Miss Fanny called?"

"Yes, milady, they are waiting for you in the smaller sitting area."

Thank heavens they had not left at her tardiness. It had been over two weeks since she had seen her friends last and she missed them dreadfully. They had agreed to meet at eleven this morning and then traverse High Holborn together and buy the latest hats printed in the fashion magazine. Stifling a groan, Maryann sat in the center of her bed, and the memory of the night slammed into her like a fist. She faltered, gripping the sheets and closing her eyes.

Oh God. That had really happened.

Last night after reaching home, she hadn't slipped into a blissful slumber. She had tossed restlessly atop her coverlets, unable to dismiss from her awareness the marquess and what he had done to her. She hadn't been able to simply think about the impropriety and folly of her reckless conduct. It was a blessing that when sleep finally claimed her, she slept undisturbed.

"Susie?" she said to her maid, who was going through the armoire selecting dresses and unmentionables.

The maid glanced over her shoulder. "Yes, milady?"

"I would like a few minutes alone."

Susie dipped in a small bob and hurried from the chamber, closing the door behind her. Maryann bit her lip and slowly tugged her nightgown to her hips and stared at the scandalous bright red mark on her inner thigh. She gingerly pressed her skin, alarmed to find that the spot ached. A dark purplish bruise made by the Marquess of Rothbury's mouth...sucking and nibbling at her tender flesh.

He was entirely *too* wicked.

Then the memory of his mouth against her sex and the awful pleasure which had quaked through her had her entire body blushing. To have done something so intimate and improper and shocking, and never even having kissed her mouth? And what excuse had Maryann? A fleeting encounter in the dark and she had surrendered all sense of propriety and allowed him such wanton liberties!

Unexpectedly, she laughed and dropped back into the mound of pillows and cushion, releasing a gusty breath. "I must be going mad," she breathed.

Something wicked this way comes. Be with ruin or banishment once it knocks on my door, dare I answer?

"What am I to do about the truth of liking you?" And she did like him very much. *Who are you, Nicolas St. Ives, and why do I so desperately want to see you...to kiss you, to just hold you to me in a hug?* The memory of how a powerful man like the marquess had trembled in her embrace had warmth spreading through her body.

With a huff, she hurriedly rang for Susie to return and quickly performed her morning ablutions. Several minutes later, Maryann felt presentably dressed in a light green high-waisted day gown and her hair caught in an artful chignon. She made her way down the winding staircase of their elegant town house.

First, she would meet with her friends, and then respond to her correspondence, and pen a letter to Kitty. Though she would not receive it right away, for Kitty's last letter said she had gone on a long honeymoon with her duke to places she always wanted to travel. A wistful ache of longing went through Maryann again, to be so in love and also free.

Maryann entered the room to see her friends sitting close together on the sofa, chatting and taking tea. A rush of affection filled Maryann on seeing Ophelia and Fanny, two more members of their sinful wallflowers' club. It always astonished her that they, too, were seen as outcasts by those in society, and for such silly and insupportable reasons. Fanny was extraordinarily pretty and a talented painter, but her connections were poor and were even deemed an embarrassment. Worse, a nobleman (Maryann couldn't bear to call him a gentleman) Fanny had fancied herself in love with had jilted her a few days before their wedding and it was her the *ton* had judged for his misconduct.

Ophelia was quite different than the rest of their merry band, for she could marry should she wish it. She owned both wealth and beauty but refused to marry, which her father scandalously indulged. Ophelia was a striking lady by any standards, yet the sharp cheekbones and generous lips, and blackest of hair wouldn't have the *ton* call her beautiful. Words they often used in her presence were arresting, handsome. And, unpardonably, wallflower.

It was Ophelia who glanced up and saw her hovering in the threshold.

Her golden eyes lit with welcome, and she smiled broadly. "Maryann, you've had us waiting an age!"

With a laugh, she sauntered inside and closed the door. "We have so much to catch up on."

"You seem to be faring well after your twice brush with scandal," Fanny said with a sniff but with a very decided twinkle in her eyes. "To have danced so publicly with Lord Rothbury! How are you still in town and not banished to Hertfordshire for the rest of the year?"

"Because despite my efforts, Lord Stamford has not withdrawn his pursuit."

"Your mother visited mine a few days ago," Ophelia said with a frown. "To garner her support in squashing the rumors."

"I suspected it would have been harder than anticipated," Maryann said. "But Stamford's persistence in the face of the rumors is very surprising to me. You recall last season when Viscount Avedon canceled his betrothal to Lady Jane because a rumor started that she was seen in Hyde Park walking without a lady maid or chaperone?"

Ophelia nodded. "Yes. Lord Stamford is not behaving in the predicted manner like most gentlemen, is he?"

"What will you do?" Fanny asked fretfully. "Lord Stamford seems determined to possess you. I cannot tell if it is flattering or frightening."

It was frightening *and* infuriating. "My father gave

me a few more weeks of freedom before the announcement. Mother seems determined to ignore that. I am thinking I shall leave for Paris or Italy before I tie myself to a man I do not want."

"Maryann!" Fanny cried, significantly alarmed. "Pray do not speak such nonsense as to alarm us. Kitty, Caroline, Ophelia, Emma, and I would be most anguished should you run away from England without any companion or money. Your very life would be in danger; the scandal of a single lady traveling alone would be…" Fanny blew out a sharp breath. "I am aghast you should even say it."

"It seems ridiculous that in an age of civilization, a lady has to so constrain her desires to please gentlemen who do nothing to temper themselves," Ophelia retorted. "Because they are the ones who set these ridiculous rules. Why can't Maryann travel alone should she wish it?"

Maryann knew that would be an even bigger scandal than kissing the marquess in public. Traveling alone would signal that she was free with her charms and not a respectable young lady at all. She perched on the armchair of one of the sofas and considered the admission she was about to make to her friends.

Ophelia's eyes narrowed. "Out with it, you are fairly bursting at the seams!"

"I am not terribly certain of the rules governing affairs, but I am thinking about having one."

The teacup on the way to Fanny's mouth froze. "Having one of what?"

Ophelia gave a perceptible start. "What kind of affair?" she breathed.

Maryann tilted her head to one side, considering the point. "There are many kinds?"

"An *affaire de coeur*?" Ophelia asked.

It was so daring, it frightened her. "Yes."

Fanny's cup clattered onto the table. "With the marquess?"

"Which one?" Maryann asked with a spurt of devilry. "If you are thinking Lord Rothbury, the very one."

Fanny looked ready to faint, then she rallied and said, "Reformed rakes do make the best husbands. I have no notion who started that nonsense, but it is that very belief why so many ladies would still marry him despite his dissipated lifestyle."

"But that is it, Fanny, I do not think he was ever a rake. He has layers to him the world has never seen. There is more to him than his reputation. I am certain of it and I am so *very* intrigued by him."

"Oh dear," Fanny cried, properly alarmed. "You have fallen under his spell and have been deceived of his true nature. You are so very sensible, Maryann, so why have you deserted your senses?"

She laughed. "I am acting no less naughty than Kitty! She went off to Scotland to be with His Grace unchaperoned! I daresay the days she spent there were not steeped in innocence but perhaps in debauchery."

Fanny blushed fiercely, while Ophelia chuckled, handing Maryann a cup of tea.

"You are distressing Fanny's sensibilities."

Their friend sniffed, but amusement glinted in her warm light-blue eyes. "Stop acting as if you are more worldly than I am. I have been kissed *twice*!"

Maryann choked on the first sip of her tea. "When? And with who? I thought we shared everything?"

"Ladies," Ophelia called, laughing, "we are digressing." She inhaled gently, and the somber expression in her eyes had Maryann frowning.

"What is it?"

"You mentioned Kitty…do you hope the outcome with Lord Rothbury the same Kitty experienced with her duke? That you might form an attachment and eventually marry?"

The hunger that clawed up inside of Maryann shocked her, and the hand that lowered the teacup trembled. All the longings she had thought buried under disillusion surged into her heart with the ferocity of a battering storm.

"I am being fanciful and reckless," she gasped, hating that tears pricked in her eyes.

She was not a silly miss to descend into tears and vapors at the slightest provocation. "He has not even kissed me…and here I am speaking about *affairs* and whatnot! I feel foolish."

Fanny came over and tugged Maryann to sit beside her. "It is not foolish to dream, Maryann. You have told me this so many times."

"I feel tossed about on churning waves, uncertain of any direction in life. Fanny, you are the most incredibly talented painter and you have a grand ambition to be known for it one day. Ophelia, you have a hidden identity, an entirely different life, and I can tell you know what wicked path you'll be pursing. Sometimes I feel that what I want cannot be known to me!"

"What about a family?" Fanny asked wistfully, painful longing in her eyes. "Your own home to manage and not to live by the whims of others who control how you eat and the clothes you wear."

A silence that felt heavy lingered.

Then Maryann said quietly, "I *do* want a family… children, a husband who I will love." The ache in her chest became a physical thing, and there was no ease in its tightening grip. "I want my husband to love me breathlessly. I want him to take me sailing, and he won't mind that I am exceptionally good at fencing, that I can ride astride and might best him in archery. I want a man who wants to hear my opinions on political matters as well as the latest gossip! I want a man who challenges me but allows me to challenge him right back. Maybe even a husband who would take me to a gambling den! I do not want a *piece* of what I hope for…I want it all," she ended with a groan, covering her face. "And maybe, just *maybe* I could have it with the marquess, because I have never met anyone who rouses me so."

Emerging from that shattering awareness, she lowered her hands and stood.

"All of that with a rake?" Fanny asked skeptically.

"Yes, with a rake," Maryann whispered. "A supposed libertine and the wickedest of them all."

But also, so much more.

"Who has vowed never to marry," Ophelia contributed.

"That very one," Maryann said, folding her arms beneath her breasts, and started pacing.

"It might be easier to get a pig to fly than a man not so puffed up with vanity that he would allow all that," Fanny said with a heavy sigh.

"The truth of it is, sometimes I do not know if I want to marry any man. The independence I have now is limited, but I relish having it, and the more advanced I get in age, the more freedom I will attain. If my father has shown me anything, it is that once I am a wife, I am not expected to have my own sense of thought, everything will be controlled by my husband and dare I protest, I will be scolded most severely!"

"But?" the always astute Fanny asked archly.

Everything inside her went soft, and achy with need. "For the right gentleman, I would happily relinquish my independence—for he would not cage me, would he? He would want to see me fly. And if I should overreach in my recklessness, the right man would catch me."

The memory of falling from the trellis into the marquess's arms flowered through her, and she bit into the soft of her lips to prevent the smile hovering in her heart. "I do not want a husband who will *allow*...but one who will share and experience with me."

Fanny wrinkled her brow thoughtfully. "You were the one who encouraged us all to stop giving a *damn* about what is expected of us and for once reach for what *we* want! So, seduce the marquess into falling in love with you."

"Fanny," Ophelia gasped, her eyes twinkling. "How rakish!"

Her friends laughed, pulling a smile to Maryann's lips. "The prospect is alluring, but also ridiculous. What do any of us know about seduction? And I am *not* consulting with Princess Cosima as Kitty did." *Unless...*

"Would he be open to your wiles?" Ophelia asked, arching a brow.

Maryann snorted, quite unladylike. "What wiles? Should I possess any, I do not know it!"

"He has not tried to steal any kisses from you," Fanny said, tapping her chin with a finger. "The first step is to determine if he is attracted to you."

"I *was* wicked with him last night in a manner I can never describe," she confessed in a rush. "I daresay he is very attracted. He just has not kissed my mouth as yet."

Ophelia made a choking sound and Fanny froze, her eyes rounding.

Oh dear.

Ophelia stood, fisting a hand on her voluptuous hip. "What do you mean—"

The door opened and her mother sailed inside, her eyes bright and determined. Fanny and Ophelia curtsied and greeted the countess.

"I must ask you ladies to cut this visit short. Maryann has a caller who wishes for an audience."

Her heart leaped. "A caller?"

"Lord Stamford. He awaits you in the drawing room."

A shock went through her. "I am to meet with him alone?"

"Perfectly permissible between an affianced pair," her mother said coolly, looking down her nose at Maryann. "The door has been left discreetly ajar. Hurry now, and do not keep the earl waiting."

"We are not affianced," she said, repeating it once more. "There has been no announcement, and Papa has promised me to wait." *But you sense he has been prevaricating*, a small voice reminded her.

Her friends were ushered out, and Maryann plodded from the small sitting room, down the hallway to the waiting earl. She recalled Nicolas's warning to be careful around the earl, then frowned, for the man was acting in a respectable manner in coming to her home. The rumors had not deterred him in any fashion.

"Mama," she said, "I would ask that you stay in the drawing room with us. I am not comfortable with Lord Stamford."

Her mother made no reply as they reached the drawing room, allowing Maryann to precede her inside.

The earl turned from the windows, and Maryann was once again taken aback by his youthful handsomeness. He came over, the look in his eyes mild and oddly warm.

She dipped into a small curtsy. "Lord Stamford."

He bowed slightly and without taking his gaze from her said, "Lady Musgrove, I bid you to allow me a few minutes alone with your lovely daughter. The proper courtesies will be upheld."

Her mother smiled radiantly and left the room without a by-your-leave glance at her daughter. Maryann supposed she could be grateful the door was left ajar. The heavy press of her heart was unbearable. Her wishes simply did not matter.

The earl waited a few beats, and when his gaze leveled on her, she took an involuntary step back. There was a hardness about his mouth and the lines of his eyes which bespoke his displeasure.

"Last night, why did you depart so suddenly from Lady Vidal's ball?"

"I beg your pardon?"

"I will only ask this once, and your reply *will* be honest, Lady Maryann. I saw you leave the conservatory in a manner I deemed suspicious. You will name the bounder you were with."

"Sir, you go too far! You have no right to question or make demands of me," she breathed, truly shocked at the man's audacity. "Your behavior is not advancing you in my graces."

His eyes went so cold, she took another step back. Not liking the discomfort curling through her, she whirled around and hurried to the door. Maryann gasped when a hand reached around her and closed it. She hadn't heard his movements. Ducking underneath his arm, she made her way toward the windows.

"You are acting very improperly, my lord. Are you fully aware that we are under my parents' roof?"

His hands snaked out and grabbed her, halting her retreat. His hold felt like she was bound in iron. She tried to withdraw her hand and he twisted his clasp. Maryann cried out as pain burned down her arms. She faltered, staring up at him in ill-concealed shock.

"It is best you understand now what I will not tolerate from you," he said calmly.

"You are hurting me," she choked out, noting her hands grew numb in his relentless clasp.

"I know," he said dispassionately.

"You are reprehensible," she said. "You will release me at once."

"Do not act the fragile flower," he replied bitingly. "What were you doing with Lord Rothbury in Lady Vidal's conservatory last night?"

Dear God! Had he seen their interlude? She closed her eyes, thrusting aside the panic. Of course he had not seen, or he would not be asking. "You may be certain my father will hear of this."

He chuckled. "Your father owes me thirty thousand pounds, Lady Maryann. I am sure it was understood with perfect clarity to be a part of your bride price."

Her throat felt thick, and there was a tightness across her chest that made it difficult to breathe. She hadn't known her family suffered any financial hardship.

Just then, the door sprang open and her mother framed the doorway. She glanced away as if she had interrupted a tender moment, a small smile about her mouth. The earl released her arms and stepped back slowly.

"I would be very remiss in my duties if I allowed this door to remain closed another minute," Lady Musgrove said lightly. "I should perceive no reason Maryann would not happily take an outing with you to Hyde Park later in the week. One can only hope this dreadfully disobliging rain will cease soon."

She glanced from her mother to the self-satisfied air about the earl. He had given her father thirty thousand pounds. It hurt, somewhere deep inside, that her family sought to use her but had not confided in her their circumstances. She remained silent when Lord Stamford bid his farewell, his departure taking the air of menace with him.

"Well," the countess said with a bright smile. "The earl certainly was most handsome today. He makes a truly dashing gentleman."

"He is the most odious creature imaginable," replied Maryann with a calmness which belied the disturbance in her heart.

Her mother's eyes flashed with anger. "You must perceive the advantages of an eligible marriage! And you cannot do better than Lord Stamford."

"I do understand such advantages, Mama, I simply do not find the earl eligible in any regards."

Her temper exacerbated, the countess slammed the door closed, hiding their vexation from the servants in the hallway. "You willful, disobliging creature!"

"Mama, you did not walk in on a…a moment between lovers!"

"Maryann!"

"He held my arms in a painful grasp and was making demands of me he had no right to do."

Her mother inhaled sharply, and for a moment her eyes softened with sympathy before her spine snapped taut. "I am doing what is best for you. I do not want to see you enduring life as a spinster."

Maryann's entire body hurt at the awareness that she was just a pawn to be used and pulled in whichever direction her parents desired with no regard for the dreams and hopes she held in her heart. "Even if I were to be bound and carted before a bishop, I would not marry that man," she said quietly, pushing her spectacles up her nose. It was then she noted her fingers trembled badly.

Her mother blanched. "Maryann! To be so willful and—"

She could not bear to hear her mother's remonstrances. "Did Lord Stamford loan Papa money? Is that why Papa is so adamant I accept the earl's offer?"

Acute distaste crossed her mother's face. "We will not be so vulgar as to discuss money," she said in repressive accents. "And it was an *investment*." The countess whirled about, flung open the door, and marched away, quite indifferent to her daughter's distress.

Through eyes blurred with tears, Maryann glanced down at the red swelling already forming on her hands. This did not augur well.

• • •

After her frightening and frustrating encounter with Lord Stamford, Maryann needed to be away from the house. Her mother had gone to call upon her dear friend the Marchioness Metcalf. Maryann normally accompanied her, genuinely enjoying the marchioness's dry wit and her love for needlework, a pastime Maryann enjoyed immensely. The marchioness's talent was incredible, though she praised Maryann's artwork, the last being a massive golden eagle intricately stitched to where he appeared lifelike. She'd pled a headache but now found it unbearable to remain inside. Needlework did not serve as a distraction, and she only had a few sore and bloody fingertips for her efforts.

She rang the bell for her lady maid and was soon dressed in a vibrant yellow carriage gown with its long-puffed sleeves and cinched waist, a matching bonnet, and her parasol in her grip. Crispin was thankfully at home and she only needed his agreement to accompany her and they would be on their way.

"You wish to go shopping?" he asked, carefully closing the ledger he'd been going over.

"Yes. I mean to purchase a few hats," she said.

His lips twitched. "Hats."

"I saw Ophelia with the most delightful hat covered with taffeta and trimmed with delicate ribbons and flowers. I thought it charming and mean to procure one for myself. And I also saw a few bonnets in the *Lady's Monthly Museum* that I might purchase."

Crispin sighed, placing the stopper over the inkwell. "And this must be done now?"

"Of course."

He slowly came to his feet, a frown on his handsome face. "You seem out of sorts. Is everything well?"

The truth of what occurred earlier hovered on her tongue, but some hot and unfamiliar emotion rose in her throat, threating to suffocate her. With a painful jolt, she recognized it to be fear and mortification that she'd not been able to defend herself. Maryann gripped her parasol to steady herself against shaking. It felt more frightening the more time passed. She did not understand why it was all so unnerving.

Lord Stamford was known as a crack shot and some months ago rumors had swirled that he was in a duel, though the entire matter was hushed. If she should confide in her brother, he would possibly challenge the man. Though she stood a better chance facing the earl with her own superior fencing skills. "I find the house very suffocating today."

Crispin said no more, and a few minutes later they were in the carriage on their way to High Holborn. The pain in her heart felt unrelenting. With money in play, no matter what she did, her parents would push to see Maryann married off to Lord Stamford. Leaning her head against the squabs, she thought on her next steps.

Inciting more scandalous encounters with Nicolas felt almost nonsensical. What more was there to do if a public dance with a supposedly notorious rake had not done it? Public carriage rides, and more dances? She softly scoffed and glanced out the windows.

Even if they tie and drag me to the bishop, my answer will be no. Even if I am dragged to the country and locked in my rooms, I will say no. And with a smile, Maryann suspected should her parents act so underhanded, her marquess would come to her rescue if she did not escape them. She resolved to slowly start selling her jewelry and prepare for the moment she might leave England.

Their equipage rumbled to a stop. The day seemed busy, and they exited the carriage early to stroll along the sidewalks so she could peer into the various shops. Even though her brother accompanied her, a footman traveled discreetly behind them.

"I thought you knew your destination," Crispin said a bit crossly. "Why did we not alight there? Instead here we are, almost fifteen minutes of walking past shops and you peering inside a few without going in."

"This is part of the art of shopping, my dear brother," she said with a light laugh. "And your gallantry in escorting me will surely be repaid!"

He groused a bit more, but she could tell he did it with fond affection.

Her fingers tightened reflexively on his lower arm. "I would…I would like to ask you a question."

Crispin cast her a curious glance. "This must be dire. You look like you swallowed a fish that is stuck in your throat. Spit it out."

Maryann frowned, gathering her thoughts. "I am wondering about pleasure…the kind I believe is supposed to exist between a man and a woman."

Her brother made a terrible choking, gurgling sound, and even stumbled in his steps. "Why are you asking about this, Maryann?" he demanded with a thunderous expression.

"Because there is no one else I can ask," she said primly, aghast at her furious blushing.

"The only person you should be addressing such questions to is your husband," her brother muttered, a red stain on his jaw.

"I might not get married until I am thirty," she said archly. "Stop being silly. I shan't do anything with the information."

"Then why do you want to know?"

"Curiosity."

He sent her a dubious glare.

"Many ladies have willingly run into ruin. I am wondering if there is an art to seduction."

"Well, you will not hear it from me."

She pinched his arm. "I suppose I could ask the

Marquess of Rothbury."

The look her brother gave her was filled with such shocked incredulity, Maryann felt sorry for him.

"You have agitated my nerves most abominably," he hissed, angered. "This is my fault. I indulged you too much over the years, and I—"

She leaned in and pressed a quick kiss to his cheek. "And I love you for it. You do not stifle me but allow me my wings, Crispin."

He deflated and raked his fingers through his hair. "You are shameless and provoking, that is what you are. It does you no benefit to be incorrigible."

She gave him an unrepentant grin. "I thought it a part of my charm and—"

Maryann cried out as someone shoved into her from behind and sent her into the path of a carriage, which suddenly seemed to increase its speed. To Maryann's mortification, it was difficult to find her balance, causing her to tumble for the world to see. Her spectacles fell from her face, and she reached for them before trying to right herself.

"Maryann!"

The earth shook beneath her, and she whipped her head up at Crispin's frantic and fear-filled scream to see two horses bearing down at her, the coachman cracking a whip to urge them to greater speed.

For one petrifying moment, her limbs remained paralyzed and her heart roared, drowning out sounds and the words shaping her brother's lips. She struggled to her feet with haste, as harsh hands grabbed her and yanked her forcefully out of harm's way. The carriage roared past her, crushing her parasol with a sharp crack.

"Goodness," she cried, terribly shaken. "That coachman has lost his senses."

Crispin stared after the carriage and then back at her. "They tried to run you over," he said, his voice heavy with shock. "My God, if I had not seen it I would have disbelieved the tale!"

The hands that ran over her arms shook fiercely.

"I am certain it was an accident," she tried to reassure him over her pounding heart.

"My Lady," a gentleman bystander exclaimed, holding on to her elbow and guiding her away from the curb. "You could have been seriously injured or crushed. It is a wonder you are alive. If this man"—he pointed at Crispin—"had not reacted so quickly, I shudder to think of the horror."

Her brother paled even further, and Maryann worried he might faint. He would never forgive himself for the shame of reacting so in public. "I am sure it wasn't anything as dire as *that*. I do thank you for your timely assistance. If you will excuse us, we must be on our way."

He removed his hat to reveal brown hair streaked with gold and bowed his head. "Sir Robert Whittingham at your service."

"Thank you, Sir Robert, I shall not forget your kindness."

All polite sallies extended, Crispin insisted on bundling her back home without procuring the hats, and soon they were back in the carriage headed to Berkeley Square. Her brother was unable to sit still, looking outside the carriage windows and muttering she had not seen how close she came to dying.

Close to dying.

The fear and pain that scythed through her heart then was so visceral, she lurched upright on the carriage seat.

"What is it?" Crispin demanded with a frown.

Dark emotions reared their heads and clogged her throat. "Nothing," she said hoarsely. "It was a silly awareness." But shattering, reshaping everything she thought she knew of herself and what she genuinely wanted.

"Tell me," he urged. "I am your brother; please know you can confide anything to me."

She tried to smile, but her mouth trembled too fiercely. "It was just a small brush with mortality."

"More than a small brush," he rejoined. "Damn scared ten years off my life."

A peculiar grief sat heavy against her heart. "I felt the keenest of regrets…the pain almost agonizing that I've never known what it is like to be kissed," she said softly, her color much heightened, "to be seen and cherished for who I am… I would have died without tasting the pulse of life." And her heart broke at the very thought of it. "Life offers no certainties, Crispin, and I must be willing to live on the dangerous edge and bear all consequences."

"You are out of sorts," he said. "You must not speak like this."

"I must have the freedom to love."

"Maryann—" he began warningly.

"Crispin, have you ever felt this certainty that more awaits you, somewhere? That there is another life for you, one perhaps filled with hope and happiness and you only need to search for it? There is a restlessness upon my heart. I have been so unsatisfied with my life. I want *more*. I never want to look back on my life and feel the ache of regret. To *wish* I had been brave enough."

"You *are* the most courageous lady I know," he said gruffly.

"Am I?" She was through with living according to society, her parents who did not give a fig about her happiness, and for her supposed future husband's expectations. It was just not simply enough to wish or *pretend* to be wicked and improper.

Maryann was decided—it was time she acted the *rakess*.

CHAPTER FOURTEEN

Nicolas entered his town house in Grosvenor Square from a very late night at his clubs. His gaze lit on several letters waiting for his perusal. One particularly caught his attention, and a dark satisfaction flowered through his gut. The wafer suggested the Duke of Farringdon had sent it.

Handing over his coat, gloves, and hat to the butler, he collected the letters and made his way to his library. He selected an armchair closest to the fire, and plucked the letter most important to him, the one from his thirteen-year-old twin sisters who currently resided with their mother at his main estate which was down in Wiltshire.

It was close to five a.m., and though he was desperate for sleep, he would read their letter first. Nicolas had promised them he would tie up his loose ends in town in a few months and return home to them. His mother had been considerably put out that he would return to town so soon and not honor the proper grieving period for his father. He had not been able to explain that he was on the cusp of completing his retribution, and the grief he felt at his father's death was not to be displayed for the world to see. Nicolas had mourned his father long before he had passed, and he had found it in himself to forgive the man's indifference to Arianna's demise.

Dearest brother,
Louisa and I miss you dreadfully, too, and we wish you would come home soon. Mama also misses you,

and always tasks us to read to her the letters you send. She even consumed some of the parcel of sweets you gifted us. I implore you next time to send three packets of sweets. We are growing girls.

The ponies were delivered from the Humphries' stud farm and we love them. It was so kind of you to send such pretty dapple grays, they are gorgeous, but we are still arguing over how to name them. We also got the beautiful dolls. I believe you've forgotten that we turned thirteen and are no longer children.

It has been over four months since Papa died and we still hear Mama crying when she believes no one is about to witness her pain. Louisa and myself fare better, and we feel a bit guilty that we are not filled with sorrow as is Mama. Papa was on his sick bed for quite some months and we had expected that he would be gone on to his reward soon. Papa also bid us not to cry and honor him by only remembering the pleasant memories. When we told Mama of this, she only cried more. I believe if you were here, this sting of pain would feel less to her.

Mama also frets incessantly about what people will say if you are cavorting about town and not honoring the period of mourning. We heard her say it to Grandmother. But Louisa and I know you must have something terribly important to do, or you should not have left us.

We miss our lessons with you most terribly. Today Lydia shot her arrow at a target at fifty feet dead in the center. I was terribly impressed. I am aiming to reach her level by the time we see you next. We are looking forward to your extended visit during Michaelmas.

We love you,
Your sisters, Lydia and Louisa.

He released a slow breath, folded the letter, opened the exquisitely carved wooden box, and placed the missive amongst the other twenty or so letters. All from Lydia and Louisa.

They had been born to his parents later in life to the marchioness's joy, for he had been an only child. Fifteen years separated him from his sisters, and though they had been small, he had missed them dreadfully during his sojourn in Paris.

Upon his return to England, he had made every effort to ensure they did not get lost in his need for retribution. He made time for them, returning to their country estate often. Despite his mother and father's shock at the time, he taught them archery and how to fence. His mother had even discovered that he was now teaching them the art of boxing.

She had scolded him most severely, but he had calmly told her he would not leave his sisters unable to defend themselves from the wolves of this world. His mother had stared at him for a long time, for she had known of the dreadful rift between father and son, and the ugly cause of it. She had simply nodded before lifting her chin and walking away.

Last year when he had gotten word of his father's illness, he had quit the season and headed home to Delacree Park, an affluent, lavish estate which held many fond memories of his childhood. For almost one year, the men he had been so close to taking down had been given a reprieve, for he had directed more of his thoughts then to his family.

Nicolas had remained in the country for several months by his father's sick bed, slowly mending the hurt that had been like a canker between them. His journey to town had been intermittent and then he would only stay for a week at most, all in the vainglory of continuing to stroke the fires under his roguish reputation. After burying his father in the family crypt, he had only stayed with the girls and his mother for three weeks before returning to town.

Dipping the ink into the well, he wrote,

Dearest Louisa and Lydia,

A day does not go by I do not think of you both and miss you. I shall be home for Michaelmas and will be there for a few weeks before I return to town. Business in town has kept me here a little longer than I had hoped. Remember to be good helpmates to our mother and give her my love. My thoughts are with you all at Delacree Park. I am sending you some lengths of material for the seamstress to make up since you are growing girls and will need new gowns.

I am glad you like the ponies and look forward to hearing how you have named them.

Your loving brother, Nicolas

The butler was summoned, and the letter given for immediate delivery to Delacree Park. Then after taking a deep breath, he plucked the duke's letter from the pile and opened it. It was an urgent request to come to his town house in Grosvenor Square for an intimate card party.

Knowledge settled low in Nicolas's gut—the moment had come for the duke to be removed from the board. Nicolas made his way to his chambers, stripped naked, and tumbled onto the well-padded mattress. The chamber was slightly chilled, just how he liked it. His valet, much used to his late-night activities and sleeping for hours in the day, had already ensured a low fire burned in the hearth and the heavy drapes had been drawn to blot out the sunlight. The night had been long, and he was tired. His lashes lowered and he breathed deeply and evenly.

The lush, sensual scent that seemed to be imprinted into Maryann's soft skin invaded his nostrils, and his mouth damn well watered at the memory of her taste on his tongue. "Not now," he murmured. "I cannot dream of you. I am bloody well tired, and I want my rest."

Whatever God he appealed to did not listen, for she stole into his dreams as she had done every night for the last several days. Keeping his eyes closed, he felt the phantom dream of her lying beside him, curved into his side, her lush mouth nuzzling into his throat.

Nicolas groaned, his cock twitching, his arms reaching out to grasp the air. It felt so damn real, as if she were really there. His dream lover bit his lower lip, then trailed that lush mouth down his neck and his chest.

Racoons do that.

That sultry murmur wrapped him in heated anticipation, and he drifted off to sleep with her tormenting him with her tongue and dry wit.

• • •

When Nicolas surged awake several hours later, his cock was heavy and straining against his belly, and his balls damn well ached. The dream was reluctant to leave—hell, he did not want it to leave, for in it, his little minx was wickedly caressing her tongue over his manhood, her beautiful eyes laughing at him and tempting him in the same breath. The memory of the wild and sensually wanton way she had come undone for him in the greenhouse rose in his thoughts. The hunger grew even as he felt discomfort with the recollection of how badly he had wanted her.

You made me tremble…my heart pounded and such cravings I've never known torment me for days.

Still lying on the bed, he threw an elbow over his forehead, and gripped his cock with his other hand. With a groan, he stroked upward, squeezing the head to prevent himself from releasing like an untried boy.

"Fucking hell," he whispered in the dark of the room. "How can I want one woman this badly?"

He willfully pictured her thighs split wide on this very bed, her delicate fingers gripping his sheets, pillows propped under her hips arching her, and he on his knees tonguing her plump cunny. His Maryann was a screamer. She would yell her pleasure, possibly even clamp his head between her thighs.

He grunted when his cock flexed at the idea. That made him wonder if she would be able to take his girth. Then he remembered how damn wet she had been that night in the conservatory and how she had trembled under the lash of his tongue. The next time he had her in his arms, he would test her tightness and…

She is a lady, you blackguard, he reminded himself fiercely, pushing aside his lustful musings. Perhaps he should take the time to figure out if she had a place in his life at the end of everything. Clearly he would not be able to simply dismiss her from his thoughts or awareness. *Nor do I want to.* He had never met another lady like her and doubted he ever would again.

"I will need a wife eventually and heirs," he said, his mind turning over the matter. Lady Maryann was a lady of quality and good-natured charm. He was sure his family would fall in love with her. *Christ*. The way his heart raced at the thought of Maryann being his wife shocked him.

She would be a suitable candidate to be his marchioness. More than suitable. He liked her. She was intelligent and had a little bit of cunning inside her. That, he appreciated more than he thought he would. She had a vibrant and unflinching spirit he admired. Her loveliness and damn smile always tossed his heart into disorder.

To court her, he would have to reshape the reputation he had in the *ton* from wild and wicked to a proper marquess. It had taken years for him to build this reputation. He couldn't imagine what he would have to do to dismantle his dastardly notoriety. Worse, he felt like that part of him stamped upon his bones was simply another facet of himself he hadn't known existed until he was forced to explore it.

Would her parents be open to his courtship even with his reputation?

What if the black Dahlia is her brother?

Ice congealed in his gut. There was no forgiveness for the men who took part in Arianna's demise, and it was beyond him to show mercy to any of them.

He released his cock, ruthlessly expelling Maryann from his mind. It was a bit damn shortsighted to even be wondering about her until the path he had set for himself was over. But when would it actually be done with? A month from now? A year? Would she still be there when he was ready, or would she be forced into marriage with Stamford or another man, and Nicolas would then lose his chance with her forever?

With a hiss of irritation, he pushed from the bed, padded to the windows overlooking the square, dragged open the massive green drapes. The sun had lowered in the sky and the night revelers were already pouring from their homes. Turning away, he rang for a tray to be sent up and a bath.

It was time to prepare for facing the duke.

An hour later, dressed in the heights of current fashion, Nicolas elected to walk to the duke's home, given that they both resided in Grosvenor Square, his silver-headed cane which held his blade in his hand. Upon entering the man's home, Nicolas handed over his coat and hat, but retained his walking cane as he made his way down the hallway to the duke's study.

The butler preceded Nicolas to announce his presence, and then he was allowed entry into the study that was well lit with gas lamps.

"I am surprised you came," the duke said, not bothering to rise from his desk.

"What is surprising about it?" Nicolas asked blandly. "Did you not invite me?"

The duke's gaze was shrewd, but desperation also lurked in the depths of his gray eyes. "I also invited three other friends over the course of the last week," he spat. "None came."

"To what do I owe the invitation to your home?" Nicolas drawled, taking in the duke's disheveled appearance.

"Sit," he commanded, still trying to retain a measure of control of those around him, as if he exercised the same powers he had done a year or more ago. The power of those in the *ton* always rested in money. If that money was threatened even temporarily, his position and reputation would be endangered.

Nicolas lowered himself into the armchair opposite the fire, and smiled, barely, but the duke's bleary eyes narrowed. The duke retrieved an enamel snuffbox from his pocket, opened it, and took a pinch.

Nicolas did not rush to fill the silence, though he suspected that was what the duke wanted. A man who fancied himself above others and had always enjoyed his superiority would find it uncommonly distressing to ask for aid in any way. But this was the place Nicolas had worked to take him, three years of systematic assault on his wealth and holdings.

"Are you by chance seeking a wife, Rothbury?" the duke finally asked after some contemplation.

Now that was interesting. "A wife?"

"Yes."

"No."

"Are you really determined to only marry when you are forty?" he asked, his brows drawing together.

"That was just idle chatter."

"I collect you, like many gentlemen, find my sister to be ravishing," the duke said, with faint amusement in his eyes. "I've entertained a number of offers for Lady Sophie's hand, but I think she needs a man of your stature, one who will be able to keep her in the elegances and luxuries she deserves."

With his back flushed against the wall, and the odds now against him, the man thought to sell his sister.

"And so, you offer her to me?"

Farringdon smiled. "I offer her to you."

"I fear you'll have to consider one of her previous suitors. I am not a contender."

The duke's jaw slackened. The man had believed Nicolas would be salivating over Lady Sophie's beauty.

"Come, man," Farringdon said with an incredulous laugh, leaning back in his wing-back chair. "Do not pretend to be unmoved by her prettiness. My sister is incomparable!"

Nicolas lifted a quizzical brow. "Incomparable? I find her to be spiteful and an undeserving creature who bullies others she deems below her. Her charms are quite lost on me."

The snuffbox dropped from the duke's hand to clatter onto the surface of his desk. "How dare you?" he slung with outrage.

"I dare whatever I want," Nicolas said with icy civility. "I am sure you did not ask me to come to discuss your sister's merits or lack thereof."

They stared at each other, and the duke grimaced.

"I was hoping to be more delicate about it, but I believed you may be obliging enough to help me remedy a spot I find myself in—but not for long, I assure you, not for long."

"I am listening."

"My initial thoughts had been my sister's hand in marriage for one hundred thousand pounds and shares in the copper mines you have in Cornwall."

The duke had clearly used up her dowry living his reckless extravagant lifestyle.

"I am not interested in marrying your sister," Nicolas said, keenly observing the duke.

"You truly do mean it," the duke said, apparently at a loss.

Another man not bent on retribution or not tied into knots over Lady Maryann might have fallen on his face to wed the ravishing creature. The only thing Nicolas felt in regard to her were thoughts of wringing her pretty but scrawny neck for the vile plot she'd set against Maryann.

Farringdon leaned forward, resting his elbows on the over polished surface of his oak desk, his mien growing serious. "If I do not find a solution soon, we will be obliged to exercise the strictest frugalities and I might even have to remove myself to the country and let the town house to stop the bank from calling in the mortgage. Sophie and I might head to the poorhouse soon, and her immediate marriage is the most sensible remedy."

"A man with three country estates and a town house can hardly believe himself to soon be poor."

The duke scrubbed a hand over his face. "You do not know the full of it," he growled. "I am damnably broke. All the money my father left: all gone. All the investments I had made over the years have fallen through. I cannot credit that much to pure bad luck." He shoved at his desk with violence, jerking the sturdy oak with the strength of his anger. "All my creditors called in at the same time and the banks refused to extend me any more credit, as if they do not know who I am. I am the bloody Duke of Farringdon, and they dared refuse me! I swear it is as if I have the very devil himself after me and all he has laid at my feet is disasters."

Dark pleasure filled Nicolas at the man's obvious fright. "What do you want from me?"

"You are filthy rich," the duke said bluntly. "I had my man of affairs check. You can easily afford to blunt me one hundred thousand pounds. I will repay it in good time, my man. That you can trust on."

The duke waited with an air of expectation. Nicolas stood and held his hands over the fire. Keeping the duke in his periphery, he replied, "No."

The man flinched. "Rothbury, if you will not take my sister in marriage, I will avail my other assets to you, of course," he said coldly, as if he had been the one offended.

Nicolas smiled mildly, satisfaction settling deep in his gut. "I would not spot you a loan when I have been the man behind your present trouble."

The duke froze. "What did you say?"

Nicolas faced him, his cane held in his hand. "You heard me."

The duke stood, fisting his hand at his side. "By God, Weychell was right. He noticed that while our finances were being dealt blow after blow you remained flushed in the pockets." He tossed his head arrogantly, a cruel sneer curving his mouth. "You would dare make enemies of us?"

"I would dare. Men stripped of their money and their connections sullied have no power. Surely you know this," he murmured, allowing the facade he wore around them to melt away, and stared at the man, not bothering to hide the hatred that lingered in his heart. "There is no way out for you. You've gambled reck-lessly, losing thousands of pounds and a few unentailed estates in your arrogant idiocy."

The duke flinched, and wariness settled over his face. He stared at Nicolas for several moments before standing with a scoff and saying, "You really expect me to believe you are the architect of the problems I am now facing."

"Of course. Did you not wonder why the navy canceled their lucrative agreement with your ships on the high seas? Or why your tin mine got flooded without any of your workers being hurt and unwilling to return working for you? A mass exodus of almost two hundred men? Or is it that all of your unentailed properties' mortgages were called in? That devil you wondered about…" He held out his hands, saying, *here*

I am, before lowering them to his side.

Nicolas waited, allowing it to resound with the duke that all his financial losses of the past three years that had taken his dukedom to this level of insolvency were all at his ends.

When it dawned, his face flushed with rage. "You goddamn bastard! Why would you do this?"

"Because the ruination of Miss Arianna Burges demands it," Nicolas said with icy contempt.

Bewilderment settled on his face. "Who?"

"The Golden Lion Inn. The only time you were ever there with your friends. All four of you were cronies from Eton who were studying at Oxford. Together you visited a friend in Wiltshire for a garden party. All five of you returned to town and stopped at the inn with plans to stay overnight. As you laughed, ate, and drank, a lone young girl entered and caught your attention."

He twirled the head of his cane, fighting down the dark rage stirring in his gut and the pain in his heart. Nicolas continued dispassionately, "She was young, sixteen years of age, and astoundingly pretty. Her clothes and the knowledge she traveled alone would have revealed her station. Not her speech. For it was I who taught her to read…to write…and to play the pianoforte. She was invited to sup at your table. Which she did…because there was a wolf amongst you whom she trusted."

The duke staggered, knowledge seeping into his gaze. His throat worked on a swallow, and he glanced away briefly into the fire before looking back at Nicolas, his gaze rage filled. "That was years ago."

"Ten," Nicolas snapped. "And three months!"

"I was but nineteen and only having a spot of fun, and for that…for *that* you have ruined me financially and my sister for a goddamn no-account gel?"

"A spot of fun," Nicolas murmured, the need to draw his sword and slice open the man's throat to let out the blood beating in his veins. He fought back the need, for he had committed no proven crime so that his family would not lose him to prison, which was where he would surely head if he killed a peer of the realm. It had also been the reason he had not challenged them to duels, not wanting to be pressed into fleeing England and to leave his sisters behind. So Nicolas had waged his well-calculated war to take the things from them they loved—their wealth, beautiful homes, and the vaunted reputations they enjoyed.

"You all violated her…except for one who stood silent, too afraid to partake, but too much of a coward to fight for her. But those who stand in the face of evil and do nothing…are just as complicit!"

The duke's throat worked. "Goddamn it, it was not like that! She…" He scrubbed a hand over his face. "We gave her coins after. It was not like that."

A sound of rage trapped behind Nicolas's throat.

My tears are like endless rainfall.

Another line from her letter left behind whispered in his head in her haunting tone.

"Which of your friends stood by and only watched, and who did she see at your table and thought a friend?"

The duke stiffened. "By God, you do not know who we really are, do you?"

Nicolas stared at him. If not for the signet ring Farringdon wore, he would not have suspected him of being Arianna's dragon. Nicolas had known them all from his days at Eton and they had been friends with several other young future lords. "Viscount Barton,

Viscount Weychell, You, Earl of Marsh…and one other. Who is he?"

Nothing in the duke's expression gave him away, and a sneer twisted his lips. "You are guessing. Lord Barton you have proven was clearly there since you've run him out of England nearly two years ago! And now me! If you were so certain that Weychell and Marsh were involved, why have you not ruined them, too? All this for a damn nobody!"

"How loyal you are," he drawled bitingly.

The first of them he'd ruined, Lord Barton, a well-loved golden boy, had been the same. Nicolas had ruthlessly taken out one of the man's teeth and given him a day to rethink his answer. Upon Nicolas's return to the man's home, he had packed and left for Europe. Nicolas hadn't wasted any time chasing the viscount.

Nicolas carefully kept his expression composed lest he revealed the doubt around the wolf's and the black Dahlia's identity. "I will see every one of you ruined without any chance of return. She was precious to me, her father, and her mother. She was precious to many friends, and her life held the same value as yours — or even more than yours, you vile shite."

Pain sliced through Nicolas's soul. "All your creditors will come calling tomorrow. All the newspapers and scandal sheets will be printing the knowledge that you are broke…and of your interest in a particular house in Soho."

Then he turned, opened the door, and walked away.

Once in the hallway, a shout of rage sounded behind him, and he turned in time to see the duke lunging at him with a rapier. He jerked back, gripping the head of his cane, twisted and drew his blade in one smooth motion. Savage satisfaction darted through Nicolas when the duke attacked him again, and he parried, all the rage and guilt carried with him for the last ten years rushing through him in a chaotic storm.

Within three moves he disarmed the duke and held the point of his rapier at his throat.

"You have ruined me," the duke said, his eyes red with tears.

"You cry, but not because you feel remorse," Nicolas said, disgusted.

A thin line of blood beaded on the tip of his blade, and several cries echoed behind them. A quick glance revealed the butler and three maids hovering in the lengthy hallway, their faces stark with horror.

"Accept the punishment for the pain and horror you inflicted on an innocent girl," he snarled. "She flung herself into the river. You have life. Be satisfied you were left with that."

Then he lowered his rapier and walked out of the man's home. Once outside, he lifted his face to the sky and breathed deeply.

The retort of a pistol shot came from inside, and then screams rode the air. Without going back inside, he knew what the duke had done. No regret soured Nicolas's gut. If Arianna's father had been a man of equal standing, he would have challenged the duke and the others to a duel of honor and would have taken their lives.

One more has been taken down. No satisfaction flowered through Nicolas, either, just a deep sense of knowing that a measure of justice had been served.

The dragon wings spread wide, a rose of coronet upon its head…how merciless this dragon was, tempting me with chances of escape only to catch me again when I tasted freedom.

"The Dragon is dead, Arianna," he said, the slight wind ripping his words into the air. A whimsical part of him wished the wind took the news to her so her haunting would stop.

He suddenly felt unbearably weary, as if something heavy sat on his shoulders. Nicolas wished he would go home to something different than an empty town house, and a bottle of whiskey. He was eight and twenty but felt as if he had lived much longer. He walked away from the commotion and started down the cobbled street.

Two footmen raced past him, no doubt to call a physician. The duke possibly lived, then, and Nicolas found himself hoping that he had not really died. That was the hardest part about his vengeance. He had made these men his cohorts. Though he had become a libertine to do it, there were days he laughed and caroused with them, and when he left their presence after a night of either gambling, playing cards, or leaving replete from a bordello, his heart would feel heavy.

He had dined at these men's homes, met their families. He had seen that there was more to them than the monstrous deed they committed at age nineteen or eighteen, but it was still not in his heart to let them off. Justice had to be served.

And there were days he bled because of it, but upon his honor he would not falter. Not even when he went for the wolf.

But I need to know beyond a shadow of a doubt that you were there.

Upon reaching his town house, a young man hovered, Ronald Jenkins formerly of Bow Street, looking a mite anxious. He was but one of a three-man team Nicolas had set to discreetly shadow Lady Maryann.

"What is it?" Nicolas demanded, his gut instantly knotting.

"The lady ye have us watching out for, a carriage almost ran her over your lordship. This afternoon on High Holborn. I did not see it, but Harry said someone pushed her into the path of the carriage, and that the two seemed to be working together. The driver waited until she was out in the street to speed up his horses. Harry tried to follow the carriage but lost 'em."

The shock and fear that tore through Nicolas rendered him silent. *Did I do this by dancing with you, by being too obvious with my attraction?* A deadly calm settled over Nicolas. "Was she hurt?"

"No, just badly shaken up."

"Have you kept watch?"

"Harry was sitting on her house, and he reported that the family is headed to a ball. He followed the carriage to a Countess Lauriston's home." Report completed, Jenkins melted away, drawing his hat lower over his forehead, his hands deep in the pockets of his coat.

Nicolas did not enter his home, but turned around, and made his way to Lady Lauriston's abode. Lady Maryann would not be a lady overset by nerves or such nonsense, and that she would attend a ball suggested she was unruffled.

Nicolas still needed to determine for himself she was well. After the raw, provoking dreams he'd been having of her, he would ensure he did not go off alone with her. A quick chat on the terrace or out in the gardens would do, then he would watch and see that she returned to the safety of the ballroom.

Do not go, something in him urged. *Ensure you are never alone with her, even for a damn minute*, it warned. But Nicolas could not fight the compulsion to go to her, and deep inside it shook him to know he did not want to examine the reasons why.

CHAPTER FIFTEEN

Somehow Maryann knew Nicolas would come to her tonight.

She sat in her bed, her back leaned against the large headboard, her feet folded beneath her. The room was well lit, with a gas lamp and a roaring fire in the hearth. The book she had tried to distract herself with had been placed by the small desk to her left. And she waited.

More than an hour had passed since she had ceased pretending to read, and by the chime of the long grandfather clock in the hallway, it was just about nine in the evening. After supper she had pled a headache and retired to her room, while the earl and countess departed an hour past to attend a ball. Crispin had headed off to his club, and the rest of the household slept.

She stiffened as a shadow passed by her window. Heart pounding, Maryann eased from the bed, and leaned against the bedpost. The window groaned but did not budge. Though she had anticipated his presence, Maryann would not leave her windows open. She had latched them firmly closed since he stopped visiting her after that first week.

Curious to see how he would bypass the latch when it was inside her room, she waited. Maryann could not tell if he was really there, or if it was her fanciful yearnings. She climbed onto the bed and lay on her side, her hand pillowed beneath her cheek as she watched the windows. A yawn startled her, and she admitted the agitation of the day and the mild headache after had exhausted her more than she'd anticipated. The ticking of the clock on her mantel revealed the slow passage of time. Her lashes fluttered closed, and she slipped away in a dreamless sleep.

I am no longer alone.

That was the first thought to enter Maryann's mind as the unknown disturbance roused her to full awareness.

He's here.

A faint stirring of pleasure or perhaps anticipation curled through Maryann, and suddenly, the beat of her heart was felt in every part of her body.

The gas lamp had been turned off, and the fireplace burned low in the grate. A silvery beam of moonlight spilled into the room, filtering through the lace curtains. She snapped her gaze to the windows, which remained closed. But she could feel his presence in her room. "How did you get inside?" she whispered without seeing him. That she could feel the power of his gaze upon her was enough.

The bed dipped ever so slightly, and with a gasp, she lurched upright and turned in the direction she felt the movement. She did not expect him to be sitting on her bed. That felt remarkably intimate and perilous. The marquess's powerful form was seated on the bottom of her bed, his shoulders resting against the bedpost.

A shadow of a smile crossed his lips and his eyes gleamed with something wicked and predatory. A knowledge passed between them that she wore his mark. That very spot ached and throbbed as if reacting to his closeness.

"I locked the windows," she said, flushing at the husky way she sounded.

He stared at her mouth for a long moment. "Very good."

"Yet you are still here," she pointed out. "How did you come in?"

"Through the front door."

Maryann's mouth parted in a soundless gasp of shock. "Surely it is not *that* easy to enter someone's abode and unnoticed, too!" She frowned. "You *were* unnoticed, weren't you?"

"Yes." Now his voice was threaded with subtle amusement. "You do not seem alarmed that I am here. Expected me, did you?"

"I…" A hair tickled along her cheek. She reached up and froze. Once again he had unpinned her hair.

Beneath his unflinching regard, a ripple of awareness went through her, and that inward alarm warned her of the peril to her virtue being so intimately enclosed with him in her bedchamber.

Yet she would not run or act like a silly ninny. If he wanted to kiss her, she would allow herself to enjoy all of his wicked advances. It was madness to even think it…yet the idea persisted. A seething cauldron of restlessness roiled through Maryann, and the shred of caution she had used to guide her life since her come out collapsed in its entirety. She actually felt frightened of what she might do, of what she might allow, without any care or worry for the consequences.

He'll not leave here until I have taken a bit of what I want.

Nicolas was staring at the spill of Maryann's hair over her shoulders and down to her waist.

"Your hair is beautiful. Your russet highlights remind me of the leaves in autumn."

The musing several weeks ago if she should cut it

into a fashionable style vanished. Not while he looked at it so. "Why did you come?" she asked huskily.

"You were not at Lady Lauriston's ball. Not finding you there, I came here. Did something happen?" His eyes held a distinct menace.

Yes. But she could not own to it. She suspected it was not wise to tempt him beyond the limits of his forbearance after recalling his vow to kill Viscount Talbot. Maryann could not have a death on her conscience. "I had no inclination for watching others dance tonight," she said with a wry smile of her lips.

"Is that all?"

His regard felt peculiarly provocative.

"A carriage almost ran you over today."

There was a curious lump in her throat that made speaking almost near to impossible. "How do you come to know of it?"

He was silent for a moment, leaving his expression strangely harsh. "I have a few men discreetly following you. One of them reported to me all that happened."

The breath went from her. "You have men *following* me?"

"Yes."

"I am duly alarmed and perhaps a second away from screaming. Have you gone mad?" She wasn't sure if she should be outraged, appalled, or charmed.

"I am in full possession of my faculties."

"You will have those men stop following me this instant."

"No."

"I—"

He caught her jaw in his hand, the grip gentle but unyielding. "You protest in vain."

"I am not yours to protect," she whispered, wanting

to strip away his layers and understand why he would guard her in such a manner.

He faltered into astounding stillness, peering down at her enigmatically. Then he released her chin but did not move. Maryann touched the corner of his mouth with her finger. "What do I mean to you?" she asked with remarkable equanimity.

"Always so bold," he murmured, his eyes never leaving her face.

"Yes, and you should be prepared to acquaint yourself with it."

"That suggests long-standing friendship."

"Is that why you are in my chamber, yet again—friendship?"

"There is an irresistible pull to you I simply cannot deny, even though I try to ignore it. I confess you interest me extraordinarily."

Maryann was suddenly breathless. Their faces were so close together, she couldn't help admiring the sheer beauty of his face. "Was it our shocking interlude that precipitated this interest?"

"No," he said softly.

"You say little when you are not playing the charming rake."

"My thoughts are constantly occupied by you." His voice grew softer still. "Is that what you wanted to hear?"

She was so thrilled by that admission, she almost hugged him. "A very disagreeable experience for you, I am sure."

"You cannot be important to me."

Her heart trembled until it ached inside her chest. She shifted closer to him, aware of his pleasing scent. "Why not?"

"Your brother might be my enemy."

That she had not expected. Her lips parted, but no words came forth. *"Crispin?"* she finally gasped.

"The very one."

There was an air of watchfulness about him, and in the gaze that stared at her lurked something dangerous. Her stomach flipped alarmingly. "I have never heard anything so silly! My brother is the best of men!"

"To others he might be a villain."

That word caught against the discomfort of her thought. "You said *might*. How certain are you?"

"About thirty percent of surety," he murmured.

"You are odd," she said, feeling an unexpected spurt of humor. "To deny oneself pleasure because of such an improbable possibility."

She gasped when he suddenly reached for her and dragged her onto his lap. The feel of the firm power of his thigh under her buttocks had her blushing, and with a hated sense of shyness she folded her hands beneath her bosom. *Oh God, I am sitting on him!*

"An improbable possibility?" he asked.

She was intensely mindful of his hand, strong and warm, on her lower back. "Of course. My brother is the best of gentlemen. It is not possible for him to do anything that might make him the enemy of anyone."

"If he did, your brother would have been a lad of seventeen."

"You do know how to hold a grudge," she cried, thumping his shoulder lightly, before quickly folding back her arms. *I am still sitting on his thigh! Are we not going to mention that at all?*

"You make light of a matter of which you are ignorant."

"Then enlighten me."

He grunted but remained silent.

Maryann peered at him from beneath her lashes. "Are you worried I will want to skewer you for my brother?"

"Should I come for him and you know it, you will stand between us like an avenging angel with your rapier—or a shovel."

"I agree," she said softly, pushing a few curls behind her ears.

"Your brother might indeed be the man I am looking for."

Her heart lurched uncomfortably. "He cannot be, I am *certain* of it," she whispered, suddenly realizing that if the marquess was her brother's enemy, Crispin's life was in danger.

"Ah, I see the understanding in your eyes finally. Should you decide to avenge your brother against me when I am finished with him, that would be a travesty. Imagine us enemies—a truly frightening prospect, especially as I believe you might win."

The look in his eyes was a frightening thing to behold—it hinted at a cunning and a strength of restrained power.

"I am astonished you think I might win against you."

His gaze lowered to her mouth and she could feel his want. The need to taste his kiss…to feel the press of his lips against hers, the yearning to feel desired rose up inside like a great hunger…or thirst. Her throat felt parched and need quivered through her.

I've never been kissed, she wanted to say, but the words were trapped in her aching throat.

"You have powers that you do not yet understand how to wield. And I must make every allowance for your sweet fierceness."

At her silence, he arched a brow. "Got your tongue, did I?"

"I admit I was stuck on sweet fierceness, wondering at the possibility of it. Are you saying that you find my manners and oddities sweet? I really must know of which you speak, my charming personality or the place between my thighs that you tasted with your tongue?"

He jerked, the motion dropping her on her arse upon the soft carpet.

Nicolas quickly stood. "Hell!"

Sprawled on the carpet, Maryann looked up at him, and the hilarity of the moment struck her. She laughed, scrambling to stand, taking the hand he held out to her for him to pull her up. Still chuckling, she peered up at him only to falter, her breath shortening. The raw hunger in his eyes was almost intimidating. A precise urging stirred low in her stomach, more potent than anything she'd ever felt. "Nicolas?" she asked tremulously.

"There is a distinct possibility your accident today was deliberate," he said a bit hoarsely.

"What?" That was the last thing she'd expect him to say given how he was staring at her. "No, that is not a sensible assumption to make. It *was* an accident. Going out was an impulse. Surely something like that would be methodically planned."

"If someone is determined and powerful enough, it could be done."

"Upon my word, you are entirely serious."

"That accident was possibly a test to see how important you are to me, if at all."

A frightening sensation dropped in her belly. What sort of man would have made such violent enemies?

"What…who are your enemies?"

"A few. But there is someone on the board I am not familiar with, and that has me unsettled, for I cannot keep him in my sights."

What was he talking about? What board? She felt a moment of pure bewilderment, and she sharply shook her head and thought about the man she knew before her. Not the rake but the dangerous, calculating lurker she often spied. He made a comparison to a chess game and possibly thought in terms of its strategies.

It struck her forcibly how much she did not know about him. "Why do you have enemies?"

"They took something from me."

"What?"

"Something precious."

The soft, regretful way he said it made her throat ache with unexpected sorrow. "A lady?" She was not sure why she asked; there might be other things this man considered to be precious: land, wealth, jewelry.

His lashes swept down for a second before he pinned her with that penetrating stare of his. "Yes."

Oh! "I am sorry," she whispered.

"It has nothing to do with you."

"I am still deeply sorry for your loss. Are you trying to…to take back what they stole?"

He took a few steps away from her, the shadows from the curtain casting him in darkness. She realized it was such a deliberate move on his part, to conceal his expression.

"Do not hide from me," she whispered. "Please, Nicolas."

He stepped into the path of the moonlight. The icy shrewdness of his look made her pulse trip in alarm.

"If they prick us, do we not bleed? If they wrong us,

do we not revenge?"

"So, it is a revenge plot then," she said lightly, painfully aware of the furious pounding of her heart. She walked over to him, lifted her hand, and cupped his jaw. He took a deep, shuddering breath, leaning slightly into her touch. "I understand the need to right the wrong done to you or someone you love. Will you tell me about it?"

His eyes lowered and he stilled. When he lifted his gaze to her, she flinched and stepped back. The eyes staring at her were indifferent, his lips almost cruel in their dispassionate curve. Nicolas's entire posture radiated coiled menace. A murderous coldness settled on his face.

"Who dared to hurt you?" he asked softly.

• • •

Maryann's unbound hair rippled in wondrous waves down her back and over the front of her nightgown. Several tendrils curled along the slope of her cheeks in a rather becoming way. She was lovely…and his heart stumbled in his chest. Her eyes were widened as if he had frightened her with his harsh whisper. An elusive sensation whispered through him, but it vanished before it shaped into a sense of tangibility.

"You silly man, I am not afraid of you."

Some of the tension left him, and with a start he realized he had needed to hear those words from her. He glanced at the dark, mottled bruises which encircled her arms. "These must be incredibly painful."

She placed her hands behind her back as if hiding candy from a toddler.

He glanced at the basin. Earlier, when he'd thought

to steal in through her windows, he'd seen her soak her hand in rosemary water, then gingerly rub an ointment on her skin.

Nicolas thought it a result of falling into the streets. But these bruises spoke of something darker, the shape of a hand...fingers perhaps. Someone had hurt her, quite deliberately. To have left such bruises, the person was precise in their brutal punishment. Her father? The earl did not seem the type. Or was it her brother? *The black Dahlia?*

He took her hand between his. The tip of her finger was not soft and feminine, her nails were cropped short and the pad of her finger rough...and prickly. "What was the cause of this?"

An almost embarrassed smile touched her mouth. "Needlepoint. It is one of my favorite pastimes, especially when I am agitated. It soothes me."

He used the tip of his finger and gently touched one of the marks above her wrists. "And who did this?"

She tried to tug her hand away, but he held onto her wrist gently.

"I thought we were friends."

She sent a mirthful look from beneath her lashes. "Friends? *I* imagined nothing of the sort."

His Maryann tried to sound snappish, but her voice trembled.

"Then what are we?"

Her face flushed a delicate, rosy hue. "I...I do not know, but I sense friendship does not define it."

His resistance to her allure was very fragile, and way down inside, in a secret place he himself did not know, he felt the barrier he was trying to erect crack. And he understood her sentiments perfectly. He felt torn between the ache of wanting her and keeping her at a safe distance. It had already been five years since he started his path of vengeance. How long could he wait before taking something for himself?

He gritted his teeth. The matter wasn't taking what her eyes so sweetly offered, it was what to do *after*.

He could not keep her or publicly woo her. Anything they did would be in secret and shadows. He'd had discreet lovers over the years who had understood they must never speak of their connection. But those women had been experienced widows or a songbird.

None had been an innocent or lady of quality with Lady Maryann's breeding and connections.

None had peered at him in such a manner—filled with longing and tender regard.

None had touched his mouth with trembling fingers.

None had made his heart quake from a smile.

None had roused the dark protectiveness surging violently in his veins.

Nicolas rubbed a soothing thumb over her racing pulse. "Please, tell me what happened. Or if you are unable to, at least tell me you've informed your father and brother."

"I...I did not."

"Why?"

The memories flashed in her gaze, and the fear he saw had icy fingers slinking down his spine. Unexpectedly, she lowered her forehead to his shoulder. An odd tenderness uncoiled inside him. For her.

He led her over to the chair by the dying fire and when he sat, he tugged her down onto his lap in the single most tender motion he had ever made in his life.

"How scandalous," she murmured, her eyes searching his face as she tried to decipher his intention.

He was damn glad she hadn't jumped away from him and chased him from her room. Nicolas didn't understand it, but he wanted…no, *needed* to be gentle with her. There was a vulnerability around her trembling mouth that gutted him to see. She was the most striking human being he had ever met. Fear wasn't something she should ever feel, not while he was in her life.

But she is not in your life…only on the edges of it.

With a sense of confusion, he realized she filled spaces he had not known were empty, and she did it so effortlessly. "Tell me," he softly coaxed.

"Why?"

"I will educate him on the error of his ways."

Her eyes flared briefly. "I think…I think he is dangerous; he is not a man with whom one trifles."

He suspected the identity of the bounder but wanted her trust. It mattered to him. Nicolas lifted her fingers to his mouth and nipped. She flushed, and her chest lifted on a sharp breath. "Am I only a feckless baboon in your sights?" he asked.

Tension crackled in the space between them.

Her cheeks turned a bit pink, and she looked away for a moment before answering. "I do not think you are a feckless baboon…but a great pretender. Sometimes I see the danger lurking in your gaze, but then it vanishes so quickly, I wonder if it was my overwrought imagination."

He was not the same boy who had loved Arianna and had lingered for years in his hapless guilt. The reputation of ruthlessness he garnered had not been lightly gained but had been another calculated and very deliberate move on his part. Some of the sins laid at his feet were well-placed rumors, but some he had committed. Only those close to him might know the truth, and with a fierce jolt Nicolas recognized he had no one close to him, yet he had never thought himself lonely.

Vengeance, and guilt, and pain had been fine company indeed.

"If not a baboon, what do you see?" he asked teasingly, hoping to get her to relax. He sensed acting the demanding brute would not work with her.

"Sometimes you remind me a bit of a hawk…or an eagle. Something in your stare. Maybe you are a more dangerous predator just to my sensibilities," she said with a teasing half smile.

He faltered into stillness. *The eagle soars indifferently while the wolf betrays…*

Nicolas studied her face carefully. "Do you trust me?"

"You are in my chamber, aren't you? I have *twice* now been sitting on your very muscular thigh," she said with clear disgruntlement.

He smiled. "My muscular thighs appreciate your trust. When did this happen?"

"Today," she admitted softly.

"Why do I hear shame in your voice?"

"I was afraid."

"A reaction that many of us feel. It warns us of the threat in the room, not that we are cowards." He gave a sigh. "As a lad of twelve, I found myself on the iced-over lake by our country estate when I was just overcome with a feeling of dread. I froze for several minutes until I pushed myself to get off the lake. Only a few seconds later, the ice collapsed in several places. That fear…whatever induced it warned me of the danger I had not yet perceived. Fear is not an indication of weakness, but that we are highly perceptive enough to sense the latent danger which surrounds us. I am certain you felt anxious before this person even acted in a vile manner."

He tugged at one of her loose curls. "You have nothing to be ashamed of, Maryann."

A quick frown chased her face, and her eyes searched his. "It is very silly, because I am not a wilting flower, and I only had to scream, and the servants would have come running. I didn't kick at him or even struggle. I…I just froze. And whenever I think of it, my heart races and I feel such anxiety."

Those softly spoken words had lodged themselves deep in Nicolas's heart and stirred something wicked and ugly inside him.

"Lord Stamford," he said, watching every nuance of her face. "It was he."

She nodded. "He is frightfully persistent. It is quite inconceivable. There are so many beautiful and well-connected ladies in society who would happily marry him."

"And because you are a wallflower, you do not think the earl could want you?"

She exuded a fire and strength he had never seen in another woman; it did not seem to occur to her how a man might crave her in his life.

"The unflattering sobriquet is meant to be such an insult, a reminder to me and my friends that we are overlooked and relegated to adorn the background of ballrooms, much like the wallpaper in this room. I choose not to be embittered at their ridiculousness or accept the role. Even with that knowledge of myself, it is astonishing the earl would pursue me in such a manner. There *are* far more beautiful women in society, who are also intelligent, who possess large dowries, who would be thrilled with the connection."

"It is because those other ladies are like roses... some red, yellow, white, all beautiful, but still roses."

"Roses are very beautiful," she murmured huskily. "Everyone loves roses. *I* love roses."

He touched the corner of her mouth, where the dimple came when she smiled, with the tip of his fingers. It was gentle enough for her to doubt the existence of the caress. Yet she closed her eyes, savoring the feel of him against her skin. Or was it he who relished the delicate softness beneath the tip of his finger?

He dragged the tip of his finger down to her lips, and gently swiped it across the fullness of her mouth. Those lips parted...and he ran his finger along the open seam of her lips. There were so many things he wanted to do with her lush mouth. Kiss it thoroughly until it bruised, and flushed the brightness of red. He also wanted to fuck that pouting mouth, coax her to take his thick length, savor the feel of her mouth as she sucked him in hot, tight pulls.

The crudity of his lust shocked him and allowed him to drop his hand to her hips. He gentled his touch, as if he held something precious in his clasp, and gave her the revealing truth. "You are the night-blooming cereus that graces us only once a year, for a single night. And on the night which you opened so beautifully, he saw you...a brewing tempest formed in his gut, and he craved you, for he knew the secret behind your unique beauty."

"And what is that?" she asked huskily, her eyes dark with indefinable emotions.

"That it wasn't just only for *one* night. That blooming fire that he saw is always there, underneath the facade of indifference you show to the world, waiting for you to show it to those you deem worthy. For one *brief* moment he saw your wit that skewered, the poignant beauty of your smile that endlessly captivated, the sensual way you saunter, the elegance of your throat as you tilt back your head and laugh, the charming way you constantly fix your spectacles, the shrewdness *and* sweetness of your tongue…and he saw that the mouse wasn't a mouse at all…but a rac—"

Her fingers, three of them, pushed against his mouth perfectly, stemming his words.

Maryann made a small, helpless sound of need. "Surely, you'll say a lioness…or a tigress," she whispered achingly. "Racoons are ugly."

A familiar craving awakened inside him, and he wanted to drag her against his chest and kiss her so badly, his teeth ached. He had to resist, for one kiss with her wouldn't be enough. He ruthlessly reminded himself, "*He who conquers others is strong, but he who conquers himself is mighty.*"

He could feel the wild flutter of her heartbeat underneath his fingers pressed into the curve of her throat. "Not *my* racoon."

His heart slammed against his chest. So close to kissing her but so far away.

"It is you…you who saw me… Since that first night you climbed up into my room, I can forever feel your gaze upon me. *You* saw."

That sumptuous mouth of hers curved with a grin that made him want to stroke his tongue at the corner of her mouth. An irrepressible dimple appeared, and he wanted to kiss it.

So he did.

CHAPTER SIXTEEN

His kiss destroyed her.

It was unexpected, it was so soft, it was unbelievably tender, and scandalously perfect, for it was just a mere meeting of their mouths, but it felt like everything. A recognition that they were more than just friends, not of ships sailing past each other in the vastness of the world.

Since the first touch of his lips to hers, neither moved. Leaning in farther, she pressed her hands to his chest, quite aware he still held a hand at her throat. Though he had not yet parted his lips, Maryann could taste him…smell him, something dark and delicious, and it stirred a violent hunger to life.

She nipped at his lower lip, and a sighing sound came from his throat. Then his lips parted, and his tongue licked along the closed seam of her mouth. With the softest of moans, she opened her mouth to him, gasping her delight when the hand gently encircling her throat, slid up and thrust into her hair, holding her firmly to him. He ravished her mouth with sensual expertise. At first with soft bites and licks, then with such demanding pressure, her lips felt bruised.

Maryann moved her mouth under his with sensual wonder, little whimpers of need puffing from her mouth to his. Their tongues met, and at first the sensations startled her, then they delighted her. With another moan she followed his lead, taking and giving in equal measure. His tongue slowly stroked hers, and she gave herself over to the heated sensations building within her.

His hands moved to grip her hips, then tightened almost painfully. As their kiss deepened and his mouth grew more demanding, moving over hers in a hot, hungry surge of possession, she trembled at the sheer pleasure he evoked.

Their mouths broke apart, and she gasped shakily.

She stared at him, her lips parted, her breath shallow. "That was my very first kiss."

Pleasure lit in his eyes, and the unguarded tenderness in his expression sent a profound ache to her heart. She lifted trembling fingers to his mouth. Nicolas leaned in and barely brushed her mouth to his.

"Open your legs and sit on me as if mounting a horse astride," he murmured at her lips.

She was scandalized by the carnal instructions, but her entire body seemed to pulse in response. The intense sensuality in his gaze stole her breath. The chair was without arm pads, and Maryann shifted, slipping one leg on the outside of his thigh and then repeated the motion with her other foot so that she sat astride him.

Their mouths were barely touching, and his eyes… God, they were so beautiful, she felt as if she were drowning in their depths. His hands shifted, but she did not break their stare, not even when he reached forward, grabbed her nightgown in his fists, and dragged it up almost to her waist.

Peering down, Maryann flushed. Her legs were split so wide to accommodate the width of his hips and the breadth of the chair. Then he unerringly pressed a thumb to that mark he had left high on her thigh. He pressed it, and she whimpered at the resulting ache felt deep inside her sex.

She hesitated, her rapid breathing mingling with his. "Frightened, Maryann?"

He kissed the exposed part of her throat, then raked his teeth against her beating pulse.

"I can feel the beat of your heart against my mouth. You *are* afraid." He sounded darkly amused, rakish. "Such sweet innocence. I am going to enjoy turning you out."

She thought it prudent to ignore what she realized was deliberate provocation. Then a sharp nip at her flesh pulled a whimper from her.

He chuckled, the hum of his pleasure lascivious. Was she meeting the full power of the libertine?

"I am most certainly not afraid," she gasped, though she could not help the shiver at that sensual threat. *Turn her out?* How properly and ominously naughty.

Maryann tilted her neck more to his questing tongue.

"Look at me." The command was low and sensually rough.

Startled, she glanced up into his fiery gaze. He gripped her hips, and tugged her almost violently to him, slamming her sex to press directly against the hardness behind his trousers. Heat blossomed in her loins as pleasure stabbed like lightning to that nub, and she gasped against his mouth and grabbed his shoulders to steady herself against the sensations.

Suddenly she wanted to be rid of all the clothes between them, to feel his entire naked body against hers, to touch that hard part of him to her aching folds. Maryann imagined this was how he would spear into her body should they ever lose themselves so, with carnal dominance. The notion was thrilling and also incredibly intimidating.

"Give me your mouth."

She helplessly responded, easing her mouth to his in an open-mouthed kiss. Maryann wrapped her hands around his neck, as he took her lips with tender desperation. He arched her, trailing his lips down her neck, licking and kissing.

"Nicolas." His name purred from her in a throaty moan.

She felt drunk on pleasure, vibrantly alive. His large hands slipped from her hips to cup her buttocks, and then he rocked her, sliding her aching sex over his hardness. When she cried out, his mouth swallowed it hungrily.

Shocked arousal blossomed through her and she grew mortifyingly wet, dampening the front of his trousers. Maryann could feel it, but somehow the awareness only heightened the primal need burning in her veins.

He did it again and again and again, never releasing her mouth from his drugging kisses. Hot, drowning pleasure gripped her and with each rock of her against him, the pleasure inside grew hotter until sweat dampened her brows.

Her breath came in gasps and pants and whimpers at the friction against that split between her thighs. Each drag back and forth ground her nub of pleasure into his hardness. That nub got harder, more sensitive, more needy. Maryann felt as if a fire had been lit from within her and she burned with reckless passion.

"Oh God, Nicolas!"

His urgings grew even rougher, and with each slide of her core over his hardened bulge, her body jerked under the burn of pleasure, eroding all rational thought until with a wild scream swallowed by his mouth, she unraveled.

The clamoring of her heartbeat seemed to drive the

air from her lungs. Maryann distantly became aware of the soft soothing kisses pressed to her forehead, and that she was quaking against him. His hands were no longer at her hips but hugging her to him while he lightly moved his hands up and down her back, gentling her body, which felt languid and unfamiliar as it came down from the stunning pleasures.

His hands seemed to move without deliberate thought and his thumbs were gently massaging her taut nipples through her night rail. Her nipples seemed to grow and harden under his supple thumbs, and she felt a rush deep inside her as her body reacted once more. She was still tight against him and she could feel the pulse within that part of him that any nice girl should not be aware of. She blushed with embarrassment at her own wantonness, but both her desires and body only wanted more—far more.

She sighed gustily against his mouth, still trembling from the pleasure. "I think I might have to marry you after this."

His lips curved. "Is that a proposal, Lady Maryann?"

She smoothed a wisp of unruly hair from his forehead. "Odd, you do not sound frightened at the prospect."

He grunted softly and pressed a kiss to her damp temple. "The prospect of spending a lifetime with a woman of your wit, beauty, and passion is not alarming."

Maryann was astonished. "Nicolas?"

"Yes?"

"So, you believe in love then?"

"I do not deny its existence, nor do I want to."

"An acceptable answer," she replied with a quick smile.

He brushed the pad of his thumb over her lower lip, which felt bruised and swollen from his kisses. "Wait on me."

Her throat closed and she felt dispossessed of all rational thoughts. Maryann was almost afraid to ask what he meant. "Wait on you to court me?"

A fleeting smile touched his mouth. "Yes."

Oh! "Why not now?"

"There are some words…some actions that can only remain in the dark. Do you understand?"

"Or else?" she whispered, her heart aching.

"If known, they become a weakness."

She turned his words over in her thoughts, unable to decipher his meaning, fearing she understood. Society must never know that he liked her…or she him.

Her chest went tight. *Shock maybe*, she dazedly thought. "For how long should I wait?" she whispered.

"I do not know. I've already been on this path for a little over five years. I only know with certainty that my enemies must never know about you." His hands tightened around her. "I am determined to end it soon. But there are certain things that cannot be rushed. It might be a few more months…maybe even a year."

She could feel her heartbeat on her tongue. "I will wait. Though I confess you might have to come and find me in France or Italy."

"You plan to run away?"

"I'll not marry Stamford."

"Do not worry about him."

Her heart lurched. "What does that mean?"

"I'll have a talk with him."

Maryann blinked. "Do you want to start a scandal?"

He took her hand and turned it over. "Do you think I'll allow him to get away with this?"

It warmed her how intensely protective he was of her. "No, I suppose not." She pressed her forehead to his. "I believe I am falling in love with you."

Maryann swore she felt the thunder of his heart, but he said nothing. "Did I frighten you?" she asked with a small smile.

"No."

He sounded *intrigued*, and her heart thrilled. Her marquess was not closed off to the notion of love. "That's good," she whispered teasingly, closing her eyes, and hoarding the sensations filling her chest close to her heart. "I do not fancy gentlemen who scare easily."

His arms tightened around her and he buried his face in her throat for long moments.

"Why were you on the ice lake?"

A fine tension entered his frame before he relaxed. "Chasing fireflies with Arianna. She loved fireflies, and the ethereal glow of their lights in the dark."

The deep throb in his voice was unfathomable.

Maryann rested her cheek against his head. "Was she the one precious to you?"

"Yes," he said gruffly.

She combed her fingers through his hair tenderly, sensing that he was not at all as relaxed as he pretended. "I can feel the tension in your body. I am sorry to stir painful memories."

A long, slow breath released from him. "Next week will mark the anniversary of her death."

Maryann stilled. She hadn't thought this person being lost meant to the grave. Sorrow crowded her thoughts. "Did she die young?"

"Sixteen."

Dear heavens. Knowing he did not want to hear

words of sympathy, she merely hugged him to her, and they stayed in their intimate embrace, listening to the pitter of rain against the windows.

His hands slid under her buttocks, and before she could react, he stood with her legs shamelessly wrapped around his hips. Maryann hurriedly released his shoulders and shimmied off him, feeling foolish to be blushing so.

Amusement lit in his gaze and he gently pinched her chin. "I must leave before your parents and brother return home."

"Do you plan to go through my windows?"

"No. The same way I came in. Through the kitchens."

"You picked the lock," she said, folding her arms about her breast.

"Hmm. Would you like me to show you how?"

"How to pick a lock?" she asked, astonished.

His teeth flashed, and how beautiful his smile was.

"It is still an age away from Mama and Papa reaching home. And Crispin normally spends the entire night at White's," she said excitedly, glancing at the clock on the mantel, astonished to see he had been in her room for over an hour. Maryann hurriedly put on a dressing gown and pushed her feet into soft slippers.

It felt natural to slip her hand between his as they left her chamber for lessons in the dark.

Certainly, it was more than an hour later, Maryann's hair streamed behind her, her nightgown twisted around her legs as she knelt in front of the library door in the hallway. Nicolas waited behind her patiently, his presence warm, protective, and the sweetest of temptations.

At first, learning to pick a lock hadn't been exciting.

He'd taken her into the library, turned on the gas lamp, and showed her a small leather pouch with various lock-picking tools. He taught her about lock levers, lift levers, throw bolts, warded locks and how to identify the types of lock she would be coaxing open.

It was an art.

On the streets of London and in the underworld, it was referred to as the Black Art.

It required patience.

It also required a swift and sharp-witted mind… and a steady hand.

"All the things you have," he'd whispered in her ear, as if anyone could hear them.

How her heart had soared, for in Nicolas she found a man who would make her fly and soar above expectations and restrictions. "The household sleeps," she'd whispered right back.

"We cannot be too careful."

That was said temptingly near her mouth, but he hadn't kissed her.

Maryann smiled when the lock on the door to the library *snicked* and opened. She stood and faced him, holding up her hairpin. "I did it," she whispered. "And with this."

Because he'd taught her that one of the most necessary skills was to be inventive.

"You've still a long way to go, but you did well, my lady."

"And you'll teach it all to me?"

"Yes. When you have learned much more, I'll introduce you to the Chubb Detector Lock. They say it cannot be picked by anyone. What a grand time we'll have trying. I can see it now, an afternoon by the lake, on blankets with wine, and a Chubb Detector Lock before us and our nefarious *and* most brilliant minds trying to pick it."

She grinned. "And you'll still respect me in the morning?"

"I'll respect you even more."

And in his tone she heard the rich admiration and pleasure. Maryann's breath hitched. *It is you*, she silently whispered.

The man who had been hovering in the shadows of her dreams, the one whom she hungered for, but he had always seemed like an impossible craving. Nicolas would catch her if she overreached in her recklessness, and do more, protect her while allowing her to live. He would not see her desires as unladylike.

"And if I want to discuss politics?" she murmured, leaning against the door that had swung back closed.

He stepped in closer, so he was right there, his body brushing the front of her nightgown.

He feathered his thumb across her bottom lip. "Then we'll discuss it—and I'll fervently pray we are on the same side."

Maryann laughed, the sound tinkling in the empty hallway. This was the man who would let her be herself, appreciate the things she was good at, talk about difficult subjects with her, and hopefully love her.

The need for that burned inside her with the ferocity of a storm.

"What if I wanted to travel?"

"Then you…we will do so in grand style. I am very wealthy. We might have to take the hellions, though."

Pleasure burst inside Maryann's chest. "I am happy you would not constrain your sisters."

"Why would I? I would like for them to also be racoons."

Maryann scowled, and before she could say "lioness," he caught her mouth with his in a burning kiss. With a soft moan, she wrapped her hands around his nape, reveling in the pleasure in his embrace. Still kissing her, he lifted her in his arms, and with a gasp she wrapped her legs around his waist, hooking her ankles at his back.

Without releasing her mouth from his intoxicating kisses, Nicolas mounted the stairs with effortless ease to her chamber. It took some fumbling to get the door open, and she lifted her lips from his, panting. He all but stumbled with her over to the bed, where he dropped her into the center. Maryann came onto her knees, staring at him, waiting with her heart pounding. His gaze dropped from her eyes, to her shoulders, and then to her breast straining through her nightgown. Her body ached for his touch.

He whirled around, and without saying a word, departed her chamber. Maryann stared at her closed door in astonishment.

So much for being a rake!

Grabbing the pillow, she threw it at the door, only for Nicolas to come back inside at the same time. The thick pillow smacked him firmly in the face. Maryann's mouth fell opened and she stared at Nicolas, whose eyebrows had shot up in surprise. He glanced at the pillow on the ground and back at her.

"Racoons do that," she said, dissolving into laughter.

The beginning of a smile lifted the corner of his mouth, and in a few strides he was there, dragging her up against him to kiss her. His touch hinted at restrained hunger, but the press of his mouth to hers was tender…beckoning, a whisper of desire. With a soft sigh, she parted her lips and slid her tongue against his. Before she could respond properly, he murmured against her lips, "Have a good sleep, Maryann."

Then he turned around and left once more.

She dropped back against her pillows in a cloud of euphoria, grabbed her pillow, and screamed her happiness in it. *Yes!*

"I am still here," he said, sounding perfectly bemused.

Maryann froze, realizing then she hadn't heard the door close. Oh! He'd just witnessed her madness. She turned her head on the sheet, staring at him, the pillow still gripped to her chest. An irresistibly devastating grin curved his mouth before he slipped through the door and it closed.

"Good night, Nicolas," she whispered, rolling over and drawing the covers to her chin.

• • •

The first thing Maryann did upon waking was to seek out her brother in the dining area. There he sat, polishing off a hearty breakfast. Thankfully, her parents were not present. They would still be sleeping, after arriving home only a few hours ago from the ball.

"You look well rested," he said, his gaze running over her critically. "Why are you blushing?"

"I was not aware that I was," she said slightly, walking over to sit in the chair opposite him.

She was such a poor enchantress, blushing like a silly miss in the light of day. It was difficult to not squirm in her chair at the memory of having him take her into his arms. She remembered his hard, sinewy body pressing against her. The wicked, luscious way he had rocked her against his throbbing manhood, and the pleasure that had torn through her.

"Well, you look frightfully pink. Are you fevered?"

"I am quite fine, Crispin!" she said, considerably disconcerted. Her purpose this morning was simple. Her brother was innocent, and she would prove it to Nicolas. Without even knowing the full of the situation, she knew Crispin deserved her belief and loyalty. And with this nonsense of them being enemies out of the way, they could get around to chatting about why he should be courting her.

She studied her brother, wondering how Nicolas could ever think he had done something so awful as to warrant revenge. He looked so boyishly charming opening the sheets of a freshly pressed newspaper, a steaming cup of coffee awaiting his attention. In this moment, he reminded her so much of their papa. Except he did not have that stern set to his mouth or the frown lines on his face.

Buttering a slice of toast, she said, "Crispin?"

"Hmm," he said distractedly, a frown on his face.

"Have you ever done anything so grievous it would make someone think of you as an enemy?"

His head snapped up. "I beg your pardon?"

She calmly repeated the question.

For a long moment, there was no reply. He slowly folded the paper and set it aside on the table. "Why would you ask such a question? Are you thinking the carriage mishap was aimed at me?"

"No, of course not," she hurriedly reassured him. "Nor do I think it was aimed at me. Odd accidents do happen."

He scowled. "It is a decidedly strange question, but that answer is no."

Maryann had been wondering if it was whatever happened to Arianna that Nicolas thought her brother might be a part of. Now she wished she had asked him more, instead of spending a rousing hour learning how to pick locks. And then those parting kisses…

"By God!" Crispin exclaimed. "You are blushing again. Whatever is the matter with you today?"

She mumbled something, biting into a treacle tart to prevent the necessity of answering.

"This bounder is completely lacking in decency!" Crispin snapped, gripping the newspaper in a tight grip. "God's blood, it is laughable the papers have declared him one of the most eligible catches of the season."

"Who are you speaking of?" she asked, lowering her fork.

"The Marquess of Rothbury."

Maryann inhaled audibly. "Nicolas?"

Her brother flinched. "I beg your pardon. Are you on an intimate name basis with this bounder?"

"What does the newspaper say?"

He carelessly tossed it atop the table. "Last evening at about eight, the marquess barged into the duke's home and had a duel with the man in his hallway!"

"A *duel*?" she demanded faintly. "Why, that cannot be true."

He jabbed a finger at the paper. "The servants were the witnesses and by their accounts it was a duel!" Crispin's visage grew dim. "I cannot imagine a gentleman conducting himself so totally without any regard for their reputation or position in society."

"I suppose he should have done it outside at one of those famous dueling fields?" she asked drily.

Her brother huffed. "There *is* a proper way to do something. And that is not the worst of it."

"What?"

"It seems Farringdon was shot. The papers are not sure how it happened, but there is speculation it might have been at Rothbury's hand, considering they were dueling."

Her belly knotted, and Maryann could only imagine how dramatic the scandal would become. Why hadn't he mentioned he fought with the duke when he saw her?

"Is…is Farringdon alive?"

"At the last report. I still cannot understand it. I thought the duke and the marquess were the chummiest of friends."

They stole something precious from me.

She pressed a palm over her heart, as if that would slow its sudden pounding. Further reflection convinced Maryann that the duke must have had something to do with the girl Nicolas lost. But then, why had they been friends? It struck her then that the facade of a dangerous rake had been adopted to inveigle himself with their set. Revenge was an art that took patience and cunning, and it seemed the marquess had that in spades. "Crispin, please do not lie to me!"

"What are you about? Lie about what?"

"Please trust me and answer me truthfully."

His eyes crinkled. "We do not lie to each other, poppet. Now what is the matter?"

"Did you…did you know someone called Arianna?"

The teacup slipped from his hand, dropped to the floor, and broke apart. A footman moved right away to clean the mess, and she could only stare at her brother's flushed countenance. The fear that rushed through Maryann made her so aghast that she feared she would swoon. "Crispin, answer me!"

"Of course not," he said. "Who…who is Arianna?"

Yet it was not her imagination that his voice trembled over the name.

"I believe her to have been a friend of Lord Rothbury."

"You've spoken to him?" he demanded sharply.

"On a number of occasions," she replied with casual ease.

"If he has the effrontery to ever approach you again…" Crispin choked on his outrage.

She would not lie to him about the attachment she felt for Nicolas. "Crispin, the marquess and I…we have an understanding of sorts. There will come a day when he will speak to Papa."

The shock of that declaration propelled her brother to half rise from his seat. "Have you lost your senses?"

"Possibly," she said gently. "And my heart is under threat as well."

He slammed back down in the chair as if he had collapsed. Crispin pointed at the paper. "Do you understand this man's reputation? He is disreputable. How…" He closed his eyes briefly. "You are to stay away from him. He is a threat to decency everywhere. This will prove to be the shabbiest affair, the worst scandal of the season, and we do not want to remind society that your names were recently associated. There is even a rumor at the club he is seeking a mistress," he hissed.

A jolt went through her. *A mistress?*

"As you said, Crispin, it is a rumor."

A black scowl settled on his face, and Maryann knew better than to agitate the matter any further, so she busied herself with slathering strawberry preserves on another slice of toast. But she did not remove her regard from her brother's narrow-eyed contemplation. She held his gaze without wavering, appearing totally at ease.

"If you do not listen to me, I will most certainly inform our parents of this unsavory attachment."

"Hmm," she said around a bite of the crunchy toast. "I am positively quaking in my boots."

His lips twitched. "Since I have been acquainted with you from the cradle, I can tell that you are decided, and I will not be able to aid you in this romance."

"Yes," she said softly. "Do you recall what I told you yesterday after the carriage mishap?"

"Yes."

"Remember it."

It took him a bit, but the tension eased from his shoulders.

"Crispin?"

He paused in the act of spearing most of a kipper onto his fork.

"Do you promise that you did not know an Arianna?"

He met her unflinching regard. "I promise it, poppet."

"Good, then might I ask you to accompany me to Vanguard Manor next week?"

"Whatever for?" he asked, disgruntled. "It is at least a two-hour ride."

Maryann was certain it was only a bit over an hour, but her brother tended to exaggerate whenever he did not want to do a task. "It is not today I wish to go, only that you add it to your calendar to take me there next week. We do not need to stay overnight. I would much prefer to journey down in the morning and come back to town in the evening."

"What nonsense did you leave there?" he asked with a heavy sigh. "And can we not send a note and have one of the footmen deliver it here?"

Maryann smiled, knowing she could always rely on her brother.

"I want to catch fireflies," she murmured, standing.

"Fireflies!"

"Yes…fireflies," she said over her shoulders, making her way to prepare for an outing with her friends in St. James Park. Their merry band of sinful wallflowers needed to be told that Nicolas St. Ives, London's wickedest rake, had asked her, Maryann Fitzwilliam, a known wallflower, to wait for him.

And she needed to desperately ask their opinion on if she was being foolish at the dreams that had blossomed through her heart last night and the frightening realization that she was indeed falling hopelessly in love with Nicolas St. Ives.

CHAPTER SEVENTEEN

Nicolas had sat in his study for the last few hours, staring at the same ledger. Well, there was some progress, for he had at least turned the first page. He was wholly distracted by thoughts of Lady Maryann and had no notion how to dismiss her from his awareness.

Lady Maryann was an unexpected, inexplicable force of chaos in his well-ordered and purpose-driven existence. Nicolas didn't trust his unfamiliar, extraordinary reaction to her, simply because he had never felt it for another. She lingered too much in his thoughts and dreams and despite his honed willpower, he could not dismiss her from his awareness. He recalled the faint evocative perfume he smelled on her skin, suspecting it was more the lady's unique fragrance.

Last night…and well into this morning had been like a dream, one he wanted to recapture and hoard deep inside his heart. Hell, it even perplexed him to be thinking about his damn heart. When he'd whispered to her to wait for him, the desire had surged from a place inside he hadn't known existed. He had ached and hungered, and for the first time he had found himself yearning for an existence he had not allowed himself to contemplate even briefly.

So, you are not afraid to love then.

How delighted she'd sounded, how mysterious and naughty that curve to her mouth had been, and that look in her eyes. He swallowed, tipping his gaze to the ceiling. And when he had lewdly dragged her quim across his aching cock without any care for her sensibilities, he'd felt the start of surprise in her body, tasted the moan of surrender.

A loud knock on the door jerked Nicolas from his reverie, and then his normally unflappable butler entered, appearing distinctly harried. "I know you are to be undisturbed, your lordship, but despite informing this gentleman you are not available to callers, he has rudely barged in and is demanding—"

A shadow loomed behind him, and a large imposing figure pushed past his butler.

"All is well, Dobson, you may leave," Nicolas murmured, staring at the Earl of Tremelle, who was Viscount Weychell's father. "To what do I owe the honor of this unprecedented visit?"

The earl took his time looking around the large study, from the wall of bookcases, to the globe tossed casually on the green and gold oriental carpet, the scrolls on the sofa closest to the fire, and then to Nicolas, who sat behind a large oak desk with a pile of ledgers before him and a half decanter of brandy.

Nicolas saw an arrogant man, slim and impeccably but conservatively tailored in almost unrelieved black. His waistcoat gave the only variation in color from the pristine black of his costume and white of his linen. A faint golden stripe was barely perceptible in its black silk cloth. Nicolas admired the conceit; it was effective. The earl's face might have once been considered handsome, although the lines now cut deep and around his thin mouth were set into a permanent expression of sour disdain.

"I have been watching you for some weeks now," the earl said, walking over to the bookshelf and taking up a small leather-bound book.

The words fell in the air, the tone of the earl a man confident in his societal power.

Nicolas leaned back in his chair, reposing at ease, one leg stretched out before him, adopting an indifferent mien. "You have been watching me," he repeated softly.

"You are a hard man to pinpoint with your erratic schedule."

"Then I tip my hat to your investigators."

The earl smiled, but his eyes were chilled. This man was furious. And he was Weychell's father.

Ah, so it's you.

The shadowed man on the board was the Earl of Tremelle. This was the man who sought his weakness... and this was the man who had ordered for Maryann to be placed in harm's way. And how unconcerned he appeared standing in Nicolas's study, casually thumbing through the pages of a book he'd plucked from the bookshelf.

"I have taken my son and removed him from your reach. He will be living abroad for the next few years."

The anger icing through Nicolas's veins felt so visceral, he had to take a few deep breaths and steady himself against the feeling. He had never been the kind of person to feel or display an excessive use of emotions, and he would not start now.

"After reading about Farringdon in the papers early this morning, I had to act with all haste."

"Did you?" Nicolas murmured, leaning back in his chair.

"As we speak, my son is boarding a ship down by the docks."

At Nicolas's silence, the earl slipped the book into its place on the shelf and walked over. The earl peered down at him, and Nicolas kept his expression inscrutable. A silence lingered, throbbing with undertones of tension. He did not rush to speak, patiently waiting, unruffled that the earl loomed above him.

"You are very different from what you present to the world," the earl said thoughtfully. "As I suspected you are not a coxcomb at all, but a man very driven and intense."

Nicolas stood and made his way to the windows overlooking the small garden of his town house. There he leaned against the wall, keeping his back to the earl. "You went to the Asylum asking about me."

"That I did."

"There is a rumor you and your son have not spoken in seventeen months."

"More than a rumor, I'm afraid. In fact, I believe it was you whispering in his ears which gave him the courage to defy me. Instead of sending that actress and his two bastards away, he instead provided them with a fortune. You were the devil on his shoulder, and he was simply too naive to see it."

Nicolas shifted so he could regard the earl fully. "And as he was about to be hooked, you ran to the rescue," he murmured with dangerous restraint.

Lord Tremelle's lips flattened. "My son might not be the brightest of them, but his spate of bad luck I could no longer ignore. He is my heir, and one day I will leave him a considerable inheritance. I would have neglected my duty if I had ignored that everything he damn well touched turned to a rotten fruit. No man is that dim-witted or has that much ill-luck. Every misfortune was from *your* machinations."

The earl's intervention was a situation Nicolas had not anticipated. The viscount himself had often lamented about the distance between himself and his father, forced even wider after his mismanagement of his sizeable allowance and the loss of a few unentailed estates his father had left in his care. Estates Nicolas had won from him while gambling, but to gain Weychell's trust, he had refused the deeds or the monies he had won.

"And of course, you did everything to save him from the devil," he said mockingly.

"My investigation took several months, and it was clear to me you were a damn snake in the garden, and they did not know about it! You have been silently stalking him for more than a year, destroying everything he tried to invest in. When the ruination of the duke began, I suspected my son would be next in your wicked scheme."

"Ah, so you are not at all curious about what he did to earn my displeasure."

The earl took a step to him. "I cannot imagine what could have happened that you would betray a fellow gentleman in such a manner."

"The manners of your son are not of someone of quality. He is in truth little more than a soft piece of turd."

The earl flushed angrily, and his gaze narrowed. "My son has some untidy habits, but nothing that requires this scheme against him."

Nicolas's brows rose in polite surprise. "Untidy habits? Never heard rape so stated before."

The earl froze. "I beg your pardon. My son would not partake in an act so vile. What need he have to force anyone? He is a future earl!"

"Yet he did. Ten years ago, he and a few of his friends did. He escaped justice then; he will not escape it now."

They stared at each other for several moments. The earl retrieved a pocket watch and peered at the time. "His ship has set sail. You will have to suffice with the many discomforts you have already caused him. Because of you, he will be living on a plantation in America, in a place called Virginia for the foreseeable future. That place is not refined like here and his life will be hard without his society."

Nicolas gently scoffed. "Your son is a traitor to the crown. With the right agitation, he will never be able to return to England's shores."

The earl's eyes grew cold. "My son never was a bloody traitor. And should you start such a scandal, I will see you finished," he roared.

"You could try," Nicolas said with infuriating calm. "I promise I will extend my arms of influence across the oceans and ensure his life is miserable. And you… you I will absolutely kill."

The earl did a credible job in retaining his composure, but Nicolas saw the flicker of apprehension in the man's gaze.

"I believe you," the earl said with a vein of shock. "I declare you are more savage than I believed. What did my son do to—"

"It was what *you* did," Nicolas hissed, pushing from the wall. "You attempted to harm Lady Maryann without any regard of her person."

"This…this is about *her*?"

An inexplicable feeling blossomed inside Nicolas when he realized all the emotions rioting through him since the earl had revealed himself and had clearly been responsible for the danger that had almost shattered Maryann. Because this man had plotted such a vicious attack against her when she was innocent in this whole mess. "You arranged for a carriage to run her over."

The earl scrubbed a hand across his face. "I gave orders that she should not be harmed. It was meant only to scare her."

"Is that so?" Nicolas said with soft menace. "If she goes to Hyde Park tomorrow, stubs her toe, falls and hurt herself, I will believe it was done by your hand. If anything happens to her, blame will be laid at your feet."

"Do not be ridiculous—"

"And I will kill you."

"You speak of murder so casually—" the earl began with seething outrage.

"I will kill you."

"By God, you mean it!" The earl frowned. "She means that much to you," he said with cold calculation.

"She means nothing to me." *Maryann is becoming my world*. But no one must know it until everything was done.

Incredulity filled the earl's gaze and he shook his head, sharply as if disconcerted. "Do you know who I am?" the earl snapped, his light gray eyes darkening. "You *dare* threaten me?"

"Of course," Nicolas said, his tone one of icy civility. "But it has become clear to me you do not know who I am. I am the man willing to do *anything* and destroy everything you hold dear if you even think to harm Lady Maryann. The only thing that is important is you believe this to be possible, Lord Tremelle."

The earl faltered, and they stared at each other, the only sound in the room the ticking of the clock on the mantel. Lord Tremelle glanced away, and a deep sigh of wariness rolled from him. "It was a mistake sending those ruffians to Lady Maryann. I assure you, such a mistake will not happen again."

The earl whirled around and walked away. His hand on the doorknob, he hesitated and said, "Let my son go out of your scheme, Rothbury."

"When your son was finished with the girl he attacked, she flung herself into a river to her death. She was only sixteen."

Lord Tremelle stiffened and he sucked in a harsh breath. "*My* son would never act with such rank dishonor."

"The lord with the blond hair and blue eyes with a scar splitting his lower lip. He laughed through my screams, 'tis a sound I shall remember on my way to hell, for I am no longer worthy of heaven. It was a sound that demeaned and ridiculed…it was a sound that found humor in my torment." A harsh chuckle slipped from Nicolas. "That is what she said in her letter about your honorable son."

The earl's knuckles whitened on the doorknob. "Let his exile from everything that he loves, his children, his mistress, his mother, and his sisters, all his vices and the balls and races to attend will be no more. I will exile him for ten years. He will feel the pain of it all. Let that be punishment enough."

Then he wrenched open the door and vanished down the hallway.

• • •

Precisely three days after Lord Tremelle's visit, Nicolas admitted himself to another town house in Mayfair gardens. Keeping his hat firmly on his head and tugged low, he padded down the hallway, and then made his way up the winding staircase. For the last few days, a man had been watching Stamford's home, while another ferreted out every detail of information about the earl's coming and goings, which an overworked but ill-favored scullery maid had gladly provided for a few coins.

Nicolas waited until after midnight before stealing inside the man's residence. The information gathered said Stamford would be home tonight, and that a lady from a bordello would soon appear in a carriage and spend the night being debauched by the earl. Nicolas had an hour before she would arrive.

He only needed five minutes.

He twisted the doorknob and opened the door soundlessly. The earl stood by the fire dressed only in a red silk banyan, sipping from a glass. Brandy perhaps. Nicolas deliberately allowed the door to creak when he pushed it wider, but Stamford did not turn around.

"You are early," he said, sounding repulsively displeased.

Nicolas padded over to the shadows cast by the man's massive four-poster bed, arching a brow at the sexual instruments laid out in a neat row on the mattress. An ivory dildo, a flogger, and a jar of cream.

"I have intruded," Nicolas said, keeping his voice low.

Stamford was not a man easily startled, for he displayed an admirably calm composure at the sound of someone in his private rooms. He turned slowly, still drinking his liquor, but his gaze unerringly went to the spot Nicolas stood. Nor did Stamford waste any time with inane questions as to how he had gained entry.

"Now that you have intruded, state what it is that you want."

"You will remove the offer you made to a certain lady's parents tomorrow. Whatever monies were paid over I will see returned to you. And this meeting will be kept in the strictest of confidence, of course."

"I see," the earl said, arching a brow.

"Do you?" Nicolas murmured.

"You have intentions in regard to my fiancée," the earl said flatly.

He pondered that cold murmur and decided the man was right. "Yes." And it settled deep inside him, Maryann was his friend, his woman, and one day she would be his countess. "It is best you understand them fully."

"I am all ears," the earl said with a mocking twist to his lips.

"You placed your hands on her and deliberately and cruelly hurt her. It shall never happen again."

The man smiled as if amused. "And she ran to you and blabbered, did she? How charming that you should sneak in here like a thief to defend her honor. Am I to name my seconds and you name our dueling location, Rothbury?"

Nicolas stepped into the light. "Turn your covetous eyes elsewhere, Stamford. She is too good for your predilections. Let this be your only warning. Should you lay your hands on her again, you will suffer more than just a broken arm."

"A broken arm? What are you blathering—"

Nicolas moved faster than the earl could anticipate, grasping his right arm and twisting with harsh strength. The snap echoed in the room, and to the earl's credit, save for a pained scream that ended abruptly, he made no other sound. Nicolas met his eyes, and whatever the man saw in his face, he blanched. Sweat beaded on his forehead and upper lip.

"This broken arm," he said with soft menace. "You are a bullying brute who would dare to try and break her spirit. How can you see something so precious and want to hurt it?"

Stamford shook his head sharply. Nicolas released him and melted away in the dark, leaving the house the way he entered. Once outside, he pinched the bridge of his nose. He had made himself another enemy tonight, one who was immensely powerful and possessed well-connected friends. The memory of Maryann soaking her wrist in warm water, the paleness of her features, and her courage in the face of another bully had stayed with him. If anything, the most she should be was another pawn in his game, but somehow, he made her to be more. And that awareness was his most profound truth.

Wait for me.

She had become so much more, something he could not stop just as he could not make water flow uphill. It was inexplicable, this need to protect her, when she had shown she was a lady of indomitable wit and strength who could walk by his side and not falter.

The day felt long, and the night promised to be longer...torturous, for he did not want to go home to his empty bed. Nor did he want to go to a gambling hell or a damn ball.

Maryann.

The thought of her whispered through his soul, and he knew exactly where he had to be.

• • •

Almost half an hour later, Nicolas stood in the dark gardens below Maryann's windows. The house appeared dark, as if everyone had gone to bed. The man he had watching her still, reported the earl and countess were home along with their daughter, but the son had gone out to a ball.

Go home, the rational side of him urged. His resistance to her allure was damnably weak, and he knew he should not put her underneath him and ravish her throughout the long night. Something he feared might happen should he climb the trellis leading to her balcony.

When he'd asked her to wait for him, there had been a throb of warning in his gut, but he had pushed it aside in his need to hold and kiss her. In his long investigation, only Crispin had matched the description of the fifth party whom Farringdon had traveled with that fateful day ten years ago. Except the viscount was not friends with the entire group and Nicolas could not find out why.

What had caused the break in friendship…if there had been a friendship?

Nicolas had probed and even asked directly if they were familiar with him, and they had denied the connection. Yet, Crispin had attended Oxford with the sorry lot, and he had been in Wiltshire at the time.

What if…just what if her brother really turned out to be the black Dahlia, and Nicolas was here asking her for promises?

Only last night, his investigators presented another gentleman who might be the black Dahlia. Nicolas had thought it unlikely, but for Maryann's sake and his, ordered his men to do a thorough investigation.

He scrubbed a hand over his face. The tug to climb

those vines and trellises beat relentlessly at him. He once again reminded himself, "*He who conquers others is strong, but he who conquers himself is mighty.*"

He was about to walk away when her windows were gently opened, and her silhouette framed the space. She did not linger but walked away. It was an invitation. *Fuck!*

I'll not kiss her, he vowed. *If I do not kiss her, all will be well.*

After a careful look to ensure no one else was about, Nicolas grabbed the trellis leading to her window and efficiently climbed up to her balcony, thankful the trellis had creepers and not climbing roses riddled with thorns.

When he slipped through the windows and stood, it was to see her in the center of her room. She appeared delightfully rosy sheathed in a pale pink gown with a ribbon tied around her waist, the simple cut displaying her generously lush figure to its best advantage. Her feet were bare, and her delicate toes curled into the carpet. Her hair was loosely pinned in a topknot with several strands tumbling over her shoulders in beautiful waves, and she nervously pushed the spectacles up her nose.

Immediately, all the tension which had invaded his body since he learned Weychell had been shipped abroad left Nicolas. He was simply powerless to control his reaction to her. "You are so very lovely."

Her cheeks pinkened and delight leaped into her eyes. "Eye of the beholder and whatnot," she said with an irrepressible grin and then a light chortle. "I am glad you came."

Her laugh was a warm, husky sound which brought pleasure to his ears.

"It is astonishing to me how often you occupied my thoughts today. I do believe I missed you."

Her words kicked him in the chest. He liked that she expressed herself so honestly. Nicolas got the sense he would always understand where he stood with her. If she were angry, or sad, or just feeling out of sorts, he would know it. She wasn't coy at all, and he had never met a lady who stared at him so directly when they spoke, as if she peered beyond the facade and stripped him down to his essence.

He liked that at a first glance she appeared the perfect picture of demure gentility, but one only had to look in her eyes to see how they sparkled with something wild and defiant.

"When I left you yesterday…I was unable to sleep upon returning home," he admitted.

"From your tone, I gather you are blaming me for that?"

This she said with a wrinkle of her nose, as if she was amused by her own assessment. She actually rolled her eyes, then that lush beautiful mouth curved in a pleased smile.

"I like you," he said, his heart pounding. Nicolas felt another surge of shock, as if something unknown inside was coming awake. "I *really* like you."

She clasped her hands before her tightly, and her toes curled into the carpet. Her eyes glittered, and he realized she withheld herself from…from what he did not know. Then he recalled her the other night screaming into the pillows. Perhaps that had been from excitement? He cleared his throat. "You can scream into the pillow should you wish it. I'll not be perturbed."

Her eyes widened and then she laughed, held out

her hands and spun into a perfect twirl. It felt as if time slowed, and he was given the rare pleasure of seeing all the smallest details that had previously eluded his senses.

He was fascinated by the small curl of hair right behind her ear.

His eyes took in how deep the dimples in her cheeks sank, reflecting the velvety softness of her skin, which was a revelation to him when she laughed with such delectable delight.

He treasured how joyously free and natural she appeared in this moment.

Her skin, and her eyes, how they glowed.

There was something about her…something almost dainty, yet he knew of her strength and fierceness.

"I like you, too," she declared, staring at him from below incredibly long lashes.

It was a look that said, "*finally you are seeing me, you buffoon*," and it endlessly charmed him. With an inward jolt to his heart, he realized that while he was just noticing her, Maryann had been aware of him for much longer. It went through him then, a jerk of fear, at the thought that he might have missed her.

"You seem anxious," she tossed in the air.

He scowled. "I am not the sort of man to feel anxiety." The thought that he might never have met her was too appalling to consider, and that was something that he knew required introspection.

She sauntered over to him. "You know that even those who are dangerous and devastatingly handsome are allowed the more delicate emotions as well. It is not a bad thing and not only unique to my sex, as some would have you believe."

"You think me dangerous?"

"Hmm, and do not forget the very handsome bit," she said huskily.

"I can be a brutal man," he said, almost uncomfortable with that assessment against her soft loveliness.

"I suppose you can be if the situation calls for it, but it does not define you, does it? I daresay you are also gentle, kind, and honorable."

Gentle. He liked that she thought a man of violence such as himself was gentle. Nicolas hoped she would believe this was true of him always. He never wanted to look in those perfect eyes and see hate or despair. He hoped only for the most tender of emotions from her.

His heart started to pound, and Nicolas wondered what the hell was wrong with him. It was probably the fear that Maryann would fall in love with him, the very anticipation she might truly do so sending a shock of hunger through his entire body.

Do I want your love, Maryann? he silently asked, drawing her into his arms, needing to just hold her for a moment.

With a sigh, she relaxed into him, as if that were where she had wanted to be all along. In his embrace, her head pillowed against his chest, her arms around his waist, and his around her shoulders. "How is your arm?"

"I got the ointment you sent to me. It hurts less and the bruises are fading."

"Good." He rested his chin against her forehead. "Stamford will no longer be a bother to you."

He felt the jerk of her heart through the layers of their clothes. She drew back and lifted her gaze to his. "How did you convince him?"

He hesitated and her eyes widened.

"Nicolas?"

At his silence, she arched a brow. "I am not a delicate creature given to hysteria or swooning, so you can tell me whatever it is."

"We had some words."

"And?"

"He listened to them."

"Nicolas!"

"I broke his arm."

Her lips parted but no words came forth, and he watched her eyes carefully. The admiration had not changed, nor did he see any fear. She lowered one of her hands from around his back and lifted it to his face. Her touch against his jaw was like the delicate brush of the wings of a butterfly.

"Thank you for defending my honor," she said, smiling tremulously. "And for alleviating my fears. I… thank you."

A slow, deep breath, he hadn't realized he'd held, released.

"Would you like to play chess with me?"

He glanced in the direction she waved, and it was then he noted the small table and the two well-padded chairs perfectly positioned by the fireplace. "You are a powerful distraction," he murmured.

Nicolas had never entered a room and not assessed every detail, calculating the threats and advantages he must be aware of. But tonight…he had only seen her.

It was Maryann who was bloody dangerous.

CHAPTER EIGHTEEN

Shortly after nine o'clock a few evenings later, Maryann stood before a particular town house on Grosvenor Square. If anyone should pass by while she went about the business of breaking into this town house, she presented as a fashionably attired woman dressed in a fully black serviceable gown and a hat with a dark veil obscuring her face. A rapier was clutched in one hand but obscured by a black cloak, and a basket rested by her feet. Her friends, when they heard of tonight's unprecedented escapade, would be green with envy at her daring.

Maryann exhaled triumphantly as the lock beneath her coaxing thumb gave way and the door opened with a *snick*. She hovered on the threshold at the Marquess of Rothbury's home, her heart pounding terribly. She had expected to encounter the butler, or a footman at least, and already had her words prepared. But the hallway was empty, with only a few wall sconces lit.

She padded down the hallway with her basket and rapier clutched in her hand to a light which spilled from a slightly ajar door. Once there, she saw that the room was a large library with floor-to-ceiling bookshelves of dark oak.

A fire roared in the hearth, and the gas lamps were lit, leaving the place pleasantly warm. Her gaze sought out the marquess.

He was sprawled in a high wing-back chair by the fire, his legs stretched out before him, his mien inscrutable. Maryann wondered that even in the privacy of his home, he hid the expressions of his musings so no one could fathom his plots and scheming. Unwatched by the masses, he was unguarded, his mien remote, a man who was inherently alone.

The fire flickered, and with it also came a shift in his expression. It was infinitesimal but Maryann saw it, a grimace of pain as if he were ravaged by some private agony.

She hovered in the doorway, staring at him as he tossed back his drink, gazing into the flickering flames. Her antics, which had been meant to impress him, now felt silly. She wanted to give him what she had gathered in the basket, but now it seemed as if she intruded on something private and haunting, something she should not be a part of. Regret coated the back of her throat and she carefully stepped away.

"You've come this far—surely you are not leaving."

Maryann blinked in uneasy surprise and then went utterly still. "I…" She closed her mouth over the rambling mess that would have bound to come out.

At her lack of response, he stood, lifted the glass to his mouth and finished his drink in a long swallow. He set it on the mantel over the fireplace, then shifted to meet her gaze.

How had he known she was there?

"I smelled you," he replied as if she had spoken. "Sweet and sultry."

Her face flamed.

"How did you get here?"

She hated the feeling that had suddenly come over her, a deep sense of uncertainty. "I walked."

He flinched, then seemed to catch the reaction. "How unconventional of you. So, my intrepid Lady Maryann does not fear footpads and undesirables."

"In Grosvenor Square?"

His expression grew even more unfathomable and nerves fluttered in her belly. She lifted the silver-handled cane which hid her rapier. "It was more sensible than an elaborate ruse to go out in the carriage alone, and I walked armed. Plus, I know you have someone watching me."

He did not deny it, but something flared in his eyes before it was quickly replaced by a shuttered mien. Maryann's awareness of Nicolas prickled against her skin like fire. He radiated such palpable sensuality with a hint of menace that it made her uncomfortable.

"Why did you come here tonight?"

"For many reasons, which seem silly now."

"Tell me," he invited smoothly, pouring amber liquid into two glasses.

"I wanted to thank you. Stamford visited my parents and, to their great shock, he withdrew his offer. My heart is relieved."

"You could have sent a note."

She flushed. "Do you wish me to leave?"

A tense silence blanketed the room.

"No."

"Then why are you berating me?"

"My heart cannot bear the thought of you hurt. The walk from your home to here might only be several minutes, but it was a dangerous deed. You act as if there is nothing to be afraid of. *Reckless!*"

It was her turn to flinch at the icy bite in his tone.

"There are many things I am afraid of, but traveling alone is not one…not when I know you are hovering in the shadows like a dragon," she whispered with a small smile. "One with dark wings unfolded over my shoulders, a force of safety I trust in. I know you are fiercely protective of me."

He simply stared at her, and she did nothing but return that unflinching regard.

"What is in the basket?"

"Something for you...and for Arianna. I recalled from one of our conversations that today is the anniversary of her death...and...and I thought I..."

He gave her a long, measuring stare. "You came to keep me company."

"Yes," she whispered. "I admit I had not thought it out fully, and I am terribly sorry to have intruded."

"I am not sorry; do not be. I am glad you came."

He radiated with visible satisfaction, and warm flutters went off in her body.

She clutched the basket to her side. "It's best I show you what is in the basket outside. Will you come with me to the garden?"

Once again, as if he could not understand her, Nicolas stared at her for long, silent moments, and she fought not to squirm under that hawkish stare. She almost blurted what she held in the basket when he prowled toward her, his long strides undeniably confident and graceful. He took the basket, and Maryann followed him silently into the drawing room which seemed as if it might also serve as a ballroom with its large folding doors. He opened one of the terrace doors, and they slipped outside into the cool night air.

The grass there was badly in need of cutting, the flowers lacked tending to, and the hedges untrimmed. The garden area was darkly shadowed by the thick tree limbs and hedges. "Why are your gardens so shabby?"

Before he could answer, Maryann saw a movement in the grass, a silver slither. With a squeak she jumped at him, clutching his shoulders.

"You are a woman of good senses," he murmured exasperatingly but with some amusement.

She sniffed. "What of it?"

"Why are you on my back, and *how* did you even reach there?"

Her entire body flushed. "There is something in the grass."

"A harmless grass snake perhaps. Come, down you go."

The moan that came from Maryann was so pitiful, he encircled her ankle and rubbed his thumb soothingly along her silk-covered leg.

"I gather you are afraid of snakes?"

"They are spawn from the bowels of hell," she said into his nape, scandalously hooking her legs around his hips.

"Ah, now I see why you involved your brother in your scheme to take down Lady Sophie. Then we shall take to the roof."

"The roof?"

"Yes."

She spun it around in her thoughts a little. "You mean for us to *climb* to the roof?"

"Afraid?"

"Of course not," she muttered against the back of his neck, quite conscious she made no effort to get off him, and he seemed contented for her to be there. He walked with her around to the side of the house, comfortable with her weight and the basket in another hand. Maryann smiled.

"I can feel that."

"I've not had this particular pleasure since I was a child with Papa. I was just thinking I should thank you for giving me the chance to ride you."

He stumbled and muttered a curse that made her cheeks burn. He came to a complete stop and a fine tension shifted through his frame. Gently he nudged her, and she eased from his back and hopped down to the much shorter grass. She rushed around to face him and glanced up. Unexpectedly, nervousness rushed through her. "Was it something I said?"

His eyes gleamed with sudden enjoyment. "No, these were more along the lines of my rakish thoughts. Come, let's climb."

And to Maryann's astonishment, there was a sort of ladder attached to the side of the house, covered with vines and trellises. He went before her and with a grin, she followed step by careful step, quite aware should they marry, this was a man who would never try to cage her.

Once he reached the top, he held out his hands and drew her up. Maryann glanced down and sucked in a sharp breath. They seemed precariously far from the ground. There was a flat surface leading to the chimney and he took her hand and led her over. At the ledge, he shrugged from his jacket and placed it there, and then assisted her to sit down. Then he lowered himself beside her.

They were positioned away from the road, and no passersby should be able to look up and see them. The view from the top was different and she looked about her, inhaling the crisp but smoky night air into her lungs.

Maryann reached for the basket, suddenly and unexpectedly nervous. "I do not know how you lost Arianna. You deeply mourn her, and I am sorry there is a pain that still lingers in your heart. If there is a heaven— Crispin says there is not, but I do not believe it to be so, why there are many philosophical arguments that—"

She broke off her rambling at the tender smile which appeared on his mouth.

"There is no need to be nervous," he said.

She laughed shakily, opened the basket which had been tightly locked. "I collected these a few hours ago."

Fireflies lifted gently into the air. At first it was just dozens of beetles flying away, grateful to be out of their captivity. Then one by one, their luminescent light began to glow.

"I read that they are really called *Lampyris noctiluca*," she said, delighted with the dozens of lights which started to blink on one by one in the dark sky. The lack of stars in the cloud-fogged city illuminated the iridescent beauty of their glow even more. "And only the males are capable of flight since they have wings."

"And the females don't?"

"Not for this type of firefly, which is more common to Europe and the United Kingdom. Isn't that interesting? I bought the book; you may read it if you wish," she said a bit shyly, glad that he was not turned off by her eclectic reading choices.

"It is very interesting, and I shall enjoy listening to you read it to me."

She turned to look at him, and the smile which had been forming died. His eyes held her in place with their unblinking intensity. Nicolas slowly lifted her veil and hat from her so he could assess every nuance of her expression. He drew her into his side, and she went, pressed intimately against him. Then he dipped his head and kissed the bridge of her nose. "Thank you for the beautiful gift of your company."

A warm silence remained as they watched the dozens of fireflies disperse. "Look," she said, pointing to the lights flickering below in the grass. "Those are the females, responding to the mating call of the males."

They watched as some of the fireflies dipped, their light creating a dance of beauty as they sank into the grass.

She wondered how much he would trust her, and if she should encourage him to speak of her. Maryann decided to merely listen and allow him to determine how much he wanted to share with her. She lightly touched his jawline. "Nicolas, will you tell me what happened to Arianna?"

• • •

His Maryann leaned her head back and gazed into his eyes. Such trust glowed in her face, such sweet kindness. When she'd entered his library earlier, the hollowness which had lingered in his gut had filled instantly. The sense of peace and happiness had just blossomed through Nicolas.

"This might be the very first year I feel an easing of the hatred in my heart…and guilt," he murmured. *And it is because of you.* Not only because he saw a future in her, but also because Nicolas felt as if he had accomplished justice for Arianna. The waiting was coming to an end.

"Five men attacked Arianna, and she…she was not able to bear it," he murmured. "She flung herself into a river."

Shock and horror blasted onto Maryann's face, and

she pressed a hand over her heart. In her eyes, he saw an awful alarm and a question: was this the heinous act he believed her brother to be a party to?

"How did you discover what had happened?"

His chest lifted on a deep, silent sigh. "She left a letter behind."

"Do you want to share its contents?" she asked hesitantly.

"*The eagle soars indifferently while the wolf betrays the dove,*" he began, glancing into the starless sky.

"You memorized it."

"It is seared behind my eyes so should I close them, it is there to remind me I deserve no rest until it is done."

"I want to weep at the guilt I hear in your voice," she said softly. "You were not the cause of it."

A harsh hiss escaped him and a burning lump formed in his throat. If his Maryann knew the heaviness of the guilt he had carried so long, she would fling herself into his arms and cry. She would try to give him even more comfort than she was doing now.

"*The black Dahlia is the cruelest,*" he said, starting the letter. "*He offered hope then silently watched as they shred my soul.*"

Her eyes widened and the gloved hand over her chest curled, gripping the material of her dress.

"*The stag with the lily in its mouth was the most brutal, for it was that one who taught me that fear and pain lie in a touch. A soothing caress on my forehead transforms to a savage squeeze of the jaw. The duality of tenderness and savagery will be impossible to erase from my heart, for I never dreamed they could belong to one.*"

The tone of the letter was dark, laced with anguish, and suddenly his Maryann seemed to realize just how they had hurt her. A cry of denial slipped from her.

"Nicolas," she said tremulously, her long lashes damp with tears. "If what you are saying is what I believe…Crispin…my brother would never use anyone so cruelly or treat anyone so shabbily. I know it with my entire heart."

He drew her closer to him and pressed a kiss to her forehead. "I am beginning to believe it is not him, either."

They stayed silent for a few minutes.

"Tell me the rest of it, please."

"Blond hair and blue eyes with a scar splitting his lower lip. He laughed through my screams, 'tis a sound I shall remember on my way to hell, for I am no longer worthy of heaven. It was a sound that demeaned and ridiculed…it was a sound that found humor in my torment."

She gripped his forearm. "Blond hair and blue eyes with a scar. Oh God. That perfectly describes Viscount Weychell."

"Yes."

Her chest lifted harshly with her ragged breaths. "He…years ago, at my debut, I danced with him. How charming and good-natured he had seemed."

"He escaped my schemes, but perhaps working on a cotton plantation in Virginia is a fit punishment. The Wolf and the black Dahlia remain."

She visibly started.

"Maryann—"

"You have borne this sorrow for years. I can bear the memory and knowing of it with you tonight."

Her strength filled him with a rush of fierce pride.

"The dragon wings spread wide, a rose of coronet upon its head…how merciless this dragon was, tempting

me with chances of escape only to catch me again when I tasted freedom. The wolf…he was all of them, cruel, brutal, unholy, and savage, yet he was more, for in him once I found love."

Maryann faltered into piercing stillness. "Someone she loved…someone she loved was there?"

The wolf…their best friend.

"My tears are like endless rainfall. How can I live with everything they stole from me? What is done is done. I have no hope, no virtue, and no will to live. May my soul find mercy and grace with thy heavenly father," Nicolas said, repeating the last of the letter.

Maryann dropped his hand as if she had been burned.

Ah, my sweet Maryann, do not cry.

Tears coursed down her cheeks, and in her eyes he spied a raw pain that echoed deep inside him. And words he had never spoken came spilling from him. "Arianna was my friend…a girl I loved with all the passion of youth," he murmured.

Nicolas realized he was trusting Maryann with every part of him, even the past which haunted him. Would she also see him guilty, as how he had seen himself? "I was eighteen to her sixteen and our stations were different. Though I had such affections for Arianna, I did not offer for her. The day she kissed me and professed her love, I told her I could not accept it."

The daughter of servants and a future marquess.

"You were young," Maryann said, swiping her cheeks. "And *scared*. That is understandable."

"I told her I needed time to speak with my father. He had plans for me to marry a friend's daughter, and I knew my duty. Arianna was hurt, and she left for London the very next day to pursue her dream of being on the stage. She would not sit around and wait for me to decide if she was worth more than duty."

A soft rumble of thunder echoed in the distance, and the air chilled. Rain felt imminent, but neither moved.

He lifted his eyes to the sky, staring at the stars for long moments, before he said, "Only a couple days after she left, I got her letter. A boy from an inn had been paid to deliver it. Terror tore through my soul when I read it. I prepared a carriage and extra horses and raced to her. But I was too late."

The pain rose, gnawing at him. "The day before, a young lady had jumped into the river abutting the inn. The young lad who had delivered her note whispered that the gentlemen who had dragged her to one of their rooms had left early that morning. They had laughed and caroused after their foul deed, secure in the knowledge they were young powerful lords and she...she had been nothing. A mere speck in their eyes."

A fat drop of rain landed on his forehead. "For months I was lost in rage and guilt. I was enraged at myself and Arianna. If I'd placed my love for her above duty and expectations, and if she had waited to see if I could convince my family, she'd still be alive. Then I realized the men who are to blame were still living their finest life. The idea was intolerable."

"Did you not report it?" Maryann asked hoarsely.

He nodded. "To my father and the local magistrate and eventually Bow Street."

"What happened?"

"There is no justice in the law. Their fathers were powerful men; the magistrate was afraid to make an arrest. They were rich and certain of their immunity from being punished. How can an ant by itself cut down a willow tree? Her father…who is he? A butler at a neighboring estate. Her mother, a maidservant in mine. Who are they in the face of future earls…a duke, and a viscount? They were nothing."

Her hand gripped his. "But you did something."

An overwhelming ache throbbed behind Nicolas's eyes. "'If you prick us, do we not bleed? If you tickle us, do we not laugh? If you poison us, do we not die? And if you wrong us, do we not revenge?'"

Looking away from the stars, he leveled his gaze on her, and the amount of pride in her expression had his damn heart near to bursting from his chest.

His Maryann admired him still.

"How did you eventually find them?" she asked tremulously.

"If a man possesses a guilty conscience, he will be startled by any sound in the night."

"So you threw rocks, and someone squealed?"

"A particular lord did, Viscount Barton. A few well-placed rumors and a letter placed strategically had him scrambling to find out what was happening. I followed the crumbs he left behind."

"How long did you follow these crumbs?"

"It has been five years. And I am not done yet. It took a significant time to gather the information I needed. I could not take my purpose lightly. These were men who had families and tenants relying on them. I had to be sure they were the men mentioned in her letters. I used private runners to go back to their school days and the inn where everything happened before I had some of the pieces of the whole. I took the time to understand their bond and who might have traveled together those years ago to Wiltshire and that inn.

Finally, I had enough to ruin Barton financially."

"You played a very long game."

I am still playing. "When dealing with powerful and connected people, it is critical to be strategic."

Her fingers toyed with the edges of her gown. "Is… is the Duke of Farringdon one of the men?"

"Yes." Nicolas's tone was flat, brutal, and unapologetic.

And still no fear showed in her. Her face was full of strength and beauty, shining with a steadfast trust and belief in his honor.

"The papers…the papers said he was shot while fighting with you."

"It was a mere flesh wound. He will live."

Her lips trembled, and her gaze was dark with emotions.

"How stricken you look," Nicolas murmured, touching her cheek. "Those I ruin do not deserve your sorrow. Those I ruin are not righteous men of conscience; these are men who believed that because Arianna was poor and unconnected, her life had little worth."

Maryann reached out and brushed her hand against his knuckles. Even with the gloves separating them, he could tell she was cold. He needed to take her home.

"You mistake the matter. All my sorrow is for Arianna…and for what you've had to do. Your restraint is admirable. If something…if something so painful had happened to me, my father would have challenged them to an outright duel and killed them."

Nicolas took back her hands in his. "My father was the second to have failed Arianna."

"And you believe you were the first to fail her. Do you think I would not understand your guilt?" she

asked when he glanced away briefly. "Your father…
what…" Her voice sounded so thick with tears she had
to take a few moments and breathe. "The bleakness I
see on your face stabs into my heart and catches like a
hook."

She rose, and shuffled so she sat in his lap, and
Nicolas hugged her to him. Bloody hell, what would he
have done without this woman?

"Father had not cared about what happened to her,
not when those committing the crimes were future
peers. The law serves only those powerful and connected."

His Maryann held herself still under the weight of
the awful truth. A young girl was driven to her death,
and no one cared because she was poor. Her connections unimportant. Her worth miniscule.

"I've been swaddled in privilege and wealth since
birth, I cannot imagine anything so terrible happening
to me, and the cry for justice would not resound in the
realm. I am *glad* you have not allowed them to escape
justice." She cupped his face between her hands and
lifted his head from her bosom. "I feel no disgust with
your actions. What I feel is admiration. At a time when
other young gentlemen were either attending universi-
ty or touring Europe for a jolly good time, you sought
retribution for the girl you loved, by any means necessary."

And Nicolas had dedicated years of his life to that
endeavor—and by his own admission would give a
lifetime more. Except what he wanted more than
anything in the world was Maryann beside him, in his
home and bed, today, tomorrow, and years from now.

How much longer can I wait? Can you wait?

"Why do you still cry?" he asked gruffly, chasing a

tear on her cheek with his thumb.

"I cannot help thinking that this time, years ago, someone died, tragically. I do not have the heart to imagine how terrified and how utterly hopeless Arianna must have been. And the only person who cared about her demise was a boy of eighteen who loved her. There is honor in your vengeance," Maryann said softly, pressing the softest of kisses to his lips.

Nicolas could not speak, not with the fierce and complex emotions burning through him. "Thank you for listening, Maryann."

She rubbed her nose on his, almost playfully. "Thank you for sharing."

"I would like to take you sailing," he said. "To stand on the deck as the boat powers through the churning waters, the fine ocean spray wetting your skin, the wind behind your back. The sense of freedom and joy is one I would love for you to experience."

A soft smile touched her mouth. "And I would love to accompany you, Nicolas."

He gently nudged her chin. "It is time for me to take you home. I can smell the rain on the air."

CHAPTER NINETEEN

Nicolas sounded…lighter, and she was incredibly glad she had risked so much to be with him tonight. A fine misting rain began to fall, and she hurriedly repinned her hat and lowered her veil. They slowly descended and made their way inside. Nicolas collected a large black umbrella, and once they were outside he opened it above their heads. The rain fell in earnest, and she inhaled, loving the dark scent of the earth and the grass.

They did not speak, simply walked closely together under the umbrella. It felt intimate, remarkably wonderful, and Maryann was glad he had not called for a carriage to be prepared. The rain heavily fell on the wide umbrella, wetting her clothes despite the covering, yet Maryann wouldn't trade this moment for a dry carriage and a warming pan.

The darkness of the night, broken by a few gas lamps here and there, the starless sky, and the fog hovering about the city appeared magical to her instead of ominous. A lone carriage rattled past them, and Nicolas caged her to his side, his gaze watchful and alert until it passed by.

She tugged off one of her gloves, immediately feeling the chill of the air against her bare hand. Then she pushed it out, collecting the cold drops in her palm, turning her hand to let the water caress against her knuckles.

"I've always loved the rain. I think I am the only one in my family who sighs with pleasure when I see the overcast sky or hear the rumble of thunder. It is the absolute best time to snuggle into my bed or a large armchair and read," she murmured, lowering her hand. "Sometimes I stand by my windows and watch as the rain falls to the ground, and against the leaves. I love hearing the sound of it on the roof."

They slowed as they approached a large puddle. Maryann barely restrained her gasp when his hand snaked around her waist, lifted her, and walked through the puddle. Then he lowered her to her feet.

"You do know we could have walked around it."

His lips tipped in a small smile. "And deny myself such a pleasure?"

By the time they crossed the third puddle, Maryann was giggling.

"You have a beautiful laugh. I enjoy hearing it."

She couldn't help it. Maryann faltered and peered up at him.

"Do not be so startled that I find you beautiful."

She said no more as he drew her closer to his side, protecting her with the umbrella against the sleeting rain.

"Let's get you home."

They continued on, and whenever they encountered a puddle, he would lift her over them with masculine ease. By the time she reached her home, Maryann was breathless with want.

"My parents have gone to a ball. And Crispin is at his club."

"It is still safer to enter from a side door. I'll pick the lock if need be."

Nicolas led her around to the gardens and opened a terraced door leading into the ballroom. She rushed from under the umbrella into the room and turned to face him. Rain ran in rivulets down his forehead, and his eyes gleamed with an emotion she was unable to decipher.

"Thank you for taking me into your confidence," she said, hoping he would hear her above the patter of the rain and the soft rumbles of thunder.

He leaned forward and pressed a kiss to her forehead. Maryann closed her eyes, savoring the feel of his cold lips against her skin. His mouth disappeared, and when she opened her eyes, it was to see the back of him walking away. She gently closed the door, resting her forehead against the glass pane for a few seconds.

Maryann hurriedly left the ballroom, traversed the long, empty hallway and then the winding staircase to the second floor. An odd awareness went down her spine, and with each step, her heart pounded, not with alarm but with an unbearable shivering excitement.

At her door, Maryann closed her eyes and sent up a silent entreaty—*please…please*. She twisted the knob of her door and entered her chamber. She scented him first, and his flavor was one of wild, dark, beautiful fire. Her gaze found him unerringly. He stood by the window, the now-folded black umbrella held loosely in his hand and dripping water on the carpet. She did not care.

He leaned the umbrella against the wall and shrugged from his coat, walking to rest it on the fireguard by the fireplace. His hair was wet and clung to his forehead, his eyes piercing and so intent on her.

"I…heard a rumor that I was not brave enough to ask you about earlier," she started.

"Ask me."

"The gossip says that you are about to procure yourself a mistress."

He froze. "It was a rumor I hinted at some days ago

while visiting White's."

Everything inside her rejected the very idea. It made no rational sense, but she accepted the burning absurdity of her emotions. "To complete your persona of a libertine? Or because you need a woman?"

His brow lifted at her boldness. "It would be another scheme, to prove I have no attachment to a young lady of quality."

"So, this mistress will be to protect me?"

"Yes."

She softly scoffed.

"Do I detect derision?"

"Will this lady be a mistress in name only?"

He thought about this. "I had not decided when I dropped the hints here and there."

"Don't you dare!"

The words lashed from her before she thought about his plan in its entirety.

Raw peril coated the silence that fell in her bedchamber. He said nothing, and Maryann did not rush to fill the quiet, merely stared at the crackling fireplace, painfully aware of his gaze upon her.

"I dare not," he quietly said. "Please be assured that scheme is now dismissed."

A gust of wind swept through the room and she shivered.

"Are you cold?"

"Unbearably so."

He looked at the dying embers in the hearth. "There's no log to rekindle the fire."

"The servants believe me to be at the ball. We are expected home in the morning. A servant will come up here at the break of dawn to rekindle the fire," Maryann said.

"How are you going to keep warm until then?"

She smiled. "You are here, aren't you?"

He closed his eyes for a long, silent minute, then turned to face the open windows. She waited, wondering if he was about to slip away once more. Thunder cracked and the rain sleeted. Reaching behind her, she closed the door with a soft *snick*. That sound seemed as if it echoed inside her chamber.

She toed off her shoes and padded softly…silently across the carpet. Her courage deserted her along the way, and she faltered. The small space between them felt like a vast chasm. A powerful need to touch him seized her, stealing her ability to breathe.

"Ah, Maryann, I wonder why there is nothing in this entire world but you that makes me happy?"

She grabbed that soft whisper and stored it in her heart.

He closed the window, shutting out the cold and the outside world. Then he faced her and held out his hand. Maryann stared at him, the dichotomy of such aching wants and fear freezing her in place. She looked up at him, and in his eyes she saw a beguiling mix of tenderness and savage desire that stole her breath.

A sudden blinding realization pierced her like a well-aimed arrow. "You waited for the day…you waited for yesterday to end."

A glance at the clock revealed it to be six minutes after midnight. He had only come to her room after the new day began.

"I wanted no past between us when I take you."

Her entire body vibrated with the awareness of him. "Take me?"

"Yes."

"Take me where?"

Silence…such wicked silence.

"The instant I touch you, you'll know."

Oh God. He was planning on ravishing her, and she knew with every fiber of her being that she would allow him *everything*. A thrill coursed through her at the thought.

Maryann licked lips that suddenly felt dry. "Arianna is not here in your thoughts now?"

"Whenever I am with you, she… Revenge does not exist."

Maryann's heart cracked at the rough guilt heard in that admission. She overshadowed Arianna in his thoughts, and Maryann could find no joy it in, not when it seemed to wreck Nicolas. "I am sorry," she gasped hoarsely.

"Do not be." He took a step toward her. "It is a struggle to recall anything else that exists in my mind once I am with you. In truth, I am lost in you."

"The prospect sounds terrifying for you."

He cupped her cheeks with his powerful hands. "You obliterate even my darkest thoughts and replace them with sunshine and want and hunger and dreams of things I've never thought about. I do not like it."

"I do!" she assured him, gripping his wrist and feeling the tripping of his pulse underneath her thumb.

He tucked a strand of wet hair behind her ear, his knuckles barely grazing her cheek. "It was a matter of honor and willpower to hold Arianna in my thoughts and speak of her yesterday when I was with you."

Only a few minutes after midnight had passed but everything felt changed, as if they had entered a different world with unlimited possibilities. "And yesterday ended."

He dragged her closer to him and dropped his

forehead to hers. "The feelings I have for you, I've never had them before, and I do not understand them."

She pushed the glasses atop her nose and stared at him wordlessly.

"Whenever you fiddle with your spectacles, while it is a most charming oddity, it tells me that you are nervous," he said, touching the bridge of her nose and then her glasses.

"I…I…being with you sometimes makes me feel nervous," she said with a shaky laugh.

"Why?"

"The feelings you rouse in me are so… I…I am not sure what they are."

"They are visceral, unforeseen, and hungry," he murmured. "They are so intense, you lie awake at night wondering at the madness of it. You are almost afraid to get close, to delve deep and understand what you feel because you are not sure what you will find. Yet there is something there luring you closer still, every day, every minute…this very second, and when you try to understand the nature of the piper…you realize it is the very one who caused that raw, chaotic need."

She swallowed, and answered the raw desire peeking down at her, "I wonder what the craving low in my belly is, and this unrelenting ache in my heart." Maryann lifted her hand and brushed a wet tendril from his forehead. "It is more than an ache…there is excitement, a sense of wonder…and a sense of fright."

His mouth curved in a beautiful smile. "What do you think it is?"

She willingly tumbled over the precipice which she had been perched on so precariously. "It must be the beginning of love, and I dare hope it is also the middle and the end."

"You speak your thoughts so boldly. Is there nothing you are afraid of?"

"I am afraid of years from now looking back on my life and feeling the keenest of regret that I had not lived. Of never feeling again the way I feel with you."

Cherished.

"You are my future." He said it so softly, Maryann wasn't certain she had heard correctly.

He leaned with space between them and kissed her. It was the briefest touch of lips to hers, but there they were, firm and supple against her mouth. She lifted her fingers to touch his cheek, astonished her hand trembled with the force of emotions working through her.

Nicolas drew back and shrugged from his waistcoat and jacket, letting them fall to the carpet.

"If you want to, and only if you want to, take off your clothes."

Oh God. The awareness of exactly what he now meant by "taking her" sent such sensations tearing through her heart, they were frightening and exquisite all at once.

Maryann untied the tapes to her cloak and shrugged it from her shoulders. Then she turned around and closed her eyes when he methodically unbuttoned her dress. His movements were so slow, as if he savored removing her clothes. She could feel the warmth of his breath against her nape and smell the wild flavor of rain and fire. After the last of her garments fell to the floor in a soft *swish*, he removed the pins holding her heavy tresses together. Her hair tumbled over her shoulders, down to her back, and his soft exhalation of satisfaction had delight coursing through her.

The silence felt thick, charged.

Maryann almost fainted when a finger ran over her back and down to the arch of her derriere. There his touch lingered before his hand fell from her buttock. Her entire body was blushing.

When she faced him again, her lips parted, and her eyes widened. Her chest went so tight, she could scarcely breathe. The marquess was stark and beautifully naked and completely distracted her from the awareness that she stood only in stockings and garters, with her hair tunneling down to her waist in a riot of curls and damp tendrils.

He watched her with an unreadable intensity that sucked all the air from her lungs, and Maryann lowered her gaze and blushed fiercely. His eyes devoured every dip and hollow of her body.

And she swallowed the cry rising in her throat when his body reacted. The statues in the museums had lied, and she had to remember to tell her friends. His manhood hung long and heavy between his brawny thighs, which were carved with such strength, he could have been one of those sculptors. His thighs and calves were thick and powerful, stomach and buttocks lean and delineated with muscle.

The very awareness that she was being so wicked with him had a familiar ache settling low in her stomach. *I have fallen in love with you*, she wanted to say, but to her shock, her mouth would not part. Maryann was never one to shy away from speaking her opinions, but at this moment she felt ridiculously vulnerable and timid.

As if he sensed the emotions rioting inside her, he came closer and pressed a kiss to her forehead. It asked for trust, and it also reassured her.

He moved away and held out his hands. And even in that action, he gave her a choice. Her marquess did not ruthlessly seduce her, using her untapped passion to assault her senses. Should she step back, he would not pressure her.

Maryann smiled tremulously up at him. To take his hand was to be forever altered, yet she reached for him.

He dragged her up against him, one hand curving to the swell of her hips and lifting so she wrapped her legs around his hips.

"I fear when I am through with you, all your sensibilities will be forever devastated," he murmured, his voice rich with hunger and arousal.

She touched his mouth with trembling fingers. "I want to be so very wicked with you."

Nicolas took her mouth in a kiss of violent tenderness that shook her. Then he ravished her lips with passionate kisses. Their tongues tangled wildly, and a long, low moan broke from her lips.

A slow, languorous ache rolled through Maryann and settled in that secret place between her thighs. She was terribly conscious of her naked breasts pressed against the smooth muscles of her marquess's chest, and that he moved with her toward the bed, never relinquishing her lips.

He tumbled them, twisting so that his back hit the mattress first and she atop him. Their mouths seduced each other with long, passionate kisses that soon had her squirming atop his hardened body, a desperate ache for more burning through her like the hottest fire.

He kissed her. Again. Over and over. As if he couldn't get enough of her taste.

Nicolas rolled with her, his large frame blanketing her much smaller one. One elbow braced above her, but his other hand did not remain still. He delved and stroked his fingers over her collarbones and down to her aching breasts. One of his palms cupped her breast, his fingers tweaking at her nipple, stabbing pleasure to the heart of her, then lightly pinched her other nipple, and the shock of that pleasurable pain had her arching sharply upward, flushing her wet sex directly against his hardened manhood.

Then he rubbed a thumb and forefinger over her throbbing peak.

Maryann never imagined a touch to her breast could illicit such a fever of need. She thrust her fingers through his hair, sobbing against his kiss that seemed to burn out of control in its ravishing wildness. Cocooned in the darkness of her chamber, Maryann became lost entirely in the taste, the scent, and the feel of him.

Finally, their mouths parted, and he dipped to kiss the soft hollow of her throat where the pulse tripped like a captive bird. Her thighs were nudged apart, and his heavy weight cradled between her splayed legs. The hand he had between them glided from her breast down to her quivering belly, and much lower. Her body flushed and her chest lifted on ragged pants as his fingertips stroked over her aching sex. She was already wantonly wet for him, and he groaned his pleasure.

Her body was wet, soft, and yielding, and she welcomed the finger he slipped deep inside her. The feeling of him there was so remarkably intimate.

Then that finger stroked in and out, and she gasped at the incredible sensation, gripping the sheets beside her. His mouth took her breast, and he sucked at her in a long, strong pull that she felt right in her belly. The sensual assault on her senses almost felt like too much, and he stroked her over and over as pleasure swelled inside Maryann until it expanded and burst forth in white-hot bliss.

Before she could come down from the high of that delight, he slipped another finger inside her snug passage, and then another. She moaned at the tight fit and the pressure. Then his fingers moved in her alarming wetness. Each stroke into her snug sex was a shock of agonizing pleasure. His head dipped and she slapped a hand over her mouth to contain the sob as he went for her pearl.

He licked her, over and over. Her nub swelled with aching hunger, and she lifted her hips helplessly against his wicked mouth as he tugged her nub between his teeth and sucked it into his mouth.

A hoarse scream slid from her mouth before she could contain it. Maryann tried to pull back from the powerful sensation. His large hands curved underneath her buttocks and held her firmly under the lash of his tongue. Maryann sobbed at the overwhelming pleasure. Her body trembled and sweat slicked her skin.

A wildness rose inside her, and with every lick and pull of his mouth, the heat in her belly grew and expanded. Maryann became a creature of carnality as she stopped trying to escape the raw, heated sensation. Instead, her thighs spilled open wider and she arched her hips more against his devasting mouth.

The shivering sensation low in her stomach felt as if she were falling, and a sense of unalterable conse-quences beat against her thoughts only to be ripped away under the shock of bliss that tore through her.

"Nicolas," she wailed, trembling. "I need you...in me!"

He crawled up over her body, dipped his head, and kissed her. It was so gentle, as if he hadn't just ravaged her senses and left her quaking. He reached between them, fisted his manhood, pressed it against her sex, and pushed.

Her breath gasped from her at the burning sensation.

"You are so damn tight," he groaned against her mouth.

She released the sheets to clasp his shoulders, hugging him close to her. He invaded her body relentlessly, and a sob hitched in her throat. Maryann found it increasingly hard to focus on anything but the stretching tightness between her thighs.

It burned.

She lowered her face and buried it in the crook of his neck, brushing featherlight kisses against the hollow of his throat. With a groan he thrust, sinking deep inside her sex. A cry tore from her throat, and she clung to his shoulders, gasping through the shock of the pleasure-pain.

A hoarse shout spilled from him, and then he convulsed inside her arms, pulling from her to spill his seed on her quivering belly.

"Bloody hell," he muttered. "I am like an untried lad. That should have been longer and far more pleasurable for you."

She giggled at the disgruntlement in his tone. "Ah, rakesses do that," she purred, feeling a powerful rush of feminine satisfaction. "I've heard rakes normally have ladies at their feet in a puddle…how wonderful that the shoe is on the other foot."

Their harsh breath mingled in the silence of the room, and it took several moments before he kissed her forehead, then pushed from the bed.

He returned with a handkerchief and tenderly

cleaned away his release.

Then he sat on the edge of the bed. "Come here," he murmured.

Maryann blinked, sensing he was not finished. Beyond curious, she shifted, containing her gasp at the discomfort between her legs. His penetration had been so abrupt and short-lived. He reached over and pulled her to him, positioning her so that she sat in his lap, her knees bracketing his hips. Her hair cascaded over her front and his chest in a curtain of simmering silk.

He reached between them to brush his knuckles over her nub. "I want to ravish you," he said, his face a grimace of arousal.

Pleasure streaked through her as nerve endings came alive from that soft caress. He dragged her so fast into a world of pure sensation, she easily became lost to him.

"Ah," she said teasingly, nipping at his chin. "Worrying about my sensibilities, are you?"

He grunted.

"I have a confession," she murmured throatily against his mouth. "I found a *very* naughty book once in the library."

"How naughty?" he groaned.

"Images…the most memorable of a buxom lady perched on her knees while a gentleman placed his mouth between her thighs."

Her marquess cursed. Maryann laughed.

He was gorgeously intense, his face almost savage in its planes and angles. "Our coming together just now should have lasted much longer…but I was too eager… too desperate for you." A dark line of color accented his cheekbones. "I am going to stroke, rub, and pinch it while you ride me."

Maryann purred. "Tell me more."

Nicolas nipped at her lip and cupped her entire sex. "Each rub of your clitoris will drive you wild, and you'll beg me to stop from the agonizing pleasure throbbing through your quim."

Her entire body flushed, sensing that this word was sensually crude, and to her shock, arousal surged hot and greedy through her body.

He brushed a kiss over her mouth again, as if to soothe. Her lips trembled in response.

He rubbed his thumb over her clitoris, once, twice, three times while he slowly impaled her onto his thick length. The relentless rub and press of his thumb against her nub had her shaking, almost mortified at how wet she got. Need coiled hot and intense through Maryann. The hand at her hips urged her down, and a wild cry tore from her throat. She felt deliciously impaled, the penetration stretching her despite the wetness of her flesh.

"Ride me."

"With pleasure," she whispered.

Holding Nicolas's brilliant gaze, she gripped his shoulders, lifted her hips, and started riding him slowly. Each glide over his thick length wreaked havoc within her body. Her mass of hair rippled down her shoulders, cascading over his chest. She fisted his hair in her hands and dragged his mouth against hers, rolling her hips against his in a greedy glide. His large hands cupped her buttocks, and he helped her, dragging her up his manhood and urging her down sometimes with slow movements, other times rough and hard.

"Ride harder," he growled against her mouth.

Maryann's heart raced, beating a harsh, driving rhythm against her breast, and a broken cry of need escaped her as she responded with wantonness. She gripped his hair and held him to her as she rode him, faster and deeper, reveling in the primal invasion of his manhood inside her aching sex. With each stroke Nicolas drove her closer to shattering.

But it was the constant stroke of his thumb against her clitoris. The sensations almost hurt, like a knot tightening low in her belly and even lower. The piercing sensation in her nub became a raw, sweet agony. She wanted to escape it, even as she never wanted him to stop that rub and press. Her world narrowed entirely onto the pleasure crowding her senses. Suddenly, hot, aching pleasure took her over. Maryann lost her breath, control of her body, and her mind as ecstasy tore her apart.

With a harsh groan, and with her still impaled on him, Nicolas twisted with her so she fell back on the bed. He thrust deep, then froze, spilling deep inside her body.

She curved into his chest, relaxing at the haven of his embrace, her lashes fluttering closed as exhaustion claimed her. Sometime later, Maryann muttered irritably when he lifted her and placed her in the center of the bed. She distantly felt that he cleaned her, and then he was there, holding her until she fell into a deep slumber.

CHAPTER TWENTY

Maryann's laughter rang into her bedchamber, charming Nicolas to no end. Playing charades with just the two of them was decidedly hilarious. Their rules had completely devolved from the original game. Each would simply think of a word, stand in the center of the room, and act it for the other to guess. Their game's most profound rule was honesty.

"I give up," she said with a gasping laugh, unable to understand what he could possibly be trying to communicate by stooping low with his hands clasped in a prayer, then to slowly rise swaying side to side, then to just explode into action by leaping high and spreading his arms wide.

She tried so ridiculously hard to not be distracted by the fact he was so casually dressed, and the open neck of his shirt revealed his throat and chest. They had been at a ball earlier, and one look from him across the expanse of the ballroom and she had pled a headache and returned home early. It hadn't been long before he had slipped in through her windows.

Her bedroom had been transformed into a place where only dreams happened. Once he crept into her room and closed the door and windows behind her, the outside world ceased to exist, the risk of discovery that he was there faded, and everything inside...every touch, smile, every kiss, every story they shared about growing up, *everything* became enchanted.

"Shh," Nicolas said, tumbling onto the carpet beside her and leaning over to nip at her ear. "Recall your parents and brother are also home. Tonight, we are living very dangerously."

"What were you acting?" she whispered.

"A volcano."

She choked on her laughter. "I am at a loss as to what goes on inside your head. How was *that* a volcano!"

He brushed a kiss over her mouth, and before he could withdraw, she snaked her hands around his nape and mashed their mouths together in a deep kiss. His groan vibrated from his mouth and she swallowed it, going with him when he curved her body into his. Heat curled low in her belly and her nipples stabbed against her nightgown.

It astonished her how easily desire kindled in her body.

"Not yet," he murmured against her mouth, biting into her soft lower lip. "I was too unrestrained with my passions and—"

"You were wonderful," she rebutted. "And it has been three days since we made love."

He smiled. "And we'll wait a few more."

She kissed his mouth again, wanting to assuage the desire rising inside. "Nicolas—"

"You were sweetly innocent, and I did not temper my passions. I should have been more considerate of your sensibilities and your body's limitations. Being lost in your taste and scent is not an excuse."

"I enjoyed everything," she said huskily.

"Of course you did, I am an excellent lover," he said with a roguish smile of such beauty, her breath audibly hitched.

Since the first night they made love, he crept into her room every evening. They would laugh, talk, play games, and read to each other. When their playful kisses exploded in raw passion, despite the arousal in her body, she had been too sore to tumble into bed with him. That very first night, he had taken her four times before he had discreetly left her room with the breaking dawn. The next morning there had been red strawberry marks everywhere on her body—breasts, stomach, and thighs. And her mouth had been swollen from his ravishing kisses and her eyes…they had glittered with carnal knowledge.

She lightly kissed over his jaw, down to the indentation at the base of his throat, and inhaled his scent into her lungs. Her marquess needed to understand that he alone would not dictate when they made love. His personality was driven and forceful, but she was not afraid of it or him, and if she wanted something, surely he must understand she would take it. With a rough groan he pushed her away from him, lurched to his feet, and lowered himself to the sofa.

Splayed at his feet, her nightgown wantonly ridden up to her thighs, she smiled at him. His gaze narrowed. Then she stood and in one graceful move removed her nightgown from her body.

He sucked in a sharp breath and clenched the arm of the sofa in a visibly tight grip. "Woman," he began warningly. "I've decided. You'll not tempt me to—"

His words died when she lowered herself to the carpet to kneel between his splayed legs.

"Oh? *You* decided?" she drawled with a smile, reaching up to release her knot of hair from the loose chignon. Her heavy tresses tumbled to her shoulders and back in riotous waves, and appreciation lit in his eyes.

Maryann loved that he loved her hair.

She rested her hands on his thighs, and the muscles bunched between her fingertips. His body reacted to her provocative position of kneeling before him and his manhood hardened behind the flap of his trousers.

"If you will recall that I had mentioned some months ago, my friends and myself accidentally came upon a book in the library. It was clear it had been hastily tucked away, and that was the driver for our curiosity."

Holding his stare and fighting to keep her blush at bay, she reached for his pants, and deftly opened the flap of his trousers. His manhood sprang into her hands, hard, heavy, and straining. His girth was such she could barely close her fingers fully around him, and it astonished her she had taken him so eagerly into her body.

"It was a very naughty book," she said mischievously. "This was before we decided to be sinful wallflowers, but wickedness must have been brewing in our hearts from then because we all hid in the library and devoured the pages. Our eyes were opened, our sensibilities mortified, the women in us intrigued."

He made no reply, merely watched her with that brilliant, hawkish gaze, a flush of color high on his cheekbones. His eyes glittered with desire, with emotions. Without saying any more, Maryann dipped her head and kissed the very tip of his manhood.

He groaned, and the fingers on the armchair tightened. She had no notion what she was about, but she had seen the pictures, and he had pleasured her in a similar manner several times. Maryann believed in the reciprocity of such delights.

This time she kissed that flared crown as if it were his lips, and when he shouted she released him to press a single finger across his lips.

"Shh," she whispered. "Remember where we are."

The lust that leaped into his gaze had such a savage cast, her heart tripped. Her breasts swelled with languorous heaviness, breathing fractured, and she shifted a bit on her knees. Then with a mischievous smile, she went back to her tender ministrations.

• • •

Nicolas thrust his fingers into Maryann's hair, bunching them away from her face. He didn't want the curtain of her hair to hide her face from him; he wanted to see every lick and teasing caress she made with her tongue against his cock. That first wicked stroke of her tongue had a rough groan slipping from him.

The minx smiled.

That wide, lush mouth was taking him with artless sensuality and decadent greed. She was so innocent in how she licked and kissed along the thick length of his cock, and Nicolas had never witnessed a more arousing sight than her knelt before him, pleasuring him, her russet glory bunched in his fingers. Pleasure rippled from his engorged length to his balls.

Each stroke of her tongue, tug of her lips, pounded lust through his veins. Nicolas felt as if he were enslaved to the stroke of her tongue, he bloody trembled, and sweat beaded his brow.

"God, you're beautiful," he said, voice so guttural with arousal he sounded unintelligible.

There was a point he thought he muttered crooning nonsense for she giggled sweetly against him. Then she sucked him into her mouth as far as she could take him. A ragged groan burst from his throat.

Unable to bear her tormenting tongue any longer, he pulled her up to him.

"I like that I drive you to losing control," she teased, her cheeks rosily flushed, and her eyes dark with desire.

Those soft words seemed to brush directly against his cock.

"I am going to make love to you," he said, his chest lifting on a harsh breath.

An engaging twinkle lit in her eyes. "That was my plan, my darling."

He felt a peculiar wrenching in the vicinity of his heart. *How and when did you slide underneath my skin?* She felt imprinted on his soul.

He shifted and placed her on her stomach on the large armchair by the fire.

"Grip the armrests, and do not let go."

She sweetly complied, then he stood and shrugged from his clothes before coming down behind her on his knees. He widened her legs slightly, pushed a hand between her body and the cushion to find her clitoris which he caressed until he felt a rush of wetness against his fingers.

It physically hurt to crave her this much.

She panted, need making her slick with welcome. Nicolas was relentless in how he stroked her clitoris over and over until she was mindless with arousal. Her fingers sank into the armchair's padded arm and her delightfully rounded arse arched in the air.

He slipped one of his hands around her hips and drew her to her knees. Nicolas had never been so unrestrained with his passions before, and despite her gentility his Maryann burned with a wild passion he hadn't dreamed possible, coaxing him to be himself in every way.

Her hands stretched above her head, gripping the armrests, she turned her face, her cheek sliding against the cushion set of the armchair. Nicolas pressed his cock at her wet sex, and slowly sank deep inside her welcoming heat. He entered her slowly, inch by deliberately slow inch, holding her still until she took his throbbing length to the hilt. A groan of shuddering satisfaction, and she swallowed him up with a muffled scream into the cushions, her back arching.

The desire that tore through him was a savage, demanding ache. She gripped his cock in the tightest, wettest clasp he'd ever experienced.

His palm found the inside of her thigh, stroked, caressed, as he savored the feeling of her softness. "I love feeling you under my hands," he murmured, caressing the globes of her arse. "I love these wanton little noises you can't help but make as I take you."

He thrust inside her sex with long, deep strokes, pleasure rippling over him like fire, gritting his teeth at the sublime ecstasy of her tight sheath. With each piercing thrust within her, a mix of tenderness and lust rose inside, and he gripped her hips, riding her harder. With each plunge, his name from her lips became a whimper, a cry, a plea, a gasp, a moan. Nicolas bent over her, delving his fingers between her thighs to find her clitoris. He pressed it with his thumb, and Maryann convulsed around his cock, gripping him so tightly he could barely move. Passion rocked his body with jarring force and with a harsh groan he tumbled with her.

Hard shudders wracking her body, he leaned forward and kissed her shoulders gently, reverently. He pulled from her, lifted her against his chest, and took her over to the bed. Then he went behind her screen to the wash basin and returned with a cloth. He gently cleaned her, finding it so amusing that she blushed.

Everything in him—every thought, every one of his senses, arrowed on that sweet, loving smile on her mouth. His heart stuttered. Love. He could see it in her eyes, feel it stirring through his soul.

"I will be speaking with your father soon."

Her eyes widened. "How soon?"

"I have made my move against the wolf. Only yesterday, I had set up a financial scheme especially for him, it is something on the lines of the South Sea bubble scandal, which was all smoke and mirrors, but it can't be traced back to me. He will learn today how much money he has lost. This will shake him from the dark."

Her throat worked on a swallow. "And the black Dahlia?"

"I am still searching."

Her brows furrowed. "Do you still believe it to be my brother?"

He hesitated. "I have not ruled out that possibility."

The words fell between them, a fiery arrow piercing their tranquility.

Something wild flashed in her gaze. "I swear to you my brother would never act with such dishonor. And I asked him if he knew Arianna and he said no. We have never lied to each other."

"So you know he has a mistress and a child?"

She froze. "I...what?"

"One of the reports that came across my desk revealed there is a home on the outskirts of London he visits once every two weeks."

"And the child?"

"A girl."

She flushed. "The bacon-brained dolt would think he is protecting my sensibilities. Why would he not marry her?"

The naivete in the question rocked through her. "Her circumstances might be inferior."

He hated seeing the hurt in her eyes. "He has a child, and he has allowed her to be born a bastard! And then he hid her existence from this family."

"All men hide their mistresses and by-blows," he calmly said. "And your mother has a reputation of being a moral prig. I am certain he would take care to not reveal it."

Using the pad of his thumb, he traced a slow line from her collarbone to the tip of her breast. *Thud, thud, thud.* How fiercely her heart jerked. "I have cast my net wider," he promised. "I already set my investigator to pay a keener attention to details. And they've already suggested another young man's name who attended both Eton and Oxford and was there at the inn."

For suddenly it was unbearable that her brother might be the man Nicolas was looking for. It would hurt her, and he couldn't imagine what it would do to their relationship. Nicolas had been relieved when they gave him the report that there was another young lord, a baron, who might be the black Dahlia. Suddenly it had made sense that he hadn't found anything linking Lord Crispin to Arianna.

She nodded, a relieved sigh slipping from her.

"Do you have a masquerade mask?"

The sleepiness that had suffused her lovely face vanished and she sat up excitedly. "Yes, why?"

"I will take you to the Asylum."

She looked about ready to faint. "The gambling den?"

"Yes."

She flung her hands around his neck and rained exuberant kisses all over his nose and mouth.

"Do you have a wig?"

She paused. "No."

"We must cover your hair. It is incredibly unique."

She laughed softly. "You are the only person who does not think my hair brown."

"Are your parents still attending Lady Burrell's ball tomorrow?"

"Yes, it is the final ball before we retire to the country."

"Plead a headache and stay home. Tomorrow, procure a black wig, and be ready for me by ten p.m."

She brushed her lips against his, then lower over his jaw. "Thank you."

His Maryann barely touched him, featherlight, but it was the most sensual sensation he'd ever experienced.

His hands framed her face, thumbs brushing her frantic pulse, then he kissed her with all the emotions brewing in his gut, hoping she would feel them, even as he struggled to express what they were.

• • •

The following night, Maryann stood inside the most notorious gambling den, staring around in awe. Her pulse had quickened alarmingly, she felt achy, terrifyingly breathless that she was here, in this den of sin.

The decor could be described as decadent luxury, blue and silver carpets covered the floor, and swaths of silver and golden drapes twined themselves around massive white Corinthian columns. Dozens of tables were scattered in an organized sprawl on this lower floor, and many lords she recognized sat at tables playing faro, Macao, whist, and *vingt-et-un*.

The clattering of dice echoed as they rolled on the tables. Raucous sounds of laughter, the downing of drinks, and snatches of conversations and smoke filled the air.

Maryann was tugged by the strains of music and they bypassed the gaming tables to the large ballroom. The glitter of the chandeliers, the dazzling array of lavish and beautifully dressed ladies, the self-indulgence and laughter, the ornate and exotic masquerade masks all assailed her senses.

"People are staring at you," she said, raising her voice to be heard over the din.

"I've never brought a lady here before."

Maryann sent him a pleased smile. "I cannot believe I am here. My friends are going to be green with envy!"

"So, I see everyone in this wallflowers club you've told me about is just as mischievous."

"Oh, we are all going to be terribly naughty, you'll see," she murmured, her hand fluttering to her throat when a waltz started.

"Dance with me," he murmured at her nape, curving his hand around her waist, and leading her to the dance floor.

With a sense of shock, she realized he touched her freely, without any worry that how closely they stood might seem improper and start a wildfire rumor.

"Here, when we dance, we can be as close as possible."

"And we can even kiss," she said faintly, staring at a couple locked in a passionate embrace near the doorway leading out to the terrace. Unexpectedly she laughed, tipping her head to the dazzling chandelier which seemed to hold a thousand candles.

The waltz leaped into life from the orchestra's bows, and he took her in his arms. Scandalously and wonderfully close. They twirled across the floor, and whenever he drew her in, Nicolas flushed her body against his. Maryann almost expired on the spot, until she realized just how free the mask and the wig she wore was. The second time he spun her away and she twirled twice, sliding her feet across the parquet floor in the intricate and sensual moves to come back to him, this time he kissed her mouth. Their dance blossomed into something sultry and decadent and so very naughty. By the time the strains of the waltz died away, Maryann was breathless and laughing.

"I am so pleased you are the only gentleman I've danced with in over two years who is not my father or brother."

"And I am damn glad you waited for me," he murmured, kissing her mouth in a quick, scandalizing kiss.

The night was perfect. And as Maryann twirled in his arms for their second waltz, an odd surge of fright darted through her heart. What if this should all end? Pushing aside that unexpected burst of raw dread, she lost herself in the moment of being so free from the restraints of society's expectations, and simply lived. And most glorious of all, Nicolas would soon approach Maryann's father for her hand, and they would be affianced.

Almost an hour later, Maryann laughingly complained of sore and tired feet. They had danced the waltz and the polka several times, but none of the strict proprieties of distance had been observed. Every move and touch had been designed to heighten the carnal awareness of being in your dance partner's arms and touching their body.

It had been remarkably intimate, freeing, and so sensual.

"Let me procure you a drink, something cool and refreshing."

"Am I allowed to explore?" she asked, looking up at him.

"Freely. No one will accost you."

She glanced around a bit skeptically. "Are you seeing the same room that I am?"

"No one would dare."

"Because they know I am with you."

His eyes darkened and her breath hitched at that tender yet starkly possessive look.

"Because they know," he murmured.

Maryann smiled when he melted away in the crowd, and she slowly walked the expanse of the room, admiring the lavish gowns and masks the ladies wore. They were all bewigged and their identities hidden. It was only the men who were allowed to indulge without any worry to their reputations.

Maryann scoffed, turning to make her way down a well-lit hallway that was conspicuously empty. She paused, intending to return to the ballroom when the distant sound of singing pulled her farther down the hallway. The closer she got to the door at the end, the more the raw beauty of the voice enchanted her.

And it was also so familiar.

Maryann came to a door and gently tested the knob. It opened soundlessly under her palm and she faltered into stunned stillness. It was a large room swathed in more shadows than light, but she saw clearly the lone man sitting in the center of that room in a large armchair. He was indolently reposed, a cheroot in his mouth and a glass in his hand. She could not discern his appearance in full, it was more an impression of power and masculine grace, and that his gaze was unflinchingly pinned on the lady before him on a raised dais.

Ophelia.

Maryann swallowed her gasp. Though her friend wore an elaborate silver-blond wig and a gold filigree mask, she would recognize her anywhere. And that voice, so pure and powerful in its sheer beauty, enveloped the room, creating a pulse of such ache inside Maryann's heart.

Ophelia's voice had always enthralled, and once when she had regaled an audience at a musicale some years ago, Maryann had felt such regret that the world might not hear what she had to sing.

But now here she was, a songbird of poignant and rare talent singing in her unique voice to an audience of one, bravely standing before a gentleman who stared at her as if he were a hungry predator. There was something about the situation that was alarming.

And suddenly Maryann knew this man—Devlin Byrne, a man so mysterious not even the scandal sheet had much to report on him other than that he was a wealthy industrialist who stood on the very edge of respectable society. His relentless rise to power and influence in the *ton* had been remarked on frequently, and his background which was shrouded in uncertainty was also whispered about.

Is he your slice of wickedness, Ophelia?

The slight shift of the man's head, a cant in her direction implied he knew they were no longer alone. Maryann stepped back from the room, closing the door. Yet her feet did not move, and she admitted it was with worry for her friend. Anything to do with a man of Devlin Byrne's ill-shrouded reputation could not be good.

She bit into her lower lip, torn between wanting to protect her friend and also celebrating whatever wickedness she was enjoying for herself. Ophelia had recently turned four and twenty, the oldest amongst their sinful wallflowers group, and for the last year or more there had lingered a shadow of pain and doubt in her eyes, something that bespoke of a private agony she had not shared with her friends.

Accepting this must be what her friend wanted, she slowly released the knob.

"Maryann?"

That shocked tone arrested her retreat and had her sharply turning around. It was Crispin.

"What are you doing *here*?"

She could think of no possible reply.

Her brother wiped his hand over his face slowly, shook his head, and stared at her unblinking.

"How did you recognize me?"

"Is that what you are concerned about?"

"Yes," she said mildly.

"You are my sister—how could I not recognize you?" he said furiously.

Crispin grabbed her hand and drew her away with rapid strides. Not wanting to cause a scene, Maryann followed him out the side doors and into the garden. They passed a few couples whose actions caused her to blush, to a small private alcove.

"How are you here?" he demanded. "I…I just cannot credit it."

"I am here with Lord Rothbury," she said honestly.

Her brother's mouth hung open. "You have irrevocably lost all sense of yourself. I cannot even think of the scandal. That bloody bounder—"

"Do not be ridiculous, Crispin," she snapped, tugging her arm from his clasp. "What scandal? I am in disguise. There is no need to worry about it."

"You reckless hoyden with no sense of—"

The soft sound of footfall crunching on leaves sounded, and they looked up to see the marquess, standing in the shadow of the gardens. He had been deliberate in alerting them to his presence.

She moved toward him, only to falter upon realizing he stared past her.

"What is it that you wear?" Nicolas murmured, his tone a purr of lethal menace.

Maryann glanced back at her brother, her gaze falling on his cravat pin.

"Oh," she said, "it is a cravat pin from our grandmother. I have the brooch to match it. They were made by a most famous London jeweler in the shape of a…"

As her heartbeat slammed deafeningly in her ears, she faltered into complete stillness. They had been done in the shape of the dahlia flower, and in the center of each jewelry was a black onyx stone.

The black Dahlia. She shook her head sharply, a place in her shattering. "Crispin?" she asked with a voice that shook.

He stumbled back and she understood; the sheer menace in Nicolas's expression was frightening.

"Are you familiar with a certain inn at Wiltshire ten years ago, and a girl who drowned?"

Her brother paled, and Maryann pressed a hand over her mouth. She whirled to face Nicolas. "There must be an explanation," she began. "Please—"

Crispin rushed past them, all but running back inside the gambling den. Nicolas whirled to follow, but she grabbed the sleeves of his jacket. "Nicolas, please, let me talk to him first."

His eyes were so chilled, she felt frightened.

"No."

"The cravat pin is not proof of his guilt!"

"Then I will ascertain it, *tonight*. Because I must know what it will mean for us."

"What it will mean for you?" she demanded shakily. "It does not have to mean anything."

His expression closed, and he peered down at her as if she were the oddest creature. She recalled then his certainty they would be enemies should her brother prove to be the black Dahlia.

"Nicolas…I…"

With an air of dark resolution about him, he pulled away from her, and she stood there, her heart a beating mess, before springing into motion and rushing after him.

CHAPTER TWENTY-ONE

She rushed through the throng in time to see Nicolas drag her brother by the back of his neck, down a darkened hallway. Crispin was trying to loosen his cravat as Nicolas's grasp was choking him. *Dear God!* The crush in the ballroom slowed her movements and it felt like it took forever to reach the passageway down which they had disappeared. Gathering the skirts of her gown, she ran down the hallway before coming to a shuddering halt.

"I told you all that you asked," her brother said shakily. "Please remove your blade from my throat."

"Please, Nicolas, please!" Maryann cried, rushing up to where he held her brother against the wall with a knife at his throat. "Why do you threaten him so?"

"It was the most effective way to loosen his tongue," Nicolas said menacingly. "Leave, now."

She gripped her gloved hands before her to prevent them from shaking. "No! You are in a dangerous mood; I will not leave!"

There was a speck of blood on the corner of her brother's mouth and his jaw appeared bruised.

"There must be an explanation, something we are missing," she said tremulously, a desperate uncertainty quaking through her heart.

A cruel curve slanted Nicolas's mouth. "He's already admitted that he was there."

Maryann's heart stopped. "No…I…what?"

Her brother had paled. "You involved my sister in your madness?" he demanded. "You damn—"

The knife sank deeper, and blood kissed the edge of the blade, stripping her brother of his verbal attack.

"You did not kill the others!" she cried, so frightened she wanted to crumple to the floor. She knew what Nicolas's retribution meant to him, and his vow that none would be spared was implacable and impenetrable. "He was only seventeen! A boy who was foolish and afraid," she said hoarsely.

"What are those who stand silent in the face of evil? How are they judged?"

His tone was a lash of rage when he asked the question.

"Answer me!"

"Guilty!" she cried, swiping at the tears which spilled over on her cheeks. "They are guilty."

"Do you wish me to treat him as I did the others?"

She pressed a hand over her mouth. "No."

Those other men had been ruined financially, stripped of the things they valued, divested of their pride, and their financial security to live their idle lives in luxury. He had broken them beyond redemption. Maryann's logical mind asserted that justice had been done for their heinous crime, but looking at the pale fright in her brother's eyes and knowing he had only been a lad almost felled her to her knees.

"He watched while she was violated, and he did *nothing*. He is just as *guilty*," Nicolas said.

"I am so damned sorry," Crispin said, tears leaking down his face, even though with speech, more blood flowed. "I have lived with that torment for years. I wished...I *wished* I had been brave enough to speak up then, to fight them off and damn the consequences. Not a day goes by that I've not thought of Miss Arianna and the pain she endured. I have tried to atone—"

"Nicolas!" Maryann screamed when the blade shifted. "Stop this right now, *please*!" When he did not respond she said, "You promised never had I to fear harm from you. Hurting him is harming me."

The very air itself became still at her desperate plea.

Nicolas stepped back from her brother and faced her. His eyes were shadowed with such agony, they almost broke her. He had warned her, but she had still gone ahead and fallen hopelessly in love with him. Yet here he stood, the enemy of her brother, and she had no notion how to fix it. Or even if she could.

"We can fix this," she said, aware of how much her mouth trembled.

Nicolas came over to her, and cupped her cheek, his thumb swiping at her tears. She closed her eyes, a trembling breath escaping her. "Maryann?"

Her lashes fluttered open. "Yes?"

"I will let him go."

Relief made her wilt into his embrace. Her lips parted, but the words of gratitude could not come. Even as his vow filled her with such profound relief, how could she accept it?

That admission cost Nicolas—his pride and his honor.

"Nicolas?"

"For you…" He closed his eyes, a shudder worked through his frame. "For you I shall let him off."

When he looked down at her, the chilling distance in his gaze shattered something deep inside her. "No," she whispered. "Nicolas, *no*! We can—"

Still cupping her cheeks, he tugged her face closer to him, their mouths mere inches apart.

"I cannot bear the idea of these eyes looking at me

with hatred, pain, and regret of ever knowing me. Do you understand?"

"Nothing could ever induce me to hate you," she cried softly. "I know what you are thinking, Nicolas, and I promise it does not have to—"

He pressed a kiss of violent tenderness against her forehead, then murmured against her flesh, "I never want to see you again."

Maryann simply froze, yet she was aware of nothing but him. The beat of his heart against her chest, his masculine scent, the tender way he framed her face, the regret felt in his touch, and the absolute promise heard in his voice.

She stepped away from him, forcing him to lower his hands. "You cannot mean it."

He angled his sleek dark head to one side and studied her with unflinching intensity. "*Never*, do you understand me? For you shall be a reminder of how much of a coward I am."

The words were a brutal strike to her heart.

"You are not a coward," she said softly, afraid that she might shatter at any moment.

"Then what am I if not a coward? I am willing to give up my honor, my vow, my pride, I am forsaking justice that is denied to her because I cannot bear the idea of hurting you."

That he had placed her before his honor and pride was an unforgivable sin for a man who already lived with the guilt of failure. Now he would have failed Miss Arianna twice. "He does not have to escape justice. He can still be punished."

"How?"

Her throat tightened.

"Should I remove his eyes, letting him live with the

pain of no sight for the rest of his life? A fit punishment that he should watch and not even run for help?"

She recoiled at the brutality of that statement.

"Or should I ruin his finances and any possibility of solvency for his future? Or should I see him sold to a press gang or exiled from his family and sent abroad without connections or money? Should I destroy his reputation, so he is not accepted by anyone in the *ton* and all his friends turn their backs on him? What punishment can I give that will not see you hurt and us enemies?"

The resolve she stared at was frightening. The awareness of how much he must have loved Arianna drove the air from Maryann's lungs. Because she saw no compromise in him that Crispin could be punished yet they still could have a future. And she had nothing to offer that might prove otherwise.

Maryann gripped his jacket, her entire body shaking. Unable to stop the sob that rose in her throat, she started crying. Pressing her forehead to his chest and gripping the lapel of his jacket as if it were a lifeline, she cried at the loss tearing through her. "I do not want to choose," she said, her shoulders shaking.

"I am not asking you to," he murmured, his chin resting on the crown of her head.

She lifted her chin and stared into his eyes.

"I choose *you*," she whispered, even knowing what it would cost. Her heart broke and more tears came. Whichever way she leaned, pain was waiting on the other side, and she could not bear the agony.

Shrewd, assessing eyes bored into Maryann. "I would never ask you to make such a choice. I've let him off. Let that be enough." He dipped his mouth to her ear. "Should there be any consequences to my damn foolishness, you will let me know immediately."

It took her precious seconds to understand, and her hands involuntarily settled on her stomach. *Dear God*. She had been so certain of every emotion brewing between them that she hadn't even thought to worry when they made love.

"And if there are consequences?"

"Our child will have the protection of my name and love."

"But I'll have nothing," she said, an aching knot in her throat, understanding his intentions. If necessary, they would marry, but only for the sake of their child and her reputation, but she must have no expectations of anything else—certainly not his love or respect.

Without glancing at Crispin, he said, "I leave your sister in your care; see her home safely and discreetly."

Then he stepped back from her, turned on his heels, and walked away.

Maryann stood there, silent tears coursing down her cheeks. She would never see him smile again, touch him, or kiss him. She had never told him about the emotions he stirred in her heart.

She ran after him; he sensed her and slowed his steps. Upon reaching him, she hugged him from behind, pressing her face into his back. She squeezed tightly. "I love you," she whispered.

He heard, for he went remarkably still.

"I think I fell in love with you even when I thought you were an unredeemable rake. Then I got to know the man you are…and I admire you most ardently. I love you, Nicolas…and…and I suspect you hold me in your sincere affections as well. Please do not walk away. If we have the same feelings for each other, we *must* find a way to work it out."

There was so much more she wanted to say, but the hopes beating against her chest warned her to tread carefully. His contemplative silence hurt. She squeezed him even tighter. "My heart is laid upon the ground. Please do not step on it," she whispered achingly.

He gripped her hands encircling his waist and pried them away. A part of her expected him to turn then and give her an answer, and she tried to brace her heart for his rejection.

But Nicolas did neither. He simply continued walking away and toward the exit of the gambling den.

The degree of her loss was incalculable. In him she had found the man she loved and respected. A man she could see herself growing old with, a man she saw walking by her side for as long as God would allow it, in this life and the next. She stood watching him, hands hugged around her middle, her heart a shredded mess until he disappeared from sight.

"If the marquess loves you as you clearly love him, he would not have walked away," a soft voice said behind her.

Turning around, she stared at her brother. She could not reconcile that the boy she loved so much growing up, the man she admired now, was guilty of the crime he was accused. Maryann had been so sure of his inherent goodness. "You lied to me."

He grimaced. "I can explain."

"Would it excuse that you did?"

They stared at each other. "You watched as your friends reduced a young girl to such pain, she took her life. If that girl had been me…you would have fought them tooth and nail to save me even at the peril to your own life."

His jaw visibly clenched. "*You* are my sister."

She flinched.

She was an ant to them, and perhaps that was giving her too much significance.

He took a tentative step toward her. "There may be a way to fix this so that…so that you and he might work."

Her sigh left her on a shaky breath. "The marquess is not a man to go back on his word." *Except just now.* Oh God, because of her he had betrayed everything that shaped him to become the person he was today. Tears pooled once more, and she furiously swiped them away.

Her brother looked off in the distance. He was nervous it seemed, and more than a little worried.

"Crispin, what is it?"

He grimaced. "She is not dead."

"Who…" Her voice came as a hoarse croak. "Who is not dead?"

"*Her.*" He closed his eyes as if pained. "I never suspected anyone would be looking for her."

Maryann's heartbeat was an awful roar in her head. "Crispin!"

He lifted a blurry gaze to her, touching the nick at his throat which came away with blood. He swayed, the import of what had just happened hitting him hard. "Arianna…she did not drown. I did not leave when they did, for I was disgusted with them *and* myself. That day shattered the bonds of friendship I had been so certain of. I wanted to help her, though I was not sure how to. We had all been drinking and carousing, but it was no excuse! I was so damn afraid they would turn on me, I just froze, Maryann."

Profound shame coated his voice, and he could not meet her regard. "I watched when she left and gave a lad a letter, then made her way to the river. I followed her and when she jumped, I dived in behind her. I saved her and took her away from there."

Something inside of Maryann shattered. "Arianna is *alive*?"

"Yes."

"We must tell Nicolas right away!" she cried, pressing a hand to her chest.

"Wait…I gave her my promise I would never betray her location or her new identity. I betrayed her once; I *cannot* do it again."

"Even from him?" she cried, anger brewing in her heart. "The man who has been tirelessly waging a campaign of retribution in her name?"

"Miss Arianna does not know that!" Crispin swallowed. "Let me take you to her…and then you can make a decision from there."

"Tonight," she said, "we go to her tonight. We have not a moment to lose."

Crispin nodded, and soon after they were in his carriage traveling south. A myriad of conflicting emotions and thoughts darted through Maryann, the predominant being a chilling shock.

"Once he sees that she lives, he might forgive my inaction and understand me a bit better," Crispin said, his eyes dark with guilt and another emotion she could not identify. "It will also give you and the marquess a chance—"

"There is no chance for us," she said, lowering the carriage curtains to stare at him. "Once he knows Miss Arianna is alive, there is no chance for us." And she desperately wanted to curl into a ball and weep.

"He loves her," Crispin said flatly.

"Yes, very much."

It was his turn to shift the curtain and peer through the windows.

A shock of realization went through her. "Do *you* love her, Crispin?"

"That does not matter."

"Why not?"

"Because she is still in love with him, even after not seeing him for ten long years."

Maryann could not speak, and she had to squeeze her fingers to prevent their trembling.

"You do not have to tell him," he said quietly.

She snapped her head up, aghast. "Surely I heard wrong."

"If you tell him, you will lose him with absolute certainty. He will want to be with her, and she will want to be with him."

Maryann had arrived at the same conclusion, but now stared at her brother, wondering who this selfish creature before her was. "I would never hurt him in such a manner. If he chooses to be with me, it must be because he is just as hopelessly in love with me, not because I hid his other choice."

Her brother gave her a pitying glance, and she gripped the edge of the seat, fighting with the useless hope lingering inside. Nicolas had walked away just now with a vow to never see her again. At their next encounter she might reunite him with a girl he had truly loved and grieved…a woman who now seemed to love him still.

There is no us nor will there ever be.

Closing her eyes, she leaned her head against the squabs, hating that silent tears coursed down her cheeks and that the pain in her heart grew with every *clip-clop* of the horses as the carriage took them closer to Nicolas's beloved.

• • •

A few hours of silence lingered in the carriage. They did not speak again until the carriage had arrived at their destination. The coach swayed over a rough patch of the ground, and the moonlight peeking through the parted carriage windows revealed Crispin wore an expression of anxiety.

"We've arrived," he said tightly.

The carriage came to a shuddering halt and the steps were knocked down. He quickly descended and aided Maryann in her descent. A charming, picturesque house rose before her, the many lit rooms appearing warm and inviting from the outside. "She lives here, alone?"

He hesitated for a moment. "Yes, with her daughter."

Maryann glanced at him, understanding his sudden discomfort. "Do you think so little of my character, that I would judge her for it? Is that why you never told me even as I grew older?"

He sighed and gruffly admitted, "I knew better, but the entire situation was just unexpected. I bought it some years ago and she made it her home. At first, she did not want it, thinking it too grand and far above her station. I told her the child she carried deserved to be cherished, and she relented."

"It is lovely," she said, faintly surprised. Maryann wasn't sure what she had expected when she set out with her brother. "Do you have a mistress?"

His head swiveled around. "What? No."

So, this was the home Nicolas's investigators had uncovered. The cruel irony pushed a jagged laugh from her throat. It would have only been information on paper; if he had just seen who actually lived here, possibly Maryann might not have known him at all.

They hurried up the front door, and before he knocked, the door was opened by a butler.

"Welcome back, Lord Crispin," he said, reaching out to take their coats, hats, and bonnets.

A lump grew in Maryann's throat. Her brother seemed to enjoy another life of which she was completely ignorant. He walked with confidence down the long hallway and opened the first door which led into a large and tastefully decorated parlor. A lady who had been reading from a book and laughing with a child lifted her eyes. Joy lit in her expression and she hurriedly stood.

"Crispin! You are back so soon, I—"

Her words faltered when she noticed Maryann.

The little girl who had been curled into her side sprang to her feet and hurtled herself at Crispin.

"Uncle Crispin!" she greeted with a huge smile, hugging him. "You're back so soon!"

He ruffled her dark blond hair. "How are you doing, poppet, feeling better?"

Poppet.

Maryann's heart started a slow, painful thud.

The lady had not taken her gaze from Maryann, and she in turn couldn't help noticing how astonishingly beautiful she was.

"Arianna," Crispin said with palpable effort, "this is my sister, Maryann. Something has happened, and we must converse immediately."

Arianna strolled to her, a cautious smile on her face, and dipped into a curtsy. "Lady Maryann, what a pleasant surprise but such an honor to meet you. I have heard many wonderful things about you."

Maryann smiled. "I have heard a lot about you as well, Miss Arianna, it is a pleasure." Yet her heart bled.

Arianna appeared at bit bemused, but she smiled, a happiness glowing in her eyes.

The little girl who appeared about nine years of age was reluctantly ushered off to bed, and Miss Arianna called for tea and some cakes. She sat on a long sofa and Crispin lowered himself beside her and gently held her hand in his.

Maryann noted the intimacy and the blush that pinkened Miss Arianna's cheeks. The awareness was mutual, yet Maryann took no comfort in that knowledge.

"Please, tell me what is wrong," Miss Arianna said. "My heart has been so anxious since you arrived. I had no expectations to see you before next week, Crispin."

He looked away as if he did not know where to start.

Maryann set her plate with small cakes on the walnut table and delicately cleared her throat. "There is a man…Lord Nicolas St. Ives…"

Miss Arianna gasped, pulling her hands from Crispin and folding them in her lap.

"Yes?" she asked tremulously at Maryann's pause.

"He believes you to be dead…and…and for the last several years has been bringing the men who hurt you to justice. They have all been made to pay as he took the life from them they value so much. That you are alive does not underscore the justice he dealt to these men. Their monstrous attack alone would have warranted it. I believe…I believe it is particularly important that Nic…Lord Rothbury be made aware that you are alive, Miss Arianna."

She paled and tears sprang to her eyes. "Oh God!" A hand was pressed over her mouth and for endless minutes she closed her eyes. A determined tear leaked from beneath her lowered lashes. "He got my letter."

"He did," Maryann said softly.

Miss Arianna appeared anxious as she demanded, "Please tell me everything."

Maryann relayed all she knew succinctly. Miss Arianna noisily sobbed and Crispin looked on help-lessly.

"He found them from the letter I left?"

"Yes."

"I did not know he cared," she whispered, raw with emotion. "I believed him cold and uncaring, his only concern his status and reputation."

"Is that why you allowed him to believe you had died?"

Crispin sent her a cautioning glance and she took a deep breath.

"He loved you...*loves* you," she said with a throat that ached. "He grieved for you, and he allowed such hatred in his heart so he could ruin the men who hurt you. His path led him to Crispin, for he was the black Dahlia."

Arianna covered her face, her shoulders shaking controllably. Several minutes passed before she lifted her head, taking the handkerchief Crispin held out and dabbing her cheek. "They...those men...I put them behind me years ago. They no longer haunt me, and from my pain I even gained my most precious gift. My child and a friendship in which I trust and treasure. I never imagined my Nicolas would have hurt so."

My Nicolas. Maryann wanted to howl her grief and pain.

"They led me to believe he did not care, that he knew what they planned, and I...I naively believed what they said. I thought him greatly indifferent. Even at such an age, I understood girls of my background only served as mistresses and Cyprians for gentlemen...and when I was reminded of that, I believed it."

Maryann stiffened. "Nicolas is the eagle?"

The eagle soars indifferent while the wolf betrays the dove.

"Yes, he is," she whispered, closing her eyes against the memory. "When I tried to use his name and position to scare them, my bravado was met with such taunting laughs. I was so silly."

As if he could wait no more, Crispin wrapped his arms around her shoulder. "I was there, and I believed it, too. Please do not be so hard on yourself, Arianna."

She looked at him with wide, wounded eyes. "Will he forgive me for doubting me?"

Crispin fell silent, but Maryann stood. "He will. The marquess will be overjoyed that you are alive and well. You must return with us to town immediately. There can be no delay in informing him of the news."

Arianna stood. "Please remain here as my guest for the night, and then tomorrow we could go to see him."

How excited and scared she seemed.

"I accept your offer and thank you. I would that a letter be sent to our parents immediately. Do you have a footman it could be entrusted with?"

Miss Arianna's hand fluttered to her throat. "I...I do not wish to see him alone," she said, looking embarrassed. "I do not have the courage to face him and...and..."

"I will go with you," Maryann said, wondering how she would bear to witness their loving reunion.

"How will we…will we call upon his house? Will he be there? Is it…is it better that we meet at a public place?"

Her nervousness was heartbreaking.

"He would never hurt you," Maryann gently assured her.

"He might shout," Arianna said, folding her arms at her front in a protective gesture. "It is unlikely if we are in public he will shout or be too disappointed in my conduct."

"He would find nothing to reproach in your behavior. Lord Rothbury will only be exceedingly glad that you are alive. That you survived a horror that many would not."

Arianna searched her face. "You know him well?"

"We are friends of a sort." *And lovers…and the man I love with every emotion in my heart.*

Relief lit in her expression, and Crispin looked away.

"I am certain he will be at a particular ball tomorrow," Maryann offered. "I have an invitation. We could all go. And once there, we send him a note to meet in the gardens. Will that do?"

"Yes," Arianna said with a warm, relieved smile. "Thank you, Lady Maryann."

Soon she was shown to a tastefully furnished room with an adjoining bath chamber. Arianna had assured her it was not too late for the servants to heat water for a bath, and Maryann had taken a long soak, where she had wept.

Now she lay in the large, comfortable bed in the dark, staring at the unadorned ceiling. What would he do when he found out Arianna lived? Marry her immediately or publicly woo her first and then make an offer? The agony of the thought was unbearable, but how could she begrudge him such a happiness?

If he had wanted Maryann, he would have stayed… and allowed them to try to find their path to happiness despite everything.

My heart is laid upon the ground. Please do not step on it.

The memory of her plea had mortification and pain clawing at her heart in equal measure. "He walked away," she whispered in the darkened room. "And I, too, need to walk away from all the hopes I've had about him."

Memories of his tongue against her, his hands pleasuring, the feel of his body deep within her, the evocative blend of pleasure and pain. Maryann could not regret living with such wanton freedom, and years from now she would not regret that she loved him with every emotion in her heart. If only the pain of it all didn't make her struggle to breathe. Inhaling deeply, she attempted to quiet her mind.

Simply put, she needed to stop loving Nicolas St. Ives.

CHAPTER TWENTY-TWO

Nicolas stood on the wide-open terrace of the Dowager Countess of Marsh's home, smoking a cheroot, the noise of the ball, the *clink* of champagne glasses, the facile laughter and chatter a distant hum in the background. He had not slept since he hovered in the shadows outside of the Asylum and watched as Maryann and Crispin entered their carriage and rumbled away. It had been almost a full day, his eyes were gritty, his jawline shadowed by an overnight beard, and his stomach unable to withstand even the simplest of food. A hollowness had blossomed through him the second the words parting them forever had left his mouth, and it had spread and settled into his bones.

He had hurt her.

My heart is laid upon the ground.

The words were stuck in Nicolas's chest like sharpened barbs and with every breath he took, they dug deeper, ripping into his belief that he could exist without her. *Fucking hell*. The raw ache that had throbbed in her voice haunted him. They existed in the same society, and he would only be able to watch that laugh on her mouth from a distance. He'd have to imagine how it would sound, dream of how she would taste, hunger for her beside him.

Nicolas dragged deep of his cheroot. He had let Crispin go. Bloody hell. Nicolas was a man like his father, without honor.

He was just a lad of seventeen.

Nicolas tried to accept that reasoning to pardon her

brother, to excuse the dishonor of not fulfilling a promise and his weakness in letting him go. But they had all been lads of eighteen or nineteen, young men on the cusp of manhood, and he had not forgiven any of the others. So how could he ignore the sins of her brother?

The memory of her wide, pleading eyes, and the fear which lingered because she understood his ruthlessness in exacting his retribution drove the air from his lungs. For her sake, he was glad he was able to walk away. For their sake…perhaps he would forever be tormented by his choice. Or perhaps there had been enough justice for Arianna.

Nicolas looked up to the star-studded sky. "If there has been enough, why am I here?"

A presence moved up beside him, holding out a glass of brandy which Nicolas took but did not drink.

The wolf…

That anguish he had buried for so long rushed to the surface and with a silent snarl, he swallowed it down. His best friend. No…his and Arianna's best friend. And the great betrayer.

"So this is where you've escaped to," David said, glancing over his shoulder into the ballroom. "Mother has been haranguing me to dance with Lady Cecily because she is perfect for me. God save us from feverish matchmaking mothers."

At Nicolas's lack of jovial or sarcastic response, David arched a brow. "Who killed your dog?"

His friend slapped him on his shoulder. "Come, man, what do you contemplate with such insouciance?"

"The things I cannot live without," he murmured, taking a sip of the drink.

"And what are those?" David asked with an arch of

his brow. "And why must they bear such weight of contemplation tonight?"

The things he could not live without—a particularly stunning smile with a dimple, a low husky laugh, a wit that skewered, a shrewd and intelligent mind, a lush body, and a sensuality that was breathtaking. His Maryann.

Something disturbingly akin to grief flashed, freezing everything inside Nicolas. It was impossible to envision a future without her in it. Simply impossible.

The loss he felt at the idea was so profound, the hand gripping the glass shook, sloshing the brandy over the side. With a muttered curse, he knocked back the drink in a long, burning swallow.

He would go to her after this. Another night must not pass with her thinking he did not love her, that he did not want her more than anything else in this world.

And as for Crispin…

That knife-like pain stabbed through Nicolas again. He had already sacrificed his honor. What more did he have to give?

And that was it, he was willing to give anything for her, even if he himself did not understand the lengths he had to traverse to achieve this state. Was it that he had to learn the complex nature of forgiveness?

He recalled saying to his father, with such hatred in his heart, "*An eye for an eye, a tooth for a tooth, pain for pain, and hatred for hatred.*"

"*And what about forgiveness?*" his father had demanded gruffly.

And Nicolas had laughed in disbelief, and demanded, "*If some minor or those poor fools suffering in London had attacked a lady of quality, would you dare to talk about forgiveness or immediately have them hanged?"*

Nicolas had never allowed forgiveness to enter his thoughts; even now something in him recoiled from the notion. Yet he had not made any allowance for their youth, simply knowing it to be a reprehensible crime that deserved punishment whether they had been young gentlemen or old men, poor men or rich men.

And he had not allowed that Crispin would be inculpable. He had held the black Dahlia in his heart with the same burning rage as the others. Nicolas had not allowed that his crime was less, and perhaps there was no dishonor in learning to forgive him. To now relinquish his anger against Crispin would not be easy, but Nicolas was willing to sacrifice anything.

For her sake. For his sake. And for theirs.

For so long, nothing else but his promise of retribution upon his honor and assuaging the guilt and rage in his heart had mattered. But then she fell into his life and he hadn't pushed her from it when he knew better.

Because with every touch, smile, and conversation she had brought such warmth, peace, pleasure, happiness to his cold existence. With her he felt things that were not guilt or hate; with her he hungered and craved a future he hadn't even dreamed could exist.

He was a damnable fool to risk such a precious treasure slipping from his grasp. Maryann was his future. It was time he laid the past to rest. And that meant there would be no long game with the wolf—the guiltiest of them all.

For Nicolas could not bear letting her wait weeks, months, years while he played the long game of merciless ruination. And not only because she deserved all happiness, but because he knew his Maryann was fierce

and indomitable enough to eradicate him from her
heart and never look back.

"I must speak to you in private," Nicolas said.

"How perfectly ominous," David mocked, but there
was an unfathomable look in his eyes, and a fine tension had invaded his frame.

"In your study, perhaps?"

He waved for Nicolas to precede him inside.

They made their way inside the ballroom, and it was
as if he felt her gaze upon him. Nicolas's steps slowed,
and the advantage of his height allowed him to scan the
crowded room until he found her. Maryann stood still,
staring at him, her eyes wide and almost afraid. A quick
scan showed no immediate threat to her, and he had to
prevent himself from going to her. He would deal with
David first and then visit her after.

She glanced away from him, and it was clear she
struggled to regain her composure. Maryann wore a
fashionable dress of vibrant green silk, which accentuated her slight but curvy figure. Her hair was piled high
atop her head in intricate curls, and a single strand of
pearls encircled her throat. Their gazes collided, and
she pushed her glasses up to her nose.

She was nervous and so breathtakingly lovely.

He looked away and continued on his path which
led him to the hallway and to David's study. Once
there, he went over to the window overlooking the
gardens. Feeling suffocated, he wrenched the windows
open and breathed the crisp night air into his lungs.

Nicolas turned when David closed the door, ambled
over to his desk, and sat on the edge of the furniture,
folding his arms.

"What did you want to talk about?"

Nicolas thrust his hands in the pocket of his trousers

and stared at his friend. A man he had loved as his
brother for so many years.

"You are the wolf…"

David frowned. "What are you talking about?"

"I never shared with you the first line of Arianna's
letter. Nor a section of the end."

David stiffened, his expression drawing tight.

"*The eagle soars indifferent while the wolf betrays
the dove.* You always called her dove. With that very
first line I knew she referred to us, even as I found the
notion improbable," Nicolas said, "*The wolf…he was all
of them, cruel, brutal, unholy, and savage, yet he was
more, for in him once I found love.*"

David flinched and scrubbed a hand over his face.
"I… There is not a day that I do not grieve for Arianna."

"The reason she sat at that table was because *you*
were there."

"I was drunk," David said hoarsely.

Nicolas flinched. "Is that the distinction you've used
to justify your cruelty to a girl you loved?"

Remorse and something darker gleamed in David's
eyes. "Where do we go from here?"

"I am certain you know it."

A sneer curved his lips and his eyes narrowed. "Do
you think I will stand idly by and watch you destroy me
as you did the others?"

"Surely you knew this reckoning was coming…or
did you really believe me ignorant of your participation? You were the enemy, David, thus the perfect
place for you was by my side. Is that why you aided me
all this time, to stay close to keep abreast of what I
knew? No, my friend, you were there by design, and
with each of your friends taken down, you worried
more. You started to hide your unentailed wealth and

assets, things I didn't even know you owned. They are now under my control."

His former friend fisted his hands at his side and surged to his feet. "You must be mad if you think I will allow you to ruin me as you did the others!"

"Alas, I am no longer interested in playing the long game. You will allow me whatever I will, for you will not be let off," Nicolas said with chilling calmness.

A spasm of anguish raked across David's face. "Is it a duel you want?"

"Most assuredly," Nicolas said with lethal iciness. "We will meet in the fighting pits of the Asylum."

"I'll not win if we meet fist to fist," David said tightly. "You are known for your bareknuckle skills."

Nicolas smiled, and whatever David saw in his face, he blanched.

"Whether we meet with fists, rapiers, or pistols, you will not win. This will be a lesson…a punishment. I will leave you shamed, bloodied, broken, and it will not even be a fraction of what you deserve. When I am done, you will crawl from the pits on your belly like the snake you are; no one will help you, and it will take months abed to recover. That is your punishment—accept it with grace."

David's chest lifted on a harsh breath. "Who appointed you our judge?" he snapped furiously.

"Arianna's pain," Nicolas calmly said.

Before David could reply, there was a knock on the door, it opened, and Maryann stepped inside. His heart jolted. "What are you doing here?" Nicolas snapped, taking a step toward her. He did not want her around David at all.

She flushed, pain darkening her eyes. "We were going to send you a note but then I…I saw you come in here which is more private. I am dreadfully sorry for the intrusion, but there is someone here who wishes to speak with you, and it must not wait a second longer."

Behind her, Nicolas spied her brother hovering in the doorway. "Leave now. I will speak with you another time."

Instead of complying, the door opened wider, and a lady stepped inside the room.

"My God," David cried, stumbling back.

Nicolas stared, his gaze moving over her black hair artfully piled atop her head, the vividness of her green eyes which glistened with unshed tears, the way her mouth trembled as if overwrought with emotions, and the tears that finally spilled onto pale cheeks.

A roar sounded in his head and he blinked, but she did not vanish. "Arianna?" he demanded gruffly.

"Oh, Nicolas!" A harsh sob tore from her and she hurtled across the room to fling herself into his arms.

CHAPTER TWENTY-THREE

Maryann almost cried out at that look of torment and profound relief on Nicolas's face when he closed his hands around Arianna and returned her embrace. Maryann whirled away, hurrying down the hallway with such speed, it was as if she ran. It was impossible to stay and watch their reunion. The anguish tearing through her heart made her want to howl.

Unexpectedly, someone grabbed her hand and pulled her to a stop. She stumbled and with shock stared up at David. He must have dashed immediately after her. "Let me go," Maryann hissed, appalled at the man's gall.

"You are coming with me." He dragged her quite violently, and she gripped her fan and smacked him across the face.

He whirled around, and his hand lifted to slap her.

"Do you *dare*?" Nicolas's voice snapped through the hallway like an icy blast.

She glanced up, surprised to see him there. He must have left the room as soon as they did. He looked at her, and something unreadable touched his gaze for a fleeting moment.

Arianna spilled from the room, running toward them, her gaze only for Nicolas.

"Don't you come closer," David snarled, reaching into his pocket.

The cock of a pistol had Maryann's heart lurching.

"Let her go," Nicolas said, his eyes and tone calm and absolutely concentrated on his former friend.

Confusion rushed through Maryann. "What is going

on?" she demanded shakily.

David dragged her with such strength, she pitched forward, a pain wrenching up her arm. They spilled inside the crowded ballroom, and Maryann slapped him again with her fan, uncaring of the scandal it would cause. A murmur swept through the throng as they drew the attention of several people.

David pushed her away and lifted his weapon to point it beyond her shoulder. She whirled around to see Nicolas and Arianna entering the ballroom. The spectacle of a man with a gun pointed on another gentleman soon swept the area, and even the orchestra stopped playing. The crowd parted, backing to the walls and exits away from the men. At least one lady swooned to the floor, but she was ignored as those remaining stared fascinated.

Neither David nor Nicolas seemed to care they were the recipients of so many avid stares. Maryann carefully shifted away from David, wanting to be out of his range of madness.

"Do not move, Lady Maryann, or I will shoot you," he snapped.

She froze, her heart twisting. Nicolas stepped forward and David swung the gun at Arianna. The stillness that blanketed the room felt perilous.

"You may not believe this," David said shakily, his eyes wild. "But I am damn glad you are alive, Arianna. I was young and foolish...I had been drinking when I asked you to be my mistress and...I did not react well to your rejection. It has *haunted* me for years."

Arianna's hand fluttered to her chest, and a wounded look entered her eyes. "We were best friends," she said softly. "And you broke that bond of friendship and trust."

"I am damnably sorry!"

Nicolas's stance was coiled readiness, the coldness in his eyes one Maryann had never seen. She tried to discreetly glance around the room for anything that could be made use of as a weapon, but all she saw were ladies and gentlemen frozen in horror as they watched the tableau unfold. None thought to interfere or perhaps look for a weapon. The damn useless fools.

"You are not going to let me off, and I do not accept that," David snarled. "And I want to hurt you how you've hurt me, Nicolas. I am going to put a bullet in a place that you will never recover from."

Maryann faltered at the change that came over Nicolas. Gone was the mien of icy indifference, of cold rage. To her shock, she realized he appeared frightened. She wanted to reassure him she would not allow him to lose Arianna twice, but he was not looking at Maryann, but at David. Arianna was staring at Maryann, her eyes wide with shock and glistening with tears.

"I know she is the *most* important thing to you," David said snidely.

Maryann watched Nicolas swallow, shaking his head in a movement that was almost vulnerable. Then he looked at her, a pleading look of torment in his beautiful eyes. Confusion rushed through her, and she stepped haltingly toward him.

It was then she noted David had taken the pistol away from Arianna and pointed it dead center at Maryann's heart. Shock and confusion blasted through her in icy waves, and she gripped her fan until her palm burned.

"Do you think me a fool?" David murmured with malicious spite. "I know the most important person to your entire world is *her*—Lady Maryann Fitzwilliam.

And her loss will torment you, drive you mad with grief…it *will* kill you."

There was a ripple through the crowd, and Maryann saw her father stiffen, his eyes going wide before his expression shuttered. And her mother reached up to grab her husband's arm as if to steady herself against a blow. Crispin had paled, and a perilous hush had fallen over the ballroom as if they had just perceived the raw extent of the danger.

In two strides, David was before her, and he pressed the point of his gun directly against her stomach. Maryann felt faint as a bitter taste of fear coated her tongue. She swung her gaze to Nicolas, and her knees weakened at the raw agony on his face.

"Please, let her go; she has nothing to do with this. You can leave. I will not come after you. This I vow upon my life and honor," Nicolas said.

Fury flashed in David's eyes. "No," he snapped tightly. "You've been a right thorn in my side these last few years. We have been friends since we were toddlers, but that meant nothing to you because you still made steps to ruin me!"

I've made moves against the wolf.

Oh God. David was the wolf. And from the conversations she'd had with Nicolas, the Earl of Marsh was a good friend. This was the man Arianna had loved, and he had betrayed her.

"I stayed by your side helping you take down the men who hurt Arianna, hoping to redeem my honor, but you would not let me."

"You were the leader of those very men."

"I have been your friend for years, and I was hoping…" David's chest lifted on a ragged breath. "I was hoping that should you learn of my hand in everything, you would allow that our friendship was more important than what happened. But you ignored our bond of brotherhood as if it meant nothing to you. She is nothing but the daughter of servants and we… we have been friends since we were small. The best of friends! And you dare to place her before me? You dare to judge that one moment of mistake against a lifetime of friendship? A fleeting moment ten bloody years ago and you have the nerve to still hold it against me!"

With his free hand, David thumped his chest. "You damn well *hurt* me, and I am going to hurt you now by taking the single most important person in your life. Her loss will cripple you in such a manner, you'll never recover to chase after me, will you? And it will also soothe this hatred in my heart for you. You took my peace for years. I'll damn well take yours, too."

Maryann's hands shook. "You are wrong," she said shakily. "He…I am not the most important…"

Her voice died at the look of disbelief on David's face, and as if someone else controlled her, she turned and stared at Nicolas. It was then the pieces fell together in her mind, that he had been right on their heels in the hallway. He hadn't lingered with Arianna but must have pushed her aside immediately to chase after them…

To protect her.

And now Maryann could read everything in his face that was so normally shadowed and inscrutable—stark fear and so much love.

"Nicolas?" she sobbed, pressing a hand over her heart.

Still he did not look at her; all his attention, his readiness was pointed at David. But that man had a primed pistol pressed against her hips. There was no room for an attack.

"David," Nicolas said, "you are right. Lady Maryann is the lady most important to me."

Behind him, Arianna closed her eyes as if pained, but then she swallowed, opened her eyes, and squared her shoulders.

Nicolas took a step forward. "I love her. She is my everything."

A few people in the crowd gasped.

"My heart is laid upon the ground…and you have the power to stomp on it and cripple me," Nicolas said, his voice throbbing with undefinable emotions.

Maryann stared at him, her heart a shivering mess. He was declaring himself in such a way before everyone. And it was not for David's benefit. He wanted her to know beyond a doubt what she meant to him, and with a jolt of fear she realized he dreaded not saving her in time.

"David," Nicolas continued. "I want you to understand something."

The hand that stabbed the gun harder against her body trembled.

"You have one chance to do damage and escape. That is not achieved by harming Maryann. You turn that pistol to me and do the damage where it will have the most effect."

"No," she cried out, raw fear filling her.

David laughed. "The most damage will be with her. You will be broken."

"Yes," Nicolas said with icy promise. "And there is nowhere you can go to escape what I will do to you. Arianna was the girl I loved in my youth, and even then I loved her as a friend more than anything else.

And you see what I did to those who hurt her."

Nicolas took another step closer. "Lady Maryann is the woman I love with every fucking emotion in my soul. Can you comprehend, you fool, what I will do to you should you harm a hair on her head?"

More gasps and a ripple of whispering went through the crowd, but nothing distracted Nicolas's hawkish and remorseless regard from David.

Anguish cast her love's expression in a savage mien. "Can you imagine the hatred I will have for you should you take her from me? Do you imagine I would be content with hunting you to the ground? You threaten everything you hold dear, my good fool. Your mother…"

David paled, his eyes widening with disbelief.

Something dark and dangerous flashed in Nicolas's gaze. "Your three sisters. Your cousins. Your mistress. They will all stand *guilty* for your crime, and they will repay life with life."

The violent promise was like a solid blow to the center of her chest. A fierce swell of intangible emotion ripped through her and left her shaking. A loud thud sounded as someone fainted, and to Maryann's shock, a smile trembled on her mouth. In his eyes, she saw the absolute truth. She felt breathless *and* terrified as she stared at Nicolas.

"I love you," she said tenderly, her eyes wet with tears.

A tiny, almost indecipherable smile touched his mouth, but he never took his regard from David.

"Pointing the gun at me is your best option. Stopping me is your only choice. Harming her will be your irrevocable downfall. All I want is her by my side—you can simply walk away."

Silence throbbed in the room like a wound. And then in one smooth motion, David turned the gun on Nicolas and fired.

Two sharp retorts, echoing closely behind each other, filled the large ballroom.

Maryann's scream mixed with the others in the room. Red bloomed on Nicolas's pristine white shirt and she hurtled toward him as he stumbled to lean weakly against the wall.

Uncaring of who might be watching them, she pressed her hand to the wound high on his shoulder, trying to contain her fear. "Nicolas," she gasped, shaking. "Oh God, please!"

Hands pulled her away, and she glanced up to see her father. "Papa," she cried, hating that she felt so frightened. "What are you doing?"

"Go with him," Nicolas said.

And it was then she noticed Viscount Montrose was by his side. And the screams behind her were from Lord Marsh's sister. David had been shot, and himself lay on the floor bleeding.

Maryann glanced around to see Crispin discreetly taking a pistol from Arianna where she held it against the folds of her skirts. He took her hand and they slipped away in the chaotic noise rising in the ballroom.

"I am coming with you," she said to Nicolas. "And you cannot stop me."

"You will do no such thing," her father said tightly.

"Go with your father," Nicolas said, swaying, sweat beading his face. "Now, Maryann."

Her father bundled her away from the scene of the greatest scandal to possibly ever rock the *ton*.

• • •

A FEW HOURS LATER...

"That man is the most odious creature; whatever was Lord Rothbury thinking to declare himself to be in love so violently and so publicly!" the countess cried with excessive passion, wearing a hole in the plush carpet on the drawing room. "You are *ruined*."

Maryann stood by the window, still clothed in the gown she had worn to the ball. The dawn broke, and pale sunlight touched on the flowers in the gardens. She pressed her hands against the chilled windows, desperation worming in her heart.

Are you well, Nicolas? What if he had died and she was not by his side?

"That man was willing to die for our daughter," the earl said with soft contemplation. "I have never seen anything as courageous."

"I will not have my daughter marry that wretch, if that is what you are insinuating!"

"My dear," her father interposed, "I believe the violence and profound nature of his declaration suggest they might need to marry sooner than later. Such a love is not borne alone from walking in the park or reading poems to each other."

"Good God, Philip, whatever are you about?" her mother asked in shocked accents. "Marry sooner than later?" She sucked in a harsh breath. "You do not mean—"

Her words faltered as if she couldn't bear to utter the scandalous suggestion.

Maryann slowly turned around from the windows. "Mama, Papa," she said with a small smile. "I must leave. I cannot stay here a moment longer."

"Wherever are you going?" the countess demanded.

"To see for myself that Lord Rothbury lives."

Her mother swayed. "My dear child, after the exceedingly scandalous spectacle you created in the ballroom last night, screaming his name and sobbing and promising to love him forever? You intend to call upon him? Have you no consideration for your good name?"

Maryann blushed and lifted her chin. "I shall return home in a few hours. If it will relieve your worry, I do not intend to walk up to his home and knock. I will break in very discreetly."

Her mother glanced at the earl, who silently watched her.

"Whose child is she?" the countess cried. "Where are her parents? We did not birth this…this…" The words stuck in her throat, threatening to choke her. Her mother swooned quite dramatically, and her father caught her against his chest and bore her to the sofa, ringing the bell for smelling salts.

Maryann gripped the skirts of her gown and hurried from the drawing room. She spilled into the hallway and faltered. Nicolas stood there, looking very pale. Despite this, his tall frame was one of powerful, lithe elegance. His dark hair was perfectly groomed, and his beautiful golden eyes ensnared her.

How wonderfully alive and beautiful he looked.

Relief blossomed through her and a love so fierce her throat went tight, and tears sprang to her eyes. She rushed toward him as he swayed, slipping her hands around his waist and holding him to her. If he should fall, she would tumble with him to the floor, but Maryann felt as if she would never let him go again.

"Why are you here? You were shot only last night," she said softly, brushing her finger over his jaw. He did not object to her tender ministration but leaned even farther into her touch. "I was coming to you, Nicolas."

"I had to come to you…to let you know I love you. You *must* know."

Alarm and joy suffused her in equal measure. "Are you dying?"

"No. I didn't want you to linger in any doubt even for a moment about how much you mean to me. I love you, Maryann."

"I know you do," she said achingly. "I love you, Nicolas, with my entire heart."

He cupped her cheeks between his large hands, bent his head, and crushed her mouth beneath his own.

"Marry me," he said against her mouth.

"Yes."

"Tomorrow."

She laughed. "I want a large wedding. We are the most scandalous couple of the *ton*. I will not disappoint their thirst for a grand spectacle, and our wedding will be the grandest."

"Ah, I suspect this has been your dream? A large wedding?"

"I have always hungered for a family of my own," she said softly. "A husband who will not cage me but love me completely. And you do, Nicolas, you do. But I think I just might be happier eloping with you."

He smiled and took her mouth in a kiss of possessive tenderness.

A throat cleared loudly, and Maryann pulled her lips from his, blushing. It was her father. Nicolas did not release her from his embrace but rested his chin atop her head.

"I believe you called, Lord Rothbury, to make a formal offer for my daughter's hand?"

Nicolas cleared his throat. "That I did."

"Offer accepted," the earl said, and then went back into the drawing room to his wife.

"Sneak me into your room," he suggested.

Maryann giggled against Nicolas's chest, happiness bursting inside her heart. "It astonishes me you think you will ever be able to enter my room again before marriage," she said with a laugh, leading him to the smaller parlor. "I am calling for our physician."

"No need. I was tended to well."

They entered the smaller parlor and went over to the large armchair by the open windows. He lowered himself onto the cushions and tugged her into his lap. She peeled back his jacket slightly and stared at his padded shoulder.

"You promise the doctor's report was good?"

His head dipped in a slight nod. Maryann slipped her hand around his nape and rested her forehead against his.

"Arianna is alive," she whispered. "I am so very glad she is."

"I gather Crispin saved her and protected her these last few years. I have not spoken to her as yet, but I am also extremely glad she lives," he said gruffly.

Maryann smiled, understanding his world had narrowed to her. He had only pushed from his bed to reassure her. Piercing emotions tore through her with the power of the fiercest storm. "Is David alive?"

"Yes. I suspect he will be leaving England soon. I will ensure that there are no legal consequences against Arianna for shooting him."

He butted against her, and she lifted her forehead from his. Nicolas cupped her cheek, his thumb brushing over her mouth. His soft caress, so light it was scarcely a breath of sensation, pierced her heart sweetly.

"Forgive me for hurting you with my careless words," he said, pressing a kiss to her mouth. His mouth gently moved over her cheek and to her hair.

"I understand your heart, and I know why you walked away."

"I want you to know that I had planned to sneak into your chambers last night, fall to my knees, and beg you to forgive my foolishness."

Maryann smiled, a lump forming in her throat. "All is forgiven."

Then he kissed her, and she sank into his embrace, knowing how irrevocably cherished she was.

EPILOGUE

Two weeks later...

Maryann grinned as Lydia lifted her rapier in salute and assumed the en garde position.

"Remember now," Maryann said, "slow and easy."

Lydia nodded, a glint of pleasure in her golden gaze, which reminded Maryann so much of Nicolas's eyes.

Maryann had been teaching Nicolas's twin sisters to fence for only three days. She had asked Nicolas's permission to secure a fencing tutor for them, which he had agreed to after speaking with his mother. The dowager marchioness had relented, but with the condition that they started in the next summer.

The girls had been disappointed but had rallied at Maryann's suggestion to teach them what she knew until their tutor arrived.

"Nicolas!" Louisa, who had been reposing on a lawn chair, awaiting her turn, shouted.

Maryann's heart lurched. She lowered her rapier and turned to see her love strolling across the lawn.

"We should stop our brother from seeing Maryann during this hour allocated to us," Lydia grumbled, putting down her sword and lowering herself to the large blanket. "They are going to make silly eyes at each other."

"Don't forget the kisses," Louisa said, laughing.

Maryann flushed but was grinning. To think they were so scandalized by those chaste kisses Nicolas seemed unable to stop himself from brushing across her mouth. He touched her at every opportunity, kissed her at least ten times each day.

Or more.

And every night…

Her skin heated at the mere thought of the wicked ways he turned her boneless with pleasure when they retired to bed. This morning had been the first he'd scandalized her senses by taking her in the library against the door. She had been so sure the household would hear her wild cries, but when they'd peeked outside in the hallway, there had been no servants.

The memory of how her beloved husband had made love to her again on the chaise had her smiling wider.

"Whatever are you thinking, Maryann?" Lydia asked.

"Practice the moves I taught you together. I will be back shortly."

"Do tell Nicolas to stay away," Louisa said. "And remember that we are going riding together soon."

Maryann strolled toward him, loving how carefree and unrestrained he appeared. Since that night, when their scandal had rocked the *ton*, she hadn't seen any more shadows in his eyes. Only burning love and such contentment.

They had married only last week by special license in the family chapel at his principal estate. Their ceremony had been well attended by their friends and families, and many of the newspapers had bemoaned that the most scandalous couple of the season had not held a grand wedding at Hanover Square.

She reached him, and he tugged her into his embrace, kissing her lightly.

"The girls do not like you distracting me from their

lessons," she chided.

Nicolas chuckled. "I've made arrangements for us to start our honeymoon next week. It will only be for three weeks, since we have to return in time for Christmas."

"Where are we going?"

His gaze gleamed. "That is a surprise. But you will enjoy every moment, I promise. There might even be some riding astride. I've already instructed your dresser to procure riding trousers and shirts in your size."

Maryann laughed and tossed her hands around his neck, kissing him a bit too enthusiastically, if the girls' overly loud and dramatic shouts were anything to go by. With a breathless laugh, she stepped back.

"This came for you," he said.

She plucked the letter from him and quickly pried it open, scanning the contents. "It is from Crispin!"

"Is all well?"

Maryann lowered the paper. "He married Arianna in a secret ceremony. Mama and Papa are not pleased with the match. I shall write to him right away and let him know he has our support."

A soft smile curved Nicolas's mouth. "She loves him truly. They will be an excellent match."

Maryann admired Arianna's strength and the love she owned for Crispin. "I am glad; I could tell he was in love with her and despairing she might not return his affections."

She folded the letter and slipped it into her pocket. "Will you join me for the rest of the lesson with the girls?"

He nodded, and they walked toward his sisters.

• • •

"No!" Lydia cried, scandalized. "My brother climbed into your chamber, and you and he had a duel?"

Louisa sent Maryann an admiring glance. "Did you trounce him?"

His marchioness laughed, the warm, sweet sound logging into his heart.

"It was more of a draw."

He arched his brow and sent her a meaningful stare. She blushed prettily, turning back to his sisters, regaling them with the tale of how they met. Nicolas hadn't dreamed that such happiness could await him in life. He hadn't dared to think his heart could have been this full, and not with guilt or need for retribution. Those emotions had vanished the night David threatened Maryann's life. Even though Nicolas loved her and wanted her for his wife, it was in that moment he had known that life without her would be impossible.

He hadn't known he could love like this…laugh like this…or that anyone would look at him the way Maryann did.

The laughter of the most important ladies in his life swirled around him, the images of them dancing and parrying with swords in dresses forever entrenched in his heart. He'd vowed to his love that she would have the best life with him. That he would never cage her and that he would love her forever. For their honeymoon, he planned to take her to Devon, a stay at Torquay, and then a trip to the Isle of Wight from Southampton. By later that night, she would manage to get the full details of the trip out of him, no doubt. Nicolas was anticipating her delightful methods to obtain the information, and so he missed whatever caused Maryann to chuckle so happily, bending over to catch her breath. Lydia was also laughing, and Louisa was grinning sheepishly.

Maryann caught his gaze and mouthed, *I love you*.

It almost shocked Nicolas to feel the raw ache in his throat. Knowing it would scandalize his sisters, he went over to his wife, swept her into his arms, and walked toward the gazebo in the distance.

"Nicolas!" the girls cried.

Maryann gasped. "You plan to debauch me."

"More like to sit with you in my arms just for a few minutes."

Her gaze softened. "I know… There are times I, too, cannot believe it is real, and I just want to hold you. Feel that you are real."

He paused, and she slipped her hands around his neck, peering into his eyes.

"I love you," he said gruffly.

She smiled and fitted her mouth perfectly to his.

The End

ACKNOWLEDGMENTS

I thank God every day for loving me with such depth and breadth. To my husband, Du'Sean, you are so damn wonderful. Your feedback and support are invaluable. I could not do this without you. ☺

Thank you to my wonderful friend and critique partner Giselle Marks. Without you, I would be lost! Thank you to Stacy Abrams for being an amazing, wonderful, and super-stupendous editor.

To my wonderful readers, thank you for picking up my book and giving me a chance! Thank you. Special THANK YOU to everyone who leaves a review— bloggers, fans, friends. I have always said reviews to authors are like a pot of gold to leprechauns. Thank you all for adding to my rainbow one review at a time.

My Fair Lady *meets* Pride and Prejudice *with a twist! Escape to Regency England with* USA Today *bestselling author Eva Devon.*

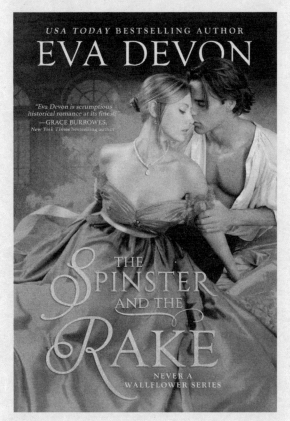

USA TODAY BESTSELLING AUTHOR
EVA DEVON

"Eva Devon is scrumptious
historical romance at its finest!"
—GRACE BURROWES,
New York Times bestselling author

THE SPINSTER AND THE RAKE

NEVER A
WALLFLOWER SERIES

Sleeping Beauty *meets* As You Like It *in this continuation of award-winning author Amalie Howard's Regency series that is sure to keep you up way past your bedtime.*

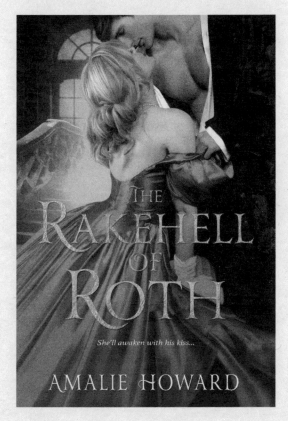

She'll awaken with his kiss...

THE RAKEHELL OF ROTH

AMALIE HOWARD

Waging war with a highlander never felt so good in this second installment of the Sons of Sinclair historical romance series.

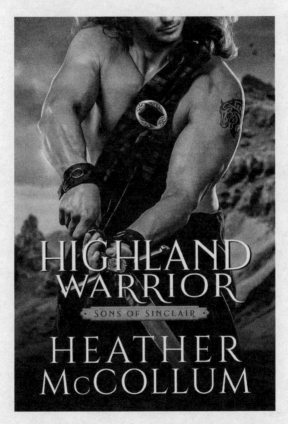

HIGHLAND WARRIOR

SONS OF SINCLAIR

HEATHER McCOLLUM